REBELLIOUS KAT...

A match struck and I saw Donovan's hard face as he held a lantern. He lit it casually, shaking out the match.

I stood frozen, staring at him, my breath coming in frightened gasps. He smiled slowly, though his eyes were still cold and hard.

"If you touch me, I'll kill you. I swear I will!" I said, though my threat sounded empty and weak.

HAD SHE MET HER MATCH?

"Touch you?" He raised his brows slightly. "I warned you about pushing me Kat. Do you remember? Well, you had your warning and you didn't listen. I'm going to do a lot more than just touch you this time. You've got this coming to you. And I'm going to give you everything you deserve."

He stripped off his shirt and tossed it onto the hay in one angry motion. His hands went to his belt buckle and I watched, stunned, as he shed his clothes.

a novel by
**FRANCINE
RIVERS**

ace books

A Division of Charter Communications Inc.
A GROSSET & DUNLAP COMPANY
51 Madison Avenue
New York, New York 10010

REBEL IN HIS ARMS

An ACE Original

First Ace Printing: August 1981
Published simultaneously in Canada

2 4 6 8 0 9 7 5 3 1
Manufactured in the United States of America

CHAPTER ONE

"Jeremy? Have you seen Papa?" I asked worriedly, entering the two-room log and sod cabin. I had checked the barn and the section where he said he would be working. There was no sign of my father, and I was becoming alarmed. He had said only this morning that he had something of vital importance to discuss with me and Jeremy and then, right after lunch, had disappeared.

Something was wrong. I felt it, and the more I looked for Papa and could not find him, the more the uneasy feeling grew. My mother had told me as a small child never to ignore intuition. Usually it guided you well. In my eighteen years, I had times when instinct served me, but never before had I had such strong feelings of trouble as I did at this moment. Where was Papa?

"On the ridge, I expect," my younger brother answered indifferently, not looking up from his arithmetic text, the thick pencil poised in his thin pale hand. Madrone was a good eight miles from our cabin, too far for a ten-year-old boy in poor health to ride to school each morning. Mama had died of childbed fever a few days after Jeremy was born. As a baby, he had suffered from severe bouts of colic without his mother's milk. Later, he had developed respiratory problems. The frequent attacks had caused me and Papa to become very protective of him.

Papa ordered textbooks from a mail order house and from them I taught Jeremy reading, writing, and arithmetic. When he was older and more skilled he could attempt the books Papa had brought from River's Bend, his family's plantation in Virginia. Already Jeremy was showing a strong bent toward the sciences, while I much preferred the humanities. He grew impatient with my insistence that he be familiar with the classics and balked stubbornly against learning Latin. My only persuasion was that the language was essential to the sciences, and grumblingly he conjugated his verbs and memorized the meanings of the suffixes and prefixes.

Jeremy scratched something out on his worksheet. "Katie, would you help me on this problem? I can't figure it any way I try!" he said with ill-concealed frustration.

"He went to the ridge again?" I asked, not hearing Jeremy's request and unable to conceal my own concerns.

"You know how Papa is. He likes to go up there to think. He can look out over the whole valley. He says he can see the Pacific right over the top of the Sierras from up there," Jeremy muttered, pushing the light brown hair back from his forehead and giving me a distant look with his hazel eyes. He had Papa's coloring, while I had inherited Mama's gold-red hair and blue eyes.

"He's never been gone this long," I mumbled to myself. It was almost four by the sun. Usually Papa was around the cabin by this time of day, or he would have told us where he could be found. This lengthy absence was not like him.

Jeremy scarcely looked up from his work. "Maybe he's hunting," he suggested, still trying to figure out his equation. "I heard a shot somewhere uphill not long ago."

I glanced quickly at the mount above the fireplace.

The long rifle was there. Papa always kept it cleaned and primed, the intricately carved stock with inlaid silver gleamed with his endless polishing. He was so proud of that gun, a reminder of his days on the Virginia plantation when money had never been a problem.

I felt a sick dread in the pit of my stomach. I had felt it twice before in my life. The first time I had been five and we had just arrived from the wagon train. A little girl, Glenda, had become a very close friend. I had this feeling shortly after she and her family left us that I would never see her again though they had planned to settle in Madrone. A few weeks later I learned that Glenda had been bitten by a rattlesnake while playing among some boulders near their cabin. She had died within hours. The second time I had this feeling was a week before Jeremy was born. All had seemed well when Mama had given birth to him. Then she had become fevered. She died a few days later, and the doctor who had come to help Papa said there was nothing they could have done. It was not uncommon for a woman to die after childbirth.

Jeremy seemed to feel my tension and looked up at me curiously, his childish features set in sudden solemnness, his arithmetic momentarily forgotten.

Papa did have a lot to think about, I reasoned desperately. I knew that money was short, but it always was this time of year. I knew also that since the owner of Tasajara, Brian Donovan, had had his accident and had called his son home, another offer for the homestead had been made. Papa had discussed it with me. I did not want to leave. Mama was buried in the redwood grove down the hill. Jeremy had been born on this land. It was our home. How could he even think of leaving? Papa had told Mace Donovan of our decision, but the offers kept coming. Mace Donovan seemed to want this land very much indeed.

Jeremy was watching my face. He stood up. "Katie?"

My eyes widened and my body started to tremble. "Katie, what's the matter?"

"It's Papa . . . something has happened . . ." I turned away, rushing out the door. I heard Jeremy shouting behind me.

The ridge was well over a mile away, all uphill through a wooded area of spruce, madrone, and digger pine. I ran without heeding my brother's cries. I tripped over my gingham skirt and fell headlong onto the trail, scraping my hands. Catching my breath, I pushed myself up and ran on, feeling an urgency I couldn't explain to get to the ridge as soon as I could. I pulled my skirts up around my knees and ran on again more swiftly.

My side ached and my lungs burned as I hurried up the narrow trail. As I was climbing over one of the many boulders on our land, I heard Jeremy behind me. He was wheezing. I stopped and turned around.

"You stay here for a few minutes," I ordered. "You'll have another attack if you go on." Strenuous exercise and excitement always brought on an attack. His face was pale and beaded with sweat as he looked up at me.

"I'm coming . . . with you," he said between breaths.

"Jeremy, please. I haven't time to worry about you. I've got to find Papa!" I pleaded with him, glancing over my shoulder at the trail leading to the ridge. "I've got to go. Now, do as I say and come slowly if you must. I . . . I may need your help."

Tears flooded his eyes and he looked terrified. He was so sensitive to anything I said and my harshness transmitted my worries to him. "What's wrong?" he cried.

"I . . . I don't know. I've got to go . . ." I climbed the last foot and dropped over the other side. Then I started to run again.

When I reached the ridge, my lungs were bursting and my heart was thudding like a racing locomotive. I looked around wildly, praying silently that my intuitions had been wrong. Papa was nowhere to be seen.

"Papa!" I called, running toward the boulders near the edge where he liked to sit. A ponderosa pine grew right out of the rocky plateau, stretching its arms toward the cloudless sky. I called again, louder now that my breath was returning. There was still no answer. I looked toward the alder grove to the south.

"Papa!" I shouted again, my voice cracking.

Then I heard something. A low moan. Pebbles bouncing off the granite face of the ridge.

"Where are you?" I cried frantically, moving closer to the edge. Hundreds of feet below the cliff was a tree-covered slope. Rocks fell away beneath me to clatter down. I dropped to my hands and knees, inching forward. Still, I did not see him.

I heard another noise. A groan. Stretching out, I moved forward again, my head and part of my shoulders over the edge. I saw Papa then, lying on a narrow ledge about fifteen feet down. His shirt front was blood-soaked. One leg was at an odd angle and his left arm was twisted unnaturally.

My body shook with the urgency to reach him. Cold sweat broke out on my skin. I searched for, and finally found, a precarious means of getting down the face of the cliff. It was a few yards north of him, and as I scrambled down rocks dislodged beneath me, cascading into the depths. My feet slipped in their thin shoes and my hands scraped over the granite surface as I barely managed to hold my balance. Looking down, I sucked in my breath, my heart accelerating. One slip and . . . I raised my eyes, concentrating on clawing my way down. I moved quickly and incautiously in my effort to reach my father in time.

I fell the last four feet, jarring my side painfully and almost colliding with a jutting boulder. The ledge was

long and narrow. Rocks broke loose, raining down the
ridge. I worked my way toward my father, clutching at
any handhold, however precarious.

"I'm coming, Papa." Tears blurred my vision, and by
the time I reached him, I was gasping for air. My bleeding hands burned like fire.

Crawling the last few feet almost on my stomach, I
reached my father. My throat closed as I looked at him.
His face was gray, his hazel eyes glassy and pinched into
slits against the glare of the late afternoon sun.

"Papa . . ."

"Katie!" Jeremy's voice came from above. He had
not had to search, hearing my voice. He stared down at
us for a second.

"How'd you get down there?" he called urgently.

"Stay there!" I shouted. "It's too dangerous . . ."

"Hon . . . ey . . ." my father tried to speak, his right
hand shaking as he moved it toward me. I clasped it,
kissing it.

"Don't talk. Don't move. You'll be all right," I said
determinedly, squeezing his hand. I tried to think of a
way to get him off this ledge before it crumbled beneath
us. But neither Jeremy nor I, nor both of us together,
had the strength to raise him up the cliff. We needed
help and fast! I looked out over the stretch of valley,
seeing the Tasajara ranch house and outbuildings in the
distance. It was three miles from the ridge, a rough, hard
ride down the trail along the ridge to the valley floor and
then through the trees on the slopes below.

"Come . . . close . . ." he rasped.

I leaned down, my eyes pleading. "Please. Papa. Save
your strength."

"No . . . time . . ."

I could hear Jeremy approaching as small rocks broke
loose, toppling down the cliff.

"Jeremy! I said stay up there!"

My father's fingers tightened on my hand. "He . . . shot . . . me . . ." Tears filled Papa's eyes as he made the tremendous effort.

"Who, Papa?" I leaned closer, putting my ear to his dry lips. "Who shot you?"

There was a gurgling sound in his throat as though he were drowning in his own blood. I straightened, terrified.

"Papa!" I cried, releasing his hand. I could see the hole just to the left center of his chest. Blood oozed out steadily as I pressed my hand over the wound, vainly trying to stop the flow. His blood came up between my fingers, and he moaned in agony as I increased the pressure.

"We'll get help! Just hang on, Papa. Please . . . hang on a little longer." I rattled on, tears running down my face.

He did not speak again, but his right hand moved slowly, with trembling determination to overcome his growing weakness. I watched. He was tracing something in the dust. A letter, shaky but almost clear. His hand continued to move, forming another letter in the dust with greater effort.

"I understand, Papa. *M . . . D . . .*" His hand stopped and he opened his eyes with difficulty. He was fighting hard to remain conscious for a little longer. I searched his face, seeing he wanted to tell me something else. He was trying so hard. He mouthed words and I began to comprehend.

Papa's final gasping word seemed to confirm my thoughts.

"Tas . . . a . . . jara . . ." His expression changed, twisting with pain. He opened his mouth to say more, but he could only move his lips. I did not understand what he said except "brother" and "Jeremy."

"I understand, Papa," I said. "Don't try to speak. I

understand. Mace Donovan shot you!"

A low moan came from deep in my father's chest and he forced his eyes open. His entire body seemed to tense. Beads of perspiration formed on his upper lip and across his forehead. The smell of blood was cloying in the hot afternoon.

"I'll take care of Jeremy, Papa. But you're going to be fine if you'd only stop. Please! You're making yourself worse."

Papa's eyes misted with tears but still his lips moved. I leaned down once again. I watched his mouth trying to form the words he wanted me so desperately to understand. No sound came. He blinked several times, then he closed his eyes and sighed deeply.

I stared at him, petrified. "Papa!?"

"Katie . . ." Jeremy whispered from behind me, having managed to climb down the cliff and crawl the last few feet to us. He looked beyond me to our father.

"He's . . . he's fainted," I said harshly. "You're going to have to stay here and press your hand over the wound, like this." I showed him. "He's bleeding badly." My voice was not my own, but high-pitched and rapid. I turned and took my brother's shoulder, my fingers leaving a blood stain.

"Don't try to move him at all. Talk to him. Let him know you're with him and that I've gone for help. We'll have him home soon."

Jeremy was looking at Papa. His expression was one of horror, tears streaming down his freckled cheeks. He didn't say anything and what was in his eyes drove me to anger.

"*He's not dead*! It's not too late!" I almost screamed at him. "Stop looking at him like that!"

His thin shoulders heaved with a sob and he stared up at me, his young face looking very old. I moved carefully around him, avoiding his eyes, and then edged along the ridge until I could begin climbing upward again. My hands were cut, fingernails broken to the quick by the time I managed to pull myself over the top and scramble to my feet.

I remember little of my ride to Madrone. In a haze of urgency and physical pain from over-exertion, I bridled our brown mare and rode bareback the eight miles to town. There was no sense in riding the shorter distance to Tasajara when my father had scratched Mace Donovan's initials in the dust.

It was dusk when I reached Doctor Walinsky's small, white house, only to learn he was out somewhere delivering a baby. His wife, Martha, sent her eldest son, Timothy, to fetch the sheriff while she forced me to drink a cup of strong, sugared tea. I was nearly hysterical with impatience by the time Sheriff Benjamin Collins arrived with two men and a buckboard. Martha Walinsky said she would send Doc out as soon as he arrived home unless we'd brought my father into town before that.

Sheriff Collins and his two deputies had difficulty keeping up with me. The buckboard had to wait at the cabin while we went to the ridge. The trail was too narrow up this way for horses. The three men followed me as quickly as they could while I ran ahead through the dark shadows of the trees.

The moon lit the ridge and I stood at the edge, looking down. Jeremy was huddled next to our father, his face buried in his arms on his knees. I hadn't enough breath to even call out to him.

Sheriff Collins came over to stand next to me. He shouted out to Jeremy who looked up, startled, his face white and angled in the moonlight. The sheriff did not need to voice his question. I dropped slowly to my knees. My grief was too deep even for tears.

"We'll drop you a rope, boy," Sheriff Collins shouted

to Jeremy. "Tie it securely around your waist and we'll bring you up."

"What about Papa?" he called and I closed my eyes.

"We'll rig pullies. Hugh Crowley will climb down and see to you. You needn't worry. We'll get your pa up."

A rope was dropped, snaking its way down to Jeremy. My brother tied it well, testing it as the sheriff instructed him to do. Julio Sanchez pulled him up while Collins dropped more rope to Hugh Crowley, now down on the narrow ledge with my father's body.

His body . . . I shuddered convulsively, biting down hard on my lip.

I could not watch while they lashed my father securely and hauled his weight up, bumping him against the rocky ledge. I could hear the thuds and wanted to vomit.

It seemed hours before we reached the cabin. Papa lay on a narrow bed in the corner, a quilt my mother had made spread over him, covering his face. I had stopped shaking, but felt cold and still inside. Jeremy stood at the table in much the same state. He kept looking at me, confusion and fear paling his face.

Sheriff Collins approached, drawing me to one side.

"We'll take him to the undertaker. You can ride in in the morning and make whatever . . ."

"No," I said flatly. "He's going to be buried next to my mother in the grove," I told him. The sheriff did not say anything for a moment.

"You'll want a funeral," he said.

"Papa said he never wanted one. He said they were an abomination, a parade of grief. He said he wanted people to remember him alive," I parroted my father's words.

Collins sighed softly. "It's up to you, ma'am." He started to say something more and then stopped and shook his head. "I'll send someone out in the morning to help you bury him." He started to step away and I clutched at his arm, straightening to stare intently into his craggy face.

"I want you to arrest Mace Donovan," I said in a low voice. Collins's dark eyes opened very wide and his bushy gray brows shot up in astonishment.

"What did you say?"

"He killed my father."

"Mace Donovan?" Collins was openly skeptical. "You can't be serious, Miss Durham."

"I *am* serious!" I said, my voice rising. Jeremy turned toward us from where he had been standing near our father, staring down at him, almost as though he was waiting for Papa to get up from resting. Julio Sanchez put his arm around the boy's shoulder.

"What makes you so sure Mace Donovan killed your father?" Collins asked, looking at me as though grief had deranged me.

"Papa wrote his initials out."

"There must be a half-dozen men around Madrone with the same initials. That's nothing to hang a man on," he dismissed my information.

"Papa said Tasajara."

"He probably wanted you to go to Donovan for help. They were friends. It would have made more sense to ride over there instead of all the way into town. It's barely three miles to the Tasajara ranch house."

"Donovan has been after our homestead," I persisted. "When my father wouldn't sell, he murdered him."

"You're overwrought and not thinking straight, if you'll pardon me saying so, ma'am," Collins said, trying for reason.

"I am thinking straight! Mace Donovan killed my father! He shot him and I want him to hang for it!"

"Good God, girl," the shieriff muttered, "pick a less dangerous enemy. Mace Donovan owns thousands of acres in the valley. Why would he kill a man for this . . .?" He swept his arm around the small, dismal cabin. "Have you ever been to the Tasajara house? Have you ever even been close to it? He was probably being charitable when he offered to buy this place."

I stiffened, but forced myself to overlook the insult. "Then you won't arrest him?" I challenged, already knowing the answer.

"Did your father say 'Mace Donovan shot me'?"

"I already told you he wrote his initials in the dust."

Collins looked at me for a long moment and then shook his head. "I wouldn't even mention it to him. I wouldn't arrest anyone on such flimsy evidence. Especially not Mace Donovan."

"High-and-mighty Donovan, is that it? You're afraid of him, aren't you?"

Collins's eyes narrowed, his gray brows coming down and making his square face harden with anger and impatience. He was an imposingly built man with massive shoulders and he made me feel suddenly vulnerable. He drew in his breath slowly, his mouth tightening.

"I know Mace Donovan, and I know his father. There was a day when his father might have taken a man's land for whatever reason he could find. But neither one of them would stoop to murder . . . especially not for a few lousy acres."

"Not a few lousy acres, sheriff. We own three hundred acres. And maybe you don't know the great Donovan as well as you think you do," I retorted, tears of frustration warningly near. "He's been very persistent about wanting our land. Would he do so out of the goodness of heart?" I demanded sarcastically. "This is the only parcel of land in the valley that Donovan doesn't own. Maybe he wanted to own it all."

"Miss Durham," Collins said in a voice hard with dismissal. "Mace isn't the murdering kind. He'd kill in a fair fight. You've met him . . ."

"I've never met him."

Collins's brows shot up at my admission. "You haven't?"

Tasajara was our closest neighbor. Mace Donovan had returned to the Sierra rancho to take control two years ago. It must have seemed very strange to Collins that I had never met the great man himself!

Sometimes it seemed strange to me, though I had been more than eager to avoid such a meeting. I had heard quite enough about Mace Donovan from my father to satisfy my curiosity. I didn't want to deal with the man himself. It seemed sometimes that all Papa could talk about was Mace Donovan and the places he had been. What was wrong with the California Sierras that he had to go searching the world for wonders? Where else could anyone find such beauty, such challenge?

Perhaps my admitted jealousy of my father's admiration for the rancher contributed to the circumstances that prevented a natural meeting between neighbors. But there was also the fact that my father seldom took me or Jeremy into Madrone with him, where he usually met with Donovan. I went to town once every few months with Papa and Jeremy to buy supplies, but those visits were short and businesslike. Other times my father met Donovan on the ridge, undoubtedly because Donovan enjoyed looking down on his empire!

Of course, Donovan had never considered coming to the log and sod cabin. I had suggested it once but my father had quickly changed the subject. I understood. As the sheriff had so kindly pointed out, there was a vast difference between the Tasajara rancho and our humble abode. But that made me no less proud. It bothered me a great deal that my father seemed so impressed with Tasajara. What was wrong with our four walls? Why should my father feel embarrassed about a house he had built with his bare hands from the earth and towering

trees of this great land? Why should he be so awed by a
man who had never built anything in his life but had, by
accident of birth, been handed an empire? This house
and land was ours by my father's sweat and love . . . and
now his blood.

"Then maybe you should meet him," Collins suggested. "And I'll give you a little friendly advice, Miss
Durham. Don't press this idea you have. I don't imagine
Donovan would appreciate your accusations. And you
might just need the help he could give you if you and
your brother plan to survive out here without your
father."

I stared at Collins in disbelief as he walked to the
door, signaling his men that they were leaving.

"Let's get on home. There's nothing more that we can
do here."

I went to the doorway, watching them mount and
turn their horses away. Collins hesitated, his saddle
creaking as he turned back. "Think about what I told
you, Miss Durham," he said.

"You do likewise, sheriff," I said, looking at him
levelly. He seemed to sigh before he headed down the
hill toward the open gate. Angry tears burned my eyes.

"Katie . . ." Jeremy whimpered behind me. I turned
and looked at his distraught face and then opened my
arms. He ran into them, burrowing against me as the
flood of grieving tears came. I smoothed back his hair,
kissing the top of his head.

"Everything will be all right," I mouthed the platitude
automatically while staring out into the darkness. The
smell of pine and cooling earth was all around us. The
old hoot owl was in the redwood grove where Mama
lay. Tomorrow Papa would be beside her. My chin
trembled and I closed my eyes, putting my head down
against my brother's as I hugged him closer.

Three miles away, the man who had murdered my

father sat in comfort waiting to take over what belonged to us. But just because the sheriff had dismissed everything, did not mean that I would do so.

Mace Donovan had murdered my father, and he was not going to get away with it!

CHAPTER TWO

The first time I met Mace Donovan, I knew he would be a fierce adversary. His presence immediately set me on edge, sending shivers of apprehension through me. Papa was gone, and with him whatever real security we had. Donovan took the rest of our illusions away with one level look.

It was midmorning, and the sheriff's man had not yet arrived to help us bury Papa in the redwood grove beside Mama. Jeremy had left the cabin, tearfully upset at watching me laying Papa out. He walked alone on the slope below the cabin, head bowed, grieving in his own way.

For me, this last act of love was a kind of salve for my grief. With a pan of warm water and soap I cleaned away the dirt from Papa's face and then shaved him. Slowly and tenderly I washed away the dried, crusted blood from his chest and arms. The gaping hole in his chest was black and I swallowed back the nausea at the smell of death in the cabin.

It was difficult to raise my father's weight enough to slip on the white shirt and then pull on the dark suit pants and finally the coat. I tied the narrow silk tie at his tanned throat and then brushed his wayward light brown hair neatly back from his face. Like Jeremy's, it had constantly fallen forward into his eyes and had to be combed back with impatient fingers. I stroked the graying temples lovingly as tears blinded me.

Looking down on that face, I tried to see Papa. I failed. Whatever it was that had made the man Roger Allan Durham was gone forever. There was little resemblance between this lifeless, settled body and my beloved father. I tried desperately through my tears to see the father I knew—the one that laughed away my irritation, sang bawdy songs leaving out words he thought unfit for a young lady to hear, teased me when I was depressed, and loved me always in spite of my faults. He was gone.

Pulling the multi-colored quilt around him, I began to sew it closed. My mother had spent many months making this with patches of materials she had saved. Papa had kept it on his bed since her death. Sometimes in the evenings, I would see his sad expression as he silently traced the stitches Mama had made. It seemed fitting that this should be his shroud.

Jeremy's shouting averted my attention. I ran to the door, trying to understand what he was yelling. It was indecipherable. He was running up the slope and a sudden surge of fright swelled inside me, turning my stomach over.

"What's wrong?" I called, running to meet him. Jeremy skidded to a stop in front of me, cheeks flushed from exertion, his breathing strained as he tried to get the words out. He pointed back toward the valley, gasping for breath.

"Some . . . someone's coming! He's riding a big sorrel stallion. The biggest horse and man I've ever seen, Katie. I . . . I think . . . I think it's Donovan!" he managed finally.

"Donovan." My eyes narrowed as I searched the slope for him and saw nothing yet. The muscles in my jaw felt stiff, and I clenched and unclenched my hands.

"I'm going to get the gun," I decided, turning with a swishing of my skirts and running toward the cabin.

Jeremy ran after me, grabbing my arm, clinging to me with the tenacity of an ivy vine.

"Let me go, Jeremy!" I ordered, trying to pry his fingers loose. "He'll be here any minute and I'm going to be ready for him!"

"Katie! You can't shoot him!"

"Oh? Why can't I!" I said sarcastically. "That's just what he did to Papa!" I yanked my arm from my brother's grip and continued toward the house, Jeremy trailing after me.

"But . . . but the sheriff will arrest you, then! They'll hang you, Katie!" he cried in alarm.

At that moment, I didn't really care what they did to me so long as Mace Donovan paid for what he had done to my father. But I looked over my shoulder at my brother's taut, frightened face. What would happen to him? And hadn't my last promise to Papa been that I would take care of my brother as I had since the day he was born?

There was no time to think about it. Someone was coming. I could hear the thunder of horse's hooves on the slope below. Without glancing back, I darted into the cabin and ran to the fireplace. Yanking the long rifle down from its mounting, I ran a shaking hand over its glass-smooth surface. All I had to do was cock and fire. It was ready and so was I. The fury and desire for revenge rose inside of me until I thought I would explode. Jeremy looked at me and his hazel eyes widened.

"Katie. You can't shoot him!" Stepping in front of me, he tried to detain me. "Don't kill him . . ."

I remembered my father's agonized, ashen face. I remembered him choking on his own blood. I turned my head and looked at the form sewn into the bright quilt.

"Katie . . ."

When I looked into my brother's face I saw his fear
and need more clearly. I reached out and cupped his
cheek.

"I won't shoot him, Jeremy. But let me go out there.
I want the gun just in case . . ." My eyes moved to the
open doorway. Jeremy stared at me intently and then
moved aside, knowing there was nothing he could do. I
walked out of the cabin into the hot sunlight. Squinting
my eyes against the glare, I watched the approach of
horse and rider. A shiver of anticipation and tension
moved down my spine.

Squaring my shoulders, I watched the man ride toward me. He sat his horse as though he were a part of it
and he looked straight at me with unwavering intensity.
It only angered me more that he could look directly at
me so easily after murdering my father. He apparently
possessed no conscience.

"Katie . . ." Jeremy said, seeing my knuckles whiten
on the gun. His voice shook with dread and expectation.
"Please, don't . . ."

"I won't kill him unless I have to," I said through taut
lips, though I badly wanted to shoot him right then. The
murdering bastard was still looking at me. I never removed my gaze from him. "Now, hush! It'll be okay.
You just stay there behind me and keep out of my way!"

The man on the stallion was bigger than I had expected. Papa had said he was tall, but Papa had been of
middling height and anyone over five feet ten was tall to
him. This man was easily several inches over six feet. He
was broad-shouldered and narrow-waisted. I could see
the strong length of muscles in his legs ripple as he di-
rected the horse's movement. Looking back up, I noted
the open collar of his shirt and an Indian turquoise
choker that should have been an effeminate display but
somehow only further emphasized his overwhelming
masculinity.

Worse than his size, this man was young, not more than thirty if even that. Papa had spoken of Donovan as a contemporary, a man to be respected. Though he did not fit the image my father had created for me, I had no doubt that this man was Mace Donovan. Papa had spoken of his eyes. Below the thick, chocolate brown hair were a set of eyes that were the color of a puma cat and just as intense. They were narrowed on me speculatively, as though he had his prey in sight and was judging its endurance and strengths. Papa had mentioned those eyes more than once. He said there couldn't be another set that color in the whole world. They were almost gold.

I studied the face, assessing the square jaw, the uncompromising set of his firm mouth, the straight nose, the high cheekbones. Aware of my appraisal, Donovan's lips curved into a half-smile that made me hate him from the very depth of my being. He was the essence of confidence, the height of arrogance, a man without any doubts about his power and position.

As he drew rein before the cabin, I slowly raised the gun and aimed it squarely and steadily at the center of his broad chest. The open shirt showed a tanned throat and thick growth of dark hair. I watched that chest rise and fall slowly. If I squeezed the trigger just a fraction harder, I could put a hole in it the size of the one he had left in my father. I could watch him blasted off the back of that stallion. Donovan did not move. He was a worthy target, I thought, clenching my jaw.

"Not much of a welcome for a friendly neighbor," he drawled with a faintly mocking tone and wry smile. His gaze moved over me curiously, lingering briefly here and there, and bringing a stinging flush of indignation to my cheeks. He made the slightest movement to dismount and I tilted my chin to meet his eyes again.

"You move," I said in a low voice, "and you'll get the

welcome you deserve." His brows shot up in surprise and then those gold eyes narrowed and darkened.

Jeremy's fingers grasped a fold of my skirt and tugged. "Katie . . ."

"Hush!" I ordered, my chin jerking upward as I felt Donovan's anger aimed at me as surely as my rifle was aimed at him. This was no time for talk. The man before me was scrutinizing my face carefully, assessing my expression, judging my weaknesses.

"I heard about Roger," he started.

My mouth curved in a travesty of a smile, my eyes glittering with challenge. "You heard about my father," I sneered. "I'll just bet you *heard.*"

"What in the hell is going on here?" Donovan snapped impatiently. "Sheriff Collins sent a man over last night to let me know what happened. He was going to send someone back this morning, but I told him that since I was a friend . . ."

"Friend . . ." I repeated caustically. "My father was shot down yesterday."

"So I was told."

"He was shoved off the ridge and left to die."

Donovan frowned.

"Was it necessary to be told all that, Mr. Donovan?" I smiled unpleasantly. His face tightened, the eyes flashed and then cooled.

"What're you getting at?"

"He isn't even in his grave yet and you come sniffing around here like some filthy scavenger trying to steal what rightly belonged to him!"

A muscle jerked in Donovan's jaw and the coldness in his gold eyes was frightening. "I'm not planning to steal anything," he said with an effort to be reasonable.

"You're right about that, Mr. Donovan," I told him. "My father told me about your offers to buy our land. You were most determined and persistent, weren't you?

Well, you can take your offers and go . . . to . . . hell!"
I enunciated clearly and insultingly. "This is my
brother's and my land now and you'll roast in Hades
before you get it!"

Something flickered across Donovan's face. "You
think I killed your father?"

"Didn't Sheriff Collins tell you?" I mocked. "I don't
think you did," I added, making my meaning clear.

"Your father was a friend," he said in a hard, unyielding voice. I did not say anything but knew my eyes spoke
volumes. His smile was derisive.

"No wonder your father kept you well hidden whenever we had our talks. You're the most unreasonable,
prejudiced little bitch I've ever run across. And that's
going some!"

I felt Jeremy's sudden movement behind me. "Don't
you call my sister names!" he cried in childish fury, darting forward, intending to attack the giant of a man. He
only succeeded in startling the restless stallion. The huge
horse reared sharply at the small apparition coming at
him and let out a high-pitched whinny of challenge, ears
flattening back menacingly.

"Jeremy!" I screamed, dropping the rifle and grabbing my brother around the waist. His impetus sent us
both into the dust beneath the horse. I rolled sharply as
the stallion's hooves crashed down inches from us. I
rolled again, keeping Jeremy's slim body locked against
mine, shielding him.

Donovan swore violently, quickly getting his mount
under control and swinging down. "Of all the asinine
things to do!" he exploded.

I hauled Jeremy up, searching his face in fear at what
had almost happened to him. "Jeremy," I cried, tears of
tension and fright blurring my vision. "What were you
trying to do? You could've been killed!" Then, hearing
Donovan's approach, I thrust him behind me and swung

around to face the man.

Too late I remembered the gun lying uselessly in the dirt several feet away. I stared up the length of the man until I met blazing eyes in a sun-browned face. The breadth of his shoulders blocked out the sun and I strained back, pressing Jeremy further behind me protectively.

"Good God!" Donovan continued to rage. "Someone ought to take you two in hand!" he growled.

"You've no right to call my sister names!" Jeremy cried, unrepentant. I tried to quell his incautious tongue with a glance, but he pulled loose to stand beside me, glaring hotly up at Donovan. Donovan looked at Jeremy in faint admiration and then smiled.

"You're absolutely right, Jeremy. And I apologize." He gave me a mocking bow and then raised one brow. "Truce, Kathryn?" Apparently, Papa had done some talking about me. How else would he know my name?

My shoulders stiffened. I was still shaking from what had just happened, and suddenly felt very vulnerable.

"I think you'd better sit down before you fall down," Donovan commented, looking at me.

The rifle was on the ground behind Donovan. I doubted if I could reach it without him stopping me. He saw the direction of my gaze and smiled tauntingly. He walked over and retrieved it. Looking at me with that infuriating smile, he handed it back.

"There, Kathryn. Does that make you feel safer?"

I blinked and then looked up at him haughtily. "Considerably," I admitted without thinking, and he laughed. My stomach tightened. The smile faded as he looked from Jeremy to me. His expression grew serious.

"I rode over to pay my respects and help you bury your father," he offered, arousing my temper again with his utter gall. "And to offer you and your brother any assistance you might need." His eyes were boring into me. "I take it from our earlier conversation, before you both tried to kill yourselves under my horse, that you intend to keep the homestead and make a go of it."

I stared at him coldly. "You take it correctly." Donovan was silent for a moment, considering both of us.

"You might want to think that decision over very, very carefully." His words sounded like a warning, even a threat.

"And just what is that supposed to mean?"

He shifted impatiently at my rude tone. "I should think it was obvious, even to you."

"You've a great deal of nerve, haven't you?" I flared. "You think because you're a big-time rancher that you can get away with anything!"

"You deliberately misunderstand me!"

"Do I indeed?" I threw back my head challengingly.

He let out his breath. "How do you expect to keep this place going by yourselves, for God's sake?"

"We'll manage."

He gave a harsh laugh. "Two children running a homestead that a man could hardly keep going," he said cuttingly. "You won't last out the year."

Calling me a child only further infuriated me. Donovan seemed to know exactly how to irritate me, and his mouth curved.

"How old are you anyway?" he asked, amused. "Your father never did say, and I always had the impression that you were still in the schoolroom."

That hurt, but I refused to dignify his taunt with an answer.

"Katie's eighteen!" Jeremy flashed defensively.

Donovan's eyes lightened.

"She's that old, hmmm?" he commented, and managed to look skeptical. His eyes flickered over me again. I knew there was nothing at all childish about my shape and felt the instinctive urge to hide myself from his measured study. It was the second time he had looked me over in just that way and I resented it greatly. It was with determination that I remained still and satisfied myself with a mocking study of his lean, well-muscled form. My eyes moved over him derisively, climbing steadily until my gaze locked onto his. There was a glinting amusement in those gold eyes that I did not like. I looked away quickly, furious to feel the growing heat in my cheeks and a hard thudding of my heart. His eyes never left me and I hated him even more.

"If you change your mind," he said, "the offer I gave your father still stands." He stated a sum that sounded more than generous and I flashed him a hateful look.

"You're *never* going to get this land away from us, Donovan!"

He looked at me for a moment longer, holding his temper with great difficulty. "I doubt if anyone else in their right mind will make you an offer for this place," he said in a clipped voice. He swung himself easily into the saddle, looking back down at me. Then he looked at Jeremy and his expression noticeably softened with sympathy.

"I'm very sorry about your father. He was a fine man. You've reason to be very proud of him."

After what he had done, how dare he come here with his patronizing condolences, lying through his teeth? My lip quivered and I bit down hard on it.

"Get off our land!" I ordered in a high-pitched voice, full of rage.

Donovan's eyes moved to mine. "I'm trying damn hard to remember that you've had a bad shock and are probably not thinking too clearly," he said tightly. "Remember what I said," He told Jeremy. "If you need help, I'm available."

With that, he turned the stallion with a mere tensing

of his leg muscles and the slightest movement of his hands on the reins. I watched him ride down the hill and only then let out my breath.

"What're we going to do, Katie?" Jeremy asked shakily.

"Just what we've been doing," I answered, lowering the gun, suddenly feeling exhausted and precariously close to a tempest of tears. I could still see Mace Donovan and there was a feeling in the pit of my stomach I did not understand or like. I pulled my eyes away from his broad, darkly-clothed back and looked down at Jeremy.

"We'll work the garden and run the cattle together. It's not going to be easy, but we've got to do it if we want to keep our land." I put my arm around Jeremy's thin shoulders. "I'm sorry, but you'll have to shelve your schoolwork for a while. I need your help."

I felt the dejection that announcement brought and squeezed him against my side. Jeremy had always preferred books to any physical labor; he had a quick mind and I knew what my last statement meant to him. Somehow we would work things out so that he would have some time for his precious books.

"I don't see how we'll do it," Jeremy sighed dismally. "Papa never let me work with the cattle. I don't know the first thing about them. And you always managed the house and garden. You don't know any more than I do."

Jeremy was right, of course. But I could not let him feel my uncertainty.

"We'll manage," I said, repeating what I had said to Donovan and sounding more assured than I felt. I looked toward the grove. There was still Papa's grave to dig, the burying to be done. I felt the tightening in my throat, the burning in my eyes.

I would have to be strong if we were going to keep our

land and survive where so many before us had failed. I could not allow myself to give in to grief or despair, nor the fears inspired by our precarious situation. Below us, all around us was Tasajara, Donovan's domain. I looked down the slope and swallowed hard.

"We'll manage, Jeremy." I forced a hardness into my voice and gave him a sure smile.

"We have to," I added silently to myself.

CHAPTER THREE

Standing over Papa's grave, I read from Mama's little white leather-bound Bible. Papa had liked the twenty-third Psalm and it seemed fitting. I sprinkled red earth over the shrouded body at the bottom of the hole and then stooped to pick up the shovel again. Jeremy put his hand on my arm.

"Let . . . let me do it, Katie," he said through a haze of tears. His face was pinched and pale.

"You're not strong enough," I said quietly.

"Your hands are bleeding. Let me."

"Jeremy . . ."

His face convulsed. "I'm his only son," he said harshly, sounding very adult for a ten-year-old boy.

I relinquished the shovel. His shoulders quivered as he pushed the blade into the pile of red-brown earth and lifted it over the grave.

I turned away, knowing if I broke down in front of Jeremy it would only make things that much harder for him. The sound of that shovel scraping and the dirt dropping onto Papa was more than I could bear. I walked away, forcing myself to go slowly though I wanted to run.

Coming out of the cool shade of the redwood grove, I stood in the warm afternoon sunlight. I stared tearfully up the hillside at the cabin. I remembered how my mother and father and I had arrived here exhausted from the seemingly endless trek across plains and mountains to the great California Sierras. Papa had turned the animals loose. Then he had turned to Mama, spreading his arms wide, laughing joyously. She ran into them and he picked her up and swung her around and around, laughing.

Papa had axed down trees, cutting them into proper lengths while Mama, with her skirts hiked up around her knees, had stomped water, red-brown earth, and grass into a thick pasty mud. She poured it with buckets into wooden frames to dry in the sun, later to be packed between the logs that formed the walls of the house. Papa chopped long wooden shingles for the roof. Glass windows were bought in Madrone and set in before winter. The fireplace was made with mortar and stones collected from the mountainside.

During the long first winter, Papa had talked endlessly of the plans he had. When Mama found she was pregnant, he drew up elaborate designs for expanding the house. Someday, he told his wife, it would be as big as that place down there in the valley, the ranch they called Tasajara.

When Mama died, the plans were folded away. For a long time, Papa did not do anything but sit in the redwood grove where Mama was buried. Eventually, as Jeremy grew stronger, Papa let go of his grief. He built the barn to the left of the sod house. After that, the corral, small because there was little stock.

I turned away, the memories filling my head. Walking around the grove of towering trees, I headed toward the western edge of our property. The grassy slope fell away gradually for a while and then dipped more steeply into a tree-covered area below. A belt of spruce grew along the property line. Beyond it were undulating hills with scattered trees that led to the rich green, yellow, and brown valley floor. I walked slowly along the trees, reaching up to break off a sprig of pine, crushing the needles between my trembling fingers. The tangy smell was a balm for my pain.

Wandering along, I looked up toward the cabin again. The vegetable garden stretched out in productive rows just east of the small house. I should be working in it now, pulling new weeds, toting buckets of water from the well to drench the drying plants. But I just wanted to walk over our land, feel it, smell it, taste the clear air. Papa's land. Ours now. Ours to hold, ours to fight for.

I crossed the rutted dirt byway to the house. The gate hinge was hanging loose and would have to be tightened. Papa had been meaning to do it. I continued upward toward the hills behind the house. The trees thickened the further I went. Once or twice they broke into broad meadows where mangy cows grazed idly in the afternoon sun. The ground was rocky in places, cutting into the thin soles of my shoes. Here and there boulders jutted out of the sun-warmed earth. Papa had once said they looked like discs and javelins heaved there eons ago by some giant primitive being.

Tired and hot, I sprawled at the edge of the upper meadow beneath the shade of a tall digger pine. I stared up through the branches at the blue, cloudless sky and listened to the birds. A squirrel on an upper branch was taking a pine cone apart, dropping the pieces almost on my head as he stuffed his furry cheeks with the nuts for his winter storage.

A fleeting image came to mind of my mother in the morning, with her long red-gold hair loose, putting bread crumbs on the glassless windowsill of our new cabin while Papa sat at the small table behind her, talking and sipping his coffee. A hard lump of pain filled my throat. I sat up abruptly and then put my head against my knees, letting the tears come.

So many times I missed my mother. Often I longed for her with something close to desperation. One time that I vividly remembered was when I found the blood stains. I had thought I was dying of some dread, unmentionable disease. I was afraid to tell my father. He questioned me about my quietness and preoccupation. After several days he cornered me into an explanation when he found me sobbing in the hayloft. I could smile about everything now, remembering his painfully embarrassed look and halting explanation of the workings of a woman's body.

He left a lot unsaid. But after our discussion, I became very curious. The rest of my worldly information came from observing various stock animals around the place. Breeding was a rather awesome though sometimes hilarious business. I didn't ask Papa any more questions, and ever grateful for that, he volunteered nothing further on the subject.

Standing, I brushed off my skirt and continued walking. The ridge beckoned me as it had my father. I walked forward slowly, standing almost at the edge. A few feet beyond, the ridge dropped away. Below was the ledge where I had found my father. I bent down, touching my fingertips to the stain on the granite where my father had been laid the night before.

Straightening, I stared outward, letting the breeze whip my hair back from my tear-wet face. Beyond lay the hills sweeping down into the valley.

Tasajara. Donovan's land. As far as I could see. To the west, to the north, to the south for miles. A green, rich land studded by pine and oak.

Pulling my eyes away, I looked up. Above me a hawk gave a cry as it dipped and soared. Darting in on the attack was a small bird. Again and again, it flashed in, aiming for the vulnerable eyes, pecking at the great bird that had threatened her territory, perhaps her nest. The hawk pulled in and dropped away, spreading its wings again to catch the wind. The small bird gave up and flew away.

Will I be like that little bird fighting a hopeless battle against the giant hawk?

The sun was low in the west. It was time to go back. Jeremy had had his time alone with Papa. He would need me now.

When I entered the cabin, the sun was just on the horizon, casting its golden haze over the slopes. The cabin would be in the sunlight until the last rays were cast over the horizon. Mama had wanted it that way.

Sunlight streamed through the thin white curtains, filling the drab room with warmth. A small table stood near the window. It was overloaded with my plants set in small, handmade adobe pots of various shapes and sizes. Clippings were in a mason jar waiting to be rooted for planting.

We did not have much furniture. A simple sofa Papa had bought in Madrone faced the windows. I had re-covered it a year before with a brown, gold, and green material that had been on sale at the general mercantile. A tanned cowhide lay spread before the fireplace. Papa had made three straight-backed chairs and I had added cushions using patches of old material from useless clothes. A bookshelf in the north end of the cabin was jammed with books Papa had sent east for.

The fireplace, built with colored stones from our land, had a nice oak mantle made by Papa. On it stood a small, beautifully carved marble and gold clock that had been a wedding gift to my parents when they were still in Virginia. During the long trek west the oxen had almost died, and every item not necessary to survival had been dumped beside the trail. Mama would not part with this precious gift from her maternal grandmother. Papa had found it hidden among the blankets when we arrived here. He had held it up, looking at his wife with a mockingly stern expression. She had spread her hands and then laughed. She had saved other things as well. At the bottom of her trunk was her wedding dress and shoes, plus several dresses she had worn to fancy parties on the plantation.

The long table at the back of the house in the kitchen doubled as Jeremy's desk. Papa had built it with leftover redwood timber. The cabinets were made of spruce and redwood.

I shared a double bed with my younger brother. It was against the northern wall of the cabin near the bookshelves. A small kerosene lantern was perched on a makeshift table on Jeremy's side because he loved to read.

The small room on the southern end of the cabin, partitioned off by a simple gingham curtain, was my father's. In it was the brass bed he had shared with Mama, a small dresser, and simple commode. Mama's trunk was at the foot of the bed covered with another tanned cowhide. On the dresser was a daguerreotype of Mama and Papa on their wedding day.

The fire was out though the woodbin by the fireplace was full. I glanced around absently, all the familiar things soothing me. It was home, yet it was empty now without Papa.

Thinking Jeremy must still be in the grove, I walked back down the slope to the redwoods. The grave was completed. Jeremy had even put the rocks over the mound of earth. A plain wood cross bearing my father's full name and the dates of his birth and death was at the head.

I went back to the cabin, wondering where my brother had gone. Then I knew. Pushing aside the gingham curtain I found Jeremy sprawled across Papa's bed, head in his arms. He had cried himself to sleep.

I stood there for a long time looking down at his thin form. I remembered the night Mama had given birth to Jeremy in this very room. Papa had kept me away. I had been frightened by Mama's low moans and the sharp cry she could not keep back when Jeremy pushed his way into the world. It had been a long labor and Mama was very weak. Papa had called me then, depositing the six-pound baby in my arms. I had just turned eight.

Sitting on the edge of the bed, I gently brushed his hair back from his pale temples. Memories flooded my grieving mind. I remembered giving Jeremy milk from the goat the doctor had brought us from Madrone. I remembered holding my tiny brother, rocking him into the early hours of morning when he cried with endless colic. I remembered the fear when his breathing attacks hit. I remembered cuddling him against me in my bed during the long, chill months of winter. I remembered the first gurgling laughs, the first teeth, the first steps, the first word. "Kay . . . Kay . . ." Not Mama. And my love for Jeremy almost suffocated me. Tears filled my eyes and spilled down my cheeks.

My brother stirred on Papa's big bed, rolling over to look up at me with red and puffy eyes. He looked so pale, so vulnerable. I smiled at him, leaning down to kiss him. He started to cry again, putting his arms up. I drew him against me as I always had when he was hurting, rocking him back and forth, rubbing his back.

Outside the old hoot owl began his nightly solo. And beyond—below—Donovan waited.

CHAPTER FOUR

The pulse in my temple began to throb and I stared with shocked dismay at the man behind the general mercantile counter. His gray eyes softened with sympathy.

"I . . . I had no idea about this, Mr. Iverson," I said faintly, apologetic, not knowing what else I could say under the circumstances.

"I'm sure you didn't, Miss Durham. Your father wouldn't have wanted to worry or burden you, I'm sure. And what could you do about it anyway? Your father said you pulled far more than your share at the homestead. But I'm afraid he owed me quite a sum. He's been unable to pay anything on the account for well over a year now."

Rummaging through some papers near the cash register he found a ledger. Pushing his spectacles up the wide bridge of his nose and rubbing his thick gray mustache, he turned the pages.

"Let me see," he muttered to himself, his face pinched in concentration. "Ah, here we are," he said, tapping his finger on a page, his muscles relaxing. He read off the amount owed him and I blanched.

"So much?" I gasped in dismay.

He nodded. "I'm afraid so. Here. See for yourself," he

said, handing me the ledger. There were slips of paper bearing my father's very distinguishable signature clipped to the opposite page. The total was staggering.

I remembered Papa bent over sheets of workpaper, scrawling numbers, adding and readding. On those occasions, he had looked very tired and gray. Whenever I had asked him if anything was wrong, he had always roused a smile for me and said it was nothing that could not be handled.

"I'm terribly sorry to have to lay this at your doorstep so soon after your father's death," Iverson cleared his throat.

"I'll pay you back somehow, Mr. Iverson," I told him, my face paling as I stared at the ledger and sheets of paper in my hand. Looking up, I handed everything back to him. He stared at my stricken face with obvious sympathy.

"Look, Miss," he said, leaning forward on the counter. "The bill has waited this long. I don't expect it will hurt anything to let it go a little while longer."

I felt very shaky and afraid, and tried desperately not to further humiliate myself by crying. This poor man was embarrassed enough as it was. I just looked at him mutely. I had no money and we needed supplies badly. What choice did I have but to accept his kind charity for the time being, until I could find a way to repay my father's debt. Iverson flushed and looked away. He cleared his throat again.

"Now, what were you and the boy needing?" he asked gruffly. "I expect you had a list with you?"

The slip of paper I had written out that morning was crumpled in my hand. I flattened it out on the counter and handed it to him wordlessly. It seemed we needed everything. He measured out flour, beans, salt, rice, sugar, and molasses and stacked it all on the counter.

"We can do without the coffee, Mr. Iverson," I said,

but he shook his head.

"Who around here can do without coffee, Miss?" he said and measured out a five-pound sack of beans. "Consider it a gift." He pushed it across the counter. Without looking at me, he glanced at the list and began taking tinned items down from the shelves. I watched the stack grow, and pushed back half a dozen items.

"We can do without these," I said, avoiding his kindly gaze. He scratched his long sideburns, looking troubled, but he didn't say anything. Finally, he sighed and then picked up the goods, restacking them on the shelf. Then he tallied the items on the counter. Looking up, he smiled.

"Would you be needing anything else, Miss?"

"No, that's all. Thank you very much."

Iverson's wife, Melinda, came from the back of the store. Seeing me, she removed her long apron and came forward.

"I'm so sorry about your father," she offered, reaching for my hand. "If there's anything we can do."

"You and your husband have done more than enough already."

"Roger was a fine man," Iverson said, clearing his throat again.

"Thank you."

"Are you and your brother planning to stay on? Or do you have relatives?" Melinda Iverson asked.

"We've relatives in Virginia," I told her. "But we plan to stay on at the homestead. It was Papa's life. Mama died there. We won't leave it."

"You've picked a hard row to hoe," Iverson said and Melinda glanced at him, troubled.

"Well, whatever you decide, we wish you God's blessing, my dear."

Joseph Iverson loaded the supplies into the buckboard. Then he handed me another slip of paper and I signed my name to the bottom, while biting my lower lip. I looked up at these two kind people and caught their pitying glance.

"I'll pay you as soon as I can," I assured them. "That's a promise."

"We know that. Don't worry about it," Melinda said.

I learned the same dismal situation existed at the feed and grain store and at the butcher's. Both Jeremiah and Harriet Bellows, and Tobias Jacobson, were as understanding and willing to hold over the bills owed as Melinda and Joseph Iverson. People could be very kind.

Stopping at the bank, I asked to speak with Charles Lambert, the president.

"I'm afraid it's quite impossible to loan you anything, Miss Durham," he said grimly. He looked very affluent in his gray suit, white shirt, and pearl-gray silk vest with a gold watchchain dangling from the pocket.

"Why? In the spring next year we should be able to repay you after the sale of our cattle."

Lambert sighed heavily, rubbing fingers along his smooth, pale jawline. He had thinning brown hair and gray eyes behind gold wire spectacles.

"Apparently your father didn't apprise you of his . . . situation . . . ."

"Situation?" I repeated blankly, feeling the tension building again in my head and stomach.

"Your homestead is already mortgaged," Lambert said flatly, seeing no easy way to state the facts. He tapped his fingers together in a pyramid, leaning back in his swivel chair.

"Oh, God . . ." I breathed miserably.

He picked up a pen and then put it down again. He opened a lower drawer in his desk, fingering through files until he found what he wanted. Pulling out a folder he flipped it open, glancing at the top sheet. He frowned.

"You'll have to make a payment on the balance in

another month, in fact. He was late with the last one."
He stated the amount due and I felt a sick lump stick in
my throat. Where was I ever going to get the money?
Why hadn't Papa confided in me about our financial
situation?

Charles Lambert was watching my face. "I sympa-
thize with your circumstances, Miss Durham. Really I
do." He leaned forward, clasping his thin, smooth hands
on the desk. The hazel eyes were keen. "If it was up to
me, I'd loan you the money. But I have to consider the
depositors. Quite frankly, you and your young brother
are very bad risks."

"What do you suggest we do, Mr. Lambert?"

Lambert thought for a long moment. He unclasped
his hands and tapped his fingers on the desk blotter.
Then he rose and paced behind his desk.

"If I were you," he said slowly, "I'd sell out. That
land's been a millstone around your father's neck for the
last five years. With the drought and then the flooding
right afterward, he lost a lot of money, and he's never
been able to recoup. I don't honestly see how you can
succeed where he failed." He hesitated and then went
on. "I understand Mace Donovan made you a fair offer
for the place."

My eyes widened and then narrowed coldly. "And
where did you become privy to that knowledge, Mr.
Lambert?" I demanded. Lambert sat down again.

"Your father mentioned it the last time he was in the
bank."

"Why would he mention that?"

"He was asking for a second mortgage. I expect he
thought that Donovan's interest in the homestead might
sway my decision. I'm afraid it didn't," he said bluntly.

"I'm not going to sell our land," I stated.

"I admire your spirit, Miss Durham," Lambert said,
his tone dubious. "But I must advise you right now that

if you are unable to meet your obligations to this bank I'll be forced to foreclose. It's not something I like doing, believe me. Especially when it's a young woman and her brother, but I've a responsibility to our bank. If the mortgage can't be paid, the place will have to be auctioned off."

"I understand," I said curtly, standing up.

"Miss Durham," he caught my distracted attention. I turned from the door and looked back at him questioningly. "I don't know if this will be any comfort to you," he said slowly, "but there are a lot of other homesteaders and ranchers around Madrone in the same situation you're in. It's a hard life and seldom a secure one unless you happen to be in Mace Donovan's or Les Bigelow's position."

Les Bigelow owned a ranch to the south of Madrone. It was almost as large as Tasajara. I had never met Bigelow, but my father had. Several times he had sold cattle to Bigelow. Papa had grumbled once about the poor price he had been given for prime stock.

"Owning the entire valley, you mean," I said dryly.

"Donovan's family came to California several generations ago. That ranch started with a Spanish land grant. Practically free land at the time. Everything was clear profit after that, or nearly so. There were some problems. There were a lot of political dealings to keep the land after we became a state . . . and gold hunters tore up the land . . . ."

"I'm not the least interested in the history of Tasajara, nor do I care to hear anything at all about Mace Donovan," I said coldly, glaring at the bank president and clenching my hands at my sides. Lambert looked momentarily stunned.

"In that case, I wish you good day, Miss Durham," he said stiffly.

I knew I had been unforgivably rude. This man

couldn't know my reasons for hating Donovan. "I'm sorry, Mr. Lambert," I said sincerely. "But I don't want to be absorbed by Tasajara. My father worked too many years and that land means too much to me to simply hand it over to . . ." I couldn't finish.

Lambert nodded, sympathetically. "I understand. Please be assured that the last thing I want to do is take your land and home away from you. I hope you'll be able to meet your payments."

"I don't expect missing them would be much good for business," I smiled wryly, "yours or mine." He smiled back.

"Neither of us would stand to make much of a profit," he agreed.

"What have you against Mace?" he asked as he opened the door for me. I gave a mirthless laugh.

"Plenty." I added no further explanation. It was very clear that Charles Lambert was a friend of the Donovans. Perhaps Donovan even owned a large part of the big brick bank building on Main Street. It would not have surprised me.

Standing outside the bank, I felt the full depressing magnitude of Jeremy's and my position. The ungodly heat of the sun and dry, dusty wind did not help to lighten my mood.

I felt sick and confused, and very afraid. I needed time to think about what to do. But there was so little time. Lambert had said one month. On top of the amount due to hold the homestead, there was still the money owed the Iversons, Bellows, and Jacobsons.

No wonder Papa had spent so much time alone on the ridge. It had been his one place of refuge, his one place of quiet and tranquility. And ironically, he had died there. Suddenly, a fierce determination filled me.

Donovan would not win! As long as I lived, he would never win!

Several townspeople stopped me to offer their condolences. I did not know all of them, but they seemed to
have known my father well. They were openly curious
about my plans. I found their questions tedious and my
responses were mechanical and evasive.

As I tried to accept the words of sympathy and summon appropriate responses, my mind was in a turmoil
about our seemingly insurmountable problems. As soon
as I was able, I excused myself, climbed aboard the half-
laden buckboard and turned it toward the north end of
town. Flicking the reins over the mare's broad back, I
started home. The slow, steady plodding of the horse
was oddly soothing to my frazzled nerves.

At the end of town, I recognized the sorrel stallion
tied in front of the three-story, garishly painted hotel. It
swished its long, silken tail impatiently, flicking at the
horse flies that buzzed annoyingly close.

What a hard life Donovan must have, I thought resentfully. So hard that he could spend time in the saloon
in late morning.

The front door opened and Donovan stood speaking
to someone on the threshold. I caught a glimpse of a
woman in a red satin dress with black lace that showed
an excess of bosom and a long length of slim brown legs.
I couldn't prevent my curiosity and stared at her. She
was pretty, with long black hair and dark eyes. She was
smiling up at Donovan.

My eyes widened in shock as I saw the woman daring-
ly caress Donovan's chest while looking into his face
seductively, speaking in a low voice. He laughed slightly,
shaking his head. He raised his hand to tuck something
deep into the cleavage of her breasts. The Mexican girl
pressed her hand over his, holding his fingers prisoner
against her skin well inside the front of her dress while
she reached up with her other hand to draw his head
down to her. Donovan did not seem to resist overmuch,

and my face grew hot as I saw her lips part. After the first second of contact he took the initiative, and I looked away, appalled.

How I hated the man! My knuckles turned white as I gripped the reins, wishing I were well past the hotel and not just drawing abreast of it. Of all the disgusting, decadent displays!

Donovan was coming down the steps as I passed. I restrained the urge to slap the mare into a faster pace. I could feel his eyes on me, and saw from the corner of my eye how he stood at the bottom of the steps, arms akimbo.

"Good morning, Miss Durham," Donovan called mockingly. My mouth tightened and I rode past without even glancing in his direction. The girl on the threshold called out something in rapid-fire Spanish and then laughed. Donovan said something back in the same language. Whatever joke they shared I did not understand nor did I care to. But the woman's name was Marcela.

I glanced around again looking at her curiously. Papa had returned once from town with the telltale smell of whiskey on his breath. He had mentioned someone named Marcel Juarez. I must have misunderstood him for I remembered the flush of his cheeks when he had stopped speaking abruptly. Had Papa been interested in *that* woman?

The girl looked back at me and raised her brow haughtily. She glanced down at Donovan again and said something else. Donovan threw back his head and laughed. Certain that they were laughing at me, I turned away humiliated, and rode on without another glance back.

For the next mile, I felt unreasonably tense, half-expecting Donovan to follow. He had been leaving the hotel and this was the road back to Tasajara as well as the homestead. When he did not make an appearance, I gradually relaxed. Perhaps he actually had *business* in town. But pleasure appeared to have been his first priority.

It was hot and my bonnet felt too tight on my head. Untying it, I pulled it off and tossed it back into the buckboard. I mopped my damp brow with a handkerchief I found in my blue gingham skirt pocket.

Another mile passed and I opened the front of my dress, loosening the tight collar. Putting my head back, I dabbed at the perspiration on my throat, then refastened the buttons. Another mile later, I heard a rider coming up fast behind me and glanced back over my shoulder.

Donovan!

Swinging my head around again, my fingers tightened defensively on the reins. He slowed his snorting stallion to a walk next to the buckboard. I did not look at him or in any way acknowledge his presence.

"You're looking hot and tired," he commented, studying my profile. "You should keep your bonnet on. You could get sunstroke, and a true lady never lets her skin get too brown."

I breathed slowly, seething.

"I stopped in at the bank," he went on after a moment. "Chuck said you were there earlier." If I had had any doubts at all about Lambert's relationship to Donovan, I did not now.

I flashed him a furious look. There was no mockery in his gaze and I jerked my head forward again. I heard him sigh.

"Listen," he said softly, "if you need some money, I'll be glad to loan it to you."

I pulled back so suddenly on the reins, the mare was startled. She took a step backwards and bumped into the harness brace before stumbling forward to stop. I swung around in the seat, facing Donovan.

"Just so you understand, Donovan," I said between clenched teeth. "I'd sooner borrow money from the devil himself than borrow a cent from you."

"Is that so?" he said. He seemed amused by my vehemence.

"That's so!" I retorted childishly.

"How do you expect to keep your head above water, Kathryn?"

"I don't remember ever giving you permission to call me that."

"Didn't you?" he baited.

"No. And don't!" I ordered.

"That is your name, isn't it?"

"It's not for your use."

"What would you prefer I call you?" he challenged, wryly twisting his lips. "You don't answer to 'Miss Durham.' "

"I won't answer to anything where you're concerned."

"You think not?" One brow cocked up, his eyes glittering.

Deciding this conversation had gone far enough, I yanked up the reins and started to urge the mare forward. Out of the corner of my eye I saw Donovan move and jerked back to avoid the hand that was coming down. In the process I released the reins. He caught them easily, leaned over, yanked up the brake and securely tied the reins around the bar. I swallowed hard.

"We're going to talk!" he said angrily. I stared at him in alarm. I wanted badly to untie those reins but did not dare, knowing full well he would stop me. I did not want him to touch me. At all cost, I did not want Mace Donovan ever to touch me.

He crossed his arms on the saddle horn and studied my defiant expression for a moment.

"You're going to have to get money from somewhere,

you know," he drawled.

"I'll get it."

"How? The bank's not going to give you another loan. You owe money every other place in town," he said in a hard voice.

"How come you know so much about *our* business?" I demanded hostilely.

"I told you once already . . . your father and I were *friends!*"

"And you're a liar!"

The gold eyes blazed and darkened. I felt the fear grow inside me, though I fought not to show it. "My father would never have confided in *you*," I added with more bravado than common sense.

"Who else did he have to confide in? A boy of ten? It's obvious he didn't confide in you. And I can understand why!"

I flinched, his words directly hitting the hurt I had felt since my first conversation with Joseph Iverson. My father certainly had not confided in me. Just how little he had told me had become depressingly clear all morning long.

"He . . . he always felt he had to protect us."

Donovan gave a harsh laugh. "More likely he was afraid of your hysterics."

My eyes burned and I averted my face. Donovan pushed agitated fingers through his hair.

"I'm sorry for that remark," he apologized and my hands fisted on my lap. "Are all Durhams this stubborn?" he asked, putting a lightness into his tone that was meant to be friendly and conciliatory. From anyone else, I would have accepted the proffered olive branch, but not from Mace Donovan.

Turning my head slightly, I looked squarely at him. "Durhams don't give up what belongs to them."

His jaw set. "Who's asking you to give up anything?"

he growled. "I'm offering you a better than fair price."

"And you offered the same to my father," I said taunt-ingly.

"I did."

"And what did he tell you?"

"You know what he said. He was far too proud. He couldn't admit defeat."

"My father was never defeated."

"Perhaps not. But you and your brother are, before you even start," he said harshly. "There's no way the two of you can cope with that homestead by yourselves. First off, you need capital. Second, you need man-power."

"We'll sell some of the cattle . . . or all if necessary," I said, making that decision impetuously.

Donovan stared at me in open frustration and anger. "You do that and you're making your first big mis-take!"

"I don't see how," I retorted. "You said we need capi-tal. That's the way to get it!"

"You sell off your cattle and you'll be bankrupt in a year, if not sooner! That's your only source of income, you little idiot! What'll you do next year or the year after? On top of that, it's the wrong season. You won't get a decent price on your stock and you'll never break even on the feed and time your father pumped into those animals."

"Oh, why don't you mind your own business!" I snapped, snatching the reins and untying them. If he tried to stop me I'd hit him with the whip.

"Someone had better help you mind yours! It's more than clear you don't know your tail from a hot rock when it comes to running cattle!"

"I know enough to keep us alive!"

"By the skin of your teeth . . . maybe . . . and for un-der a year I'll wager."

"You're never going to get our land," I protested firmly.

"If I want your land as badly as you seem to think I do, all I have to do is wait around for the public auction in six months . . . right after taxes fall due."

My face paled. I stared at him. We had no secret from this man, and his assurance made me shake with growing fury.

"I'll see you burn in hell before you take our land away from us," I said through my teeth.

"You won't have a word to say on the matter."

"Don't count too heavily on that, Donovan!"

He straightened and gave me a broad, taunting smile. "We'll talk again when you're more reasonable."

"We've nothing more to talk about!"

Donovan was still looking down at me, smiling. His cat-gold eyes narrowed as they flicked over me. "We haven't even begun yet, Kat." Tipping his hat, he rode off.

CHAPTER FIVE

Once Donovan rode off and left me in peace, I grudgingly admitted to myself that what he had said made sense. I could not sell all of Papa's herd because I would have nothing left come next year.

Yet, as far as I could see, there was no choice but to sell the cattle. My father had outstanding debts, debts that had been allowed to lapse for a year or more on the goodwill of his friends. Worse, another mortgage payment was due soon. To raise money, I would have to sell the cattle. They were our only asset.

Perhaps if I kept Casanova, the handsome black bull Papa had bought with hard-earned savings seven years before, I would have something to start with in the spring. Constance had dropped a number of fine calves. There was no reason she could not drop us a few more, and her milk would be an additional benefit.

Another possibility entered my head. Jeremy and I could farm part of the land. The south slope was rich enough. There weren't as many rocks there and it had yielded well for me over the years. We could expand the vegetable garden, put in several acres of corn with the old rusted plow. On another few acres, I could plant vegetables not usually grown in private gardens. The produce I harvested, I could take into town for sale.

What did not sell, I could store for our own use in winter.

My spirits rose. For the first time since I'd left the bank, I felt hope. We would manage. Somehow we would survive and hold our land. We had to!

My thoughts turned to Papa again. I remembered the times he had taken me to the harvest fair in Madrone where the people displayed their wares and expertise in various homecrafts. I remembered the bright starburst quilts, the knitted shawls, the crocheted bedspreads, the embroidered tablecloths. He had carried Jeremy perched on his shoulders one year while I trailed along behind. Throngs of people had clustered about the game booths. Once he had even won a pretty green glass cup by throwing balls through brightly painted rings. I still had that cup. It was on top of the bookshelf where I had put it years before to keep it safe from Jeremy's curious fingers.

I cherished my memories of Papa. He had been gay, lively, full of laughter. It was only after Mama died that he had withdrawn slightly, spending a little time each day by himself. Each year he had gone more and more frequently to the ridge. This last year he had been a quiet man, his smile infrequent. Tears choked me as I now understood why. The homestead was the one place on earth that had belonged to him and he loved it, yet each year brought closer the danger of losing it.

I was not going to let our land go without a fight. My parents lay together in the grove, and the thought of leaving them filled me with dread. Logic told me their essence was gone, but it was no use. At least during times of intense loneliness I could go to the grove and find a measure of peace.

I felt close to Papa now, as I remembered our last few days together. His final words had been of my brother though. I had to remember that Jeremy was in the middle of this battle between me and Donovan. He was the vulnerable one. The land was his, not mine.

It had been a Durham custom for generations that the eldest son inherited everything so that property would not be divided and lessened. That was the reason Papa had left Virginia after marrying my mother. Papa had been one of four sons, the third to be born. His chance of inheriting the rich plantation would have been remote at best. So he decided to seek his fortune in the west. He came ten years after the gold rush and had bought this land cheap from a family that had come with the forty-niners. They wanted to go back home to Missouri.

Now Papa was dead. It was up to me and Jeremy to hold onto what Papa had slaved over for more than ten years. I looked around me as I rode on, loving the smell of pine and sun-warmed earth. I knew nothing of Virginia, but did not believe it could possibly surpass the beauty of the California Sierras. There was a wild beauty about the grassy slopes, wooded mountains, jutting boulders, wild flowers, and a sky that was so blue it looked painted on a canvas.

Papa had been at home here, but my mother had never seemed to really belong. I remembered the stories she told about the gowns she wore, the social life she led, and the convent school she had attended in Richmond. After she spoke of Virginia, Mama was always sad-eyed with longing. Papa would then draw her onto his lap, stroking her cheek and shoulder, and pressing a kiss to the curve of her neck. Mama had always smiled at him, a gentle, private smile that he returned.

Sometimes they talked laughingly of how they had met outside the theater in Richmond. Mama's parents had taken her for her sixteenth birthday. Papa had been a handsome young man of twenty, and Mama had fallen in love with him immediately. They were married in the spring. The following year they left Virginia to come west. Mama's family had been greatly chagrined by their decision, knowing that they would never again see their only child nor her children. But there was no future in Virginia for them.

My first real memories of the trek west were of Papa holding me in front of him on his horse as he rode beside the wagon coming from Colorado. And of little Glenda, my friend who died before having had a chance to live.

For the first time, I wondered if Mama and Papa's families ever thought of us. Mama had come from a small merchant family with few uncles and aunts, so I did not know if she still had any relations in Virginia. Papa's three brothers would be married by now and there must be a gaggle of cousins at River's Bend. Somehow, the thought was comforting. We were not entirely alone in the world, though distance cut us off from any communication or knowledge of them personally.

I never remembered Papa writing to his family or my mother's. I never gave it much thought before, but now it seemed strange. I considered writing to River's Bend to inform them of my father's death and then decided against it. Papa must have had some reason for his silence.

I knew so little about Papa's family. Mama had once said I took after my grandfather Durham, which I found curious. She laughed at my expression. "It's not a slight, sweetheart. I only mean that you have a determined streak in you . . . and your temper . . ." She had shaken her head at me. "Quick to burn and slow to cool. Your grandfather all over again."

Jeremy was different. He had my mother's serious, quiet nature, yet sometimes his laugh sounded so much like Papa's. And he looked like Papa, too. His love of books came from Mama while my love for the land came from Papa.

The bend in the road that came just before the homestead was in view now and I sighed. Flicking the reins, I hastened the mare's easy pace. As I rounded the curve and looked up the hill I sucked in my breath in angry exclamation.

"Damnit!" I muttered, furious. The gate was just ahead and I jumped down, throwing it open and pulling the mare through before slamming it shut behind the buckboard. I grazed my hand in my impatience and swore again. I hit the mare's rump, sending her at a startled trot toward the barn with the buckboard rattling behind, and taking the whip I ran toward the vegetable garden.

"Jeremy!" I shouted. *"Jeremy!!"*

He was nowhere to be seen and the cattle were trampling all over the vegetables, crushing down those plants they were not pulling up to eat. They munched in ruinous delight on my crop, flicking their tails at flies, dropping their meadow muffins all over my planted rows.

"Jeremy!!" I screamed in abject frustration, taking the whip to the closest steer. It jumped forward, startled, and let out a loud bellow. The steers began to mill around nervously, rolling their big brown eyes at me while doing even more damage.

It was as one swishing tail almost hit me in the face that I noticed the brand. Donovan's stock! I swung the whip again across the hide of another steer. This one was expecting me and took a hefty swing with its horned head so that I had to jump back. I shoved and kicked at the beast and it finally moved to the side, looking at me balefully.

I waved my arms and shouted, and slowly the steers meandered despondently from their feast. They stood just beyond the broken mesh barrier waiting for me to go away so that they could complete their repast. I stared around me with tears of angry frustration. Then I sank down and put my head in my hands.

Hearing a rider coming, I jerked up, expecting to see
Donovan's gloating face. A stranger on a large pinto
was approaching. He was dressed in the work clothes of
a cowhand, leather vest, chaps and jangling spurs. A
wide-brimmed hat obscured his face. Drawing rein just
beyond the fence, he tipped his hat back, staring with
obvious dismay at the damage the steers had wrought to
my garden.

"Ma'am, I'm sorry about this," the man apologized,
rubbing the back of his neck and looking around again,
his eyes still not fixing on mine. "They've really torn it
up, haven't they?"

"Oh, no, just a wee bit of damage," I snapped, fum-
ing. "What are those damn beasts of Donovan's doing
up here on our land, anyway?"

The cowhand pointed down the slope. "The fence is
down. Looks like they just pushed through. Probably
some time this morning."

"There was nothing wrong with that fence a few days
ago," I said suspiciously. Had Donovan sent someone
up to deliberately cut the fence so that his cattle could
do all this damage?

"Did the steers do it, or did Donovan?" I asked
aloud.

The cowhand looked surprised. "Why would he do
that?"

"Oh, forget it. Just round up these dumb animals and
get them away from my garden and off our land," I said,
finding it difficult to contain my tears of frustration as I
looked around me again. So much work and time spent
for nothing! All the plans I had made on the way home
from town were shattered. I picked up a limp tomato
plant and then dropped it back to the ground. Everything would have to be dug under before a new garden
could be replanted.

Damn Donovan!

It took the cowhand only a matter of minutes to group the steers together. He hesitated, pushing his hat back to dangle by the cords between his shoulders. He was handsome, with longish, sandy brown hair, hazel eyes and an attractive smile. I could tell he was only a few years older than I.

"I'll tell the boss about all this," he said. "I'm sure he'll want to pay you for the damage."

"I wouldn't bother," I commented bitterly. "I'm sure Donovan's already more than aware of it."

"He's not God," the man said, and I heard a familiar drawl that reminded me piercingly of Papa.

"You're from the South," I said with certainty.

"Pecos, Texas, ma'am," he said still smiling, seemingly in no great hurry to leave. He was looking me over admiringly and it bolstered my sagging spirits considerably.

"You're a long way from home, cowboy."

"Home's where I put my hat," he shrugged. "This place is as good as any," he jerked his head toward Tasajara. "And a lot better than some I've worked."

Putting my fingers to my hair, I tried to tidy myself. "I'm Kathryn Durham," I smiled tentatively.

"I know who you are, ma'am," he admitted surprisingly. "Anybody who's been around Madrone a week hears about you."

"How's that?" I frowned. He grinned down at me. "The prettiest unmarried girl in two counties."

"My father must have started that rumor," I said, taking his compliment lightly. "And you *are* from Texas, aren't you, Mr. . . ."

"Saunders, ma'am. John Saunders," he supplied, touching his brow in a salute. "Sorry I didn't introduce myself sooner." It slipped my mind. He looked me over in such a way as to imply that my pulchritude might have been the cause for his momentary lapse of memory.

He was flirting with me, the first man ever to do so, and I was enjoying it.

"How long have you been at Tasajara, Mr. Saunders?"

"Two weeks." He leaned on the saddle horn after casting a quick glance at the steers, now moving slowly down the slope, nibbling at grass along the way. Saunders's pinto shifted, letting out a snort before lowering its head to take the steers' example. One of my crushed lettuces disappeared down its gullet.

"How do you like it?"

"Well enough. Good pay, good food, good bunk. Enough time off." He seemed to be giving me a message with his last words. He smiled broadly, showing straight white teeth and deep smile creases in his lean cheeks. I felt as though I had known him for a long time. "The company could be better," he added.

"The other cowhands aren't friendly?" I asked and he laughed.

"I wasn't thinking of cowhands, ma'am. Tasajara is a ways from town, and the only women on the ranch are Mexican, with one exception, Hattie McFadden. She works at the big house."

I had met few people from Tasajara. It seemed important now to know someone so that I could learn what was happening. Since Sheriff Collins would not arrest Donovan for my father's murder without more proof, I needed to know what my enemy was planning. I wondered how much Saunders had gleaned about Tasajara's activities in two short weeks.

"Would you like to stay for coffee?" I asked, smiling up at him while my mind worked furiously.

"I'd be much obliged," he accepted without hesitation, swinging down from his mount. He moved easily, his head at a proud angle. There was no bow to his strong legs and he was big, though not as big as Donovan.

"It'll take a few minutes to prepare," I said, admitting to a nervous flutter. I had never entertained a man before. Papa had never invited any out to the homestead, and not going to town frequently, I had not known many well.

Glancing down the hill at the steers, I asked if they would be all right on their own. "I don't want them trampling my garden anymore."

"They're fine. Looks like they've got other fields in mind besides your carrots and beans," he drawled pleasantly. "Now they're on this side of the fence, the other side will look tastier."

Saunders sat at the table while I made coffee. I could feel him watching my movements when he was not looking around the room. There was not much to see in our sod cabin. Saunders' eyes lingered on the gun above the mantle.

"That's a mighty handsome rifle," he commented.

"It was a gift to my father from his father, just before he and Mama left Virginia."

"That your mother?" Saunders pointed to the small oval portrait to the right of the mantle. I nodded.

"You look like her."

"That's what Papa used to say," I commented sadly. "I can't see it." Turning, I glanced at the likeness of my mother. She was so delicately beautiful and I simply could not think of myself in those terms.

I poured out the strong brew in two blue china cups my mother had brought from New Orleans, and pushed a plate of macaroons toward my guest. I did not know how to approach the subject of Mace Donovan. Subterfuge was not my strong point. I did much better speaking bluntly.

Saunders was smiling, glancing at me speculatively over the rim of his cup. "Good coffee, ma'am."

"Thank you," I said, wondering how to be subtle. I

glanced at him through my lashes. "What do you think of Donovan?"

"As a boss, ma'am . . . or as a man?" he asked dryly.

I flushed at his implication. "I'm not in the least interested in him as . . . well, you understand!" I said crossly. "I want to know about him because he wants this homestead. He wants it very badly. And I don't want him to get it!"

"Well, then, I'd say you're in a peck of trouble. Donovan gets what he wants, from all I've heard about him. I don't know him all that well, you understand. Haven't been at Tasajara long enough. But from what I've seen . . . I wouldn't want to be on the opposite side of him."

I sighed heavily. "Well, he's not going to get what he wants this time," I said grimly.

Saunders looked from his coffee cup to me. "You could have asked me that without going to the trouble of making coffee," he said quietly.

I flushed again. "It was no trouble. And I don't often have company." Not at all, in fact, except for Donovan . . . and he was not "company"!

Saunders did not say anything for a long time, but he watched my face. There was something at work behind the bemused expression.

"There's nothing much I can tell you about Donovan," he said finally. "He pays me and I'm beholden to him for my room and board. It wouldn't be loyal to turn spy on him."

"I didn't ask you to," I said slowly, surprised by his perception. There was nothing dense about this man, and put into words, my thoughts sounded dreadful.

"No. Not outright, maybe. But you're a little desperate, aren't you?"

"I want to hold our land!" I said defensively.

"I can't see Donovan as the type to try and take land

belonging to a young woman and a boy."

"You've met Jeremy?" I looked up.

"I haven't had the honor," he drawled. "But word travels fast about what happened up here a week ago."

I flinched at the reminder of Papa's murder. "What would you think if I told you Donovan murdered my father?"

Saunders' eyes opened wide and glittered. "What does the sheriff say about it?"

"The sheriff is a friend of Donovan's. I doubt he'd arrest him if he had witnessed the killing himself," I said in a voice heavy with defeat.

"What makes you so sure Donovan killed your father."

I studied the young face opposite me. Strangely, I felt I knew him well enough to trust him. "Papa wrote his initials in the dust and mentioned Tasajara before he died," I confided.

"My God!"

"And he had a motive. He wants our land. He made several offers for it and Papa turned him down. Papa never wanted to leave here."

"And the sheriff still wouldn't believe it?"

"No. Now you understand why it's important for me to know as much as I can about Donovan's doings? I've got to protect myself. Papa said Jeremy was in danger."

Saunders' mouth tightened. "I wouldn't think so, ma'am. He's just a boy."

"I can't take the chance that Donovan has a thread of decency in him. Anyone who would shoot a man who called him friend, and then push him off a ridge to die isn't human."

"No," Saunders said, sipping his coffee. "I expect not. Seems to me Donovan could have just bought you out, though."

"Papa wouldn't sell."

"What's so special about this place? It's lousy for running stock. Too many places for the animals to hide."

"Maybe he wants it because it's the last parcel of land in the valley that doesn't belong to him."

"That's not enough reason to kill a man, though I suppose some have killed for less," Saunders said in deep concentration.

"You think there might be another reason he wants the land?"

"There's got to be," he said, glancing up at me.

"Maybe he'd like the ridge so that he could look down at his valley," I said unpleasantly. "The Lord Almighty of the Land!"

"You really hate him, don't you?"

"I've every reason in the world to hate him, wouldn't you say?" I retorted defensively.

Saunders finished his coffee in silence. His eyes narrowed thoughtfully, his mouth a firm, hard line. "I'll keep my eyes and ears open," he told me, getting up.

"I'd certainly appreciate it," I sighed in relief, feeling I had at least one ally in my battle against Donovan.

Saunders stood up and we walked out into the afternoon sun. Jeremy was just riding up the hill on Dionysus. Papa had named the horse for its stumbling gait. My brother had a look of curious alarm on his face.

"What happened to the garden, Katie?" he asked, jumping down from the horse. He eyed Saunders warily. The cowhand returned the cool appraisal.

"Donovan's steers broke through the fence," I answered with a wry twist of my mouth. "Strickly accidental, of courses. This is John Saunders, Jeremy. One of Tasajara's cowhands." I looked at John and smiled. "He's a friend." I received a smiling look back.

Jeremy was staring at Saunders, but gave no welcome greeting. There was nothing remotely friendly in his expression. Saunders glanced at him briefly and then walked over to remount his pinto, tipping his hat to me again.

"Sorry we had to meet under such unpleasant circumstances, Miss Kathryn," he drawled. "I'll be by." He rode off down the hill and Jeremy turned to watch him, his stance belligerent.

"You weren't exactly polite," I commented.

"Why should I be? He should have kept those cows on the other side of the fence."

"It was hardly all his fault," I defended Saunders.

Jeremy turned and looked up at me. "I don't like him."

"For heaven's sake, Jeremy! You don't even know him."

Jeremy's mouth tightened mutinously. "He likes you," he said insinuatingly. "Papa wouldn't have liked him coming around here. He would have told him just where to go."

My brother's expression surprised me and suddenly I understood.

"Oh, Jeremy," I said, hugging him until he protested. My little brother was jealous!

CHAPTER SIX

Long before dawn I awakened with a pounding headache, having dreamt about Mace Donovan and my father on the ridge. I lay in the dark fretting about it, and then my thoughts turned to Jeremy's and my financial situation. We had so much work ahead of us just to hang onto our land. There was no one to help us but ourselves. We owed everyone, and Donovan hung over us like a vulture waiting for its prey.

Before light, I dressed and lit the fire. I could not sleep any longer and there seemed little sense in tossing about when so much had to be done. I made bread dough and left it to rise on the table while I went to the barn to gather eggs and feed the chickens. Constance lowed at me as I milked her. On the way back to the cabin, with a basket of eggs under one arm and a sloshing bucket of milk in the other, I stopped to survey again the damage to my garden.

It was a total loss. The beans had been ripped up and eaten, the potato plants were trampled. The carrots, radishes, beets, and rhubarb were mangled. The tomatoes and lettuce were wilted and broken down. I stalked into the cabin to leave the eggs and milk and put on my gardening gloves. Papa had bought them for me, saying that a girl shouldn't ruin her hands in the dirt.

Cursing Donovan, I went back out and began my

work. Pulling everything up, I cast it all on the compost pile behind the barn. Then I hoed the ground. On my hands and knees I began making the grooves and mounds for the new seedlings I always kept growing in flats in the barn. By the time first light came, I was one-third of the way through the planting.

The cabin door opened. "How long you been up, Katie?" Jeremy asked, rubbing sleep-filled eyes.

"Hours. I couldn't sleep."

Jeremy stared at the garden. "You've replanted."

"I've still a long way to go," I sighed, sitting back on my heels and wiping the perspiration from my forehead with the back of my hand. "Thanks to Donovan."

"You mean thanks to Saunders," Jeremy retorted.

"He didn't do it. The steers did it . . . after Donovan cut the fence."

"If Saunders had been doing his job, the steers wouldn't have tromped up here. Where was he when the cattle broke through? It must have taken them a while to wander up here to the garden. He was probably sleeping under a tree some place."

"Donovan has a big herd. You can't expect John Saunders to see where they all are."

"Seems to me you make plenty of excuses for that cowhand who was responsible and blame Donovan when he wasn't even anywhere around."

"Jeremy Durham!" I cried, infuriated, rising to my feet. "How can you defend that man? He killed Papa."

"You say so."

I felt as though he had slapped me. "Papa said so before he died."

Jeremy flinched. "You never told me that . . ." he said chokingly. "What did he say?"

I told him. My brother looked pale and sick.

"Are you all right, Jeremy?" I asked. He nodded slowly.

"It's just that . . . well, I saw Donovan yesterday for a while. He talked . . . and, well . . ." Jeremy looked up at me, his eyes glistening with unshed tears. "I liked him."

"He wants you to like him," I said harshly.

"Couldn't Papa have meant someone else on Tasajara?"

"No." I pressed Jeremy against me, smoothing down the thatch of thick hair. "You can't trust him, Jeremy."

"I wish Papa were here." His shoulders shook. I swallowed hard.

"So do I, sweetheart."

"Why would Donovan want to shoot him?"

"To take away what belongs to him. This land. It's yours now, Jeremy. And we're going to have to fight to keep it."

"Fight Donovan, you mean," Jeremy said depressingly.

"Yes."

There was a lot more than Donovan we would have to fight, I thought despairingly. Somehow we would have to pay off our debts and find a means of supporting ourselves, while still increasing our herd over the next few years. It seemed an impossible task. But I couldn't put those worries on Jeremy's young shoulders.

"It's more your land than mine, Katie," Jeremy said, drawing back to look at me. "You love it like Papa always did."

"And don't you?" I said, faintly accusing. I knew, of course, what my brother meant. He loved his books more than the land. There would be no heartache for him if we were forced to sell.

"It just seems like we can't win."

"Donovan isn't God," I said in a hard voice. "He's a man, and now that we know what kind of man he is, we'll be less trustful than Papa was."

I squeezed Jeremy again and then released him. "I'll fix us some breakfast and bake the bread. Then you can fix the fence while I finish replanting the garden," I told him, drawing him toward the cabin.

The smell of baking bread soon filled the cabin, and I watched as Jeremy, reading a book, pushed his scrambled eggs around on the plate. Slowly, he took a few mouthfuls, the hunger of a young and growing body taking thankful precedence over his unhappiness.

"Jeremy, would you please draw the water from the well?" I asked. "I've got some washing to do this morning, as soon as the garden is set to rights."

"Sure," he agreed, picking up the bucket just outside the door.

Bread baked, I returned to the garden. It would take a long time for the water to be hot enough for a good wash, and that gave me plenty of time for replanting. Jeremy worked at the fence, propping it up with stakes and hammering them back into the ground. When he finished, he went back into the cabin to get a hunk of bread and some cheese.

"I'll go out and look at the cattle again," he said in a grown-up tone that surprised me. He went off to the barn to saddle Dionysus and a few minutes later I saw him ride off up the hill. I didn't expect to see him again until the afternoon.

Finishing the replanting, I filled the furrows with water. Then I went into the cabin. The fire had burned low, but had kept the water hot enough for washing. I toted heavy bucketsful to the washbasin out back, dumping them in with the stringent soap. Then, on my knees, I scrubbed the clothes against the metal washboard. It was hard work and my back ached after half an hour.

Wringing out the garments, I set them in a pile on a flat rock and gently poured the sudsy water on the seedlings, bucket by bucket. Soap would keep the bugs away. Then I refilled the washtub with fresh warm water for rinsing. I was almost finished with the chore when I heard a noise behind me.

"How's the stock, Jeremy?" I asked, glancing up at the sun and realizing it was later than I thought. There was no answer and I turned my head slightly, while sloshing the last shirt up and down. I saw Donovan leaning negligently against the cabin, watching me. I stared in shocked silence, a flutter of tension coiling in my stomach. Then, I dropped the shirt with a splash and stood up to face him, hands on hips.

"What're you doing here, Donovan?"

He smiled easily. "I heard my steers ruined your vegetable garden."

"No great surprise to you, I'm sure."

The gold eyes narrowed slightly. "I came to make amends," he said dryly, no apology in his tone.

"The only thing I want mended is your fence," I shot back. "The next time one of your steers comes onto our land, I'll shoot it. We could use the extra meat."

He pushed away from the wall looking wholly amused, which irritated me all the more.

"That wouldn't be very wise, Kat."

I controlled the impulse to tell him not to call me that, but knew it was useless. It would be more effective to ignore him entirely—but that seemed utterly impossible.

"You could always add them to your herd," he suggested smoothly.

"You'd like that, wouldn't you? Then you could claim I rustled your miserable animals."

"I wouldn't slander such a . . . charming . . . little lady," he said, and there was something in his tone that increased my indignation.

"You've had your gloat, now go away!"

A flicker of impatience entered his eyes. "It won't happen again."

I laughed. "I'm sure *that* won't happen again. But something else most assuredly will. Won't it, Donovan?"

He stood still for a moment, then decided to let the jibe pass. He took a few steps closer, making me feel decidedly uneasy. I was forced to throw my head back to look up at him and I felt at a definite disadvantage. I wanted to back away, but refused to let him see how nervous his presence made me. I did not like the way he looked me over, from head to foot, and I especially did not like that smile he wore!

"About your garden . . ."

"It's replanted," I interrupted.

"So I noticed when I rode up. You don't waste time, do you?" he grinned.

"There's no time to waste."

"It'll be a while before you get any yield from it," he went on, infuriatingly reasonable despite my derision. I wanted to make him lose his temper, not thinking of the possible consequences of such an action.

"No thanks to you, Mr. Donovan."

The gold eyes flared then. He breathed in slowly. I could feel the tension in him even as he controlled it. It gave me an odd sense of triumph and excitement.

"Tasajara has a sizable garden," he went on doggedly. "I'll have one of the hands bring a share over to you until yours is producing again."

His offer caught me off-guard. I opened my mouth and then clamped my teeth together. I almost accepted his offer gratefully, then my eyes lit with suspicion.

What was he after? He looked sincere enough. But he had murdered my father. There must be a reason for this small kindness he was showing us. I did not like it. He either was salving his conscience or planning something. Whatever was in his mind, it was to benefit Mace Donovan.

Squaring my shoulders and tilting my chin up, I
stared straight into his questioning eyes.

"Go to hell, Donovan," I said distinctly.

There was no mistaking the anger in him now, as the
muscles knotted in his jaw and the smile he wore became
a simple baring of his even teeth.

"You needn't worry that I might add the cost of the
handout to your other outstanding debts in town," he
taunted, bringing a painful flush of humiliation into my
cheeks.

"Keep your charity," I managed through the constriction in my throat, fighting for control. Donovan looked
at me and then raked his fingers back through his hair.

"It isn't charity, for God's sake. My steers ruined
your garden. I owe you something."

"Well, well" I snapped, blinking fast to prevent tears
from coming. "You, the great Donovan, owner of the
valley Tasajara, owing someone. Do you like it?"

"I'm sorry for that remark, all right?" he relented
harshly. "Will you accept my offer?"

"No."

Donovan's mouth hardened at my unyielding decision. A muscle tightened in his cheek and worked
there. "Why not?" he bit out after a pause.

I smiled sweetly, cocking my head to one side. "Because, Donovan, there might just be more in your offering than meets the eye."

"What's that supposed to mean?"

"There might be something in the basket besides vegetables."

Surprisingly, he grinned at the intended insult. "Such
as a rattler, I presume? Or possibly a nice fat tarantula?"

"We don't need your brand of help," I told him, cold-
eyed. "And we don't want it."

There was a certain grimness in his face. "Pride isn't
much of a meal, Kat."

"We'll manage."

Something finally snapped in him. "On what? You didn't buy any produce in town yesterday. In fact, you didn't buy much of anything in the way of supplies."

"How would you know what I bought? Did you look in my wagon?" I sneered.

"As a matter of fact, I did," he admitted, unabashed.

"Then I'd better re-inventory what I brought home after you stopped me."

His face darkened ominously and he swore violently under his breath. "I wonder if giving you a good hiding would help " he muttered, taking a step closer. I did back up then. There was enough fire in his gaze to make me frightened.

"You are going to accept my offer, Kat," he ordered imperiously, his face lowering to within inches of mine. The black pupils widened. "Whether you like it or not."

My heart was thudding wildly in my chest and I was having difficulty breathing with him so close. He stared into my face for a moment longer, his eyes dropping briefly to my mouth before he straightened abruptly. He turned away, rubbing the back of his neck in agitation, and then he swung around again.

"One of these days, you'll learn not to provoke me. The consequences might not be to your liking."

"I've already learned the consequences of going against your desires, Donovan," I managed, thinking of my father.

"You think so?"

I did not answer, but hoped my expression was clear enough. His eyes narrowed on my face. His gaze was impossible to hold after a moment, and I looked away, feeling a curious heat run through my body.

"The basket will be delivered right to your door, ma'am," he announced mockingly, his eyes challenging.

"We're always in need of more compost or feed for

the animals," I said with a cloying smile. Donovan's face was rigid, and I waited for the explosion.

"What a bloody little fool you are."

My temper flared. "What did you expect, Donovan? That with your offer of a few beans and tomatoes, I'd forget that you murdered my father? You think I'm fool enough to trust you an inch? My father trusted you. He liked you. And what did it get him? A bullet hole in his chest and broken bones from being shoved down a cliff." I was shaking violently with anger and pain, but fear was churning inside me as well. Donovan watched my face. His lack of guilt infuriated me all the more.

"There's nothing human about you," I cried. "You don't even feel the least remorse!"

"Why should I?"

I stared at him. "My God, how I hate you!" I whispered chokingly. "You actually think you've gotten away with it."

"I told you once . . ." he started and then stopped. "Oh, what the hell's the use!" he growled harshly. He turned and strode off, disappearing around the corner of the cabin. I heard his horse thundering off seconds later.

I stood shaking for a moment. Then I fell to my knees and started to cry.

"He'll pay, Papa! I swear it! He will pay!"

CHAPTER SEVEN

The day after Donovan came to the homestead, I worked the cattle with Jeremy. We managed after a full day's hard work to corral twenty head. There were still more than a dozen somewhere in the hills and ravines and we would have to search them out tomorrow. I had decided to approach Les Bigelow, the rancher south of Madrone, who was building his herd to match Donovan's. Surely he would buy our head. Jeremy was dubious about my decision, but agreed after some discussion.

John Saunders came by the following morning with a basket of vegetables from Tasajara. There were several leafy heads of lettuce, radishes, onions, potatoes, huge red beef tomatoes and even a bag of beans. Whoever managed the garden at Tasajara had a green thumb. However, I told John to take the basket back. He refused, saying it would cost him his job. Relenting, I invited him in for coffee and bread. I would dump the offering on the compost pile later. John tried to talk me into keeping the basket, but I was adamant. I would accept nothing from Donovan even if it meant we had to search out roots in the forest.

"He does owe you. Actually, I do, because I was the one watching the cattle," John reasoned.

"Let's drop the subject. My mind is made up."

"You're as stubborn as my father . . ." he gave a harsh laugh, "as a mule, actually, if you'll pardon my saying so."

I mentioned the fact that Jeremy and I planned to sell the cattle. Saunders suggested I approach Donovan.

"You could get a little revenge on him by gouging him for the price of your beef. Put the price up."

I thought about it and was tempted for a moment. Then I decided against it. I did not want anything of Papa's to belong to Donovan, even if he paid a price for it. Saunders left, saying he would be back again as soon as he could. He did not ask after Jeremy.

Jeremy and I fell into our beds that night, exhausted. The work seemed unending. How had Papa managed so much by himself? He had always left me only the household chores to do, and Jeremy was left free for his studies. Yet, Papa always seemed to have time enough to linger on the ridge, looking down at the valley. Were we doing something wrong?

It took three days to find all the cattle and I was sure that there must be more than the mangy herd that filled the corral. I was awake for a long time the night after we brought them all in. Tomorrow I would ride over to Bigelow's ranch and present our proposition. He would then inspect the herd and set a price. I hoped he was a reasonable man, because aside from our daily expenses, we needed so much money for our debts and the mortgage. Papa had not liked Les Bigelow, I recalled with dismay. But then Papa had liked Donovan, and to me, that didn't say much for his judge of character.

Late that night, I was awakened by the high-pitched screams of our two horses. Dazed with exhaustion, I sat up in bed and listened, wondering if I had been dreaming. I heard the screams again, and this time could also hear the cattle lowing and the thudding of nervous hooves in the corral.

"Jeremy," I cried in alarm, and leaped out of bed. He had been awakened by the noise too and we both headed toward the door.

Smoke was billowing out of the barn and I saw the flicker of flames inside.

"You get water while I get the animals out!" I cried, running toward the barn in my long nightgown. The night air was chilling, but inside the barn it was as warm as summer.

After a fight, I managed to get the bridle on Dionysus and led him out. Handing the reins to Jeremy, he took him to the far end of the field, while I went back in the barn for the mare that pulled the buckboard. The flames leaping ever higher into the rafters made the heat unbearable and the mare paced nervously, but I managed to drag her out after throwing a blanket over her head.

The chickens had scattered and the cattle, in panic, had broken down part of the corral fence and were heading back up into the hills again. The wagon was a loss, consumed by the flames. I could smell roasting oats and barley feed, mentally tallying the money burning before my smoke-filled eyes. And there was nothing I could do!

Standing just inside the barn, I felt the heat growing to an inferno. The flames licked the roof and I looked around to see if there was anything more that could be salvaged. The smoke was suffocating. There was a loud crack and Jeremy screamed behind me.

"Katie! Katie! Get out! The roof's falling in!"

I ran out, coughing and stumbling. Jeremy's thin, but strong arms came around my waist as he valiantly tried to help me. We both fell at the edge of the garden fence, turning in time to see the barn collapse in a ball of exploding flames. Staring at the blaze, I felt numb.

What else can happen? I wondered despondently.

"How do you suppose it started?" Jeremy asked, his eyes fixed on the burning rubble.

"How do you think?" I said tearfully, frustration and

anger welling inside me. "Donovan, of course, who else?"

I buried my head in my knees, pressing my forehead against my scorched nightgown. "Damn him!" I moaned. "Why won't he just leave us alone?"

"What're we going to do now?" Jeremy asked in a small, frightened voice.

I sighed heavily, feeling the full weight of responsibilities. Reaching over, I put my arm around my brother's shoulders.

"First thing tomorrow, we're going to look everything over and see if we can come up with some solid evidence that this is Donovan's doing. Then, I'm going in to see Sheriff Collins again."

"The sheriff? But Katie . . ."

"He'll listen if we have proof," I anticipated his question.

"Then what?"

I smiled slightly. "Then we'll round up the cattle again."

Jeremy groaned and I felt his shoulders droop.

"I know," I said with empathy. "But it's got to be done and there's no one but us to do it. I'll approach Bigelow as soon as the cattle are corralled. Maybe John will help us."

Jeremy's head came up, his eyes flashing with anger. "No! I don't want him around here."

"Now, be reasonable. We could use his help."

"I . . . I don't like him!" Jeremy stated out.

"Why not? He's been perfectly cordial to you."

"I don't like the way he looks at you," Jeremy said. "Besides," he went on in a more hopeful note, "he might not come by for a couple of days, and I can't see you riding over to Tasajara to ask for the loan of his time. He does work for Donovan, doesn't he?"

"Yes, but he's our friend. You're right, though. I

wouldn't ride over there and ask him to come." I wouldn't set foot on Tasajara for any reason. "But John said he'd be coming by again in a day or two. If we haven't finished bringing the herd in, we'll ask for his help then. Agreed?"

Jeremy paused. "I don't see why he should help. You've got me. We managed without him before." Seeing my expression, he relented grudgingly. "Oh, all right!"

The following morning, Jeremy and I walked through the blackened ruins that had been our barn. Both of us carried buckets to douse any remaining embers. There was little left but a pile of charred timbers and boards. A few feet beyond where the back of the barn had stood, I spied an unfamiliar kerosene can. I ran to pick it up and the Tasajara marking on it boldly confirmed my earlier suspicions. I smiled grimly as I waved it at Jeremy.

"This time Donovan isn't getting away with anything," I announced, triumphantly. "I'm going to town to see the sheriff."

Dionysus was sweating by the time I reached Madrone. I reined in sharply at the sheriff's office and jumped down, not caring if anyone disapproved of my riding astride in a gingham skirt. Tying Dionysus, I was sure this time that something would be done about Donovan and I felt immeasurably relieved that the fight was nearly over.

Sheriff Collins looked up from his desk as I opened the door. Standing up, he smiled.

"Hello, Miss Durham. What brings you into Madrone?"

"This!" I snapped, thrusting the can forward for him to see, but not relinquishing it.

"A kerosene can?"

"Donovan burned our barn down last night," I said without further preamble.

Collins looked suddenly impatient. "You're not going to start all that again, now are you?" he asked coolly, sitting down. I stared at him in disbelief.

"You still don't believe me? Here! Look at this! It's got the Tasajara marking on it. It's Donovan's! I found it in the bushes behind where our barn *used* to be. Now, you've *got* to do something about it! Only a couple of days ago, Donovan's fence mysteriously broke down," I went on derisively, "and his steers marched all over my garden, ruining everything. Then, the barn burns down. That's a little much for coincidence, don't you think? What else do you want on top of my father's murder and what he told me before he died? What does it take before you'll do something? Does Donovan have to kill me and my brother too?"

"Calm down, Miss Durham!"

"Calm down? How can I when you keep ignoring what's going on. My father named his killer and you won't believe me!"

"We've been over that before."

"What about my garden and the barn?"

"All right," he relented with a raised hand. "I take it you want to swear out a complaint against Donovan?"

"You take it correctly," I said, relaxing slightly. Collins looked at me for a long moment and then opened a drawer and took out some forms.

"Fill these out then," he said, sliding them across to me. I did so and handed them back.

"When will you go to Tasajara and arrest him?" I wanted to know.

"I'll go and *question* Donovan this afternoon," he answered patiently. "I'll make your complaint known."

"My ride in here accomplished about as much as telling you who killed my father," I said coldly.

The sheriff's face turned a mottled red at my accusation. "Your father's murder isn't forgotten, Miss Durham," he said tautly.

"Not by me and my brother," I muttered, standing up, fighting back tears.

"Believe me, Miss Durham," Collins said softly, "it's not forgotten. Your father was well-liked and respected in Madrone. We'll do all we can to find his killer. I've already questioned half a dozen men with the initials M.D. But so far I haven't come up with anything. These things take time."

"Have you questioned Donovan?" I asked, trying to keep the bitterness from my tone.

He sighed heavily. "I'll question him, all right? This afternoon. I won't accuse him, but I'll feel him out about the situation that existed between he and your father." He did not seem overly enthused about the prospect and I smiled.

"Thank you." I turned to leave, but Collins stood up.

"Miss Durham, there's something I want you to think on."

"Yes?"

"Aside from the initials your father scratched out, there's no evidence that Donovan committed the murder. Is there anyone else who might have had a grudge against your father?"

"No one."

"You answered too quickly. I said I want you to think on it. And there's something else . . ."

"What else?" I asked stiffly.

"This kerosene can," he indicated the can sitting on his desk. "Donovan is an intelligent man. Don't you think it's a bit too obvious to leave it behind after burning a barn?"

"Maybe he was in a hurry."

"Donovan never does anything in haste. He evaluates, thinks things out. That's why he's such a successful rancher."

"Maybe this time he didn't think."

Collins looked very doubtful. "If he did burn your barn, and I'm saying a big *if* . . . he wouldn't have been stupid enough to leave something as blatant as this lying around."

"Well, maybe he feels he's such an important man that he doesn't need to worry about little details like a kerosene can," I suggested sarcastically.

"Or maybe someone is trying hard to make it look like Mace Donovan is responsible," Collins countered.

I had not considered that. But that did not explain away my father's message and the look on his face just before he died. *Betrayal.* I looked at Collins.

"Who have you questioned?"

"Michael Downs at the Bar J. Morgan Devonshire and Matt Daniels at Bigelow's. Mark Dirkson at Rafer Woodhouse's Stoneridge. And Mercer Dumont at Graff Hardings ranch."

"That's five. You said you had spoken to half a dozen," I reminded him.

Collins smiled slightly. "Well, I still haven't questioned Milan Davis, but I seriously doubt if he murdered your father."

"Who's Milan Davis?"

"He's an old drunk who lives under the bridge at the end of town . . . when I haven't got him locked in one of my cells sleeping off the booze."

"Oh."

"Have you heard of any of those other men, Miss Durham?" Collins asked.

"No. I'm afraid I haven't."

"Well, your father probably knew all of them. They've been around for a good amount of time, and your father came into town frequently. He probably met most of them at the hotel."

I had never really thought of my father spending much time at the hotel and the idea was somewhat unsettling. I pushed it away.

"That still doesn't give any of them a reason to murder my father. Why would any of them want to kill him?"

"That's what I'll have to find out."

"You're not forgetting Donovan? He does have a motive."

"Your land," Collins said wryly.

"Yes, our land," I said, not liking his tone. "It's the last parcel in the valley that Donovan doesn't own. And he wants it. He offered a lot to buy it again."

Collins rubbed his fingers against his temple, his mouth pursed in concentration. "Well, I suppose that could be motive for some. But I know Mace . . . and I know Brian, his father. He's still alive, you know, but he's been sick a long time. Hasn't been into town in two years."

The nerves in my stomach tautened painfully. I waited.

"We'll see what comes out of my talk with Mace this afternoon," Collins told me, standing up, as a gesture of dismissal.

"Will you please tell me what happens? I've got Jeremy to think of and I have to be prepared if you don't arrest him."

"Prepared for what?"

"Prepared for Donovan. Whatever the law says, he won't give up until he gets what he wants. And right now Donovan wants our land."

Collins looked at me soberly, then he nodded. "I'll ride over to your place when I'm finished at Tasajara," He assured me. "And it might not be foolish for me to send someone out periodically just to check on the two of you. I doubt it's Donovan . . . but someone is up to no good."

CHAPTER EIGHT

Sheriff Collins came by in mid-afternoon. Jeremy was out in the hills looking for the scattered herd. I had managed to find most of the chickens and penned them in an enclosure I made from the extra fencing from the garden. When the sheriff rode up, I was hammering on the corral fence broken by the cattle.

"What happened?" I asked, setting the hammer on the fence post and pocketing the nails.

"Not much," Collins admitted, not getting down from his bay gelding. "Seems he was at the ranch house all of that day. Hattie McFadden verified it. She said he went into the study early that morning to work on the ranch accounts. Brian saw him later on. He didn't eat the lunch Hattie took in to him, and he was still hard at work when she went in at dinner."

"What about between lunch and dinner?" I asked, wondering if he could have slipped out of the house for a few spare hours.

"If you're thinking he left the ranch, it'd be nearly impossible. Someone would have seen him." He looked down at me, his arms crossed over the saddle horn. "You neglected to tell me of Mace's offer to share yield from Tasajara's garden."

"I didn't trust his sudden kindness," I answered dryly, unable to keep the flush from crawling into my cheeks.

Collins shook his head, his expression impatient.

"Have you been thinking about what I asked you this morning?" he asked.

"Yes, if you mean about someone else possibly wanting my father dead." I had thought of little else since leaving Madrone, and had come up with nothing.

"And?"

"There isn't anyone, except . . ."

"Yes, I know," Collins cut me off, lifting his reins. "Donovan. Good day, Miss Durham." He turned his horse and trotted down the hill toward the gate.

Who was Hattie McFadden? And what was Donovan to her that she would supply him with a ready alibi? My mouth tightened angrily as I hammered a nail into the fence railing. How many others were there that would take up Donovan's defense, and leave Jeremy and I without any?

John Saunders rode up an hour after Collins had left.

"Good God!" he exclaimed, looking around. "What happened here?" He stared at the blackened pile that had been our barn.

"The barn burned down last night," I stated the obvious.

"Somebody was mighty careless, I'd say," he drawled, eyeing me questioningly. I was too tired to argue and let him believe it was an accident.

"Ever feel like the good Lord was against you?" he asked with a slight laugh. I looked up at him, leaning against the fence.

"The good Lord has nothing to do with it."

"Can I help?"

"Are you on Tasajara time or your own?"

"My own," he smiled.

"You could ride up and help Jeremy round up the stock again. They broke through the corral in a panic during the fire."

John did not seem enthusiastic about my suggestion. There was a withdrawn look in his eyes. "Your brother doesn't cotton to me."

"He'll get over it once he gets to know you," I assured him, smiling.

"You think so," he said dryly, the smile quirking slightly.

"Why shouldn't he?"

"He'd probably like me enough if I wasn't so interested in his beautiful big sister," John said, leaning down so that his warm breath fanned my cheek. His eyes moved over my face and then dropped suggestively to my mouth. Putting up a restraining hand, I leaned back away from him.

"Will you help?" I asked, wanting to get back to the point.

"First things first, hmm?"

"We have to sell those cattle to keep this place."

"All right," he sighed overemphatically. "I'll go help little brother and put up with his sullen looks." He pushed away from the fence and straightened in his saddle.

"I appreciate it, John," I smiled up at him.

"I'll come back later to find out how much," he grinned, turning his horse toward the hills.

"I'll make you dinner," I called after him, laughing. He laughed back, taking off his hat and hitting the pinto across the rump to set it galloping up the slope.

Still smiling, I went into the house. There was a lot to be done before sundown.

A pot of stew was boiling over the fire and I was kneading bread dough when the door burst open with a crash. I jerked upward in frightened surprise, my eyes large. Mace Donovan stood there, his face anything but friendly.

"I think it's about time we had a little understanding," he said, striding into the room as though he owned it. My mouth opened to protest.

"For once in your life, just shut your mouth and listen." He stopped on the other side of the table, glowering at me. I blinked, too stunned by his sudden intrusion to think straight.

"I was at Tasajara all day the day your father was killed," he told me through his teeth. "There are half a dozen people who can verify it."

I started to say something and his hand shot across the table to clamp shut my jaw.

"I said," he told me in a slow, deep voice, "not to open your mouth." His eyes glittered and my heart began to knock against my ribs as he came closer. I knew his fingers would leave marks on my face. He stared at me for a long moment and then dropped his hand. His eyes moved slowly over my face, his breathing slowing from its angry pace.

"My God, but you can make me so mad I can't think," he said. Then he went on harshly, "I did not kill your father! Furthermore, I did not tear down my fence and allow my steers to trample your precious, bug-ridden garden, nor did I burn down your damn rickety barn! And as for that kerosene can, I loaned half a dozen to your father which he never returned. He didn't have to. I gave them to him because he didn't have the money to buy some from Kirst, and Kirst doesn't give credit."

My face paled under his onslaught, which seemed to be growing fiercer.

"And I don't want this miserable rock pile you call land!" he finished.

That did it. "Don't you really?" I said sarcastically, leaning across the table, my chin jutting out stubbornly. "Then why did you make so many generous offers to my father, Donovan?"

"He was going under and he wanted out."

"If that were true," I said derisively, "he would have accepted your offer on the spot, which he didn't!"

"He was as full of pride as you are, Kat. Eyebrow deep in it. Choking on it. It was pride that made him leave Virginia and it was pride that kept him from admitting his mistake and going back!"

"What do you know about it?"

"A damn sight more than you do, apparently!"

"There's nothing wrong with pride," I said, my voice losing its hardness and sounding vulnerable.

"That's true, if it's not the only thing holding your back straight," he said dryly.

"My father wasn't like that!"

"He wasn't a bad man, just a damn foolish one. This land, for example. Anyone wanting to make a go of a homestead or a ranch wouldn't have picked a couple hundred acres of rocky slopes, peppered with trees, a good fifty or more acres made worthless by a ridge and cliffs. He'd have bought good grazing land, or land he could farm."

My eyes were swimming in tears. "Stop it! Don't you dare speak about my father disrespectfully."

"Someone on God's green earth has to make you see sense!"

"My father was murdered!" I cried.

Some of the steam went out of Donovan and he sighed. "Yes," he agreed. "But not by me, young Kat!"

"If not by you, then who else had a reason?"

"You think a couple of offers for your land gives me a reason to kill your father?" he mocked. "It'd take a lot more reason than that to make me kill."

"I don't expect you to admit it," I sniffed.

Donovan swore under his breath, raking one hand back through his thick, clean, dark hair. The firelight caught the red highlights.

"Why don't you just confess, Donovan?" I leaned forward again. "You say the land is practically useless. Then why waste your money to buy it? Just to help out my father? I don't believe that story for an instant. You aren't my idea of a philanthropist."

Donovan put his hands flat on the table, almost touching mine. His golden gaze locked onto mine.

"I said it before," he whispered. "What an unreasonable little bitch you are."

I drew back my hand to slap him across the face. He caught my wrist and twisted it, bringing me forward so that I almost fell over the table against him. It had been so easily done, I was sure he had baited me deliberately. His hold was unyielding as he drew me around the table slowly, his eyes moving over my face and lingering overlong on my mouth. The look in his eyes sent a frightening shiver of excitement through me.

"Let me go, damn you!" I cried, swinging at him with my other hand and finding that one captured as well. I could smell the soap he used and the masculine scent of his body was like a tantalizing drug. I jerked back again, only to be yanked forward, this time fully against him so that I felt the hard muscles of his thighs through my gingham skirt.

"A wise girl knows not to push a man too far," he whispered softly against my ear. "You're not very wise, are you?"

"Let go!"

"You deserve a good spanking, but there are other more pleasurable ways of making you listen to reason. Shall I show you some?"

The insidious softness of his voice against my hair aroused the first bubble of panic inside me.

"What you need, Kat, is to be kissed into silence," he said and my body stiffened in resistance and fear. "Then you'll listen." His mouth moved caressingly down the curve of my neck as I strained away from him. The shock that went through me made me kick hard at his shin. He let out a startled gasp and released me.

"Go kiss that woman you have in town!" I spat at him, putting the table between us again.

Donovan grinned devilishly. "It's eight miles to Madrone. Ten from Tasajara. It's just a little over two miles to get here."

"Well, what you want you won't get from me."

"What do I want, Kat?"

I flushed brightly and he laughed. "Are you afraid you'll be lacking as a woman?" he taunted. He moved slowly along the table and I backed toward the fireplace and the mounted rifle.

"I'm woman enough with the right man," I said, implying experience I did not have.

Donovan's mouth tightened. "That just begs the issue, Kat," he drawled, looking at me in a way that tightened the muscles in my stomach.

The sound of beating hooves drew our attention to the cabin door, which still stood open. Relief flooded me and I darted toward the yard. John expertly herded three steers into the corral and shut the gate on them. Then he swung down from his pinto and strode across the yard toward me. He was grinning expectantly.

"Now, about that appreciation," he drawled suggestively, stopping just in front of me and running his hands caressingly down my arms. Under different circumstances I would not have allowed the liberty, but I was still shaking from my encounter with Donovan. Saunders felt me trembling and frowned slightly.

"What's the matter, Kathryn?"

I glanced back over my shoulder. John looked up and I felt him stiffen as his eyes stopped on the tall man leaning in the doorway of the cabin. He looked back at me questioningly.

"Believe me, I didn't invite him," I told him shakily, my eyes pleading.

Donovan straightened away from the doorjamb and came forward slowly. John's face flushed to the roots of his hair, and he suddenly looked very young.

"What the hell are you doing here, Saunders?" Donovan demanded in a low voice.

"I was helping Miss Durham out, boss," he explained too quickly. "Her barn burned down and the cattle scattered back up into the hills."

"Correct me if I'm wrong, but didn't Hal McFadden put you on the line?" he asked, those gold eyes cutting.

"Yes, sir," John answered, flicking me an embarrassed glance.

"If you'd been doing your job properly, my steers wouldn't have gotten into our fair neighbor's yard the other day," he went on relentlessly.

"Now, just a minute," I blurted out, unable to stand by silently and listen to Donovan upbraid John Saunders. "You've miles of fence and hundreds of steers. How can you expect . . ."

"Be quiet!" Donovan ordered, glaring down at me. "This is Tasajara business and none of yours!" His blistering gaze swung back on his cowhand. "I suggest that if you want to keep your job, Saunders, you'll mount your horse and get back where you belong. Help Miss Durham on your own time, not on mine!"

John had little choice but to obey. I followed him back to his pinto, feeling miserable.

"I'm sorry, John," I said, touching his leg as he sat above me.

"It was my own fault. I didn't think I'd be missed for a couple of hours," he admitted with a rueful smile.

"You'll come back some other time for your dinner?" I asked, forcing a smile.

"You can bet on it," he agreed, his finger outlining my jaw.

"John," I detained him again. "Where's Jeremy?"

John shrugged. "I didn't see him."

I frowned, worried. Jeremy had been gone for a long time. "I wonder what's keeping him?"

"Steers, no doubt," John smiled. "He's got his job cut out for him finding your herd." I could hear Donovan approaching, and John gave me a quick good-bye before turning away and riding down the hill toward Tasajara.

"In another second I'd have fired him," Donovan said from behind me. Swinging around, I looked up at him.

"I was asking him if he'd seen Jeremy," I said stiffly, knowing the explanation was necessary if John Saunders were not to get into further trouble.

"And?"

I looked past Donovan toward the hills. "That's Durham business and none of yours," I repeated his previous words.

There was a moment of cold, still silence before Donovan spoke again. "Would you like me to ride up and look for him?" he asked gently.

Why was it that Donovan could always surprise me? I looked up at him searchingly. Blinking, I looked away.

"He's all right. He's bringing in more steers, that's all," I said with more conviction than I felt. Donovan smiled.

"You're sure you're not just being contrary?" He moved his head, indicating the far hills. "The sun is almost down. It'll be dark in less than an hour."

Chewing my lower lip, I thought of how long Jeremy had been gone. If Donovan left, I could go searching myself. But what if Jeremy was hurt and needed help? There was no one but Donovan now that Saunders was gone.

Glancing up through my lashes at the man who was studying my face with an odd intensity, I still hesitated, afraid to trust him. But what choice did I have?

"I'll ride up and take a look around for him," Donovan said, deciding for me.

"He'd never answer to you, Donovan, even if he needed help," I told him brutally, concern for my brother overriding any toward this man's feelings. Jeremy was all I had left in the world other than our distant relations who, as far as I knew, had never shown any interest in us.

"No. I don't suppose he would at that." His face was enigmatic.

"I'll come with you."

"Where are you going?"

"For the mare," I called back over my shoulder, running toward the makeshift corral.

"Forget it. We can ride double and save time."

I pretended not to hear. After what had almost happened in the cabin, I couldn't allow myself to be too close to Donovan again. I bridled the mare, tied up my skirt and mounted. Then I rode back to where Donovan was waiting.

"Where's your saddle?" he asked critically, before his eyes dropped and widened at my thin slippers, bare ankles, and exposed calves. I flushed red at the smile he gave me.

"It burned in the barn," I snapped, pulling the horse around and setting her at a gallop up the hill.

Donovan took the lead almost immediately, his stallion stronger and faster. I'd never seen a man sit a horse better and felt a tinge of resentment at that silent admission.

My thoughts returned to Jeremy and I shut my eyes for an instant. A picture of my father flickered in my mind and I remembered his plea for me to watch over my brother. Now Jeremy was missing and possibly hurt. And it was my fault.

"Please, God. Don't let anything happen to Jeremy," I whispered, riding into the trees and up the hill behind Donovan.

CHAPTER NINE

"Jeremy!" I called again, my voice cracking. It was dusk, and still we had not found any sign of my brother.

"Jeremy! Jeremy, where are you?" I cried tearfully.

"Calm down, Kat. Hysterics aren't going to help us find him," Donovan said sternly. I kicked the mare and moved away from him. How could he possibly understand what I felt for my baby brother? How could he know?

"Jeremy!"

"Wait a minute!" Donovan ordered. "I heard something. Call again!" I obeyed. Sitting as still as I could I strained my ears for the slightest sound. All I heard was the evening wind in the trees, the restless snorting and stomping of our horses, and the creak of Donovan's saddle leather as he shifted his weight.

"Come on," Donovan urged, turning his stallion southeast and climbing upward through some digger pines. "Call him again," he commanded. I ducked under the branches and did as he asked.

"Katie . . ."

Immense relief flooded me. "Jeremy! Where are you?"

Donovan did not wait but moved on ahead through the trees, around a pile of jutting boulders. Just beyond,

I spotted Dionysus standing on a grassy incline. He was favoring one leg badly. Jeremy lay several yards away.

Drawing rein, Donovan waited for me to move up next to him. Then he reached out and took hold of the reins to stop me. I stared at him questioningly.

"You'd better go ahead. We don't want to scare him with my arrival. But don't move him! Understand?"

I tried to pull the reins away from him, in a hurry to reach Jeremy and find out what had happened.

"Kat!" Donovan growled. "He might be badly hurt! Don't make it worse by grabbing him!"

I blinked, surprised at the concern I saw in his face. "All right." He released me and I rode the mare ahead several yards before dismounting and running across the open space to Jeremy. His face was white and pinched, beads of perspiration clustered on his forehead and upper lip. His eyes widened painfully as I approached and he put up a detaining hand.

"It . . . it hurts," he said, tears flooding his eyes. I sank down beside him, looking over him and trying to keep my voice steady when I spoke.

"Where, sweetheart?"

Jeremy did not answer. He was looking past me to Donovan, eyes round. Then he looked at me again, a worried question in his eyes.

"There was no one else around," I explained softly.

Donovan hunkered down on the other side of my brother and looked at him intently.

"Where?"

"It's my leg. It hurts awfully bad," Jeremy answered without hesitation. His chin was trembling, but he contained the tears. He was trying so hard to be manly and I was having difficulty controlling my own emotions. They felt ragged after the past hour of searching; so many nightmarish thoughts had raised their ugly heads. I took Jeremy's hand and squeezed it comfortingly.

"I'm going to have to touch you, Jeremy," Donovan told him. "I'll be as quick and as gentle as I can." Jeremy nodded. Donovan moved his hands over Jeremy's leg. Jeremy winced and bit down hard on his lower lip. Then he gasped and let out a groan of agony as Donovan tested the area above the knee.

It's broken all right," Donovan said, glancing across at me.

Jeremy groaned. He looked at me through his tears. "What about rounding up the cattle?"

"Don't worry about that now, sweetheart," I told him.

"We're going to have to splint it before we can take him down the mountain," Donovan told me. He looked at Jeremy, smiling gently in encouragement. "I won't lie to you. It's going to hurt like hell, but there's nothing we can do about it. I'll make it quick. We've got to get you down off this mountain before it's too dark to see."

"Go ahead," Jeremy said bravely, swallowing hard.

Donovan looked at me clutching my brother's hand. "Find some straight branches. I'll rig a stretcher."

I scurried away, finding it difficult to see anything in the growing darkness. Breaking off several branches from a pine, I stripped off the small stems and needles and carried them back to Donovan.

He was working on a rough stretcher using two long branches and rope from his saddle.

"We can lash one end to your mare and carry the other so Jeremy won't be bumped all the way down," he said, working quickly. I watched his hands, powerful, long-fingered hands that had a quick sureness. I wondered how those hands would feel . . . I banished the thought at once, horrified that it had even risen.

Donovan stripped off his leather vest and laid it across the rope. "Have you anything on under that skirt?" he asked, glancing up at me, causing a hot, indignant flush to course through my body.

"What do you think?"

"Then take it off and tear it into strips. We need the slip to splint your brother's leg." He gave me an impatient look when I hesitated. "This is no time for modesty. Do it!"

Lifting my skirt, I ripped a band of my petticoat into long strips, and stiffly handed them to him.

"That should do it," he said, smiling slightly at my expression. He looked at me thoughtfully, unconsciously fingering the fabric. Seeing my curious look, he turned away and walked to my brother.

"All right, Kat. You're going to have to hold him down. This isn't going to be easy . . . on any of us."

Jeremy looked nervously between the two of us, his eyes widening. "I . . . I won't move, Mr. Donovan."

"Call me Mace."

"Katie doesn't have to hold me down."

"You won't want to move, Jeremy," Donovan said grimly. "But sometimes, it can't be prevented. Don't be afraid to cry out. It doesn't mean you're less a man." He looked at me. "Kat?"

"I'm ready," I swallowed, forcing my voice to a calmness I didn't feel. Smiling encouragement, I bent down over my brother. His body jerked rigidly when Donovan started to straighten his leg, but he didn't cry out. I heard his teeth grinding together, and tears started in my eyes as I murmured to him to hold on. His breathing grew rapid and when Donovan pulled the leg to align the bones, Jeremy jerked against me, crying out for him to stop. My brother's fingers dug painfully into my shoulder as I pressed him back, holding him still.

"Almost done, Jeremy," Donovan said. He expertly tied the strips of white material around the branches that held Jeremy's leg straight.

"Jeremy," I whispered, stroking his damp forehead. "Honey? It's over." I pushed the wayward hair back from his pale face. "Jeremy?"

His eyes were closed and he was limp in my arms. I straightened, looking at Donovan beseechingly.

"He isn't . . ."

Donovan leaned over, his arm brushing hard against my breasts as he reached past me to check Jeremy's pulse. I felt a tingling shock run through me and stared at him as he turned his head toward me.

"He's fainted," he said flatly. "That's best, Kat, believe me. It's going to be hard enough on him going down this mountain." He straightened. "Get on your horse," he ordered. I did not hesitate to do what he bid. He had taken command in this situation and oddly, I trusted him.

We did not speak on the way down. Jeremy stirred several times, moaning in pain when we couldn't help jarring him. Donovan was at the other end of the stretcher, walking behind the mare. His stallion moved behind us, following his master like a pet dog.

The cabin was warm, and softly lit by the coals of the fire. Donovan carried Jeremy in and carefully laid him on Papa's big bed.

"I don't think it's wise to risk taking him into town," he commented in a low voice, touching Jeremy's forehead with the back of his hand. "He's in shock."

"What can I do?" I looked up at Donovan, eyes wide and tear-filled. Donovan reached out, caressing my cheek.

"Keep him warm and quiet."

"Shouldn't he have something to eat? He hasn't eaten since early this morning." I moved away slightly, finding Donovan's touch disturbing.

Donovan smiled in wry amusement. "Just like a woman. Feed a man and cure him. If Jeremy wants something to eat, give it to him. But don't press him about it."

I nodded, looking down at my little brother. He was

so pale and small on Papa's big bed. When I touched him he lay still. I pressed my knuckles to my lips and took a shaky breath.

"He's all I have, Donovan."

"He's going to be all right, Kat," Donovan said harshly, laying a hand on my shoulder. Again I moved away from him. His expression grew grim.

"I'll be back as soon as I can," he told me, striding to the door.

Jeremy revived a few minutes after Donovan had ridden away. He moaned and moved restlessly on the bed, his forehead beading with cold sweat. I pulled the quilt up and tucked it around him securely.

"You're back at the cabin, Jeremy. Donovan's gone for Doc. They'll be back in a few hours," I said soothingly, wiping the moisture from his face.

"It hurts," he said, opening his eyes and looking at me for some cure to his pain.

"I know. I wish there was something I could do about it. Do you want something to drink?"

"I'm not thirsty."

"I mean Papa's brandy. They give brandy to men that are in pain, don't they?"

"I guess . . ." he groaned and I went to the cabinet where Papa had kept the bottle of French brandy. I poured a large measure into a glass and brought it back to Jeremy.

Jeremy choked on it, his eyes watering. "It tastes awful."

"It's supposed to be the best," I smiled. He managed to get down the rest.

"Can you tell me what happened?"

"I'm not sure," he sighed. "One minute I was riding along looking for steers and the next Dionysus reared and bolted. He must have seen something . . . a snake maybe. When he threw me, I couldn't get up. I knew I had broken my leg." He shut his eyes. "It still hurts, Katie . . ."

I poured some more brandy for him. It seemed to go down easier this time. His eyes were beginning to look very strange.

"Ugh!" he said after finishing the brandy. "How's Dionysus?"

"I'm not sure. He was favoring his front leg. I'm not sure which one. I wasn't paying much attention," I smiled. "I'll go up for him tomorrow if he hasn't come back down. The main thing is that you're all right."

"With a broken leg? A lot of help I'll be to you," he said glumly.

"Look at the bright side. You can go back to your studies." That seemed to brighten him a bit.

Jeremy gave a big yawn. "Mush have been a snake . . ." he slurred sleepily.

"How long ago did you fall?"

"Don't member. On my way back. Even had a coupla steers. Probably back in the hills by now."

"Don't worry about it. You're more important than any steers."

His eyelids were heavy as he tried to focus on me.

"Are you feeling all right, Jeremy?" I asked, concerned.

"I feel good . . . just sleepy."

"Then close your eyes, sweetheart." I leaned down and kissed him on the forehead. "I love you."

He tried to say something but the words were indistinct. He smiled and went to sleep. Surprisingly, he snored rather loudly.

While Jeremy slept, I puttered about the cabin, straightening things up. The stew was done and I had previously moved it to one side of the fire so that it wouldn't overcook. I drew it over the warmth again. The bread dough was ruined and I tossed it out and started a fresh batch. Every few minutes I went over to look in on Jeremy. He was sleeping soundly, his breathing deep and normal. I thanked God.

It was several long hours later that I heard Mace Donovan returning, a carriage in his wake. I raced toward the door, throwing it open. Doc, in all his rotund glory, climbed down and smiled reassuringly at me. Donovan headed straight for the small back room, standing aside for Doc to set his black bag down beside Jeremy.

"He smells of brandy," Walinsky observed with surprise.

"I thought it might ease his pain. It did."

Doc and Donovan looked at me. "How much did you give him?" Doc asked curiously, glancing again at the sleeping boy. I lifted the glass from the dresser.

"This much. Wasn't it enough? He seemed to feel better, even good, he said. And he's sleeping soundly."

Doc and Donovan looked at one another and burst out laughing. I glanced at Jeremy in concern, afraid their loud amusement would awaken him. He didn't move.

"It was enough all right," Donovan grinned. "He may even have a hell of a hangover tomorrow."

Doc began to tend to Jeremy and I watched, holding the brass bed frame tightly, afraid the pain would awaken him. He slept on. Returning to the main room I sat down at the table, feeling slightly faint. I let out my breath slowly.

"I'll go up for your horse tomorrow," Donovan said in a low voice. I glanced up at him.

"That's not necessary. I can go for him. There's no need for you to come back here again."

His face hardened and became inscrutable. "My usefulness is at an end, I take it."

I flushed. "I'm grateful to you for helping me find

Jeremy and bringing him down off the mountain. I'm grateful too that you went for Doc," I said, my voice cracking under the strain of the whole episode. How many things could possibly go wrong?

"That damn near choked you, didn't it?" he said bitterly. He came forward, leaning down, hands on the table. "I thought things were changing," he said in a hard voice, for my ears only. "I thought, just for a few minutes, you were beginning to trust me."

"I can't help how I feel," I whispered defensively, flashing him an angry look.

"The devil's assistance was better than no assistance at all, hmmmm?" he taunted. With an effort, I held my tongue. He laughed low and sardonically.

"Dear Kat. Even I have my lapses of humanity, is that it?" he went on in a hard, mocking voice. "Especially when it concerns a ten-year-old boy."

My hands fisted on my lap. "This isn't the time to argue your humanity, Mr. Donovan," I said tautly, refusing to look up at him again. "If you want coffee or stew, it's there on the fire," I offered ungraciously. Donovan straightened.

"How many tablespoons of rat poison did you lace it with before making that offer?" he asked dryly, and not waiting for an answer, turned away. Looking into the small bedroom at Jeremy, he spoke to Doc.

"How's he doing?"

"He'll do just fine. The brandy made it easy. And your splint is as good as anything I've ever done. It's a clean break. Could have been a lot worse. He's young and the young mend quickly."

"Good. I'll be on my way, then," Donovan said. He leaned down and touched Jeremy lightly. I felt my throat tighten as I watched Donovan's face from my position at the doorway. What I saw did not sit well with my image of the man. There was nothing cold in his face now, nothing to indicate a man who would kill for any reason, except perhaps self-defense. My stomach tightened. I moved quickly aside when he came back out.

Donovan strode to the door without a look in my direction. I could feel the anger in him. I followed, grabbing my shawl from the hook by the door. Standing at the rail, I watched Donovan mount his restless stallion.

"Donovan . . ."

He looked down at me with cold derision. "You've already thanked me for my help and offered me your fine southern hospitality," he said sarcastically. "Don't overdo yourself!"

His remark hurt more than I wanted to admit. "I'm sorry. But what you did for us tonight doesn't alter the facts about what happened to my father."

Donovan's face grew even harder. "Are you so damnably sure you've got all your facts straight?" he snarled.

I looked up at him, searching his face.

It was becoming increasingly hard to believe he had murdered my father. Sometimes I almost believed he did care about me and Jeremy. Why else would he have helped me find my brother tonight? Why would he have tended to him so carefully and gone for the doctor? And why had he offered recompense for the damage done to our garden?

None of it made any sense if he wanted us off our land.

But I could not put aside the damning facts. Papa had written his initials in the dust when I asked him who had shot him. M . . . D . . . No mistake there. And Papa had said Tasajara. He had said Jeremy was in danger.

Donovan watched my face as he waited for me to say something. Then, muttering something unmentionable under his breath, he turned the horse sharply and rode off down the hill. I stood listening to the thundering hooves for several moments, feeling strangely bereft. Then I went back into the cabin.

CHAPTER TEN

It was well over two weeks before I had all our cattle in the corral and ready for sale. They were a scraggly lot and I was depressingly aware that they would not bring a high price.

Setting out before dawn, I made the long ride to Bigelow's ranch. I rehearsed my proposition a dozen times before reaching the sprawling white ranch house surrounded by well-manicured gardens. Several Mexicans were tending them and I smiled a greeting as I reined in. A plump woman with gray hair greeted me, looking me over with frank curiosity when I told her that I wanted to see Lester Bigelow. She ushered me into the parlor at the front of the house and said she would send for him. I had well over an hour to look around at the rather opulent room with its rich, oak paneling, dark-marble fireplace, velvet drapes, and heavy wood furnishings.

When Lester Bigelow came into the room he was beating the dust off his denim pants with his hat and wiping his damp forehead with the back of his arm. So much for the expensive imported carpet, I thought, watching him stride across the room in his boots and jangling spurs.

Bigelow was my father's age or perhaps older, his brown hair streaked with gray. He was of middling height, strongly built, with the most piercing blue eyes I had ever seen. I noticed that they were doing a thorough study of me from head to foot, a smile slowly spread across his face. I smiled back nervously.

"What brings you to see me, Miss Durham?" he asked, pouring liquor into a crystal glass. I declined his offer for sherry and bluntly explained my business, stating my price for the fifty cattle.

Thick brows shot up in surprise. "That's a tidy sum you're asking. You know you're selling at the wrong time of the year. You'd do better to get your price later on, say in six months."

"I can't wait six months," I answered frankly. "Are you saying you're not interested?"

"Now, I didn't say that, ma'am," he shook his head, smiling again over the rim of his glass. "I just said you'd do better by waiting for the right time of year."

I could see what was coming and there was very little I could do about it. The mortgage payment was due in a few days.

"How much would you be willing to pay for my herd now?"

He considered me for a long time and I felt as though I was one of the cattle he was thinking of buying. The feeling was uncanny and rather distressing.

"I might see my way clear to paying . . ." he stated an amount which brought a frown of disappointment to my face. I stood up.

"I'm wasting your time," I said flatly. "I need at least my asking price to pay off some debts and keep my brother and me going for another year."

Bigelow raised his brows again at my admission. "Things are as bad as that?"

"About as bad as they can get. My brother broke his leg two weeks ago, so there's only me to do the work until he's mended."

The expression in the blue eyes changed, though I could not fathom what it was. "Would you like to sell out entirely?"

"No."

"You sound pretty definite," he smiled.

"I am."

Bigelow looked me up and down. "Sit down, please, Miss Kathryn. We might be able to work something out."

I sat and waited.

"Why are you so definite about not selling out?"

"My father worked for years to keep that homestead going, and I'm not going to sell out just a month after someone murdered him."

"Any idea who did it?" he asked and there was a strange look in his eyes again.

"I'm not at liberty to say. I have my own ideas, but the sheriff doesn't agree."

Bigelow smiled. "There are other ways of solving your problems, you know."

"Such as?"

"Why don't you find some man and settle down?"

I laughed. "Just like that!" The only men I knew were John Saunders, Sheriff Collins, and Mace Donovan. Papa had kept me well sheltered.

"It ought to be damn easy for a girl with your obvious assets," he said, his eyes lowering slightly to indicate his meaning. I flushed with embarrassment, but did not feel in any way threatened or uneasy by Bigelow's comment. Not the way I felt when Donovan looked at me in the same way.

"There aren't many women around these parts with your looks. You're intelligent, too."

"I also have excellent teeth," I boasted mockingly, baring them as though for inspection. Bigelow laughed loudly.

"Only one thing, Mr. Bigelow," I added. "I'm not looking for a husband."

"Why not? You look old enough to have a family of your own," he commented thoughtfully. "What are you? Eighteen? Twenty?"

"Nineteen . . . or I will be, soon. If that makes any difference," I smiled.

"Hmmmm. It might," he said seriously. "I'll tell you what. I'll pay your price on one condition."

"What condition?"

The blue eyes flickered as he smiled again. "That you allow me to court you."

My eyes widened with unconcealed surprise. Why would a man of Bigelow's stature want to court me, I wondered frantically. He was old enough to be my father, in fact he was older than my father had been.

True, he had a certain easy charm about him that I liked. But to say he could court me was to indicate that I was interested seriously in him as a possible husband. Was I?

Bigelow chuckled. "Is there a problem about it?"

"I . . . I don't know what to say," I said frankly.

"Why don't you ask me to dinner?" he suggested.

"I find it . . . surprising that you would be interested in me . . . in that way. And we've nothing but a sod cabin . . . ."

Bigelow waved his hand airily. "I started in a sod cabin myself. And as for you . . . I find you very attractive." He paused. "Do we have a deal?"

Did I have any choice?

"What would you like for dinner?" I asked, smiling.

"Surprise me." He said it as though it didn't matter at all.

"You may be more surprised than you wish to be," I said dryly. "Do you like rabbit or squirrel?"

"I've eaten it in my time."

"Did you like it?"

"Are you trying to discourage me, Kathryn?" he asked in amusement. He said my Christian name easily, I thought, remembering that I had not given him permission to use it.

"I'm not sure."

"You're honest to a fault. But I like that."

"Mr. Bigelow . . ."

"Les. Mr. Bigelow sounds damnably old. Is that what's bothering you?"

"Partially."

"We'll get to the rest later. Now, how would you like your money."

"I'd like a draft on your account. A goodly sum will be remaining with Mr. Lambert anyway," I said.

"You're mortgaged to the hilt as well then?" he asked.

"Yes," I answered, not feeling it necessary to be evasive with this man. He looked at me for another long, pensive moment and then walked to his desk in the adjoining room. I followed and stood watching as he wrote out the draft. He waved it in the air absentmindedly until it was dry, still concentrating on some private thought that narrowed his blue eyes. Then he stood up, smiled at me charmingly, and handed over the slip of paper. I read the amount and folded it twice before pocketing it.

"Thank you. When can we expect you for dinner?"

"Saturday," he said without hesitation. That was two days away. Les Bigelow did not waste any time.

"Fine. We'll be expecting you."

"When can you make delivery on the steers?"

I flushed to the roots of my hair. "I . . . I can't. I thought you would send a couple of your men over to collect them. I'm afraid I'm sorely lacking as a cowhand. It took me two weeks to round them up. It would probably take me six months to drive them over here."

Bigelow chuckled. "I'll send Matt Daniels over

tomorrow. He's got his dog to help him out," he said, walking me to the door. Matt Daniels, I thought. One of the men Sheriff Collins had questioned about my father's murder.

"Is something wrong?" Bigelow asked, seeing my expression. I forced a smile.

"No. Nothing." I offered him my hand in farewell. "Thank you . . . Les. This money should keep us in business for a while longer."

His fingers tightened on my hand, his thumb making a caressing movement as he looked directly into my eyes. "Long enough for something better to come along. I'll be looking forward to Saturday, Kathryn."

The smile on my face felt brittle.

The first thing I did was ride into Madrone to see Charles Lambert. He was surprised, but pleased that I had the money for the mortgage payment; however, he warned me that there were more payments to come in the future. I had not thought of that, and did my best not to show my alarm and depression as I left his office.

"You said you'd square the account," Iverson beamed at me over the mercantile counter. "But we didn't expect it so soon. How'd you do it?"

"A little business dealing," I hedged.

Jeremiah Bellows was grateful for the money. He admitted that he himself was in need of it, though he had been loathe to press me, knowing the situation at the homestead. His daughter was returning from the East, where she had been attending school.

Sadie and Tobias Jacobson said I needn't pay them. They did not mind the running account if I wanted to pay a small sum as good faith. I told them I preferred cash and carry, especially since I did not know what my financial situation would be in a couple of months. The less I owed, the better I felt.

Jeremy was at his books when I got home. I was exhausted from all the riding and yet I still had a day's chores ahead of me. Washing, cooking, candle making, so much to do. I smiled across the table at Jeremy, while I sipped some hot coffee. We hadn't much left and I was going to enjoy it while it lasted.

"How're you feeling?" I asked.

Jeremy looked up, his eyes blurry from his reading. "It itches. It nearly drives me crazy sometimes."

"Doc warned you about that. Otherwise?"

"It's fine. Hurts if I move too fast. Those crutches are more trouble than they're worth," he said glumly.

"You'll live," I teased him, downing the last bit of coffee. "Well, I'd better get to work." Jeremy looked back down at his book. He had not even been interested enough to ask what had happened at Bigelow's. I felt a twinge of hurt and annoyance.

"Study hard. When you've got that cast off your leg, you'll have to help me again," I said bleakly.

"Yeah. I know," he said dismally. I left the cabin before I said more.

I worked for more than an hour on the garden, pulling up weeds, thinning out plants, and watering. Then I fed the chickens and gathered the eggs. There weren't many. We had a fat fox somewhere up in the hills that was making a nuisance of himself.

The cattle needed to be fed and watered. After that there was still the washing. It was almost dusk when I finished hanging the things on the line behind the house. Jeremy peeked out the back door.

"I'm hungry, Katie . . . ." he said and I almost told him to fix something for both of us. But that wouldn't have been fair. He couldn't help the accident, nor his love of books. I smiled.

"I'll be right in."

As I finished hanging up the last shirt, a voice greeted me from the side of the sod cabin.

"John! Oh, it's good to see you!" I laughed and he grinned at me.

"That's a nice welcome. I shouldn't have stayed away so long."

"Why did you?"

"Duty calls. I think the boss is keeping me at the opposite side of the valley on purpose."

"Can you stay for dinner?" I asked. "I was just going to start cooking."

"This time I am on my own time and I accept your offer gratefully," he grinned. "I've got two days off and money burning a hole in my pants."

"Must be nice," I smiled ruefully.

"I'd like to take you into town for dinner tomorrow," he said seriously. Then he glanced toward the house. "Or would the little lord in there throw a tantrum?"

"Don't call him that!" I said defensively.

"Just joking," he mended, but I could tell he had not been. "I heard about his accident. How's he doing?"

"Fine," I snapped, still annoyed with his comment about Jeremy. "He's restless."

"Understandable. No kid wants to be limited to the house." He stopped me with a hand on my arm. "I'm sorry, Kathryn. I suppose I overreact to his hostility."

I smiled up at him. "Let's go inside. I've got to get things on to cook or we won't eat 'til midnight."

Jeremy was not pleased to see John Saunders. He looked up from his books, saw the man coming in behind me, and studiously ignored him. John shot me an amused, sardonic glance.

Laying the table, I looked between my brother and John Saunders. There was a certain likeness about them. They both had a stubborn set to their jaws.

Jeremy was jealous and it appeared that John was as well. My brother's dislike was almost tangible.

"Wash up, Jeremy. We'll eat in ten minutes," I said,

then looked at John with a raised brow. "If you'll excuse me for a few minutes, I'll do likewise and change into something a little less of the earth and sun."

John grinned. "You look mighty pretty to me just as you are." Jeremy muttered something as he went out the door.

Our meal was eaten in virtual silence. Jeremy barely looked up, but put away two helpings of rabbit stew and half a dozen rolls.

"At least there's nothing wrong with your appetite," I hissed, picking up his empty plate. He did not answer. "There's berry pie, John. Would you like some?"

"Only if you twist my arm," he said, holding out his plate.

I prepared enough coffee for the three of us and served John a mugful. John and I talked while Jeremy remained doggedly silent.

"Would you mind if I took your sister into town for dinner tomorrow night, Jeremy? She's been working hard all by herself. I think she could do with a special evening out."

Put like that, Jeremy could hardly object without looking small and spiteful. I gave John a severe look but he still looked at Jeremy with a closed expression.

"Why're you asking me? She can answer for herself," Jeremy retorted ungraciously.

Irritation flickered in Saunders' eyes. "You're the man of the house, aren't you?" Jeremy's shoulders stiffened.

"It's up to Katie."

John turned and smiled at me triumphantly. "Kathryn?" I looked at Jeremy, annoyed at his continued rudeness.

"I don't think I should leave Jeremy on his own."

Jeremy's blue eyes flashed with indignation. "I'm old enough to take care of myself!" he exclaimed, stung.

"I didn't mean . . ."

"Go to town. I don't care." Jeremy said harshly.

"Then it's settled," John interceded. "You can't disobey the master of the house, now can you?"

Jeremy glanced between us and then got up from the table, snatching up his crutches.

"He doesn't like me very much, does he?" John said, watching Jeremy disappear through the door.

"I'm sorry. I don't understand it. He's never been like that."

"Forget it. He's just a boy. And you are going out with me tomorrow. That's all I care about at the moment. Let him sulk."

It was cool and clear outside. I put on my shawl and walked with John to the fence the steers had so recently broken down. He didn't say anything and I was loathe to break the silence. Stopping, we stared down into the valley. There was a faint light off in the distance that wouldn't have been visible from the cabin. I thought of Donovan and wondered what he was doing.

"Tasajara," John said.

"Yes." I resented the way my thoughts drifted to Donovan from time to time.

"Do you still hate him?"

"Why do you ask?"

"He helped Jeremy. I thought that might have changed things between you," he said, casting me a curious glance.

"Yes, he helped Jeremy," I sighed, looking down at the light again. "But it doesn't alter anything. It just makes me wonder what sort of man he really is."

John didn't say anything for a moment. "Has he made an offer for the homestead again?"

"No." But then he wouldn't have to if things went according to his expectations. We would miss our mortgage payments and Lambert would foreclose. The homestead would go up on public auction. Donovan would be there, ready and waiting for the land to fall right into his lap.

"Let's not talk about Donovan," I said, turning away from the light in the distance to look at John standing close by me. I liked him. There was something about him that was almost brotherly, though I knew he did not look at me in a similar light. I cocked my head to one side, looking at him curiously. Sometimes he seemed so troubled, especially when I caught him looking at me, deep in thought.

"You're so pretty," he breathed. "You make a man want to forget everything."

"Like what?"

"Who I am . . . what I am . . ." he smiled. "Jeremy. Everything. You're just so damn pretty . . . ."

"Jeremy's jealous. We're very close. I raised him after Mama died."

John wasn't listening. He was staring at me intently. "I suppose he has reason to be jealous," he said, apparently having heard me after all.

"He says he doesn't like the way you look at me."

"I don't expect he would," John mumbled, stepping closer. He raised his hand, as though unable to prevent himself, and stroked my cheek with rough fingers. "You're so soft," he murmured. I stepped away slightly, frightened by his husky tone. He dropped his hand.

"I'm sorry."

"Sometimes, I'm not sure I understand you," I whispered.

"No? There's a lot I wish I didn't understand so well," he smiled. "Listen to me," he said suddenly, in self-contempt. "You must think me mad. But sometimes when I look at you I forget that I'm just a cowpoke with no home, no future . . . at least not yet." He shook his head and I tried to understand what he was telling me.

"I'd better go before you think better of going into town with me tomorrow. I'll come by around three. I'm going to do it right . . . rent a carriage, take you to that little restaurant that belongs to Halasey's."

"Don't spend all your wages on me," I laughed.

"Why not?" he grinned. "Better on you than a poker game."

He walked me back to the cabin and then left. When I came inside, Jeremy looked up at me accusingly.

"You sure put on a spread for him," he said.

"I'd appreciate it if you would be a little more cordial to him in the future," I said sternly. "He's the only friend I have."

"You've got me!" Jeremy cried. "Aren't I enough?"

"In some ways, you are, Jeremy," I said gently. "But in others, no."

Jeremy didn't look at all happy with my answer.

CHAPTER ELEVEN

Matt Daniels came by the following morning with his big, black dog, obviously trained from a pup to herd cattle. I carefully studied the tall, lean man with weather-beaten features and shy gray eyes, and found nothing at all suspicious about him. When I asked him if he had known my father, he admitted he had heard of the killing and had been questioned about it. Yes, he had known my father, but not well. They had talked at the saloon in town.

I watched with respect as Daniels and his dog got to work. The cattle remained tightly together, like properly trained sheep, and moved off down the hill toward Bigelow's. Had I a small portion of Daniels's skill, it would have taken me only a couple of days to round up the unruly beasts, and Jeremy might never have been hurt.

Excited about the evening in Madrone, I next grappled with the problem of what to wear. It had been a long time since I had been given any material for a new dress. Those I had were well worn and unsuitable for a restaurant.

After some thought, I went to Mama's leather trunk. I had never opened it, but Papa had said that the contents were mine when I was old enough. Curious now, I unlatched it and peered inside. It smelled strongly of mothballs, but as I lifted garment after garment out, I realized that this was my mother's precious trousseau. She had mentioned it to me once years ago, saying that it was tucked away, for there was no earthly use in California for the things she had brought from Richmond. Papa had never let her discard the trunk, even during their troubles on the trek west. It was a last link with the old life she had led as a girl, and Papa never wanted her to lose it.

Now, holding up each gown, I stared in awe at the delicate workmanship, the soft fabrics, and elaborate styling that had kept so well over the years. I tried on a green silk and found it fit almost perfectly but needed to be lengthened. It would need a small tuck at the waist and the neckline was lower and more snug than I was used to. My breasts swelled and pressed against the soft fabric. I wondered how Mace Donovan would react . . .

Blushing furiously at the thought, I laid the silk aside, certain that it was hardly the fare of Madrone. I pulled out other things, a mauve organdy, a rose velvet, a pale, dove-gray gown of a fabric I was entirely unfamiliar with. At the bottom of the trunk was Mama's wedding gown, carefully wrapped. The veil was filmy, with silk embroidered flowers along the edge. I felt suddenly sad looking at that dress. It was exquisite. I put the wrapping back around it and returned it to the trunk.

I settled finally on a soft cotton dress with pink rose buds and fine lace trim around a low neckline. With a few minor alterations it would be fashionable and not too formal. The rest of the gowns I refolded and laid back into the trunk with great care. Closing the lid was like closing a door on time. I could almost see my mother dancing in those dresses, my father's arms around her. Why had they left such genteel surroundings for the rigors of the West? And no wonder there had been a wistful sadness in Mama's eyes when she thought of Richmond.

Airing the dress, I then ironed it with care. It was fresh and scented with verbena. Jeremy came in and glowered at my painstaking efforts. I tried hard to ignore his sullenness. I had never been into town for a special occasion like this. Papa had always kept me at the homestead, preferring to take Jeremy or go on his own when carrying out his business. Suddenly, I wondered why. How much time had he spent at the hotel?

"Is that Mama's?" he asked, faint accusation tinging his tone.

"Yes. Papa said that her things belonged to me," I answered. Water was warming on the stove for my bath and Jeremy glanced at the tub. He left without another word.

When he returned, I had finished bathing and washing my hair. I was sitting at the table, brushing the thick, waist-length waves with long, hard strokes. My hair gleamed like copper now and I tried to bind it up and failed. Finally, I satisfied myself with braiding it and twisting it at the back of my neck. It was a severe style but not unattractive.

John came in mid-afternoon and looked strange in his suit, white shirt, and thin black tie. His coat was opened, revealing a vest. Strange also that he should look so natural and at ease. He grinned when he saw me, and his eyes swept me up and down admiringly. Jeremy stayed inside the cabin and I peered back in.

"Are you sure you'll be all right on your own?" I asked. He looked up at me angrily.

"Why not?"

"We won't be very late."

As John and I rode down the trail in the rented carriage, I was angry with Jeremy. I had so little enjoyment, why should he begrudge me this? I resolved to put aside my brother's unfriendliness towards John and enjoy myself. This was the first evening I'd ever had in town with a man, and I was not going to allow my brother's peevishness to cloud it.

We talked of many things on the ride to town. John could be very entertaining, I found, and he had me laughing often. He made me forget my worries for awhile and I recounted to him the good times with Papa. When we arrived at Madrone's restaurant, I found the white table cloths and bud vases boasting fresh carnations enchanting. The proprietor seated us near the window overlooking Main Street.

"Order anything you want, Kathryn," John told me over the top of the menu. "Don't be shy."

He must have seen the way my eyes took in the price of each dinner first, only allowing myself to look at the meal afterwards. Looking up at him, I flushed slightly and smiled.

"You're absolutely sure?" Everything seemed so expensive. Jeremy and I could eat for a week on what he would spend for one evening.

John grinned. "I'm even going to order wine to go with dinner."

"I've never had wine. Maybe I won't like it and you'll be wasting your money."

"Maybe I should make it champagne then. If they have it." He closed the menu. "Have you decided?"

"No . . ."

"Let me order for you then." He seemed so much at home that I was reassured. I blanched however, when he told the waiter he wanted two Texas steaks with all the trimmings. That had been the most expensive dinner on the menu.

"I'm not sure I can eat all that," I said quickly.

"What you can't eat, they'll wrap up and you can take it back to Jeremy for a snack," he said. "Maybe a little steak would help him forgive me for taking his sister away from him."

"It might at that," I answered, though I doubted it. Again I felt assailed by guilt at leaving my brother.

The meal was delicious, and though I was so hungry I could have eaten everything, I saved half for Jeremy. Apple pie, ice cream and a final cup of rich, aromatic coffee with a dash of pure, thick cream topped off the meal. I felt as though I had just visited heaven.

When we left the pleasant atmosphere of the restaurant, John suggested we go to the park, where there was going to be a small festival put on by some out-of-town entertainers passing through Madrone. I agreed excitedly. It was early and I didn't want to go home yet.

Smiling, I watched people dancing to the lively music as vendors selling taffy and fruit moved among the onlookers. John produced a small blanket from beneath the seat of the carriage and laid it out on the grass.

After a while, he took my hand. "Would you like to dance?" he asked, seeing how intently I watched the people moving about so gaily.

"No," I shook my head quickly.

"Why not?"

"I . . . I'm afraid I don't know how."

He looked surprised and then smiled. "Let me teach you, then. It's easy enough."

When I started to protest, he stood up, drawing me up with him. I thought he intended to take me among the other dancers but we stayed in the solitude of the trees. It was near dusk and the light was fading fast.

"No one is watching us," he said reassuringly, drawing me into his arms beneath the canopy of leafy branches and smiling down into my anxious face. "Relax, Kathryn. It really is easy. Just do as I do."

He took my hand and put it on his shoulder. "That's right. You're still tense. Loosen your muscles. Better. Now, follow me." He chuckled after a moment, and I looked up, embarrassed.

"Am I terrible?"

"You're doing beautifully . . . just stop looking down at our feet. Close your eyes and move with me. That's right."

He whirled me around the grass and it did seem easy. When the music stopped, I was breathless and smiling with triumph.

"It's so much fun!"

John stood still for a moment, looking down at me in the darkness. The light was in my up-turned face and I could not see his expression. He moved forward again, drawing me back into his arms when the music started once more. I waited but he didn't move. He seemed to be trembling. His hand pressed at my lower spine, forcing me to arch backwards to see his face. While I looked up questioningly, he kissed me. I was so surprised I did not move away and his mouth moved more demandingly over mine. He pressed his body urgently against mine, trying to pry my lips open with his tongue. I began to struggle and pushed myself free, repulsed by his sudden and unexpected display of passion.

His breathing was ragged, but he stepped back immediately, as though stung by my touch. "Kathryn . . ." His voice was pained. "Oh, God," he said, putting a hand to his forehead. "I never meant to do that. I didn't plan to feel this way about you."

He turned away and I thought I saw someone just beyond us, standing in the shadows of the trees. John turned back, blocking my view of the intruder.

"I'm sorry," he said flatly. "It won't happen again."

"Let's just forget about it," I said, unable to keep the distaste from my voice. I wondered who had been watching us. When John moved again, there was no one there and I wondered if the shadows had played a trick on me.

John did not say anything, but guided me back to the

blanket a few feet away. He looked at me several times as we sat down, and I forced a smile at him. Reaching across the blanket, I touched his hand to draw him out of his dismal thoughts.

"I'm not angry. I suppose I'm rather flattered. I didn't expect it, and . . . well . . ."

"I shouldn't have touched you," he said abruptly, his face a curious mixture of frustration and self-contempt. "I'll get us something to drink. Excuse me."

I watched him walk away and frowned. Granted, I had been repulsed by his zealous kiss, but why was he so upset about it? I wanted to put it behind us and remain friends.

My attention wandered to the dancers and merrymakers under the colored lanterns. I wrapped my shawl around my shoulders and rested my chin on my knees.

After awhile, I had the uncanny feeling that someone was watching me. Glancing around, I saw Mace Donovan leaning against a tree not far away. His face was in the shadows, but there was no mistaking the casual strength of his body, the breadth of his shoulders, or the way his hair lay forward. He straightened and walked toward me. I looked away quickly, trying to spot John in the crowd. He was nowhere to be seen.

Donovan stopped at the edge of the blanket, looming over me. I glanced up the length of him, feeling my body tense.

"Aren't you even going to ask me to sit down?" he drawled tauntingly. There was an edge of anger in his voice.

"No, I am not," I answered stiffly.

"Then, I will anyway, without your invitation," he said, and stretched his length out beside me. My heart began to pound. He turned his head to look into my face and smiled slightly, as though aware of just how disturbing his presence was to me.

"Where's your escort?" he asked sneeringly.

"John's gone to get us something to drink."

"John, is it?" he mocked. I searched the crowd again, wondering where John had gone and why he was taking so long.

"You'd better not get serious about him," Donovan warned and I flashed him a hateful look.

"What business is it of yours what I feel for John?"

Donovan's mouth tightened into a hard line. "He's a tumbleweed, Kat. He hasn't been in Madrone three months, and I doubt if he'll be staying longer than six. So keep it to chaste kisses in the *daylight* so you won't have any regrets later. Got that?"

"*You* were the one spying on us!" I accused.

"From my vantage point, not much was happening," he drawled derisively.

"And what were you expecting?" I demanded, trying to keep my temper in check.

"You'd better quit while you're ahead, Kat," Donovan said in a low voice that sent a shiver through me. I looked at him quizzically, and then quickly looked away.

"How's Jeremy?" he asked when the silence had become almost unbearable.

"Fine," I bit out tersely.

Donovan glanced at me. "How does he feel about his sister gallivanting around only two and a half months after his father was murdered?"

"You bastard!" I cried, sudden tears welling as I took a furious swing at him, toppling over onto him from the force of my anger. He hit my hand away, and before I knew it, I was swung flat onto my back, with Donovan on top of me. Both my wrists were pinned to the ground above my head and my legs were effectively immobilized by Donovan's. I could feel his hard muscles down the length of me and his obvious maleness pressing into the upper part of my thigh. My eyes widened as I stared up at him, my heart beating furiously against my chest.

"One of these days, you're going to push me too far," he breathed through teeth bared almost in a snarl. The glitter in his eyes was hot as he drew back enough to allow me to breathe, but not to escape.

"Let me go," I pleaded, sounding curiously breathless. I was feeling a strange tingling sensation in my lower body and wanted him to release me. Donovan looked down at me relentlessly, his eyes moving slowly to my mouth. He ran his tongue along his upper lip and I watched the action, mesmerized.

"In a minute," he whispered. "There's something else . . ."

I struggled frantically, squirming beneath him, trying more to escape the feeling he aroused in me than Donovan himself.

"Stop it, Kat," Donovan said hoarsely. "If you're wise, you won't move at all until I've said my piece."

The expression on his face and the sudden tension in his body made me obey.

"Les Bigelow tells me he's having dinner with you tomorrow night . . . at your place," he said softly, his eyes growing cold and hard again. "Is that right?"

All defiance seemed to have seeped from me. I nodded.

"You're making fast time. Do you think you can handle it?"

"I don't know what you're talking about."

"John Saunders and Les Bigelow in one week. What are you after? A husband to take over the homestead?"

Anger flared again and I jerked in protest. "I don't need a husband."

The smile lurked unpleasantly on Donovan's face. "Then, if it's just a man you want, why don't you look closer to home? I'm younger than Les and I've more to offer than Saunders!"

My eyes widened and the color left my cheeks. "You're . . . you're disgusting . . ." I said tremulously.

Donovan laughed silently. "Maybe I am . . . or just a little insane at the moment." He lowered his head and my mouth suddenly went dry. I stared at him, frightened by the look in his cat-gold eyes. He smiled again, slowly.

"You feel damn good, Kat," he breathed, moving his hips against mine and sending flashes of heat through me. "Damn good. I wonder what you'd feel like without anything on . . ." he sighed, burying his face in my neck.

"No . . ." I protested, twisting beneath him, and succeeding in nothing. Still his lips moved across my skin. He lifted his head an inch, stopping just above my mouth. I could feel his warm breath mingling with mine. I stopped moving, my body rigid with awareness and a frightening expectancy. He was searching my face intently and I could not look away or close my eyes.

"No," he said, letting his breath out slowly. "No, I don't think I will. You're not ready for it . . . yet."

As suddenly as I had found myself pinned to the ground, I was free. Donovan stood above me, and there was a roguish grin splitting his handsome face. I had never hated him so much as I did then.

"Good night, little cat," he said and strode away toward the light and music. I trembled, tears blinding me and emotions churning inside, until I was totally confused by what I felt.

John was still nowhere to be seen and I wanted desperately to leave Madrone and go back to the security of the homestead.

My eyes drifted unwillingly to Mace Donovan. He laughed, talked, and danced with several young townswomen. One he paid particular attention to was Charlene Bellows, Jeremiah's pretty daughter who had recently returned from the East. When she left with her parents, Donovan stood off by himself watching the festivities. A woman approached him through the shadows, and I recognized her as the woman from the hotel. They talked for a few minutes and then left together. I felt sick.

It was almost half an hour later when John reappeared, and he was slightly drunk. He offered me no explanation for his long absence and said nothing on the long ride back to the homestead. I did not care, for I felt miserable myself and did not want to think of the reasons underlying my mood. The evening that had begun so well had ended dreadfully. I wished I had never gone and vowed I would never do so again.

By the time we reached the homestead, John was stone sober. Stopping the carriage, he jumped down and helped me to the ground. His hands lingered at my waist and then he pulled them away abruptly as though realizing what he was doing.

"I'm sorry," he said lamely, obviously trying to apologize for his behavior throughout the evening. Then he climbed back into the carriage and turned away.

I stared after John Saunders, feeling angry, disillusioned, and vaguely disturbed.

From that night on, I dreamed of Mace Donovan in a different light. I awakened several times, my body flushed and aching, my mind filled with thoughts that would not go away.

CHAPTER TWELVE

A beautiful bouquet of roses, brought by Les Bigelow, adorned the table and its embroidered linen table cloth, which I had found in Mama's trunk. After some debate with myself, I had decided to use it in honor of our guest. After all, I reasoned, if it had not been for Les Bigelow, Jeremy and I would still owe money all over town. There was some satisfaction in knowing that we had only the debt to the Madrone Bank to pay off, doubtful though it was that we could do so.

Les Bigelow came in his best Sunday suit. He had even had a haircut. I felt oddly touched by his efforts for such a simple evening at a poor homestead.

From the beginning, Les set out to make friends with Jeremy. Jeremy responded to the man's easy banter and interest in his studies. Bigelow said he respected a man who was educated and that being educated did not mean a man had to go to school, one could absorb knowledge on one's own. The two went on to discuss fishing, hunting, cattle, and, finally, the homestead and Papa, while I set dinner on the table.

As I poured coffee and cleared away the dishes, I was aware that their conversation had not lulled much. Jeremy was doing most of the talking now, and I smiled, proud of his varied knowledge. He was telling Les about the battles in the *Iliad*. Ironically, John Saunders was more to my liking, and Jeremy openly despised him. Yet this man, who intended to court me for marriage, was charming my little brother into confiding many of his private interests.

Jeremy asked numerous questions about raising cattle and building a herd. I was surprised at my brother's interest and turned to look at him. I caught Les watching me intently, his eyes seldom on my face, and felt my cheeks flush with embarrassment. The man had just eaten a big dinner and he looked hungry!

"Would you mind if I took your sister for a walk, Jeremy?" Les asked. Jeremy glanced at me and back at Les curiously. He shrugged.

"I suppose you'd like to see the homestead."

Les grinned. "Something like that."

Jeremy was no fool and there was a faint frown on his face as he looked at Les Bigelow again. Then he looked at me. Taking my shawl, I went outside with Les.

"You seem to be getting along well with my brother," I commented as we walked down the slope past the grove of redwoods and on toward the property line. It was a warm night, lit by the moon and brightly shining stars. Les gave me a sidelong look and there was a sheen in his eyes.

"He's a fine boy. A bit too bookish, but he'll learn to put that aside as he gets older."

So much for all Les Bigelow had said about admiring a self-educated man, I thought wryly.

"When he comes to live at my ranch, he'll learn a lot of more important things . . . things he'll be able to use as a man."

I shot Les a startled glance. "Aren't you going a bit fast?"

"Why did you think I wrangled this invitation out of you, Kathryn?" he asked bluntly. It was not a rhetorical question.

"I'm not entirely sure. I thought perhaps you might just want an evening out . . ." I said lamely.

Les Bigelow laughed low, eyes glinting. "Don't hedge, my dear. You knew very well what I had in mind the minute I set eyes on you. You should be married."

"Oh, for heaven's sake. As if that's a solution to anything," I said impatiently.

"It could be. If you married the right man, that is."

Meaning him, of course. My mouth tightened. We continued walking, finally stopping near a towering spruce. Les stood with his feet splayed, hands clasped behind his back, looking out over Donovan's land. I snapped off some pine needles, crushing them between my fingers and smelling the tangy scent. It was something I always did, since I derived peace from the earthy aroma. I felt Les watching me and looked at him. He was appraising me, and obviously liked what he saw. I definitely did not like the proprietorial gleam in his eyes.

"I've been married before," he told me.

"You have?"

"My wife died ten years ago in childbirth. My son died as well. She was too small boned to have babies apparently."

"I'm sorry," I murmured, thinking of my mother and Jeremy, thanking God again for having spared my brother.

"I've been a long time without a wife. I need sons to carry on my ranch," he went on seriously. "The first time I saw you standing there in my den, so proud and pretty, I decided I was going to marry you."

"What?" I gasped. I knew that he was interested, but had not expected him to make his offer of matrimony quite so soon. I had hoped to dissuade him, become friends while making him realize that the idea of marriage was out of the question.

"Close your mouth, my dear. It's not the least bit flattering that you're so damned surprised. What did you think I had in mind?"

"I didn't think."

Les smiled, disbelieving. "But I told you outright."

"I didn't think you were really that serious."

"I am very serious."

"But why would you want to marry me?" I was years younger and practically indigent. What would a man like Les Bigelow with a huge ranch, money in the bank, and years of experience want with someone like me?

Les gave me a purely male smile. "Because I am very attracted to you and that—with a little encouragement and time together—can lead to a solid marriage."

My eyes widened at his bluntness and I felt the slow flush of embarrassment creep into my cheeks.

"I don't suppose you thought a man in his early forties capable of those kinds of feelings, did you?" he said, amused at my innocence. "Let me assure you, Kathryn, I am still young enough to function rather well, and I'm old enough to have all the experience necessary to satisfy any cravings a young woman might have . . . perhaps better than a younger man."

I pressed my hands to my burning cheeks. "I . . . I don't think you should be saying these things to me."

"I'm not a man to mince words and waste time, as you will learn."

I gave a nervous laugh. "No, I shouldn't think you were. But I think you are rushing me . . . ."

"Why wait? Think about it, Kathryn. I'd pay all your debts. We could hold onto this land for Jeremy when he got old enough to take it over, if he wanted to. Otherwise, he could stay working for me at my ranch. I've got a lot to offer besides what I just told you. Jeremy could manage the ranch for our sons. He'd have a future."

There was nothing wrong with Les Bigelow's self-confidence, I thought wryly. Did he think Jeremy was studying hard so that he could become someone's foreman?

Since he was being frank with me, I would be with him.

"I just don't love you, Les." I did not add that I did not share his physical attraction either. I didn't think his male pride would like such a low blow. And I had the feeling already that Les Bigelow could be a hard enemy.

"Love doesn't necessarily make a good marriage," he said easily, not the least daunted by my statement. "You don't dislike me. I know that much."

"No . . ." I had to admit. I looked at him and then decided to be completely honest. "I think you're too old for me. And I'm too young for you."

"Out here, things like that don't matter. I may be twenty-five years your senior, but it doesn't mean a thing. I still want you and given the chance, I could make you want me."

"You're older than my father, Les."

"Your father was a very young man when he married."

I gave a slight laugh. "You have an answer for everything."

"A man in my position didn't get there by letting a good thing get away."

"I'm not a prize cow on the market," I said in growing irritation. Why was he so persistent? I had told him how I felt. Couldn't he take no for an answer? Les was laughing at me.

"Oh, Kathryn. You might as well get used to the idea," he told me, the sparkle of determination shining out of those intense blue eyes. He unnerved me.

"Can you imagine what everyone in Madrone would say if I were to marry you? They'd think I was . . ."

"They'd be saying how smart you were to land yourself such a catch," he interrupted. "The only man around these parts that has more land, money, or cattle is Donovan. And I'll surpass him one day."

"Donovan!" I muttered under my breath.

"And you don't like the man much, do you?" He already knew the answer to that question. "Now, come here, Kathryn." His voice was silky. I looked at him warily.

"What for?"

"A little enticement, in case you need more convincing."

"I don't."

But he gave me no choice. He was strong as a bear. I thought briefly of struggling and then knew I would accomplish nothing, except perhaps to bring on repercussions I could not deal with. I stood placidly in his arms as he lowered his mouth to mine. It was not an unpleasant feeling, but it did not arouse any desire in me. His hand moved down from my back to my waist to press me more tightly against him, and although I knew that his kiss was not arousing me, I became very aware that the same was not true of him. He made no effort to hide my effect on him, pressing an obvious male hardness into my thigh. I quickly thrust my hands against his chest. Forty-four was not so very old after all.

Les stepped back and surveyed my face. His mouth turned up at the corners.

"Did that shock you?"

I did not know what to say, embarrassed by his candor.

"Maybe now you understand why I don't want to wait," he said, running a caressing hand down my arm. "We'd have fine sons, you and I."

I looked at him curiously and then cocked my head. "I might be barren."

The blue eyes narrowed and then looked me over again. "Do you have any reason for thinking that?"

If I had had any doubts about why he wanted to marry me, there were none now. I could always lie and say I did have reasons.

"A woman never knows until she conceives."

"You're just trying to put me off, and it won't work," he said, smiling. "I'll give you a little rein for a while, but don't think I'm going to change my mind."

His eyes had a steely quality that was frightening. He was not a man to give up what he wanted.

"I suggest we change the subject."

"There is no one else I want, Kathryn. Just you . . . and you are going to be my wife. I want sons with your copper hair and blue eyes, and that indomitable will to survive. Men need that in this country."

So did women. "Like it or not, Les, the decision is going to be mine, not yours. And right now, my answer is no. Furthermore, I don't see it changing in the future."

"We'll see about that. You may not have much choice later on," he said, patting my cheek. My heart lurched in sudden trepidation. What did he mean by that?

Jeremy looked between the two of us when we returned. He frowned at the drawn look on my face. Les left right away, but he said he would be back and that our discussion wasn't finished. I thanked him with stiff politeness for the flowers and shut the door.

Resting my head against the pine panels, I sighed heavily.

"What's wrong, Katie?"

"He wants to marry me."

"He does? But why?" There was such surprise in those two questions that I felt insulted. I turned and looked at my brother, eyebrows drawing together.

"Am I really that undesirable?" I asked him, feeling indignant.

He considered me. "No, I suppose not," he admitted,

raising my ire even more. "But Katie . . . he's . . . he's old. Older than Papa."

"Yes. And I don't want to marry him."

Jeremy relaxed visibly. "Then there's no problem."

"He won't take no for an answer," I said dismally.

"You'll just have to keep telling him, that's all."

"If he'll listen." I kept thinking of what he had said about my not having any choice later on. What had he meant?

The following morning I did my usual chores. Then, smiling slightly, I put Constance in with Casanova. We might as well get a start on another herd, I thought. Casanova seemed to enjoy his work, but Constance was dubious of the entire affair and eyed him warily. The bull bellowed and moved in a wide circle around the corral, keeping his goal clearly in sight. The smile faded from my face as the situation reminded me of Les Bigelow and myself.

It was Sunday and I took flowers to the redwood grove where Mama and Papa were buried. Kneeling down, I readjusted the cross which had tilted, using a stone to pound it more securely into the damp earth. It was cool in the grove, and quiet. I looked up through the trees arched over me. Most of them were so big that I could not put my arms around their trunks. Papa had cut some of them down when we first arrived. Their trunks still protruded from the ground on the western slope. Oddly enough, seed had taken root and had grown out of one or two decaying stumps. Life coming from death. The infant tree taking its nutrients and gaining strength from the dead parent.

I thought of Papa again, and his death on the ridge. As usual, my thoughts then swung to Donovan. As long as I was away from him, I could believe that he had murdered my father. But faced with the man, I felt many doubts. He aroused feelings and instincts in me that were new and confusing. I was supposed to despise him. But I could not deny that my senses reeled when I saw him. Even thinking of him disturbed me more than a little. I remembered how it felt to have him close to me, his body pressing against mine as it had been on the night of the festival. I hated Donovan more than ever now, despite my growing doubts that he was a killer.

What was he after? Why did he keep coming over here? Why couldn't he just leave well enough alone? Did he still want the homestead? Or was he just biding his time, waiting for us to fail so he could walk in and take over?

I sat by the graves for a long time. Then I decided to go up on the ridge and conquer my fear of the place. I hadn't been there since the day we buried Papa. It was part of the homestead, and a place Papa had loved. I had to remember that and forget the rest.

The sun was warm on the boulder where Papa used to sit. I took his position, my heart beating nervously as I looked down into the valley. It would be easy for someone to fall from here. All they had to do was move a step too close to the crumbling edge and over they would go, crashing down against the jagged rocks.

Birds were singing all around me, and after a while I began to relax, putting away the memory of Papa's death and soaking in the beauty and tranquility of the place. No wonder Papa had loved it here. You could see for miles.

The wind caught my hair, cooling my heated temples. I breathed in deeply, closing my eyes and listening to the rustling branches.

I thought of Les Bigelow's proposal and then pushed it determinedly away. I did not want to marry him. Whatever assurances he gave me about his sexual prowess, I had felt nothing at all when he touched me. The thought of having his child filled me with revulsion and fear. Like Casanova, Les Bigelow would probably greatly enjoy his work. Women did marry without love, of course, but I would not be one of them; better never to marry at all.

Movement below caught my eye. A rider was coming up the ridge trail. I stood and peered down curiously. My heart started a quick hard thumping in my chest. There was no mistaking the man's carriage, nor the stallion he rode.

Without thinking, I stepped closer to the edge, staring down at him resentfully. He turned his head, looking straight across at me and my heart pounded harder. Damn him! What was he doing coming up here? Then I didn't care. Recalling the night he had pinned me to the ground, and Papa's murder here on the ridge, made me want to be as far away from this place and Donovan as I could. Swinging around, I jumped down from the boulder and began to run down the trail to the homestead. I knew I didn't have much time.

My skirts hindered my progress and I snatched them up, running wildly between the trees and rocks, ever downward toward the meadow and the cabin. The sound of hooves followed me. Not stopping to look back or to hide, I ran on, breathing in short, painful rasps. I could hear nothing now but the beating of my own heart, sounding like thunder in my ears.

A few yards from me was the upper meadow. I raced on, my hair coming loose, my skirts flying. I could smell Donovan's lathered horse. Suddenly an arm came looping down around my waist and hauled me up over the saddle like a sack of potatoes. I struggled frantically and the stallion started to rear.

"Whoa, boy!" Donovan commanded. "And you settle down!" he told me, his hand coming down with a resounding slap across my rear end. Then he deposited me back onto the ground in a heap. I was breathing hard and fast from my run and blinked up at him from where

I was sitting, legs outstretched, afraid and angry at the same time.

Dismounting, Donovan grinned down at me.

"You provocative little witch! Don't you know better than to run like that from any man! It only makes him want to give chase! There's the hunter's instinct in all of us."

He reached down and hauled me up, pulling me against him. I put my hands up protectively and stumbled back in my effort to avoid touching him. His eyes glittered with laughter as he took in my flushed, defiant face.

Sucking in my breath, I finally found my voice. "You're on our land, Donovan!" I accused bitingly.

He looked around and then back. "So I am," he said casually, his eyes dancing in enjoyment of my agitated state.

"I want you off. Now!"

"What you want and what you get are two different things," he drawled smoothly.

"I'm warning you!"

"What are you going to do, Kat? Throw me off bodily?" he taunted. He held his arms wide, taking a step toward me. "Come on, then." My heart thudded and I stepped back sharply. Swinging around with a flurry of skirts, I started down the hill again. He matched my pace, striding easily as I soon became breathless again. The stallion followed.

"That animal of yours is just like a lap dog," I said as insultingly as I could. Donovan merely chuckled.

"Diablo? Hardly. But I did train him well, didn't I?" He glanced at my tight expression. "I could do as well with you. And using similar methods." His tone was insinuating and I seethed.

"A carrot and lump of sugar, I suppose," I said, still not looking at him.

"Animals are much the same as humans in many

ways. They respond to gentle treatment. They like being cared for, having soft words spoken to them . . . someone caressing them . . ."

I shot him a startled look and caught the gleam in his eyes. He had not forgotten the other night either. My eyes widened in alarm, then I bolted down the hill, intent on nothing other than getting as far away from him as I could. Donovan laughed. I heard him coming after me again and almost panicked. Catching my wrist, he stopped and my momentum made me jolt backwards, into him.

"What's the all-fired hurry, Kat? Are you afraid of me?" he taunted.

"No!" I denied hotly, twisting myself free, and knowing when I was, that it was because he had permitted it.

"The hell you're not," he said, his eyes narrowing. "I think I put a damn good fright into you the other night." The laughter was gone from his expression.

"I've . . . I've got work to do," I said shakily, "Even if you've got people to do yours for you."

Donovan smiled slightly. "You're never at a loss for an insult, are you?"

I turned away. If I had hoped Donovan would tire of whatever game he was playing, I was sadly disappointed. He was not going to leave me alone. He walked with me down the hill to the cabin. Coming around the side of the house, my eyes took in the scene in the corral and I turned bright red with embarrassment. Apparently, Constance's coyness had been overcome. If cows could smile, she was beaming!

Donovan stood next to me and I felt him looking at my appalled expression. He laughed, and then to make matters worse, walked straight to the corral to watch the festivities, not the least bit embarrassed.

"Building up your herd again, Kat?" he needled, his mouth twitching.

"What's wrong with that?" I retorted, looking away and trying not to show how entirely flustered I was. How could Donovan stand watching it all so casually?

"I'm afraid your bull lacks staying power," Donovan said crossing his arms on the top fence railing while resting one foot on the bottom. I turned and looked in the corral. Constance had changed her mind again. Maybe she didn't like an audience. Casanova bellowed his frustration and moved after her. I raised a hand to hide the sudden urge to laugh. Donovan glanced over his shoulder and saw my expression. His eyes lightened briefly and then narrowed again, cooling rapidly.

"The same will be true of Les Bigelow."

I flushed again and glared at him. "He said he has the experience a young man lacks."

"Is that a challenge?" Donovan asked, straightening from the fence and looking at me in such a way that I had difficulty breathing.

"Hardly!"

"Hmmmmm. What a damn shame," he drawled, leaning back against the rails and straining the material across his chest. My stomach muscles tightened. "How was your *tête-à-tête?*" His question was tinged with sarcasm.

"He wants to marry me," I blurted out, more in self-defense than a desire to admit to the proposal. Donovan's face hardened and he looked at me derisively.

"Does he? He's not wasting any time, is he? But then how many more good years does he have?"

"He's not that old," I said in Les Bigelow's behalf.

Donovan raised his brows slightly and his eyes grew cold. "Congratulations are in order then, I take it."

I frowned, confused.

"Everything neat and tidy the way you want it, hmmm? Bigelow will pay all your debts, open a nice fat account for you and Jeremy, you'll keep this piece of land if you still want it . . . and all he'll expect of you is what you expect of your cow. That you drop him a baby, preferably a boy, once a year."

My mouth dropped open and my face paled. "You're . . . you're revolting!"

His shoulders stiffened and his face whitened in anger. "Deny any of it!"

"I didn't say I was marrying Les Bigelow, only that he asked me to!" I flared. Donovan relaxed slightly and smiled unpleasantly.

"So the siege has just begun, then. Give him time. He may look the kindly gentleman, but there's a streak of ruthlessness in him. He'll use every inducement he can to get what he wants. And he wants you."

I swallowed, knowing there was a good deal of truth in what Donovan was saying. Hadn't I seen it myself last night?

Aware that he was scrutinizing my face, I tried hard to control my expression, hiding all the doubts and fears I was feeling.

"I'm not going to marry him. I'm not going to marry anyone. I don't need a man to hold onto what belongs to Jeremy and me. We'll do it on our own. And just for your information, Donovan, we don't have any debts. I paid them off with the money I made from the cattle I sold to Les Bigelow."

Donovan let out his breath angrily. "And what do you have left? Nothing, I'll wager. Your mortgage isn't paid off. You just met the quarterly payment. You'll have another and another after that. And you've forgotten something else in your zeal for independence. Taxes are coming due. How're you going to pay them?"

I froze inside and stared at him miserably.

"Now you're beginning to understand what I mean by the inducements Les will use to get you," he said quietly.

"When you can't come up with the money to pay the tax collector or Lambert at the Madrone Bank and Trust, Les will buy this place right out from under you. He'll have you just where he wants you. You won't have much choice then when he comes around with his proposition, now will you?" There was a hard, cold edge to his voice that hurt far more than the words he was saying.

I was shaking, unable to look away from Donovan. He was telling the truth and I knew it. And there was nothing I could do to prevent it unless the homestead miraculously began to make money.

"I told you, you were making fast time," Donovan said dryly, not looking at all pleased that he had been correct. "You should have studied your quarry before you tried to snare it."

"I went to Bigelow to sell my cattle, not me!" I cried angrily.

"You should have come to me . . . I would not have put conditions on the sale," he said quietly.

"You'll never get anything that belonged to my father," I said, glaring at him. He looked at me, long and hard.

"Neither will you or Jeremy," he retorted stingingly, his eyes blazing. "Bigelow will have everything . . . and you with it . . . not to mention having Jeremy as an extra cowhand."

"I hate you!" I railed, unable to prevent my eyes from clouding with tears.

"You hate the truth, not me!" he snapped loudly. "It's going to be very interesting to see if you can get yourself out of this one, Kat," he said more quietly. "I warned you about selling off all your assets. But you wouldn't listen. Now, you've made your bed, and Les Bigelow is going to do his damndest to help you sleep . . . or should I say play . . . in it!"

CHAPTER THIRTEEN

Donovan was right about Les Bigelow's siege. He came by twice a week, always bearing gifts. Once he brought a box of expensive chocolate, another time the more practical gift of three laying hens. Always, he had flowers and arguments as to why I should marry him "without wasting anymore time."

The pressure he exerted was nerve-racking. No matter how often I told him no, he still asked again, or prophesized my ultimate acceptance. Several times he attempted a physical advance, which he allowed me to ward off. For all his arrogance, he was still a gentleman.

John Saunders came by once. Our conversation was stilted and he left as soon as possible. I wondered if he would be back and felt that our friendship was deteriorating fast.

Doc came out to look at Jeremy's leg while he was on his way to Tasajara to see Brian Donovan. He told me that the cast would be coming off in a couple of weeks. That was the only good news we had had in a long time.

I went to town to sell some of our produce and did surprisingly well. I put the hard-earned money in the mason jar I kept hidden in a kitchen cabinet. If things continued to go like this, we might, with luck, make the next mortgage payment.

Donovan did not come by the homestead for several weeks. When he did come, he brought a basket of vegetables from the Tasajara gardens. "Good afternoon, Kat," he said coolly. He dismounted and carried the basket across the yard to deposit it by the front door. Straightening, he looked at my face, waiting expectantly. I wanted badly to throw the offering back at him, but knew it was time to check my temper and use a little more common sense. I had done a lot of thinking about Donovan. Though I was no closer in my understanding of the man, I had decided it would be best not to antagonize him. We needed no more disasters, and Donovan was a worthy adversary.

"You plan to use that for your compost pile again?" he drawled, his mouth curving up slightly.

I glanced down at the succulent vegetables, far larger than the ones I had succeeded in growing in our rocky soil. I had stripped the garden yesterday and would now have to wait another week before harvesting more carrots, lettuce, beans, tomatoes, squash, and cabbage. Maybe longer.

"No," I answered frankly. "The stew pot. But you needn't send over any more, Donovan. Our garden is beginning to yield again."

Donovan's eyes flickered at my politeness. He looked as wary as I felt and I almost smiled. "Why the sudden change of heart, Kat?"

"You were right in the first place," I admitted. "Your steers did destroy my garden. You do owe us."

Donovan grinned maliciously. "As always . . . graciously said." I flushed and looked away.

"How're things otherwise?" he asked, looking around the homestead. Nothing much had changed. I had built a rough shelter for Constance and a separate one for the ever-amorous Casanova. There was a new, if somewhat poorly constructed, chicken coop that housed the chickens Les had brought, plus our own motley group.

Donovan knew very well how things were going and I saw no reason to answer him. He glanced at me, eyes narrowing.

"You look tired." It was a flat observation and not a taunt.

"I suppose I am," I shrugged. "There's a lot to do around here. Jeremy will be able to help again in a few weeks."

Donovan frowned, looking vaguely irritated. "What's he been doing?"

"Studying. He could pass the eighth-grade level now," I said proudly. Donovan did not look impressed.

"How's Bigelow's courtship progressing?" he asked after a moment.

"About the way you said it would."

"And what does that mean?" he demanded sharply.

"He won't take no for an answer."

"So you've taken the easy way out and said yes?"

"No, I haven't," I snapped. "But he hasn't given up either."

Donovan laughed. "You've always shown me you had a will of your own. Give him the sharp edge of your tongue. Maybe that will cool his ardor a little."

"I don't need any more enemies. Jeremy and I have enough to contend with without Les Bigelow's added animosity. And I have a feeling he could be very . . ."

"Vindictive?"

I sighed. "Maybe."

"I can assure you he would be."

"It's nice to know when one is right," I said dryly and walked away from him toward the garden. I bent down and plucked a couple of newly sprung weeds. Donovan's shadow fell across the row of carrots.

"Did your bull's seed take?"

I couldn't keep the color from flooding my cheeks.

"How would I know? I'm not God!"

Donovan laughed. "Don't get so red about it, Kat. If you're going to stay in the cattle business, you'd better learn to be a little less squeamish on the subject of reproduction."

"It doesn't have to be bandied about like the weather!" I snapped.

"It's as ever-present and as important," he grinned.

Hiding my embarrassment, I yanked up some crowded seedlings. "You want me to check her?" Donovan asked, and I glanced up at him in surprise.

"You could really tell something?"

"Possibly." He strode across the yard and I trotted after him, hating myself for doing so. Donovan swung himself over the fence and I watched in fascination as he ran expert hands over her. He straightened after a minute and walked back over to the fence.

"I think you'd better put your bull back in with her again. I don't think she's taken."

"Casanova hasn't been feeling well."

"Overexertion, probably," he commented and then stopped and looked at me, eyes opening wide. "What did you call him?"

"Casanova," I repeated defensively. Donovan threw back his head and roared with laughter.

"Good Lord! If that isn't the limit!" He was still laughing and having difficulty in controlling it. I had always thought it rather funny myself and was having trouble not laughing as well. But I didn't want to share laughter with Donovan.

"Papa named him," I told Donovan, my memories of my father softening my expression.

"No doubt about that," Donovan agreed, still smiling, eyes brilliant. "Roger wasn't one to pass up a laugh."

My face paled as I heard Donovan use my father's

Christian name. He was not looking at me, but staring down the hill as though filled with his own pleasant memories, and I felt a twisting in my chest. Sensing that something was wrong, Donovan looked down at me and the warmth and softening in his eyes confused me more than I ever had been before. I kept looking at him, trying to place the look on his face.

"You were saying something about Casanova," he said, smiling at the name again.

"He's . . . he's been acting strangely," I stammered.

"I'll take a look at him while I'm here."

Casanova was not as willing to be inspected as Constance had been. He was not cooperative and several times bellowed warningly at Donovan, who ignored the threat and sidestepped the horns.

"He's sick all right," Donovan agreed dismally. Casanova lay down and wheezed, eyeing Donovan balefully.

"What's wrong with him?" I asked worriedly.

He told me, but I did not understand the words nor what they meant.

"What does all that mean?"

Donovan hesitated. "I doubt if you're going to want to hear it."

"Tell me!" I said, trying to control my growing impatience.

He sighed. "It means you're going to have to shoot him unless you want him to suffer or infect your heifer."

I stared at him blankly. "Shoot him?" I looked at Casanova and back at Donovan. "But I can't shoot him! He's the only bull we've got. How are we supposed to get our herd started without him?"

"You can hardly build an entire herd on one cow and one bull, Kat."

"But it would be a start," I snapped. I looked back at the bull and bit down hard on my lip to keep it from quivering. "I . . . I can't shoot him."

"He's going to die anyway. And it won't be long by the way he's breathing. Look at him."

"Oh, God . . ." I turned away.

"You don't believe me, is that it?" Donovan demanded angrily. "Don't take my word for it, then. Ask Les Bigelow! He knows cattle. Do what he tells you!" His voice was ragged and angry, laced with impatience and frustration. I stared into the pen again at Casanova and felt miserable.

"I . . . I just can't shoot him," I said tremulously.

"He's not just your last bull, is he, Kat? You've made him a pet! My God, what a cattlewoman you are," he said harshly. I turned my head and glared up at him, tears trickling down my cheeks.

"It's not fair! It's just not fair. Not with everything else!" I cried bitterly.

"Nothing is fair in this business. What did you think you were getting yourself into?"

Unable to stand anymore, I turned away and ran from him, heading for the solitude of the redwood grove where my parents were buried.

"Kat!"

I didn't stop. Entering the shaded wood, I slowed and finally stopped to look down at the graves, feeling bereft. If I ever needed my parents, I needed them now. No matter how hard I tried, everything seemed to be falling apart, slipping through my hands.

Donovan came up behind me. "Leave things as they are. Maybe I'm wrong," he said, but I could tell from his voice that he didn't think so. I knew he was right. I had seen it myself, but had not wanted to recognize the facts before my eyes. When an animal is dying, you know it.

I felt so tired. I just wanted to find a place to lay my head and not worry anymore, not fight. But I couldn't give up. There was Jeremy. This was all his and I couldn't lose it. But how could I hold it until he was old enough to take over?

I pressed my fingers against my aching temples. "Just leave me alone," I said, devoid of emotion. "I'll handle it."

"Whether you let him die . . . or shoot him, the carcass should be burned so the disease won't spread," Donovan said flatly.

Something inside me snapped at his cold instructions about an animal my father and I had loved. I turned on him, my hands clenched into fists at my side.

"Yes, Donovan! By all means, Donovan! Don't worry yourself about it! I won't allow Casanova to infect your precious Tasajara stock!"

Donovan's hands came up, grasping my shoulders painfully as he shook me like a rag doll. "You unreasonable little . . ." he cut himself off forceably. "Is this just something else you're going to lay on my head? Do you think I came over here and hexed your damn bull? You think I'm sitting at Tasajara rubbing my hands together while I watch you go under? Let me tell you something . . ."

I was gritting my teeth against the pain his fingers inflicted, tears glistening in my eyes. Donovan froze for an instant and stared at me. He released me so abruptly I stumbled back against a redwood and grazed my elbow. Donovan continued to stare at my face, obviously restraining himself until a shudder froze his features into a mask of contempt.

"To hell with you! Give your damn bull chicken soup!" he said and left me standing in the grove.

The following afternoon, when Casanova's breathing became agonized, I shot him. It was the hardest thing I had had to do so far. As Donovan dictated, I burned the carcass. John Saunders rode up, having been sent by Donovan to help bury what remained after the burning.

I should have been thankful but I wasn't. I did not sleep that night.

Les Bigelow came by the next day. I was in no mood for his arguments and said so little to him that he left after an hour with a disgruntled look. He spoke a few words to Jeremy outside and my brother explained about the bull. I had hoped Bigelow would take my silence as a personal rebuff, but after Jeremy's helpful assurances he put it off as preoccupation with the homestead. He seemed very content with that supposition, as though my misfortunes assured his own success. I was beginning to heartily dislike Lester Bigelow.

I arose early the following morning, still unable to sleep for all my worrying. Constance had not shown signs of the disease yet, but there was still time for her to fall victim to it. It seemed like days since I had been able to sleep soundly and my body ached with fatigue. When I did manage to sleep, nightmares made me toss and turn. I felt sick, disheartened, and defeated. There seemed nothing more to do but to wait for the bank to foreclose, or the county to put us up for auction when we could not pay the taxes. Where had all my hopes gone? Was this how Papa had felt when he had worked over those endless papers? Had Casanova been the last straw? Or had it been the finality of Donovan's cutting words to me in the grove? I hated to think that he could be a part of moodiness.

Finishing my garden work and feeding the chickens and Constance, I sat exhausted at the table in the sod cabin. Jeremy was reclined on my bed, reading. He had not looked up from his book since breakfast.

Our diet had been mainly vegetables lately, with very little meat. Perhaps a little hunting would take my mind off our worries. I had seldom gone with Papa, as he had always taken Jeremy with him. But Jeremy couldn't hunt now and a rabbit or squirrel would be a welcome change to our diet. There was a river on Tasajara, but I would not beg Donovan's permission to fish, a pastime I had enjoyed on occasion.

Taking up the rifle, I left Jeremy reading and went out to see if luck would find me a deer. I might as well dream big. I loved venison and Papa had shot a buck several months before he was killed. That buck had lasted us a long while.

I walked up and down the hills looking for deer and saw nothing but signs of where they had been. The rabbits and squirrels did not seem worried about me and after shooting at a big gray squirrel I knew I would need a bigger target than that. Preferably something the size of a barn!

After a couple of hours I was too tired to hunt anymore. I sat down by a pine and leaned back to rest for a while. It was a hot day and the heat had sapped my remaining strength. I closed my eyes and listened to the birds and the warm breeze moving through the trees. I would have liked to stay here forever, putting everything out of my mind, if that were possible.

It was not possible. I had to remind myself of my responsibilities, will myself to open my eyes again.

When I did, they widened in surprise. Not a hundred yards from me stood a buck with a magnificent rack of at least eight points. The rifle lay across my lap and carefully, silently, I lifted it and aimed it at the animal. Through the sight, I looked at large, soulful eyes.

When the buck moved, I watched the sleek body, the shiny coat of tan fur, the white-tipped tail. The animal was majestic. What had it ever done to anyone that it should be killed? We were hungry for meat, yes, but he was so beautiful.

Tears blurred my vision and I rubbed them away with the back of my hand before taking careful aim again. I had him. All I had to do was slowly pull the trigger.

"Don't jerk it, Katie. Squeeze. Squeeze. That's right. Now you've got it." I remembered Papa teaching me to shoot behind the cabin.

That buck would drop with a bullet through his heart. A quick, painless death. Then I would have to cut the soft hide from the sleek body, gut him, butcher him for eating. There would be no more graceful, beautiful buck roaming free up here in the woods, but we would have venison for our table.

After a moment, I put the gun down in my lap again. As though sensing my presence, the buck turned his head, saw me, and with one mighty thrust of his hind legs bounded into the trees. Watching it go, I felt utterly useless. I could not even shoot a buck when we so desperately needed the meat. I leaned back against the tree and closed my eyes. I was so tired. If only I could sleep, sleep without dreaming.

Later I felt something brush against my hair. I stirred but did not open my eyes. Then the weight of the rifle was lifted from my lap. My eyelids felt heavy as I opened them to look up at the man bending over me. I was too tired to feel even alarmed or afraid.

"Just lie back and relax for a while, Kat."

"What are you doing up here, Donovan?" I asked, watching him lean the rifle against the tree and stretch his length out beside me, only a few feet away. I was reminded of the night in town and sat up. Pulling pine needles from my hair, I watched him warily. He smiled.

"Looking for you."

"And caught me napping," I quipped. Then I sighed, blinking several times to try to completely focus my vision, still drowsy from sleep.

"Did you have any luck?" he asked indicating the rifle. I shook my head and then sighed heavily.

"I had a beautiful buck in my sights, but I just couldn't shoot him," I admitted. I glanced at Donovan, expecting him to laugh over that sentimental admission. But he didn't. He was looking at me in an oddly intent way. Blinking, I looked away from him, very confused by the feelings stirring inside me. Leaning forward, I wrapped my arms tightly around my knees.

I didn't know what was wrong with me. Was it being so tired that made me want to curl up and cry? Or was it because I had held it all in for so long? Oh, God, how I missed Papa right now! Missed his laughter, his teasing, his easy smile. And I missed his love most of all. The security I had felt when he was alive had been a carefully constructed illusion, but it was there all the same.

Swallowing hard, I struggled to keep the tears back and stared up through the trees on the hillside.

"There's nothing wrong with crying, Kat," Donovan said gently.

"No? If I started now, Donovan, I'd never stop," I said, turning my head away from him to bite down hard on my lip. My chest ached and my throat hurt so badly from holding it in, but I was not going to cry now . . . not in front of Donovan. What was wrong with me?

"Do you think it's a sign of weakness?" he asked, deliberately pushing me closer to the breaking point. For a long time, I couldn't answer him. Then the pain receded and I was able to look at him in the eye.

"I've got Jeremy to think of. If I sat around weeping, what good would it do him? And there isn't time for it, Donovan."

"You think a few hours for yourself will make all the difference in the success and failure of this place?" he asked, the muscles hardening in his face.

"If you think I need your reminders about . . ." I stopped, afraid to trust my voice to finish.

Donovan didn't say anything for a long moment. Then he spoke gently. "You've had your share of bad luck."

I laughed slightly, putting my forehead on my knees. "Do tell, Donovan."

"Things could change for the better if you'd accept a little help," he said. I turned my head and looked at him.

"Such as credit from the mercantile? Or the feed and grain? Maybe a little charity from the church for indigent children? And what do I do, Donovan, if we can't make this place pay?" I meant it all to sound cutting, but it came out all wrong, my voice wobbly. "No," I said more clearly, shaking my head again and averting my face. "Papa's friends helped him and those debts are paid back. I'm not going to ask any more of those people and take the chance of leaving them in the lurch if I can't hold on. We've got to make it on our own."

Donovan frowned. "Kat . . ." He started to say something and then thought better of it. He just sat watching me. I was so tired, I didn't care. And it was quiet. I tried to arouse the protective anger but I couldn't. I was having trouble just keeping my eyes open.

"Donovan?" My voice sounded husky with exhaustion.

"Hmmm?"

"When I asked my father who shot him, he scratched your initials in the dust. His last word was Tasajara." I turned my head, forcing my eyes open to look at him. It was hard to focus. "Why would he do that?"

Donovan's face was pale and he was frowning. "I don't know, Kat. Unless he meant for you to come to me for help."

"He knew what I was asking," I said, tears welling again and blinding me. Then nothing mattered but to close my eyes and surrender to the enveloping darkness.

I felt Donovan's arms slide around me, lifting me easily from the ground. I forced my eyes open and stared sleepily up into his golden ones.

"Put me down, Donovan. I can walk," I said thickly.

"About two or three steps, . . . maybe," he answered. The rifle was already slung over his shoulder. He felt warm and hard, strangely comforting. I knew there was danger in giving in to him in the slightest.

"Donovan . . ."

"Just once, Kat, don't argue with me," he said in a low voice against my hair.

"I hope you strain your back," I murmured. I felt the rumble of his laughter. "You think everything is already settled and you're going to win . . ."

"Go to sleep, Kat," he ordered. There wasn't much else I could do, and I couldn't fight the exhaustion anymore. He murmured something as my eyes closed.

"I am going to win. There's too much at stake," I thought he said.

When I awakened, I found myself on Papa's big bed with a blanket over me. I could hear Donovan's voice raised in anger.

"A broken leg doesn't mean you can't do anything around this place!"

"What can I do?" Jeremy asked.

"Get off your little butt for one thing," Donovan said harshly. "You're sitting there like a little lord while your sister is out carrying everything on her shoulders."

"I don't see what I can do. And Katie . . ."

"No excuses, Jeremy," Donovan snapped angrily. "I'll bet you haven't raised your head long enough to take a good look at her lately. She's dead on her feet while you entertain yourself with your books on King Arthur and the Knights of the Round Table." I heard the thud of something against the wall and tried to rouse myself. What was happening now?

"If you can manage to sit a chair in here to read, you damn well can manage to sit a stool to milk that cow out there! Then you can sit and pull a few weeds in the garden, if any have managed to be overlooked by Kat!

For God's sake, Jeremy, do you want her to get sick? Have you taken a good look at her lately. She's . . ."

"Stop it!" I croaked, standing in the doorway with the gingham curtain shoved aside. I had to lean against the door frame as I glared into the main room. "Leave my brother alone, Donovan! And get out of here! Who do you think you are, anyway?" My head felt light.

Jeremy hobbled over on his crutches and took my arm. "He's right," he said, chin quivering, his hazel eyes tear-filled. "I didn't think about it. You just said to study and I didn't think about anything else."

"It's not easy to take in everything in those books," I said gently, brushing the hair back from his forehead. I looked up at Donovan, eyes glittering in challenge. "He's been doing his part, working in his own way . . ."

Donovan's mouth tightened.

"But not in a way that'll keep us going," Jeremy said, casting a look over his shoulder at the man looming close by.

"Donovan doesn't give any orders on this place, Jeremy. You and I decide what our jobs are," I said, still looking at the man. "Leave him alone." It sounded more like a plea than a demand. I was too tired to argue any more, but stared at Donovan until he turned away and walked out the door. I leaned back.

"Go back to bed, Katie," Jeremy said, and I didn't need anymore encouragement than that.

"Wake me in a couple of hours, all right?"

Later, I thought I heard voices in the other room. Then it was quiet.

When I awakened, it was still dark. I sat up and looked around, disoriented. I was in Papa's bed. Where was my brother sleeping?

"Jeremy?" I pushed myself up and went into the main room. Jeremy looked up from the table where he had been reading. He grinned broadly.

"Welcome back to the living," he said, pushing his book aside.

"How long have I been sleeping?" I asked, stretching and ruffling my hair. The headache was gone though I felt very fuzzy with sleep.

"Round the clock plus a few hours."

"What?" I exclaimed, staring at him and looking at the mantle clock. "I couldn't have!"

"You did. You might just as well lie down again. It's dark and there's nothing you can do this time of night."

"Why didn't you wake me up!"

"Mace said to leave you alone and let you sleep it out. You were dead tired, Katie. He sure was right about that. I never realized anyone could sleep so long."

"I thought Donovan left," I said stonily. "You didn't have to listen to him."

"Why not?" Jeremy countered. "He makes a lot of sense. I managed to do a lot of work around here on my own yesterday. I milked Constance, fed the chickens, and weeded and watered the garden. It took me longer than it would you, but I managed it by myself." He was proud of it!

"Mace did some work around here for us, too," he went on, making my brows go up as though on strings.

"He did?" Then I grew suspicious. "What kind of work?"

Jeremy laughed. "He wasn't very impressed with your chicken coop or the rails you nailed up on the corral. It's all fixed now. It didn't take him long, but then he knew what he was doing."

"Thanks a lot, Jeremy."

"I didn't mean anything by it," Jeremy flushed. "Besides, how would you know how to build a corral or chicken coop? And Papa never taught me how to do it. Now that I know, I can help out more when things need fixing."

"All thanks to the great Donovan," I said bitterly.

"He's not a bad man," Jeremy said defensively. "And I'm not forgetting what you said about Papa and Donovan on the ridge. I just don't believe it. Why would he want to kill Papa? It doesn't make sense."

"Maybe he still wants this land," I said, resentful that Jeremy was now also voicing doubts about Donovan's guilt. If Donovan hadn't murdered Papa, who had? Who else was there on Tasajara that had the initials MD? Or was Donovan right that Papa had been trying to tell me to go to him for help?

"Has he made an offer for our land since the first day we saw him? What's he done to keep you convinced he murdered Papa?"

"Why do you have to get so friendly with him, Jeremy?" I appealed to him.

"I like him. I trust him."

"Well, I don't!"

"Why not? He's a lot better than that Saunders fellow that keeps buzzing around you like a hawk!"

"I can't explain it. I just don't like Donovan," I said stubbornly, irritated by Jeremy's reaction to John Saunders.

"I think you're afraid of him."

My eyes narrowed angrily. "I am not!"

Jeremy did not look convinced. I turned back toward the bed in the other corner. "I don't feel like talking about him anyway," I said tightly.

"Why do you hate him so much? He's tried to be nice," Jeremy said, agitated.

"He's the kind of man that has a reason for everything he does. And whatever it is, it's for the benefit of Mace Donovan. Not you! Not me!"

"I think you're wrong about him," Jeremy said doggedly. My mouth trembled.

"One day of work with the man and you're singing his praises from the rafters."

Jeremy grimaced in anger. He pulled his book back toward him, flipping a page. I felt hurt and jealous. I could understand Jeremy missing Papa and needing a man to talk to, but why did he have to pick Donovan. Why couldn't he like John Saunders? Even Les Bigelow would have been preferable.

"Jeremy?"

His mouth tightened even more. "Bigelow came by while you were sleeping. Donovan talked to him. I think he was mad when he left." Just what I needed to hear.

"What'd Donovan say to him?" I asked bleakly.

"I don't know. They didn't say much to each other. Bigelow didn't say if he was coming back."

I sighed. What else could possibly happen? Not particularly anxious to think of the possibilities, I went to my bed and pulled the blanket over my head.

CHAPTER FOURTEEN

Les Bigelow's face was flushed with anger. "What was Mace doing here working on your corral?" he demanded belligerently, as though he alone had the right to such questions and their answers. I stared at him, taking immediate offense.

"When?" I asked, keeping my voice casual.

"Yesterday! Or does he make a habit of coming by?" he snapped. "I came by yesterday afternoon and there he was, big as you please, nailing up rails on your corral. Now, I want to know what's going on!"

My mouth tightened mutinously. "I don't like your tone, Les."

"I don't care if you don't like my tone. You're going to answer my questions. What was he doing here? Is there something going on between you two that I don't know about? I thought I read you right when you said you didn't like him. Now, I'm beginning to wonder!"

"What exactly do you mean?" I cried, growing angrier by the minute. Just who did Les Bigelow think he was to talk to me like this and make his nasty little insinuations about my nonexistent relationship with Mace Donovan!

"Oh, come on!" he said sarcastically. "You're not that stupid, and neither am I, though you apparently

think I am! He had the unmitigated gall to tell *me* you
weren't available! Now, what in hell blazes does that
sound like?"

I drew in my breath through my teeth. "Donovan was
right. I wasn't available. I happened to be asleep. It's
been a very hard week!"

"And I'm supposed to believe that?" he snorted derisively. "More likely you just weren't available to me,
but you were more than available to Mace Donovan!
That's it, isn't it?" he sneered. I had never seen such an
unpleasant face in my life and my own reddened with
growing anger.

"And you're even blushing about it! Who'd think you
could still blush after all this!" he accused.

"I don't like what you're inferring!" I said coldly.

He gave a harsh, insulting laugh. "I'll just bet you
don't. And I thought you were worth my time! You
were encouraging enough."

My eyes flashed in disbelief. "Encouraging?" I exclaimed with derision to equal his own. "You thought
you bought me along with my cattle! I *never* encouraged
you. You had to make your courtship a *condition of* our
cattle deal. You knew I had no choice because I had to
sell. Encourage you! I told you at the beginning that we
weren't suited. But Les Bigelow, big man with an even
bigger head, wouldn't listen!"

"I'm damn well listening now and seeing a lot I
missed before! You're nothing but a scheming little
shrew playing one man against the other to see how
much you can get!"

"I think you'd better go home," I said, speaking to
him as though he were a sulky child. His eyes narrowed.

"And you can look for your breeding cow elsewhere,"
I added for good measure. His face grew livid with rage
and he took a step toward me. I backed away and he
turned suddenly and stalked to his horse, mounting in a

hurry. I winced at the kick he gave the poor animal.

"Don't think I'll come back after this!" he shouted over his shoulder at me. I drew in enough air to call back to him in a cloyingly caustic tone.

"It was nice knowing you, Mr. Bigelow." He galloped down the hill. As he disappeared through the trees, I let out my breath in vexation.

"And good riddance to you, you horny old bastard!" I added quietly and then stuck out my tongue. It gave me childish satisfaction. I felt a wave of relief at his departure. I would have to thank Donovan for that!

The following afternoon, my opportunity came when he rode up the hill, leading a calf. I stood up from the garden and walked out to meet him, curious about the young animal.

Donovan stopped a few yards from me and the calf lowed loudly. Constance looked up from the corral in sudden interest.

"Lost its mother," Donovan told me curtly, not meeting my questioning gaze. "Thought you could do something with it."

"It's a bull calf," I noticed.

Donovan's face split with a grin. "So it is! At least you can tell the difference!" I turned pink but remembered my resolution to be polite.

"Do you want him?" Donovan asked.

"Yes."

The grin twisted mockingly. "Even if it's Tasajara stock?"

"I'll overlook that deficiency this once," I said, my mouth twitching as I looked up at Donovan through my lashes. He chuckled.

"Well, he's all yours then. Let him in to your cow there. He's hungry."

"Constance might kick him," I disagreed. His eyes danced.

"Constance?" he repeated. "Well, Constance might, but unless you want to feed the little fellow six times a day with a bottle, you'd better try them together."

I pushed the calf into the corral and watched as Constance eyed him balefully. The calf lowed again plaintively and approached her. Constance shifted and looked as though she were about to give him a resounding kick. I opened the gate to go in and take the calf out, but Donovan stayed me with a hand on my shoulder.

"Give them a chance."

I held my breath, watching, fingers crossed behind my back. The calf was not shy and tripped forward nosing against Constance's warm side. He latched hungrily onto a teat and began to suck eagerly. Constance shifted again and let out a moo.

"She's going to kick him!" I cried, fearing for the calf.

"Hold on a minute," Donovan kept his hand hard on my shoulder.

Constance turned her head and looked at the calf, big brown eyes rolling over him. She mooed again, but did not kick him. The calf never stopped drinking. Constance turned her head forward again and ignored him. Her only movement was the swishing of her tail, keeping the flies away.

I turned to Donovan and laughed joyously. I almost threw my arms around his neck, but caught myself. "She accepted him!"

Donovan smiled down at me, his gold eyes softening. "Seems your Constance has a loving nature. He ought to be all right now." He glanced over me to the pair in the corral, a devilish look in his eyes.

"What're you going to name him?" he teased. I looked the calf over and then grinned.

"Don Juan."

Donovan laughed. I stared up at him, disturbed by the rush of my senses. All my muscles were tightening and there was a pleasant tingling sensation in my body. I looked away from him and squared my shoulders.

"I've something else to thank you for," I said.

The softness left Donovan's face. "What have I done this time?"

"Les Bigelow."

"What about him?" There was an immediate defensiveness in his tone and stance.

"What exactly did you say to him?"

"Why? What did he say I said?"

I sniffed. "He said a lot. He was furious. He's decided not to come back to call."

Donovan's eyes flickered. "And you're upset about that," he said flatly. I smiled slightly, flicking a glance at him.

"Now, I didn't exactly say that."

He looked at me for a moment. "Well, are you?" he demanded.

"I'm relieved he's not coming back. But I didn't like the way he was talking."

"What'd he say?" Donovan's voice hardened in impatience.

"He wanted to know what you were doing here and if you and I were . . . well . . . he insinuated . . ." I let out my breath in frustration and then shrugged, embarrassed.

"Insinuated what?" Donovan asked silkily, his mouth curving upward.

"You can well guess! He implied there was a . . . a relationship between us." I looked away from his wry expression.

"Did he now? And what did you say to that?" He was openly laughing now.

"What do you think I said?" I retorted in irritation. "I didn't owe him any explanations and I told him to go find his breeding cow somewhere else."

Donovan's smile faded with his astonishment. "You said what?"

"You heard me."

When he didn't say anything, I looked up at him. He shook his head and then laughed low in his throat.

"I can well imagine old Les's reaction to that!"

"Well, it was true! You were right again, Donovan! You ought to glory in that!"

Donovan's face hardened at my sarcasm. "You might have been just a tad more diplomatic about your refusal."

"He wasn't very diplomatic about his accusations! Why should I show him any courtesy after he almost called me a . . . a . . . oh, never mind!"

Donovan's eyes darkened. "He went that far?"

"Just about."

"A scorned man isn't much different than a scorned woman, Kat," Donovan warned.

"He wasn't interested in me as a person . . . only as a female capable of . . . how was it you put it so delicately . . . 'dropping him a baby, preferably a boy, once a year.' "

"There might have been compensations," Donovan drawled.

"Such as his vast sexual experience," I said dryly and Donovan's mouth twitched.

"You consider that a compensation?" he raised a brow and moved a foot closer. Then he added before I could say anything. "I meant his money . . ."

I moved back a step and tilted my chin. "I didn't feel much like selling myself. I suppose if I had explained everything like a dutiful little mouse he would have been more reasonable. But I detest his arrogance and conceit! He acted as though he had bought me along with our cattle, and the way he talked . . . as though you and I were carrying on behind his back . . . ."

"Absurd thought," Donovan murmured, looking away from me and in at Constance. "That'd be about as healthy as bedding down with a wolverine."

"What did you say?"

"You want me to set him straight?" he asked.

I searched his face and then considered his offer. "You might just say enough so that my reputation won't be destroyed, but not enough to make him want to come back," I accepted.

"Tall order," Donovan smiled.

"Well, you didn't have to hang around here and make him think something might be going on."

"All right, I'll talk to him."

I took a deep breath. Shifting my weight from one foot to the other I tried to gather enough courage to finish what I had started. Donovan was watching my face curiously. I reached up and held onto the fence rail. I sighed.

"What is it?"

"Thank you for the other day . . . the corral and chicken coop . . . and for the bull calf." I was relieved once it was out.

"My, my," Donovan grinned wickedly. He turned and leaned back against the corral railing, crossing his arms over his chest. His eyes took in my flushed cheeks. Looking up in irritation, I became increasingly aware of his masculinity and the undeniable attraction he held for me. I felt shaky and dry mouthed, and I certainly did not like the way my heart was pounding. I looked away.

"I'm sure you have a motive for everything," I added stiffly.

"Now, don't go and spoil it," he drawled.

My resolve was breaking down rapidly. I knew what I would do if he were any other neighbor. I took another slow breath.

"Would you like some coffee?" I asked slowly.

Donovan's eyes widened. He considered me for a second before making his decision.

"I'd love some," he said, his expression veiled. He followed me into the cabin and watched me rekindle the fire. I had just made some cinnamon snails the previous evening and set some on a plate before him. Donovan looked at them and then at me. He did not look the least bit trustful and I couldn't help but smile at his expression. He smiled as well, but his was sardonic.

"I'll have one . . . after you," he said. Understanding his implication, I grinned tauntingly and picked one up after looking them over with exaggerated relish. I ate it, licking my fingers one after another.

"Satisfied?"

He chuckled. "I'll chance one." I waited until he had finished the whole thing. Then I turned away, hiding a grin. I hummed as I sashayed back to the fireplace to get the coffeepot.

"What're you humming about?" Donovan asked dubiously.

I looked at him, laughing over my shoulder. "That one had the arsenic in it!" I teased.

Donovan gave an exaggerated sigh. "Too late to worry about it now. Just send the body back to Tasajara for burial."

I poured some coffee and set the mug in front of him. "There. That'll help dissolve it faster. Sugar or cream?" I asked sweetly.

"Black is fine," he said, eyeing me curiously. He looked very confused.

"What's the matter, Donovan?"

"I'm not sure yet," he said seriously.

I poured myself some coffee and sat down opposite him. It had been a long time since I had allowed myself the luxury and I sighed after a sip of the heavenly brew.

"Are you thawing?" Donovan queried, raising his

brows above the rim of his cup.

"Jeremy doesn't think you killed Papa," I said frankly.

"And you?" His gaze sharpened.

"I don't know what I believe about you anymore."

Donovan drank his coffee thoughtfully. When he looked at me there was something new in his eyes that sent a tremor of instinctive unease through me. What was he thinking now? I tried not to look at him, keeping my eyes glued to my cup, studying the blue willow design.

"Kat, I detest killing. I've only done it when it was forced on me, and then it was face-to-face, man-to-man. There's no place in the world for a back-shooter who'd shove a wounded man off a cliff and leave him to die."

I looked squarely into those gold eyes. Then, unable to hold my gaze, I looked down again. Restless, I got up, checked the coffee over the fire and moved it away. Anything to keep moving, to stay away from the table, to avoid that look that turned me into a mass of tingling nerves. What was happening to me? Donovan's eyes followed my movements and, glancing back at him, I felt as though he were actually touching me.

The door opened and Jeremy came hobbling in. His eyes widened in surprise to see Donovan sitting at the table, the coffee mug dwarfed in his hands.

"Did you check the hens?" I asked, grateful for my brother's arrival.

"Nothing. The weasel got in and there were shells all over the place and feathers too, but at least all the chickens are there. They seem okay." He looked at Donovan and smiled. "Hello."

Donovan smiled a greeting, casting me an amused look. "Your brother seems surprised to see me sitting here . . . and still alive."

I ignored the comment. "Did you reset the trap?"

"Sure, a lot of good it'll do though," he prophesized dismally. "The critter is just too smart."

"What you need is a dog," Donovan suggested. "We've got one or two to spare at Tasajara."

Wonderful! Jeremy had been wanting a dog for years, but he also wheezed himself into a fit whenever he was around one.

"A dog is just another mouth to feed," I told him, annoyed by his interference.

"Feed him scraps off the table. The rest he can find for himself," Donovan said, undaunted by my glowering look. Jeremy laughed.

"What scraps? There's never anything left!"

Donovan looked at my brother questioningly and I gave Jeremy an exasperated look. He flushed slightly. Donovan glanced between the two of us.

"How's hunting, Jeremy?"

Jeremy glanced at me again and then looked down. "So-so," he evaded with a shrug.

"No deer?"

"I can't track them with my leg," Jeremy said flatly.

"And your sister hasn't the heart for it," Donovan commented with a wry look at me. Vaguely I remembered telling him something when he carried me down from the hills. I flushed with annoyance.

"We're not starving, Donovan."

"I'd better be going," he said, rising. "That was a good cup of coffee, Kat. And so were the rolls." His smile was taunting. "We'll see if I live through the night."

I did not see him to the door, but listened as he rode away.

"Have you changed your mind about him, Katie?" Jeremy asked, shaking me from my private reverie about Donovan. I glanced up blankly.

"What did you say?"

"Have you changed your mind about Mace?" he repeated.

Mace. I rubbed the back of my neck wearily. "I'm just plain tired of fighting," I answered.

But was that really the whole truth?

CHAPTER FIFTEEN

After Donovan stayed for coffee the first time, he began to ride by the homestead at least twice a week to see how things were going. He always had a ready compliment and a taunting grin that only increased my basic antagonism towards him. He seemed to enjoy tormenting me, sensing the whirlwind of feelings that simmered just below a strained veneer of politeness. I heartily wished that he would tire of whatever game he was playing and leave me in peace. I had enough to do without trying to contend with the confused feelings he always managed to stir up inside me.

Doc rode out and removed the cast from Jeremy's leg. My brother began taking on more chores around the homestead and his studies once again were relegated to late evening.

The garden was in full production now and my sales in town were going well. I had enough money stashed in the mason jar to meet the next mortgage payment. But there would be more to come, and winter would bring a temporary end to my garden. We would have to live from one month to the next in hopes that the good Lord would see us through until spring.

Les Bigelow had started an ugly rumor in town about Mace Donovan and me. I did not know about it for some time, but was aware of people looking at me with curious speculation. Once Sadie Jacobson had nerve enough to ask me how Donovan was. I told her that he rode by on occasion to check on us, but that I was not friendly with him. She did not look convinced and I did not care to go into a lengthy defense concerning our relationship. I wasn't sure what I felt about him anymore and it was none of her business anyway.

As for Les Bigelow, I saw him once riding into town. Thankfully, it was at a distance, for if I had been closer I would have had words with him, regardless of who heard.

The morning I learned from Sadie Jacobson about the rumors concerning me and my imperialistic neighbor, I made a decision about Donovan. When he rode over later that week, I found much to do outside while he sat inside talking with Jeremy. He came out a few minutes later, lounging against the doorjamb, his eyes on my bent back as I zealously worked on my garden.

My mouth tightened and I kept my head down, yanking up small weeds with unnecessary force and pinching off bug-ridden portions of plants. Donovan continued to watch me, saying nothing. His presence behind me began to wear on my nerves.

"Your garden is in full swing," he observed. "Jeremy says sales are going well."

I saw no point in commenting. Jeremy had said enough about our business and, as for the garden, Donovan could see for himself that things were going well again. I stood up, picked up my weed bucket, and stepped across the row of lettuce to begin work on the beets.

Donovan pushed away from the door and walked forward slowly until I could see his splayed legs out of the corner of my eyes. Still, I did not look up at him, and I could feel his growing irritation.

Let him be irritated! Damn blast him anyway! If it were not for him, my reputation wouldn't be in such jeopardy and I wouldn't be receiving such speculative looks from every sheep-brained male in town!

"What's the matter now, Kat?" he demanded tersely.

I honored him with a contemptuous glance. "Go away and leave me alone!" I snapped. Standing up, I stepped over the beets to get away from him. He followed me.

"Jeremy said you went into town early this week. And you came home in a foul temper. It doesn't seem to have improved any."

I worked on in silence. Donovan swore under his breath and hunkered down next to me.

"Out with it, Kat!"

"When was the last time you went into town?" I asked, not looking at him. I plucked another weed and flung it into the bucket. I could feel the tension in him as he watched my hands.

"Will you stop that for five seconds?" he grasped my wrist. I did look at him then, a tingling sensation traveling up my arm into my chest, to drop into the pit of my stomach. I wrenched my arm away.

"When did you last go to town?" I demanded, my voice coming out even more sharply.

"Last week. Why?"

"Then I'm sure you're aware of the whole ugly business!" I stood up, intent on getting away from him. Donovan stood with me, standing barely a foot away, overwhelming me once again with his size and masculinity.

"Just a damn minute!" he said harshly. "What am I supposed to make out of that?"

"Did you ever have that talk with Les Bigelow you promised to have? Because if you did, you either said too much or not enough."

Donovan's face hardened. "What do you mean?"

"What do you think I mean?" I turned away, stepping over another row and then another to the carrots. Even that distance didn't seem to lessen his effect on me very much.

"People are talking about us?"

"Talking? Talking!?" I laughed harshly. "They're talking so fast their tongues are choking them. Damn you! I didn't need this on top of everything else!"

Donovan did not say anything and his sudden silence fanned my anger into a full rage.

"I'm sure it does your male pride an immense amount of good having people saying what they are. But I hate it! Do you hear me?"

"I hear you quite well." He smiled slightly. "I'll take out a full-page ad in the *Madrone Gazette*. 'There's nothing going on between Miss Kathryn Durham of Rock Hill Estate and Mr. Mace Donovan of Tasajara.' How's that suit you, sweetheart? Does it meet with your approval?"

I glared at him bitterly, knowing how futile it was to try to get Donovan to take me seriously. I lifted my skirt hem slightly and jumped over several more rows until I reached the end of the garden. Then I ran off toward the hills. He could have the place to himself for a while. I'd come back when he was gone!

Donovan was not finished, however, and easily caught up with me. He stopped me with an iron-like grip around my arm.

"Cool down!" he ordered. "It'll all blow over in a few days when something else comes up for them to talk about. Be thankful they smile about it. If they thought we were doing something immoral up here, they wouldn't buy your produce!"

My cheeks flamed at the very thought. "Give them time!"

Donovan's mouth twitched. "Don't sound so cynical. It doesn't become you."

"You may think it's funny, but I don't!"

"The less said the better," he told me seriously. "The more you try to defend yourself, the more suspicious people will become."

"You make it sound as though something is going on! Well, listen to me, Donovan! They would stop talking a lot faster if you stayed clear of our homestead," I said, putting another step between us. His fingers retained their hold and he moved a step closer. His thumb began a circular caress on the inside of my arm. I yanked hard and put my hands on my hips, my chin jerking up.

"I may have stopped openly warring with you, but that doesn't mean I like you any better!"

Donovan's smile broadened considerably. "That's precisely why I'm riding over here."

"To make things worse?"

"To change your low opinion of me. At least you've stopped gunning for me and have had the courtesy to listen to what I have to say . . . on infrequent occasion."

"I don't remember hearing anything important," I retorted.

Nothing phased him apparently. "I haven't really said anything important yet," he drawled. "All in due time. Besides, Kat. I think you'd miss me if I stopped coming."

"Don't count on it!"

"Someone has to keep an eye on you two," he added smoothly, looking at my flushed, indignant face with a wry smile.

"If I have a choice, I'm asking for John," I said. The gold eyes glittered suddenly and narrowed.

"You're still interested in that drifter?"

"John Saunders is very nice," I said clearly. "He reminds me of my father."

"Because of his charming southern drawl, I suppose," Donovan sneered in a snide imitation of John's easy speech. "Or is it moonlight kissing you crave?"

Donovan seemed too close suddenly and the sensuous tilt of his mouth frightened me so that I stepped back instinctively.

"Don't be ridiculous!" I exclaimed, flinging my head back.

"Did you enjoy yourself the night of the festival?" he asked smoothly. He moved forward again. I blinked, feeling my senses rush at the look in his eyes as they dropped to my mouth. I could barely breathe with the growing constriction in my chest. My stomach was doing alarming things and my knees felt wobbly.

"Come here, Kat, and I'll show you what kissing is all about," he whispered. My eyes widened and I stepped back quickly to avoid his caressing hand. He caught my wrist. I pulled. His fingers were gentle but unyielding.

"Don't look so frightened," he smiled lazily. "It won't hurt a bit."

"Let go, Donovan," I said through my teeth, annoyed to hear how my voice shook.

"Soft as silk," he said, his thumb lightly stroking my inner wrist. I was sure he was aware of my rapid pulse.

"Don't." I pulled harder, but was unable to break free.

"Don't what?" His free hand moved to my shoulder, beginning again an increasingly familiar caress over my exposed collarbone. My mouth felt dry and I ran my tongue along my parched lips. Donovan watched intently.

"I don't like you touching me," I managed.

"You don't? Well, I like it. I like it very much," he said, and I felt his hand slowly drawing me toward him. I stiffened in resistance.

"Let go of me, Donovan," I ordered, my voice unable

to rise above a hoarse croak.

"What are you really afraid of, Kat?" His eyes gleamed, and he bared his teeth in a daring smile.

"I don't like you touching me!" I repeated doggedly.

"You let Saunders have the privilege."

"That was different."

"How?" The question was clipped.

"How was I to know he was going to kiss me?"

Donovan gave a faint laugh. "Come on. Most women aren't caught that unaware."

"I said I didn't know he was going to kiss me," I repeated defensively. "And I didn't like it."

Eyebrows shot up, eyes sparkling with laughter. "You didn't? Well, with me, it might just be different."

With a sudden hard yank and twist of my wrist, I gained my freedom. His arrogance infuriated me. "I'm not the least bit interested in making any comparisons."

Donovan considered me for a moment, smiling leisurely. He seemed to be trying to make up his mind what to do next. My heart thumped wildly against my ribs as I considered the possibilities. His eyes roved over my face again and then moved slowly down to the rapid rise and fall of my breasts, where they lingered. He smiled, but did not say anything.

"Another time, perhaps . . . when you're more willing."

"I'll never be willing!"

He still smiled and I felt the anger rising inside me. "Donovan," I said, stepping forward and thrusting my chin out. "I don't want you coming here anymore."

His eyes became veiled. "Indeed. Any special reason?"

More than I could count and not enough time to list them all, I thought furiously. "I've already told you. I don't like the talk in town!" I settled for that excuse.

Donovan shifted, putting his hand against the trunk

of a tree and leaning against it negligently. "I'm not sure I agree. I'd get bored without our fights."

"Fight with someone else then!"

"Care to make a suggestion?" he drawled, his eyes lighting with amusement.

"Why not that woman in town . . . the one you were giving money to at the hotel?" I suggested, stiffly. "Aren't you two friends or something?"

Donovan grinned. "Or something . . ." he said suggestively. "But Marcela doesn't have a fighting nature," he added wickedly. "In fact, *she* goes out of her way to make a man feel welcome."

I wanted very badly to hit him across the face. Instead I spun around. "I haven't got time for this," I snapped, stalking toward the cabin. Stopping, I looked back at him.

"The next time you come up here, Donovan, there's going to be no one home to you," I warned him.

"And all this time I thought we had a truce . . ." he said with a little too much ruefulness. He was laughing again.

"There's a truce as long as you stay on your own side of the wire."

"Are you going to be packing that rifle again, Kat?" he called after me as I stalked away. I passed Jeremy who had watched us curiously from the chicken coop. Upon reaching the cabin, I slammed the door furiously behind me.

It was a while later when I heard Donovan mounting his horse out front. Jeremy was talking to him, and I resented the easy rapport they shared. Jeremy seemed to be moving more and more away from me. And that just added to the hostility I felt towards Donovan.

It was on my next visit to Madrone that I saw Donovan. He was lounging against a post in front of the bank building. Standing next to him, gazing up at him was pretty, green-eyed Charlene Bellows. She was smiling and talking animatedly, obviously flattered by his attention. I lifted the crate of produce out of the back of my one-horse cart and carried it up the steps of the general mercantile, where I had a standing order from Joseph Iverson. Donovan did not even look in my direction. I hated him all over again.

When I left Madrone, Donovan was still talking with Charlene Bellows, and he even had his hat in his hand! Thankfully, I did not have to pass him since I was going in the opposite direction.

John Saunders began to come by regularly again. He had regained his previous gaiety and I found myself beginning to enjoy his company. He helped sometimes with the heavier work and then would putter around while I did what he laughingly called "women's work." I began to look forward to his visits. Jeremy went off someplace at first glimpse of Saunders, yet he worked close enough to keep a cool eye on my guest.

One afternoon, John was watching me do the washing. "Rumor has it that the boss is seeing a lot of a girl in town," he volunteered. I glanced up from the sudsy water, a tight knot forming in my stomach. "The whole crew is beginning to make bets about how long it'll be before Tasajara has a mistress," he added.

"They're getting married, then?" I asked casually, rubbing Jeremy's denim pants up and down against the washboard.

"Who?"

"Donovan and Charlene Bellows."

"So you've already heard about it," John said, looking at me curiously.

"I haven't heard anything. I just saw them in town together," I shrugged indifferently. "It wasn't hard to fill in the rest of the information."

"There's no engagement yet," John said, sitting back

against a boulder to watch me wring out the pants and set them aside. "But I wouldn't be surprised if it happens pretty soon. He's twenty-nine after all. He'll want to get married and have a son one of these days to take over Tasajara."

"Is that the way all men think out here?" I snapped.

John chuckled. "Well, Charlene Bellows is a pretty girl as well, Kathryn. She doesn't cast a shadow to you though. But she comes from good stock. He could do a lot worse."

I dropped a washed shirt into the rinse bucket.

"So he'll be happy as long as she drops him a baby, preferably a boy, once a year," I commented, remembering what Donovan had said to me about Les Bigelow. And he should talk!

John's brows shot up in surprise. "I've never heard you talk like that," he commented.

I laughed lightly, pretending to be amused. "Just a thought. Something he said about Les."

John was watching my face, and I looked away. "You're old enough to be thinking of settling down yourself, John."

"Hmmm. I've thought about it," he drawled, his eyes moving leisurely over me. "But there are certain obstacles."

I glanced at him curiously. He stared back at me, eyes darkening. I could see a rapid pulse beating in his temple and looked away, finishing the last of the washing and pinning it up on the line. John watched intently from his position on the ground. As I put up the last garment, he stood up and moved behind me, putting his hands at my waist.

"You're so beautiful with that shiny copper hair of yours and those big, blue eyes," he murmured huskily against my neck. "Sometimes, Kathryn, I want to forget every . . . start building a place of my own."

The ardor in his voice bothered me and I certainly did not like him kissing my neck. I turned around, moving away from his touch. "Forget what, John?"

His hand trembled as he reached out to touch my face. "Forget I have to go home soon."

"To Texas?"

He looked bemused. "Yes," he nodded, after a pause.

"When?"

"The next few weeks will decide it."

Donovan had said John Saunders would not stay more than six months. I frowned, feeling depressed. Donovan had left a gap in my life when he stopped coming over . . . just as he had predicted he would. But at least John had filled in part of it.

"I'm going back to claim what rightfully belongs to me."

"Land?"

"And a lot more. It's mine by right of birth. I've worked and waited for it and it's not going to slip through my fingers no matter who stands in my way." His face had a fierceness in it I had never seen before and I shivered.

"Someone has, I take it."

"Only for the time being. They won't have it for long," he said, looking into the distance in a distracted way. Then, with what seemed great effort, he wrenched himself from his thoughts and looked down at me again, smiling apologetically.

"It probably doesn't make a lot of sense to you," he admitted quietly.

"I think I understand very well. It's like this place. I love it. But I've got to fight every day to keep it."

"This place is in your blood, just like my home is in mine," he agreed.

"I wish you luck, John," I smiled, "in whatever it is you have to do. I hope you get what you want." He looked down at me with a look I could not fathom, and then he shook his head.

"Kathryn," he sighed. "I'm never likely to forget you. Ever."

"I should hope not," I said lightly, smiling up at him. "We've been good friends."

A faint grimace touched his face and his lips twisted slightly. "We should have been a lot more than friends," he said quietly, looking away from me.

"I'm going to miss you," I said, touching his arm and feeling quick tears of regret. His eyes flared and I was unprepared for the suddenness of his embrace and the passion of his kiss. Before I had time to react, he released me and walked away, mounting his horse and riding off without looking back.

Jeremy was standing at the edge of the cabin. "If I ever see him touch you again, I'm going to shoot him!" he announced, red-faced with anger.

"He was saying good-bye, Jeremy," I said watching him ride down the slope.

"He could have shook hands!"

"He's leaving the valley."

Jeremy let out a deep breath. "In that case, good riddance."

I gave my brother an impatient look and returned to my chores.

CHAPTER SIXTEEN

Donovan rode over several days later and as I had promised, the door remained closed. Jeremy was out hunting and therefore posed no arguments. Donovan did not give up as easily as I had expected.

"I know you're in there," he called through the door. "I saw your skirts flying as I came up the hill. You might as well open the door, Kat." He sounded amused and I almost shouted at him to leave me in peace and go visit his pretty Charlene. When I remained silent, he knocked again, harder.

"Kat!" He wasn't amused anymore. "This is damn stupid! I want to talk to you!"

Still, I remained silent. Just for good measure, I walked to the door and noisily slid the bolt into position.

"Damn it!" Donovan shouted, slamming his fist against the closed portal. "What a stubborn little witch you are!"

Hearing him walk away, I could not control the desire to peer out at him from behind the parted curtains. Donovan was standing at the well. He remained there for a minute with his back to me and then pulled up the bucket, taking a drink from the tin cup.

As though feeling my eyes on his back, he turned

slightly and looked toward the cabin. I dodged back quickly, afraid he would see me spying on him. He smiled, a tight-lipped, unpleasant sort of smile that did not spell defeat. Striding to his horse, he mounted in one swift, angry motion.

After he had left, I opened the door and went back to my work. After a while, I went back into the cabin to clean and cut vegetables for rabbit stew.

Jeremy came home hot and tired. He stopped at the well, splashing water in his face and drinking deeply from the bucket.

When he came into the cabin, he was hungry. He had had poor luck hunting and lounged in a chair at the table while I put a bowl of stew out for him. Sitting opposite him, we talked about the work ahead of us in the morning.

Before Jeremy had finished eating, he grimaced with sudden pain. I looked at him questioningly and he put his hand to his throat.

"What's wrong?" I asked, standing up to go around the table and lean over him in concern.

He groaned. "My throat burns. My stomach . . ." He stood up and bolted out the door to the outhouse. I followed, worried. Standing outside the door, I heard him retching.

"Jeremy . . ." I called, tapping the door. He opened it after a moment and his face was pale and drawn. He was stooping slightly, gripping his stomach. I put my arm around him and helped him back to the house, wondering what had hit him so suddenly.

We were not back five minutes when he vomited again, this time into the chamber pot by my bed. He lay back again, exhausted but still nauseated. I wiped his brow with a damp cloth, my hand shaking. I had barely finished when he retched again, the pain of an obviously emptied stomach increasing his agony. Severe abdominal cramps hit him and his bowels emptied.

"Jeremy, did you eat something while you were out hunting?"

"No," he groaned, shaking his head back and forth, face pinched. "So thirsty . . ." I gave him a small sip of water, hoping the cramps that were torturing him would let up. Almost immediately, every drop I had given him came back up. I gave him more. When I started to bundle him up to take him to the doctor, he begged me to leave him alone.

I had nothing but the small cart and it was hardly big enough to transport him into town unless he was sitting up. And he couldn't do that.

After a few hours, I was exhausted from worry and the effort of lifting Jeremy to wash him down. I went to the well and rinsed my face, hoping the cool water would revive me. I drank from the cup, thinking of Donovan. Looking down into the valley, I thought of going to him for help. But it was dark now and the ride would be hazardous. I couldn't take the chance with Jeremy but I couldn't leave him alone. I drank a second cup of water and then went back to the cabin, toting a full bucket. I stripped both the bed and Jeremy again. He was sleeping heavily and his skin felt moist and cold.

"Jeremy?"

He did not awaken and I shook him, suddenly terrified. "Jeremy!!" His eyelids fluttered. He groaned, doubling up on his side.

"Make it stop, Katie . . ." I pulled a blanket around him and drew him into my arms, rocking him back and forth as I had when he was a baby. He fainted.

Twenty minutes later, the pains hit me. My throat felt on fire and so did my stomach. I felt nauseous. I lay Jeremy back and stumbled across the room to vomit into a bucket by the door. The pain and vomiting continued, draining my strength. I knew I had to get to Doc.

Jeremy was worse, having passed from semi-consciousness to total collapse.

If I could just make it to Tasajara, they could send someone for Doc. But when I tried to bridle the mare, I shook so badly, I couldn't buckle the strap. The spasms hit me again and again, racking my body until I lay on the ground moaning.

It was no use. Even if I could manage to bridle the mare, I couldn't mount her or stay on until I reached Tasajara.

Stumbling back to the cabin, I passed the chicken coop. Every one of the six hens and the one cocky rooster were dead. I stared at them, wondering distractedly if the weasel had finally won. But there was no blood anywhere, no feathers torn from the bodies.

The spasms hit me yet again as I tried to bathe Jeremy's cold, sweating body. He was still now, his breathing shallow and slow. I remembered all the times I had sat with him through his breathing attacks, but nothing had ever been like this. He looked so pale, the muscles of his face still grimacing as though even in unconsciousness there was no relief to the pain in his stomach and intestines.

There was nothing left in my stomach but the vomiting did not stop. The spasms increased when I tried to slake my growing thirst and, doubling over, I lay on the floor, groaning. I forgot about Jeremy lying unconscious on my bed. At moments when the pain was at its height, I even wished for death.

I must have fainted because when I next opened my eyes the cabin was filled with light. There was no fire and it was cold. I did not care. There was a pounding in my head that drove pain through my skull.

"Kat!"

Donovan's angry voice reverberated through my brain. "Enough of this damned nonsense! Open the door!" he shouted. He pounded again. "I'm going to talk to you if I have to break it down," he warned.

"Donovan," I whispered, my throat parched. He had come back. Thank God, he had come back. The pain was still there, agonizing as ever. I tried but could not move.

"Kat! Damn it, open this door!" He rattled the latch and slammed his fist against the door in frustration. I had slid the bolt last night out of habit.

I heard Donovan's angry strides away from the cabin and closed my eyes in weary defeat.

"Jeremy!" Donovan shouted. His voice the next time he called was even further away. For a long time, there was silence.

Donovan was back outside the door. "Kat! Jeremy!" His tone was different. "Kat!!" He rattled the door harder and there was a loud bang as though he were trying to break through. I could not summon enough strength to care. A moment later I heard shattering glass.

A hand beneath my shoulders and one at my knees lifted me. I felt myself carried and laid on the couch. I retched violently, doubling up with agony. The spasm increased until I thought my stomach would burst. When it stopped, I opened my eyes with an effort, seeing Donovan bending over me. His hand was unsteady as he pushed the wild, damp hair back from my perspiring face. His hand seemed hot against my cold brow.

"Jer . . . Jeremy . . . ." I managed, tears blinding me. He looked back over his shoulder and then down at me. His face was pale and drawn. My eyes widened in fright.

"Jeremy . . ." I repeated, trying to sit up. I couldn't lose him.

"Lie still, Kat." He pushed me back. Turning my head I tried desperately to see my little brother.

"Oh, God, please . . . not Jeremy, too . . ."

Donovan straightened, crossed the room, and leaned over my brother. After a moment, he came back. He lifted me again and carried me to my bed, laying me next to Jeremy. I looked at his small pale face and heard his faint, slow breathing. Then I looked up at Donovan beseechingly.

"Please . . . don't let him die. Donovan, please do something for him . . ."

He touched my face, stroking the hair back from my temples. "I've got to get you both to Tasajara and send someone for Doc."

"Jeremy . . . first."

He knew there was no choice, but I could see emotions flickering across his face so fast I could not read them. "I can't leave you here alone," he said chokingly.

"Take Jeremy . . . Donovan, please. He's all I've got . . . please . . ." I begged.

Donovan hesitated and then lifted Jeremy, deftly wrapping him in a quilt. My brother looked so small in his arms, his oval face white against Donovan's plaid shirt. He strode from the cabin with Jeremy and a moment later I heard him thundering off.

I closed my eyes and everything around me receded. Sometime later, I felt Donovan lifting me.

"So . . . thirsty . . ." I moaned. He laid me back and a moment later let me sip cool water. I drank deeply. When I finished he began bundling me into a blanket. Shortly after he lifted me again, the cramps hit. My mind dimmed, filling with terrifying images as my body was racked with convulsions. Someone held me tightly through the worst and when it passed I was being lifted onto a horse. For a long time, I felt tortured by the pounding ride and then I heard and saw nothing.

"Where's Doc?" I vaguely recognized Donovan's deep voice.

"There's not been enough time for him to get here,

Mace," a strange woman's voice said. I tried to comprehend what was happening and where I was, but all I could feel was the pain eating me alive.

"It'll be another couple of hours at least," she continued.

"She needs him now!" Donovan said harshly.

"It's ten miles from here to Madrone, and another ten back out," the woman said calmly. "Don't be expecting miracles on winged feet."

I could hear someone moving about close by. "We've got to do something now, Hattie. She'll die. God! What is it? I've never seen anything like this before!"

"I don't know. I thought cholera at first, though I didn't dare breathe the word. People would run hell-bent-for-leather if they ever heard mention of it."

I twisted against the pain, moaning. Cold sweat broke out on my body. Someone wiped my forehead and I forced my eyes open. Sitting on the bed, stroking my hair back, was Donovan. I stared up at him.

"Jeremy . . ."

The pain tore at my insides and I closed my eyes tightly, my fingers clutching the bedclothes.

"What'd she say?" the woman asked, approaching.

"She wants to know about her brother," Donovan said flatly.

"He's still unconscious," the woman said quietly.

"No," I moaned. I prayed that I would faint to escape the pain.

"We've got to do something for her!" Donovan said, not hearing the woman. His hand was shaking as he left it against my brow. I opened my eyes again, staring up into a soft, cream-colored canopy. From another corner of the room I heard dim voices.

Donovan's face wavered into my vision again.

"Kat?" he said huskily, bending over me. "How and when did this start?"

I tried to concentrate, to remember. "Jeremy . . . first . . . afternoon . . ." I stared up at him. "So . . . thirsty . . ."

"She just vomits it up. I'm not sure we should give her anything . . ." Donovan said to someone behind him.

"We've got to get some liquid into her or she'll die of dehydration. That's what kills most cholera victims," the woman said. She bent down. "Miss Durham," she said softly, wiping my forehead and face with a clean dampened towel. "Can you tell us anything about the symptoms? It will help Doc find out what's wrong with you and your brother."

"Throat . . . burns . . . stomach cramps . . . pain . . ." I strained to say more. "Jeremy?"

She did not answer but continued to ask me questions. "Were you feeling ill yesterday? Did it start gradually?"

"Jeremy . . ." My eyes were wide, frightened.

"We don't know," the woman said hesitantly.

"Oh, no . . ." I whimpered.

"Help us. We have to know what it is to help him." She repeated her questions. I tried to think if Jeremy had felt sick when he returned from hunting. He had been tired but not ill. "Started suddenly . . ."

"Leave her alone, Hattie," Donovan ordered. "For God's sake, she's too sick for this interrogation!"

"We've no choice," she said. "Anything else?" she questioned me.

"Chickens all dead," I sighed, exhausted. Donovan turned, his face livid with anger.

"Damn the chickens! What's this about chickens!" he said in frustration.

"She said the chickens were all dead," Hattie repeated blankly, searching my face curiously.

I had watered the chickens before Jeremy returned. I opened my eyes wide and stared up at Hattie fixedly.

The well. Jeremy had drunk from the well when he returned from hunting. The cramps and vomiting had hit
him not long afterward. I had not drunk from the well
until later that night. Donovan moved from the foot of
the bed to stand over me. Hattie bent down closer to
hear what I was trying to say.

"What'd she say?" Donovan asked, his eyes holding
mine. I closed them, shaking my head, tears wetting my
cheeks.

"Something about the well. I couldn't make it out.
Could it be the water that did this?"

Donovan frowned heavily. "I drank from her well
yesterday myself."

All the old fears and feelings of helplessness churned
inside me once again. Had the well been poisoned? But
who would do such a thing? Donovan? Oh, God, not
Donovan! Who then? *Who?*

"Her pulse is awfully fast," Hattie said, holding my
wrist.

The pain wiped out my thoughts and I closed my eyes,
blackness swirling around me, threatening to choke me.

"She's getting worse, Mace," Hattie said dismally.
"The doctor better get here fast."

CHAPTER SEVENTEEN

Coffee trickled across my lips and down my burning throat to lay in my stomach like a hot brick. I vomited, and again the liquid was poured down my throat.

"This is all we can do. This . . . and wait," a voice said, as more coffee was poured into me. It sounded like Doc.

"Jeremy . . ." I groaned.

"Worry about yourself, girl," he said harshly. "Your brother will hold his own if God is willing." Then at least I knew he was not dead.

The bed moved as Doc got up. "You can start with the olive oil and milk now, Hattie. Plenty of water as well. She's badly dehydrated from the vomiting and diarrhea."

Something warm and heavy lay on my stomach. The abdominal cramps eased slightly.

"Give her opium later."

"How long will this go on?" Donovan asked hoarsely. "She can't stand much more."

Hattie bent over me, pressing a glass of milk to my parched lips. I retched on it and she wiped my face with a damp rag. "Try again, Kathryn." I looked up at her round, kindly face with its crinkly brown eyes. She had a wide mouth and smiled at me encouragingly. Her hair was pulled back into a neat, full bun and there was gray at her temples. She looked so motherly as she stroked my face. I tried again.

"Later give her bismuth and chalk." The voice dropped and droned on for a minute, giving further instructions. The door opened and closed. The room was quiet, Hattie sitting next to me. I closed my eyes slowly and drifted.

I dreamed I was running across the lower meadow to Papa. Laughing, I threw my arms around his waist. "Mama said yes. She said we can go to the fair if you'll agree. Please, Papa? Please!"

He laughed down at me. Then lifting me high in the air and swinging me around, he agreed. "Anything for my princess."

It was hard to breathe. I was so tired. Voices and memories clouded in and out of my dream. Jeremy laughing at me as I sat in a puddle of muddy rain water after being pitched there by our new mare. Papa admonishing me for trying to ride her before she had been broken to the saddle.

I was on the ridge again, stretching my arms out to my father as he lay beyond reach. "Papa . . . Papa!" I cried over and over, trying to get to him. "Don't die. Don't leave me!"

"Shhhhh . . . it's all right," someone said, wiping my brow again. How many times had I said those words to my brother?

"Jeremy . . . Jeremy . . ."

I dreamed of my father scratching the initials into the dust. I heard him choking on his blood, whispering Tasajara. He opened sightless eyes and stared up at the sky at a hawk being pursued by a sparrow. I was crying, the tears wetting his ashen, dead face.

"Donovan . . ."

"I'm here, Kat," he said, bending over me. The

tanned, handsome face, dominated by cat-gold eyes, seemed frighteningly close.

"I won't leave you," he assured me as I stared up at him. "It'll all be over soon."

Our land. *Our land.* I moaned, moving my head back and forth on the dampened pillow. I remembered the well and felt my heart begin a terrified clammering inside me. Someone did it. Who? How could I protect Jeremy? Was he still alive? Whom could I trust?

"Drink this," Donovan said, putting a cup of foul-tasting stuff to my lips. More poison? I clamped my jaws tightly shut, despite the painful dryness of my throat.

"Drink it!" he repeated, harshly. When I did not, he tried to force me, but I let the liquid spill over my lips and down my neck. He stared at me and then got up abruptly. When he came back, he had more of his vile brew.

"You'll drink this if I have to drown you in it," he threatened and when I still did not obey, he pinched my nostrils shut and poured it into my mouth as I gasped for air. I choked and coughed, trying to slap the cup away but was too weak even to lift my hand from the blanket.

"Mace, for God's sake, what are you doing to the girl!" Hattie said from behind him, her voice shocked and distressed.

"I'm not going to let her die just because she's so damned stubborn!" He was not satisfied until he had poured another cup of the horrible chalky substance down my throat. I lay back against the pillows, exhausted. I waited for the pain. It seemed to be receding slightly. I kept looking at Donovan, unable to look away, and my eyes filled.

"Sleep, Kat," he said quietly.

I did. I dreamt of a huddled form in the chair by our table. The broad shoulders shook with sobs.

"Don't, Papa," I pleaded. "Mama wouldn't have wanted you to cry so."

"Your mother's dead," he said, looking up at me through red-rimmed, stricken eyes. "I killed her giving her that baby over there. He'll die too . . . without her. He'll starve. I should have listened to her and taken her home to Virginia. She wanted to go home but I wouldn't listen. What was there for me?"

"Papa, don't . . . ." My father's grief and lack of control only made my own grief more unbearable. I needed his strength. I needed him to hold me and tell me everything would be all right.

Gentle hands lifted me. I wrapped my arms around hard shoulders, felt the warmth of a broad chest. After a while, I lay back.

"Her gown's soaked again." Gentle hands shifted me.

"We've got to get more water into her or she'll sweat herself into dust," Donovan muttered.

"Drink," Hattie said and I obeyed her, tasting the same chalky brew Donovan had forced on me. Not poison . . .

"You'd better go now, Mace. I'm going to change her gown and bathe her."

"I'm not unfamiliar with a woman's body," he said impatiently.

"You are with this one," Hattie said indignantly. "And she's not the likes of that Juarez woman you visit in town. Now, get out of this room, if you please, Mace Donovan!"

"It doesn't please, but I'll go," he agreed reluctantly.

"You'd better have something to eat and coffee while you're gone," Hattie told him severely. The door slammed behind him. Hattie looked down at my frightened face and smiled. She murmured words of assurance to me as she unfastened the buttons and stripped the gown away to replace it with a fresh one. Before donning the new one, she sponged my body with scented water.

"Jeremy . . ." My throat hurt and my voice sounded harsh. I searched her face.

"I think he's going to make it," she smiled. "He's better off than you, so don't go worrying yourself anymore about your young brother. He's in good hands upstairs. Doc spent a long time with him."

I sighed in relief and smiled at her with effort. Later, the heat grew unbearable and I kicked at the heavy offending bedclothes that weighed me down. A warmed brick wrapped in a thick cloth still lay on my stomach. I pushed it off and it thudded on the floor beside the bed. Coolness seemed unattainable.

Shoving my disheveled hair back, I sat up, feeling shaky with weakness. Looking down, I saw that I was in yet another pastel gown and already this one was damp. Hattie was gone from the room.

For the first time, I looked curiously around at my surroundings. I was in a large room with wooden floors polished to a high, glossy sheen. The bed had a cream-colored, lace canopy supported by four carved oak pillars. A French provincial desk stood to the left wall with a needlepointed straight-back chair. The other wall was dominated by a huge wardrobe taller than Donovan himself. There were several painted pictures on the flower-papered walls. Two small side tables stood on either side of the double bed, each with its own polished brass and crystal lamp. There was only one rug in the room and it was made of several thick skins of combed lambswool.

A pleasant room, definitely a woman's. But whose? Hattie McFadden's? Surely not, for its very mood did not fit the bustling, practical woman I had come to know.

I struggled to free my legs from the sheets and

touched bare feet to the floor. The wood was refreshingly cool. When I stood, my legs wobbled beneath me. My head felt light. I waited for a moment before moving carefully toward the closed double windows.

The latch would not give under my trembling fingers and I struggled with growing frustration. Finally, the lock gave and the window burst outward. I almost toppled out into the garden below me, and caught the sill frantically. I clutched it tightly as I leaned out precariously. The rush of night air hit me hard, cooling my burning face. I could smell pine and drank the scent in. There was also a sweetness in the air—honeysuckle and roses mingled with jasmine. Oh, such air, I thought, closing my eyes and breathing in deeply, heedless of my trembling weakness.

Behind me, the door was flung open. I heard a muffled oath and footsteps crossing the room. I turned to ward off Donovan and almost propelled myself backwards out the window. He grasped my shoulders in a punishing grip, yanking me forward against him.

"Are you trying to kill yourself?" he demanded accusingly, dropping his arms from me long enough to scoop me up like a recalcitrant child. He continued to berate me as he crossed the room to deposit me, none too gently, on the bed. The air I had fought so hard to get was knocked out of me at the sight of his angry face. He loomed over me with blazing golden eyes. I shrank back against the pillows.

"What in hell are you trying to do?" he raged, putting a hand on either side of my head. He looked pale and tired.

"Do I have to sit on you, Kat?" His voice grew ominously quiet. He leaned forward and I flinched.

"Get away from me!" I sounded as frightened as I was and a quick frown cooled the anger from his face.

"The hell I will," he said flatly. "As soon as I walk out

that door, you'll be hanging out that damn window again catching a good case of pneumonia. That is, if you didn't first manage to fall out and break your damn-fool neck!" His shirt was open to his waist, displaying a muscled, tanned chest covered with dark hair. I swallowed convulsively, pressing a hand to my quivering stomach.

"Please, leave me alone," I begged and his frown deepened at the faint rise of panic in my voice. He brushed the hair back from my face.

"I'm not going to hurt you, Kat," he said soothingly. "I'm sorry I tore into you like that, but I saw you from the garden and was afraid by the time I got up here you'd have fallen out."

I was shaking badly. "If I did fall out, everything would go just as you want, wouldn't it? You'd get the homestead."

The gold eyes burned and a vein pulsated in his neck. "Self-pity from little Kathryn Durham?" he mocked cruelly.

"I don't know why you'd want it now," I went on though the light in his eyes should have warned me to stop. "There's nothing left. Not even a bucket of water fit enough for animals to drink. You knew you'd win. You said you intended to win that day you brought me down to the cabin. But I'm not dead yet, Donovan. You didn't . . ." What was I saying?

His fingers curved around my neck and tightened, the gold of his eyes almost obliterated by pupils darkened with fury.

"You think I wanted you dead? Is that what you're saying now? If that were the truth, I could do it right now. Or I could have left you and Jeremy to die at the homestead. Or I could have let you kill yourself on your own just a minute ago. What about the time you and your brother fell beneath my horse, for God's sake?"

I shook my head. His hands remained loosely at my throat, caressing me. "Damn you, Kat," he murmured. His hands moved again gently, then abruptly, he pulled them away. He stood up, turning away to rub his neck. "One of these days, you'll push me a little too far."

"I don't understand you," I said tremulously. "I saw you drinking at the well. Why didn't you get sick? It was the well, wasn't it?"

"Yes, it was your well. But I didn't put poison in it, if that's what you're thinking now."

"Then who?"

He looked at me angrily. "You bought rat poison a few weeks ago, didn't you?"

"Yes, but I didn't put it in the well!"

"I didn't say you did. A couple of rats fell in trying to get some water after they had gorged themselves on the stuff."

I blinked and then closed my eyes. "Then it's all my fault. I almost killed Jeremy . . . ." I breathed deeply and slowly, not wanting to cry in front of Donovan. I looked up at him standing in the shadows. "I'm sorry . . . ."

"You ought to be!" he agreed flatly. "God! You've accused me of damn near everything!"

I turned my head away. "I don't know who to fight anymore . . . ."

"You've never had to fight me," he said quietly. He stood beside the bed again, looking down at me with that dry smile.

"Haven't I?" I was ashamed to find myself crying silently, unable to stop. I put my arm up across my face and felt Donovan sit on the side of the bed, his weight sinking the mattress slightly. I felt his hand touch my hair, his fingers delving through the lank thickness to my tingling scalp and then tightening slightly.

Ridiculously, I wished my hair was clean. But I had

not washed it since becoming ill. From the look in his eyes, he did not seem to notice. My heart raced and I put my arm back against the pillow to stare warily up at him. I lowered my hands, curling my fingers into the bedclothes, frightened by the tumult of emotions raging inside me.

What was wrong with me? This was Donovan! *Donovan!*

"If you'd only stop fighting, you might find all your worries were over," he whispered, eyes intent on mine.

And what did that mean?

Suddenly Charlene Bellows came to my mind. I remembered Donovan with his hat in his hand talking to her. I closed my eyes with a grimace, wondering vaguely why the very thought of him with her hurt me so much. I couldn't hate him anymore. But I didn't want to like him either. I didn't want to feel anything for him. I snatched at anything to save myself.

"I could always solve all my problems and take the course so many other women have," I said.

Donovan smiled slightly. "And what's that?" He actually sounded amused.

"After he knows the truth, I could probably still sell myself to Les Bigelow."

There was a sudden stillness in the room that sent a warning chill through me. Donovan's fingers twisted the hair in his hand until I cried out in pain. He looked like the very devil glaring down at me.

"Goddamn you!" he said raggedly. He turned sideways, throwing himself almost on top of me, his eyes glittering dangerously. "I *could* kill you sometimes. I swear it!"

One hand still tangled painfully in my hair, he used the other to grip my jaw and raise it as his mouth began its descent.

"No!" I cried in panic, arching up in an effort to

shove him off and escape his pinning weight, more afraid of his kiss than his fury. He must have seen the primeval fear in my face for he stopped, barely inches from me, his parted lips showing the white edge of his teeth and his tongue.

"I . . . I didn't mean what I said. Please, Donovan, don't . . ." I pleaded. His mouth twisted mockingly and he pressed a quick brotherly kiss to my forehead, releasing me abruptly. The bed moved as he stood up. He stared down at me derisively.

"It's going to come down to it, Kat. You keep pushing me, thinking there are no consequences." He leaned down again. "One of these days you'll push so far, that wide-eyed, frightened-virgin look isn't going to help you one damn bit!"

I blinked, my breath coming fast, my fingers clenched into fists at my sides. "What do you expect me to do, Donovan? Just give up and let you take over everything and run things your way?" I asked, controlling the quiver in my voice.

"The fire's back already, hmmm?" he taunted. His eyes made a slow, insolent appraisal of the thin, barely concealing gown I wore. I snatched at the bedclothes, pulling them up all the way, feeling hot color fill my cheeks. He grinned.

"Get out of here! I hate you!" I breathed, feeling perilously close to tears again. His eyes flickered and then narrowed.

"This is my house. Don't challenge me, Kat. Right now, I'm damn close to throwing what little control I have left to the winds."

He slammed the door on his way out. I sighed in relief and closed my eyes tightly, feeling I had escaped something horrible. I waited for my heart to slow its frantic beat.

Crossing swords with Mace Donovan accomplished

nothing and always left me feeling drained and more frightened than I cared to admit. The sooner I was off Tasajara, the better.

CHAPTER EIGHTEEN

When I awakened, I heard a rooster crowing over and over from somewhere in the yard below. The house was already bustling with activity for I could hear men's voices and the sounds of animals outside.

Later, the door opened and Hattie McFadden came in, carrying a tray. A pitcher of milk, several slices of barley bread, and beaten egg whites. I made a face and she smiled sympathetically.

"Doctor's orders," Hattie apologized. "You'll be getting something more substantial in the next few days. But you've got to start slowly. Your stomach has been through the wars."

"A couple at least," I sighed in agreement. I felt so weak it was alarming. Looking up at the elderly woman, I decided I liked her very much. She had a warm, motherly face and a big-boned, matronly body. She dressed simply in dark blue with a long white apron. Her touch was very gentle, I remembered, but she possessed a voice that could be quite tyrannical at times. Mace Donovan listened when she spoke. So she had my utmost respect and awe.

"How's Jeremy?" I asked before sipping some milk or touching the barley bread. Hattie sat down in the chair by the bed.

"Not much happier about his diet than you are," she twinkled. "But by Friday, you both should be up to prime beef and potatoes."

"Rabbit stew should do nicely," I said. "By Friday, I plan to have us back at the homestead, if not before then."

"You won't be up to going back there that soon," she said bluntly. "What's the hurry, Kathryn?"

I didn't trust Donovan, but I could hardly tell this woman that. She was loyal to him and any criticism of him would surely be staunchly defended. Besides, Donovan had been responsible for bringing us back here and saving our lives. She would wonder why I wasn't grateful.

"I can't let things go," I said, which was partly the truth. "There are the animals, and my garden needs daily tending. I have to take produce into town to sell . . ."

"All good reasons, I imagine. But you'd better decide what's more important, dear," Hattie shook her head. "That garden of yours, or your and your brother's health. You didn't have a stomachache, you know. You simply are not up to work like that. And you won't be for a while yet."

"There's not much choice, Mrs. McFadden." Just when things were a slight turn for the better, this had to happen. There wasn't time to waste in lying around.

"Hattie, please. Everyone on Tasajara calls me Hattie."

"Please call me Katie, then."

"I prefer Kathryn, if you don't mind. It's a pretty, English name and suits you nicely."

"Papa liked it." Tears blurred my vision and I looked away, embarrassed by my show of emotion. "I'm sorry. I'm making such a fool and nuisance of myself," I sniffed. "I don't know what's wrong with me lately."

"You're no fool because you cry for your father, my

girl. And as for a nuisance, you aren't that either. As soon as you're up and about, I'll give you something to keep you busy and take your mind off your grief."

"But I'm not staying here," I insisted. "You talk as though I am."

"Not indefinitely, perhaps," she agreed. "But you're certainly welcome to stay as long as you like."

I gave a faint laugh. "I wonder what Donovan would say if he heard you giving that invitation."

"Donovan the elder, or Donovan the younger?" she asked.

"Either one," I hedged. She studied my face briefly and smiled slightly.

"Well, I can tell you for certain that Mister Brian has been wanting to meet you for some time. And you do seem to have quite an effect on Mace."

"No doubt," I said wryly, and she looked at me curiously. She would know everything anyway as soon as she was in the same room with Donovan and me and the sparks began to fly.

"I do not like Mace Donovan," I told her frankly.

Hattie's mouth curved up in a quick grin. "Do tell. I'd say your feelings were a little stronger than that milque-toast description."

"I've got my reasons," I said defensively. Putting them into words was difficult, however. I was not exactly sure what it was about Mace Donovan that raised my hackles and made my blood boil.

Hattie slapped her thighs and stood up. "Well, that's your business and none of mine. You needn't feel you have to explain to me. It's up to Mace to fight his own battles and win them."

"He's not going to win this one."

Hattie seemed about to say something and then decided against it. "You look tired, Kathryn," she offered conciliatorily. "When you finish all that, you should try to get more sleep. Sleep is an age-old cure. That and God's goodwill of course."

"Thank you, Hattie," I smiled, reaching out to take her hand. "Thank you for everything."

She cocked her head and gave me a rueful smile. "It's not me you should be thanking though, now is it?"

I flinched at her criticism and she squeezed my hand to soften it. "Whatever is going on between you two to cause such antagonism on your part . . . well, it doesn't alter the facts, now does it? Mace is the one responsible for saving your life . . . and your brother's."

She was right. I felt depressed and confused. I knew I should be grateful, but thanking Mace Donovan for anything stuck in my craw!

Nothing made sense to me anymore. There was something in me that wanted desperately to reach out to Mace Donovan, to trust him, while at the same time the thought of getting close to him was frightening. Donovan did nothing without a reason and I had not learned yet what his reasons were for saving us.

What was he after?

Donovan did not seem interested in purchasing the homestead now unless he was still waiting for us to go under so he could get it for next to nothing. He once had said that that was what he intended to do. "All I have to do is wait for taxes to fall due . . . ." Or for us to fall behind in our mortgage payments. If Donovan didn't buy the homestead, Les Bigelow probably would just to put me off our land for what I had dared to say to him.

As far as Donovan being interested in me as a woman, that supposition was ridiculous and I wondered what made me even think of it. He had viewed me as nothing more than an irritating child on our first meeting. Since then he had taken every available opportunity to point out my mistakes, mock, tease, and generally needle me into a state of confusion and bitter resentment. Besides

all that, Donovan obviously had the woman at the hotel
for his pleasure while Charlene Bellows waited in the
wings to become his wife and the mother of his children.

So why did Donovan continue to plague me, turning
me inside out every chance he had? Why couldn't he just
leave me in peace and allow me to get on with the business of survival?

There were other more important things that bothered me about him. He must have paid for Doc's visits
to Tasajara and yet had never mentioned them. It had
cost us hard-earned cash to have Jeremy's leg set in a
cast and more when it had been removed. Not much
money, perhaps, by Tasajara standards, judging from
the appearance of this comfortable room, but by
Jeremy's and my standards, a small fortune desperately
needed to meet mortgage payments.

When and how would Donovan call in that debt? And
how would it involve the homestead? Somehow I had to
make some money or work off the debt I owed Donovan
while I was here at Tasajara!

For the next two days, I did exactly as Hattie instructed. I ate what she brought without comment, I
bathed in the luxuriously warm, scented water that filled
the metal tub and I concentrated on Jeremy's and my
dilemma. No solution presented itself. All I could think
about was my father's murder and my sick brother lying
upstairs somewhere. Jeremy needed me, depended on
me. His future would be decided by what I did now. But
I didn't know what to do.

Thoughts of my father filled my mind and made me
long for his company and counsel. There were so many
things I would have asked him, so many things I would
have wanted to learn. Now, it was too late and I was
having to cope with everything alone. Jeremy had found
solace in burying himself in his studies when time
permitted. There had not been time for me to do that
and my only compensation had been to work until I was

too tired to remember finding Papa's broken body on the ridge, or to feel the pain of his loss.

On the third day of my convalescence, I could stand the inactivity no longer. My clothes had been cleaned and pressed. I found them in the tall wardrobe and dressed at first light. I wanted desperately to see Jeremy. Hattie had kept me well informed of his progress, but I missed him terribly. I needed to see him, to touch him, to know he was really all right.

My faded gingham dress fitted me loosely and I tied the wide sash more snugly around my waist. Opening the door quietly, I peered out into the corridor. The stairs were at the far end of the airy, paneled hall.

Barefoot, I tiptoed out of my room, closing the door silently behind me. I still felt weak and shaky and waited a few seconds until the faintness passed. Then I scampered down the hall and up the stairs. The house was cool, but it would be comfortably warm later in the day. I thought of the heat that built up in the sod cabin in late summer, until it sometimes seemed like an earthen oven.

On the third floor of the ranch house, I stood confused. There were closed doors to the right and left of me. Taking a nervous breath, I carefully opened the first one, peering in and praying silently that if Jeremy were not there, no one else would be. It was a storage closet filled with fresh linen. I closed it. The next was a small bedroom, unoccupied and starkly furnished. It looked as though it had not been used in some time. The next room was a large bedroom, well furnished and obviously occupied though the occupant was not in evidence. The bedclothes were rumpled. It was a man's room, and without knowing why, I was certain it was Mace Donovan's. I shut the door hastily and there was an audible click. I moved quickly to another door and then another. The last door on the left was occupied by my little brother.

I tiptoed in and looked down at his sleeping form. He

was curled on his side and looked so young and vulnerable I felt choked with emotion. Sitting down on the
edge of the bed, I reached out to gently push the thatch
of dark hair back from his pale forehead. Then I bent
forward to kiss him. His cheeks were warm and flushed
with sleep, and he moved restlessly.

I smiled as he slowly opened his eyes and looked up at
me blearily. "Katie . . . . ?" he murmured and then
stretched and yawned. "Where have you been?" he
asked, pushing himself up into a sitting position. I
looked him over, noticing that he had lost weight but
looked so much better than a few days ago. He was in
cotton pajamas and I wondered where they had come
from.

"Downstairs. I've been recuperating just like you.
How are you, sweetheart?" I caressed his flushed cheek,
smiling at him, so grateful that he was all right.

"Why are you crying?"

I laughed slightly. "I'm just so happy to see you and
know for myself that you're going to be fine."

"Donovan said another day and I'll be almost as good
as new," he grinned. "Did you see what he brought?"
He indicated a table close to the bed. It was loaded with
books. "He brought my books from the homestead and
he even loaned me some from his library. Look at this
one," Jeremy said, reaching across to grab one from the
pile. It was leather-bound. "It's all about Richard the
Lion Hearted. That one over there is about
Charlemagne."

"So you're keeping up with your studies." I was not at
all pleased to learn that Donovan had been snooping
around in our cabin.

"I'm way ahead now. That's all I've been doing for
the past couple of days." And he looked as though he
had been thoroughly enjoying himself. "Mace brought
me some workbooks from the Madrone school. And

lots and lots of paper, too. I haven't had to worry about
running out of it here."

"How nice of him," I said quietly, my mouth tightening slightly.

"I was having a lot of trouble with my algebra but
Mace helped me with it. He's a wizard at mathematics,
Katie. And he knows his Latin too. He's real smart."

Donovan! Donovan! Donovan!

"He's been spending a lot of time with you, then?"

"Not as much as I wish he would. But he's got a lot
to do." His hazel eyes were wide and excited. "Have you
ever seen anything like this place, Katie? Look at this
room. It's as big as our whole cabin. It even smells different. Wax, Hattie told me. Wax and wood."

"There's nothing to be ashamed of about our sod and
log cabin, Jeremy," I said angrily. "Papa built it himself.
He cut every timber for it and Mama made the sod
blocks to go between them."

"I wasn't saying there was anything wrong with it,
exactly," Jeremy said sheepishly. "But . . . but, well,
there's just no comparison to this."

He was as impressed as Papa had been and I felt depressed. I stood up. "We'll be going home soon."
Jeremy did not look very pleased at that, and I frowned.
"This might all be very grand to you, Jeremy. But those
three hundred acres across the valley *belong* to you.
Papa worked them and died for them. And if we don't
go home and work, we'll lose it all."

"The land should belong to you, Katie," he said
bleakly. "You're the one that loves it so much."

"You love it too, Jeremy," I said, alarmed at his sudden gloominess. He looked up at me and I had never
seen him so miserable.

"I don't want to spend the rest of my life working
cattle or tending a garden, feeding chickens or fixing
fences. And I don't want to always live in a cabin."

I felt as though he had struck me. "What *do* you want?" I asked, hurt and angry at the same time. How could he so easily dismiss everything Papa had worked and died for? "Something like this, I suppose? A few Hattie McFaddens to wait on you hand and foot? Jeremy, we're here out of charity and the sooner we leave the better for everyone. Remember that! And remember too that all we do have, or are likely to have, is what's over there against those mountains."

"Katie," he said quietly, eyes filling with tears. "It's got nothing to do with Tasajara or with how much I loved Papa. It's me." He sounded so adult, he frightened me. "It's this." He lifted the book and held it out at me. "I want to live in a city someday . . . a city where I can go to a university and really study something. Maybe be a doctor . . . or a lawyer. I don't know what. But land doesn't mean anything to me . . . ." His face crumpled. "Don't hate me, Katie. I can't help it."

I drew him into my arms and rocked him as I always had. "Hush, it's all right."

"I wish you could understand . . . ."

"I do, sweetheart. Only it's not possible . . . not now at least. Maybe someday . . ." But how would I ever have the kind of money it took to pay for such studies?

Jeremy looked up at me through his tears. "I love you, Katie."

"I know," I smiled. "And I love you, too. You're all I've got, in case you didn't know." He looked as though I had laid a heavy burden on his shoulders by saying that. I squeezed him affectionately. "We'll work it all out. There are a few years between now and when you'd be going to a university, you know." I'd give him the moon if I could, but I knew in my heart that I would probably not even succeed in saving his inheritance from Papa. Not unless we returned to the homestead as quickly as possible.

Closing the door carefully behind me, I started down the hall, feeling a lonely heaviness in my heart. I had not gone more than two steps when I noticed an open door and Mace Donovan lounging inside on the bed, indolently watching me. My face flushed as I saw he was not wearing a shirt but had a towel slung casually around his neck. The broad expanse of his tanned chest, covered with dark hair that reached down to his navel, stunned my senses. He straightened and I stepped back against the corridor wall.

"Did you find him all right?" he asked casually, his eyes taking in my bare feet and rising up slowly over my now thinner body to linger on the tumble of hair which I had not taken the time to bind. I pushed it back self-consciously and met his gaze with increasing difficulty.

"Yes. He's looking very well," I stammered. I could smell the tangy soap he used. His dark hair was damp.

"He should be up and about tomorrow at the latest. I think he'd be happy to stay in that room forever though," he drawled, a slight smile curving his mouth. "I take it that was you peeking into my bedroom a while ago." His manner was lightly teasing.

"I didn't know which room he was in," I said stiffly. I looked toward the stairs, wanting badly to go back to my room. My last encounter with Mace was still fresh in my mind though it had happened three days before. I felt nervous, tense and all too aware of him. Even more, I wanted to escape the golden-eyed scrutiny he was inflicting upon me.

"Don't run away," he grinned, reading my thoughts disconcertingly. "Since you're up, why don't you come downstairs and join me for breakfast."

The thought of remaining any longer near that bedroom was unbearable, and yet sitting with Donovan would be unnervingly worse. I wondered if I would be able to eat, let alone to think, while aware of his eyes on me, scrutinizing my every move, every hint of emotion.

He didn't wait for my answer. Reentering his room, he picked up his shirt. The smooth hard muscles in his arms rippled as he put it on. I swallowed hard and looked away. When he reappeared in the doorway he gave me a curious look. I tilted my chin slightly.

"I thought you'd bolt for your room," he admitted.

"It's about time Hattie stopped waiting on me," I answered.

"She's going to disagree with you there. She's totally maternal and hasn't had anyone around here to mother since I was a boy."

He put his hand beneath my elbow and my startled jerk made him smile and raise a mocking brow.

"I'll explain how we happen to be coming downstairs together from my bedroom, just so there won't be any misunderstandings," he needled, his implication all too clear. My flush darkened and I pulled my arm away.

"After breakfast, I'd like to make plans to go back to the homestead," I told him, walking beside him. He stopped at the top of the stairs and looked at me, his mouth hardening.

"It's a little early yet for that."

"No, it is not. I've got work to do. And the sooner Jeremy gets his head out of the clouds and back down to our land, the better."

"You've got no well. Or have you forgotten that tiny little detail? It's out of the question for you and Jeremy to go back until one is dug."

"It's not going to get dug with me over here," I protested, cutting him off with an annoyed glance as I started down the stairs.

"Don't be an utter fool, Kat. What do you think you'll do . . . dig it by hand? It takes equipment which you don't have." He grabbed my arm, halting our progress on the stairs, and my muscles tensed instinctively. He felt it and gave me a cold look.

"I'll have to see that it gets done, then, won't I?" I
retorted testily.

"Cash on the barrel for that kind of work," he bit out.
"Have you got it?"

I felt the color draining from my face. How I resented
him! He knew damn well I did not have the money! He
was just jabbing into my pride again, twisting the knife.

"Never mind. I'll take care of having it done," he decided. "I've got the equipment and my own men can do
the job so it won't cost you a single dime. But you're
going to have to accept . . . and gracefully, mind you,
. . . that you and Jeremy are staying here, as my guests,
until the job is done."

"And how long will that be?" The thought of being in
Mace Donovan's house another day was alarming.

"Two weeks . . . possibly more."

"Two weeks!" I gasped, stopping and staring up at
him aghast. "You can't mean it will take that long to dig
one well!"

"I'm not going to stop my own business to take care
of yours."

I flushed painfully, feeling completely humiliated and
ashamed. "I . . . I didn't mean that you should," I stammered. "But I can't stay here for two weeks! I just
can't!"

"Why not? Aren't you comfortable enough?" His
tone was faintly sarcastic and I took immediate offense.

"I prefer my own home. And besides," I went on
rapidly. "What about Constance and Don Juan . . . and
Dionysus and the mare."

"Dionysus?" The irritation immediately left
Donovan's face and his mouth twitched upward.

"The gelding," I snapped, tiring of his amusement.
"Papa named him for his stumbling gait."

Donovan laughed. I drew up my shoulders. "It isn't

funny. I have my own work to do. I can't let everything go. I'll lose everything.''

Donovan's fingers slipped around my arm again, drawing me down the stairs and into the foyer.

"Donovan!" I said in exasperation.

"It's all taken care of, so you needn't worry."

I yanked my arm from his hand again. "What do you mean, it's all taken care of?"

"I sent Saunders over to your place. He drove Constance and Don Juan into my herd. Your . . . Dionysus and the mare are gorging themselves in my barn."

"John what!?" I flashed furiously, barely able to control myself.

"He'll cut them back out for you when the time comes," Donovan said casually. "Don't worry, Kat. I'm not stealing your . . . herd, or your livestock."

I stood there shaking. "How dare you give orders concerning our property!" I stamped my foot, angry enough to hit him but sure there that would bring horrendous consequences.

"You didn't expect me to leave them at the homestead to starve or die of thirst, did you?" he demanded, bringing his face down close to mine. My chin jerked up.

"They would not have died of thirst!" I railed. "There was a full trough of water for them . . . uncontaminated! And enough feed for another couple of days."

"You've already been here a couple of days," he reminded me angrily.

"Yes . . . and thank you very much for your fine hospitality," I said, sounding anything but thankful. "But I want to go home now. I can take care of my own business without your constant interference . . . ."

"Like my interference of a few days ago, you mean!"

"What in Hades is going on out here?" growled a deep voice. I swung around, not having heard anyone approach from behind the stairs. In a doorway that opened off to the left, sat a man in a wheelchair. I knew immediately who he was, for he had Donovan's eyes, though they lacked his fierceness. His hands were gnarled with arthritis and he was thin to the point of emaciation. Only his thick gray hair gave the impression of strength.

"Dad. Meet Kathryn Durham," Mace boomed from behind me as I stared at the older man. His father looked me up and down, his brows rising slightly.

"So this is the little spitfire that's been giving you so much trouble."

My eyes narrowed as my mouth tightened into a firm line. "I beg your pardon, sir," I said, "but *he* has been giving *me* the trouble."

Brian Donovan chuckled as though the thought gave him much pleasure and satisfaction. "Nothing you can't handle, I'm sure, young lady."

"I would like very much to go back to my own home," I told him bluntly. "Though I'm very grateful for all you've done for Jeremy and me."

Brian Donovan was smiling, flicking a secretive look at his stony-faced son. Mace caught the look and grinned.

"I'm the one that brought you back here," he reminded me. "In fact, you owe *me* your life. Why don't you give me your blessing, Kat?" He was laughing at me, but there was a coolness behind his eyes.

I smiled at him sweetly while my eyes crackled. "Will it precipitate my departure from Tasajara?"

"Not in the least."

"Mr. Donovan, please . . ." I appealed to the older man, but he merely smiled and glanced at his son.

"I'm afraid once Mace makes up his mind about something, there's not a damn thing on this earth I can do about it. You might as well relax and enjoy yourself, Miss Durham."

"Her name is Kathryn, Dad," Mace said, obviously trying to arouse my anger further. I smiled at the older man warmly.

"But *you* may call me Katie."

Mace threw back his head and laughed loudly. Then he looked at me menacingly. "You miserable little witch," he growled tauntingly. "When do I get permission to call you Katie?"

"When the devil builds a snowman!" I said scathingly.

Brian Donovan was watching our exchange with amused interest. He turned the wheelchair slightly and I saw a thoughtful look on his face.

How much did the father know about the son? Why didn't I feel the distrust for Brian Donovan that festered inside me regarding his son? What was it about Mace that challenged and awoke every defense I had, and still made me feel vulnerable?

CHAPTER NINETEEN

"Come on in here, you two," Brian Donovan said over his shoulder. "You might as well carry on over breakfast instead of standing out there hollering at one another on empty stomachs."

Covered plates were set out on a shining mahogany sideboard. The lids were silver and I thought that a couple of them would probably pay off all my debts. A long table covered with an embroidered cloth dominated the room, surrounded on three sides by walls consisting of tall windows. It was a bright and cheerful room with potted flowers on another long narrow table at the far end of the room. A woman's touch. Hattie McFadden's, or the long-deceased Carolyn Donovan's?

Mace put his hand on the small of my back and pushed slightly, indicating that I was to take a plate and serve myself whatever I wanted. I felt suddenly nervous and out of place. Brian Donovan lifted away the lids, displaying a mound of scrambled eggs, freshly baked bread, sweet rolls with sugar and cinnamon, enough bacon to feed an army, a bowl of what looked like oatmeal, and a stack of pancakes. There was butter and several types of homemade jellies. I had never in my life seen so much food.

Picking up a slice of bread and pouring myself some

strong coffee, I sat down at the table. Mace was looking
at me with obvious annoyance. He picked up a plate,
slapped some eggs on it, several slices of bacon, and a
sweet roll, and shoved it in front of me, snatching away
the plate with my slice of bread.

"I can't eat all that!" I protested. "And I won't!"

"You will. Or I'll cram every last crumb down your
stubborn little throat!" he threatened. Mister
Donovan's face was averted, but I had the distinct impression that he was suppressing a laugh with great difficulty.

"I can't remember ever eating that much at one sitting!" I told him stiffly.

"Probably because you never had it before."

I shoved the plate back and stood up. We weren't rich
but we had never starved and I detested his arrogant,
insufferable attitude. Just because his father had given
him a ranch like Tasajara did not mean that my father
had failed us!

"Sit down!" he boomed, stepped in front of me. My
eyes widened at the flare of anger in his gold eyes. Shakily, I sat.

"Now eat!" he ordered. My hands fisted defiantly in
my lap as I stared furiously at the laden plate. Mace
leaned down, his mouth almost brushing my ear, sending goose bumps over my flesh. He said with ominous
softness, "It was not an idle threat." I picked up my
fork.

Mister Donovan wheeled himself around to the other
side of the table. Mace put another plate, heavily laden,
in front of his father. I looked up and met the kindly,
almost sympathetic gaze of the older man.

"How do you stand him?" I asked despondently.

"It's too late to throw him back," Mister Donovan
grinned with a shrug. He dug into his breakfast. Seeing
how much he ate, I wondered why he was still so painfully thin.

Mace sat down at the head of the table, a curious place since his father was still alive, I thought critically. He looked at me and waited. I lifted my fork and put a small portion of eggs into my mouth, chewing them while looking at Mace resentfully. His eyes sparkled with amusement again.

I was much hungrier than I imagined and finished everything on my plate. Mace watched, sipping coffee.

"Would you like more?" he asked dryly when I finally put the fork down and dabbed my mouth with the linen napkin that had been set out in a silver holder.

"No, thank you." I blushed furiously.

Conversation had been sparse, but the silences had been comfortable. Mister Donovan had finished a second plateful of eggs and was now relaxing over coffee lightened with thick cream. These men ate more food in one meal than my father had in three. I glanced surreptitiously at Donovan, though it was hardly necessary to reassure myself that he had not a spare ounce of fat on him. He was rock hard—inside as well as out!

"You still look tired," Mace commented, his eyes moving over my face appraisingly. "You should rest . . . ."

"Rest! I've done nothing but rest, eat, and think for the past five days!"

"Think about what?" he raised his brows. I looked away quickly.

"About my father, mostly . . . and Jeremy."

"You father was a good man," Mister Donovan volunteered to fill the silence. "I only met him half a dozen times. But you could tell he came from refined stock." He set his cup down. "He sure wasn't much of a homesteader."

My hackles rose. "He did his best," I retorted defensively.

"No doubt about that, Katie. But some men aren't cut out for it. And your father was one of those. He would have been better off and much happier behind a counter in a town business." Just as Jeremy would be happier in a city, I thought with sudden depression.

"Papa loved the land. His family were landholders in the South, and in England before that," I insisted.

"I'm not slighting your father or his efforts," Mister Donovan said quietly. "Merely stating the facts as I see them."

"We did well enough until the last five years," I told him, wanting him to understand and feeling Donovan watching me. I wished he would stop it. "First the flooding, then the drought . . ." Mister Donovan nodded.

"We felt it here, too," he informed me. Yet, I could see no evidence that they had suffered any hardship. My expression must have said a great deal, for Mister Donovan spoke again.

"We lost several hundred head of cattle the first year, and even more the second. Almost a thousand all told."

"A thousand!" My face registered my shock. Mace spoke from the end of the table.

"I don't think Kat has any idea how many head we run, Dad. Nor," he drawled, seeing my glance, "do I think she cares."

"We feed a lot of people," Mister Donovan went on proudly. "Much of our beef is shipped by rail back East."

I smiled shakily, realizing like a blow to the head just how powerful these men were. "We just manage to feed ourselves," I admitted.

"Most people started out that way. Tasajara wasn't always lucrative. In fact, until Mace took over for me, I was having some pretty big problems keeping things together. And after breaking my hip in a fall from a horse, there was no chance for me to make things better."

Mace stood up. "Kat isn't interest in anything to do with Tasajara," he said curtly and his father looked at him with a faint, quizzical rise of his brows.

I glared at Donovan. Who did he think he was to say what I was or was not interested in?!

"Oh, but I am," I disagreed, looking back at Mister Donovan. I did it mainly to be contrary. Mace understood and gave me a wry look.

"Are you indeed?" he said and I had to look back at him. "Then maybe you'd like the complete tour and rundown of our business?"

He was serious and I knew instantly that I had unwittingly fallen right into his trap. Then, I managed a docile, innocent smile.

"You needn't worry that I'd put your father out so much, Donovan. He can just tell me a little about Tasajara right here while we drink our coffee. You can get on with your chores."

Brian Donovan laughed. Turning the wheels of his chair abruptly, he made for the door.

"Excuse me, but I'm getting myself out of the middle of this," he announced and before I could beg him to stay, he was out the door and down the hall. Holding my breath, I looked back at Mace warily. There was an odd smile on his lips and his eyes never wavered from mine. My heart started thudding heavily.

"Are you ready then?"

It was a direct challenge and one that would make me lose all face if I declined. He would know exactly how much he unnerved me and that, I was sure, would make matters even worse. I searched my mind for a way out, disgarded several possibilities, then gave in impatiently.

"I suppose so," I said ungraciously.

"Such enthusiasm," he drawled, pushing his chair back and coming around the table toward me. He pulled my chair out for me and I glanced up over my shoulder at him tensely. When he started to take my arm again, I deftly avoided his touch, throwing him a quelling look

in an attempt to cover the sudden faster hammering of
my pulse. His mocking smile raised my temper and lowered my control.

"Just lead the way, Donovan, and I'll follow," I said
without thinking.

"Ah," he grinned eloquently. "I've been hoping for
that concession for a long time."

I flushed to the roots of my hair and cursed him silently. He was looking me over and grinning even more
broadly, if that were possible.

"Are you sure you're ready?"

"Of course!" I said, wondering what he was up to.

"What about your shoes?"

I looked down at my bare feet, remembering suddenly
that I had left my shoes upstairs so that I would not be
heard in my search for Jeremy. My fingers went to my
hair and I wanted to die of embarrassment. What must
Brian Donovan have thought of me coming downstairs
bare-footed, with my hair unbound? Well, it was too late
now to correct whatever impression he had, thanks to
Donovan's ability to render me brainless.

"I do need my shoes," I agreed, giving up. Then I
smiled slightly, suddenly seeing the chance to avoid
Mace's company entirely. "You needn't wait for me.
I'll . . ."

"No. I'll go up with you," he said, undaunted.

"You'll what?" I stared at him.

"Don't think I don't know what's going on inside
your head, Kat. You'd go up, lock you door and sit in
that room until hell froze over . . . or until you got me to
agree to let you and Jeremy go back to your homestead.
Well, you're not going to get that chance. You . . ." he
leaned forward intimately, ". . . and I, are going to walk
over Tasajara this morning . . . together."

I leaned away from him. "Why are you so determined
that I see Tasajara? I can see it from our ridge! And as

soon as Jeremy and I leave here, we'll look at it there if that would satisfy you. And once we leave here, we're never coming back . . . for any reason."

His smile was tight lipped. "Don't count on that," he said softly.

"On what? Leaving or coming back?" I flared defiantly.

"Both."

"You can't keep us prisoners here!"

"That's rather strong. I'm only a concerned neighbor." I did not like the way he said that and glared up at him futilely. Turning, I stormed out of the dining room and up the stairs. Mace moved leisurely behind me. He stood in the doorway of the bedroom while I brushed my hair, tied it at the nape of my neck and sat on the edge of the bed to put on my shoes. They were low and thin, suited for housework, not for trekking around a ranch. My boots were at home. I might as well go barefoot, I thought thunderously.

"You have very nice ankles," Donovan observed with an amused expression, and I knew he was deliberately trying to bait me. I stood up, letting my skirt drop again, ignoring his comment with difficulty.

"Well, let's get this farcical tour over with, shall we?"

"Are you always so touchy when you get up in the morning?" he asked as I stood staring at him, hands on hips. He moved back, indicating that I was to precede him down the hall to the stairs. I walked swiftly past him, stiffly erect.

Coming down the stairs together, he gave me a sidelong glance. "Since you've already toured the house on your own, we'll start with the stables, barns, corrals and then take a walk around the heart of the ranch."

Stinging color burned in my cheeks as I remembered peering into his bedroom. He was not going to let me forget anything.

Standing in the front yard, I looked back at the ranchhouse. It was three stories high, white with wood trim around the windows and beneath the eaves. The veranda stretched around the house on both sides, offering a cool, welcome place for people to rest and look over the domain that was Tasajara. Several huge pines, easily older than the house itself, stood near by like sentinels on guard. Other trees grew closer to the house and were of a variety unfamiliar to me, apparently imported and planted to give shade and soft fragrance to the austere world of a western ranch.

The gardens to the back and side of the house were large and profuse enough to feed all of Madrone. Bordering them was a multi-colored labyrinth of flowers that I longed to explore. From these came the fresh bouquets that graced all the rooms in the house.

However, there the softness of Tasajara ended. The barns, stables, and corrals were purely functional, freshly painted white, and neat to the point of starkness. Tasajara was like a small town unto itself. There was a blacksmith, tackroom, butcher, sheds containing enough feed for a year or more, equipment of every sort for maintaining a working, high-paying enterprise, stables filled with cow ponies and high-bred riding horses like Mace's devil stallion, and corrals boasting prime stock being readied for market. There was even a small chapel set back within a copse of trees to serve those employees of a religious spirit.

Resentfully, I was impressed. And again, a little frightened at the power all this represented. How could I hope to fight a man like Mace Donovan? All this was overwhelming . . . an empire. Our little parcel of rocky land looked pathetic next to Tasajara. I wondered bitterly if that was the sole purpose of Mace's insistence on this tour. He wanted to show me just how insignificant we were, how useless it was to fight him.

I felt suddenly very cold and tired. Papa's dear face flashed in my mind again and I closed my eyes, trying to ward off the all too familiar pain and the fear of being alone, fighting against immense odds.

"You look ready to pass out," Donovan said and I felt his hand firmly beneath my elbow. In a second, he lifted me easily into his arms. I stiffened defensively and then relaxed, too exhausted to fight or argue with him anymore. He walked a ways and put me down on some grass beneath the shade of a honey locust. Pulling my knees up, I rested my head in the cross of my arms. I strongly felt Donovan's presence and, strangely, I wanted to cry.

"Are you all right? I shouldn't have pushed you so far."

I did not trust myself to speak.

"Kat?" His fingers touched my hair and I flinched, nodding quickly.

He stood and moved away. I hoped he would just go away and leave me alone until I could get myself in control again. I hurt inside. Some of the pain I understood, but some I didn't and it frightened me. It all had to do with Mace Donovan and the differences between us. I wished, not for the first time, that I had never laid eyes on him.

There was silence for so long that I thought he had gone. I straightened, taking a shaky breath and reaching up to push wayward strands of hair back from my temples. Donovan was leaning against the tree, watching me. I stared up at him troubled.

There must be some way to fight him and win, I thought desperately, and looked away from the growing intensity of those golden eyes. Perhaps not fighting him was the answer. Perhaps a better strategy of survival would be to wait until all the pieces of the puzzle fit together by themselves. Open hostility and defiance got me nowhere. Mace thrived on it, baiting me continually, and in every confrontation I had had with him, I had lost.

Sugar catches more flies than vinegar, the old saying went. But I did not want to catch Mace Donovan. I just wanted peace. Pitting my meager experience with the opposite sex against Donovan's obvious expertise with women would be disastrous. I remembered the Spanish woman at the hotel, Marcela Juarez. I remembered the way she had invited his invading kiss. I remembered all too clearly the way Donovan's mouth had taken hers, and a surge of feeling swept through me.

Never, *never* did I want Donovan to touch me like that! The thought of such intimacy sent hot and cold shivers down my spine and tightened every muscle in my body.

Donovan moved and inwardly I tensed, keeping my eyes averted from him. But I could *feel* his position as keenly as if he were touching me.

"You look scared half to death," he said strangely. "What in hell do you think I plan to do to you, anyway?"

"I don't think you plan to do anything," I said, my voice taut to my own ears, harshened somehow.

Donovan sat down beside me and leaned back on one elbow.

"Your ranch is very impressive, Donovan," I said to fill the uncomfortable silence.

"Thanks," he said flatly.

"It makes me wonder why with all this," I waved my hand about, "you're so interested in having our homestead."

I could feel his anger without looking at him. "I thought," he said slowly, "that once you saw Tasajara, you would get it into your thick head that I *don't* want your land . . . and never have. I offered for it for the reasons I've stated."

Turning my head I looked at him, feeling very vulnerable. I knew that I had to get away from this man now, today, or my life was never going to be the same again.

"If that's true," I said, my voice sounding strained and humiliatingly close to tears, "you'll let Jeremy and me go home . . . today. Now. And you'll stay away from us."

Mace's eyes narrowed. "You know I can't do that. You've got no water. And I can't see you toting it three miles from the river . . . which by the way belongs to me. You're just going to have to adapt to the idea of staying here, Kat."

I put my head in my arms again. "I want to go home, Donovan." I knew how childish that sounded, and how unreasonable in the face of his undeniable logic. But it was true. I felt safe at the homestead, safe away from Mace Donovan.

"I don't think you know what you want yet."

Coiled like a spring, I stood up, glaring down at him. "You think you're going to tell me what I want? I *know* exactly what I want! I want to be left alone! I want Jeremy to have his land when he comes of age!"

Mace stood up in one lithe movement to tower over me. "Does Jeremy really want that miserable hunk of land?" he demanded derisively. "And if he does . . . or doesn't . . . what happens to you ten years from now after you've worked yourself to death to hold onto that place? If you do manage to hold it, that is! What about it, Kat? What do *you* want?"

My eyes filled. "I want you to leave me alone," I said chokingly.

"I'm not going to make myself a stranger in my own home. And you're not going to sit in that room upstairs hiding from me," he said harshly.

"Then let us go!"

"Kat, you're safe here," he said, moving closer, his voice quiet and gentle. "For a few weeks you can just relax, take things easy, let people do for you . . . ."

I pressed my fingertips to my throbbing temples, feeling white and faint, completely exhausted. "I can't . . . relax," I admitted quietly. "I've got so much to think of. I've got the mortgage and taxes and . . ."

"Just forget all that for a while. It'll all work out."

I wanted to believe that, but could not. How could things work out on their own while I remained idle on Tasajara. My garden was dying and our last hopes of raising money with it.

"I don't have any choice, do I?" I said tiredly.

"None whatsoever," he agreed bluntly.

"Then put me to work," I said. "I don't want to owe you anything when Jeremy and I leave here."

Mace's eyes twinkled in private amusement. "What can you do?"

"Housework, gardening, tending animals, cleaning stables . . ."

"Your list of qualifications is endless," he drawled, teasing. "Anything else that might interest me?"

"I could ride fence," I added, undaunted.

"And that would get you out from under my feet, too, wouldn't it?" he said. "But no, you won't ride fence. And we'll talk about this in a few days when you're better able to make good on your offer."

"I can make good on it for you now," I insisted.

"I'm sure," Mace said, his eyes leaving mine and lingering for the briefest, most disturbing moment on my mouth. A muscle tightened in his jaw and he looked away. "Come on. I think you've had more than you can handle for one day."

We walked back to the ranch house in silence.

CHAPTER TWENTY

I was far more tired than I had realized. After having lunch, I slept the afternoon away. When I awakened, I splashed cool water on my face and then vigorously brushed my hair and tied it back. I went upstairs to visit with Jeremy. He was out somewhere, so I went in search of Hattie. I found her in the kitchen measuring out flour for pie crusts. Seeing a spare apron, I donned it. She glanced up at me curiously and then grinned.

"Getting bored, are you?"

"Extremely," I agreed. "Where's Jeremy?"

"Mace took him out for a ride." I wasn't sure I liked that. Jeremy was getting entirely too attached to Mace Donovan for my comfort.

"Where do I start?"

"The vegetables are in the basin over there," she indicated and I set to work, peeling and cutting.

"You are looking better," Hattie observed while kneading the dough and sprinkling more flour in it to get the proper consistency.

"Much. I've got to do something since I won't be allowed to go home for the next two weeks."

"Allowed?" she questioned my choice of words with a quick frown.

I sighed, relenting. "Donovan said it would be a while

before a well could be dug, and until then, Jeremy and I must stay here."

"You don't sound particularly enthusiastic about the idea," Hattie said dryly. She began rolling out the dough expertly.

"I'd rather be home," I told her frankly. "There's so much to do." I looked at the energetic woman and smiled weakly. "I'm afraid the truth is the longer I have to stay here, the closer I come to losing the homestead. That garden was our only means of making any money . . . and we need money to pay off our mortgage and taxes. If it dies out completely, we're really in trouble."

"Oh, you needn't worry," she said as casually as though I were discussing the time of day. "I'm sure Mace would advance you the money to meet your obligations. You could pay him back as things got better."

She placed dough around the pie plates and pressed it down into the center.

"I'd never borrow money from him, Hattie," I said harshly, stopping my work. Hattie tapped a fork around the inside of the pie plates, puncturing the dough to keep it from bubbling while baking. She glanced up.

"Why should you be more proud than your father?"

"What did you say?" I stammered.

"Your father borrowed money from Mace for the taxes last year. I don't see why you shouldn't do the same. Mace would be more than glad to help out, I'm sure."

"You're wrong!" I said chokingly, my face white.

"I'm sure I'm not," she disagreed gently. "He wouldn't mind making you a loan."

"No! No, I don't mean that. I mean about Papa!" I exclaimed. "My father couldn't have borrowed money from him."

Hattie stopped her incessant work and looked at my distraught face. "I heard him thanking Mace for the loan of the tax money myself, Kathryn. He said he'd pay it back as soon as he could, so no doubt it's all taken care of by now."

How could it be paid back? There had been no spare money during the past year. I had learned all too well that dismal fact after my father's death.

"It's nothing to be so upset about, Kathryn," Hattie continued. "There are a lot of small ranchers that are in trouble. Mister Brian and Mace have made loans to quite a few."

Hattie poured peeled, sliced apples and the seasoning into the six pie plates and then put strips of dough decoratively across the tops of each. Finally, she pinched the edges into a lacy circle. As she pushed them into a huge oven, I worked mechanically over the potatoes and carrots, questions whirling madly through my mind.

While I was still working on the vegetables for the beef stew, Hattie rolled chunks of meat in flour and seasoning, placing them in a sizzling cast iron pan. After they had browned, she transferred them into a deep pot and put more wood in the stove. I was just finishing the carrots when she approached and put an arm around my shoulders.

"You're worrying yourself about too many things at once, child," she said sympathetically. My eyes were swimming and I gave her a bleak smile.

She patted my shoulder again and then took up the bowl of finished vegetables. She dumped them into the deep pot and poured on more water, adding pinches of herbs that soon filled the kitchen with a delectable aroma. I sat down at the table and put my head in my arms.

If what Hattie said was true, when would the axe fall? How soon would Mace tell me that the homestead belonged to him? And where could we go then? Would those distant relatives in Virginia be willing to loan us the money to keep the homestead on our promise that we would pay them back as quickly as possible?

I straightened, my head aching again with tension. Hattie was stacking out dishes for the dining room. Another stack was larger, for the cowhands. The food and dishes would be taken to the bunkhouse and brought back later for washing.

Standing up, I went over to her. "Here, let me do that. I can't just sit around anymore." She smiled, allowing me to take over.

"Just take them on into the dining room. Dinner is a little more formal so we set the table instead of having things laid out on the sideboard."

I arranged the dishes and silverware on the damask tablecloth. Someone had put a huge bouquet of flowers in the center of the table. The sunset was casting soft-colored lights through the window.

"So you've been put to work," Brian Donovan's voice came from the doorway. His hands were poised on the wheels as though he had been moving down the corridor and chanced to see me.

"I was getting too used to being waited upon," I smiled. I finished setting out the last knife, fork, and spoon while he watched.

"I'd think you would welcome a long vacation after the way Mace tells me you've been burning yourself out on that homestead. Why don't you just sell out?"

My eyes narrowed on him distrustfully. "I don't want to sell. It's our land and it's going to stay our land."

Mister Donovan raised his brows at my vehemence. "Well, that's your business. I'm sorry I said anything."

I calmed. "It's our home, Mister Donovan. And it's my father's. Jeremy will inherit it when he comes of age, if I can keep it going that long."

"How did the tour go this morning?" he asked, his eyes twinkling.

"Tasajara is very impressive. But I didn't need anyone

to show me that. I can look over the whole empire from our ridge," I said, deliberately avoiding any mention of Mace.

Mister Donovan chuckled. "You and my son seem to strike sparks off each other."

I did not see any reason to respond to that. It would be the height of rudeness to tell him just how much I loathed and distrusted his son.

"May I get you anything?" I asked instead.

"No, but you can keep an old man company in the parlor for a while. It's been a long time since I've had the chance to sit and talk with a beautiful young woman."

I flushed. "Your tongue is pretty glib, Mister Donovan."

He laughed and wheeled himself down the hall and turned left. I followed. We came into a large room at the front of the house. There were several large windows opening out onto the veranda. The room was richly decorated in light wooden furniture, green and gold fabrics, and subdued beige wallpaper that blended well with the natural wood of the door and window frames.

"Pour yourself some sherry," he said, indicating a tray of decanters near the window.

"No, thank you. I don't drink."

"Then how about pouring me some bourbon. I'm afraid I do drink." He was rubbing his hip as though it hurt, and looking at his distorted hands I realized with sympathy that this man certainly had had his share of troubles. I went to the table and looked at the many crystal decanters in confusion.

"The tall square one to the right," he instructed. "And make it a good dose."

I did as he told me, carrying the glass back to him. He took a healthy swig and sighed contentedly.

"God, that's good. Mace has it shipped in from the Carolinas. The Southerners sure know how to make bourbon." He looked up at me. "Sit down. Sit down. You're not in here to wait on me."

I sat uneasily on the sofa, hands folded in my lap.

"Your father was a Southerner," Mister Donovan stated over his drink.

"Yes. From Virginia. His family had a plantation outside Richmond called River's Bend."

"Why did he leave? Seems he gave up something worthwhile to slave on something worthless."

"Apparently he didn't think so," I answered stiffly. "And besides, it's a family custom that the eldest son inherit everything . . . or his issue if he should die. My father was the third of four sons."

Mister Donovan smiled and nodded. "Now, I understand. He came out here to make his own fortune."

"I suppose." But he never did. All he had found was back-breaking work, grief, and a violent death.

"It's unfortunate that we've had so little to do with you, living as close as we do. I used to do a lot of riding before I started getting crippled up this way." He raised a gnarled hand. But I was always too busy to be socializing and later, when things were going better, I was set in my ways. Now Mace is a better administrator than me and I'm glad he has the time to make up for my bad habits." He looked at me, waiting.

"I understand he and your father used to meet on the ridge occasionally," he said after a pause.

"Yes," I said grimly.

"Mace has only been back on Tasajara for the past two years, otherwise I'm sure he would have made your acquaintance some time ago."

I saw that his glass was nearly empty. "Would you like me to get you something more?" I asked, not enjoying the turn the conversation had taken. Mister Donovan seemed distracted.

"Mace had the idea that you were a lot younger from what your father told him."

"Really?"

"Pretty curious, I'd say. Oh, I suppose I can understand why your father was so protective . . . especially since you're quite a looker."

"There was nothing curious about any of it," I said firmly, sensing some criticism of my father again. "My mother died two days after Jeremy was born. I became a mother to him and had to take over the house and garden so that my father was free to manage the homestead. It wasn't that my father was hiding me away or anything. I went into town occasionally. It was simply necessary that I stay home most of the time."

"What about your schooling?" he asked. "Though I don't expect a girl needs much anyway."

I laughed slightly at his blatant male arrogance. "I'd match my education to any man's. My father taught me to read, write, and cipher, and ordered books on history, science, and social studies. He was a very well-read man himself. My mother taught me the rudiments of the feminine arts before she died, . . . sewing, cooking, some crocheting though I've never been very good at it. Jeremy will have an excellent education as well. Papa bought, and we've both read, many of the classics."

"Seems like a mighty waste of money and time," Mister Donovan commented. "Your brother seems more interested in reading than working the land."

My face tightened. "What makes you say that?" I did not think he even knew Jeremy.

"Something Mace said when he came back from your house once. He said you were working yourself into an early grave while your brother sat around dreaming over his books."

"He hasn't any right to say such a thing!" I said heatedly. "Jeremy helps out quite a lot! And when he was sitting around, as Donovan puts it, it was because he had a broken leg!"

"Hold on now," Mister Donovan raised an arthritic

hand. "Don't start a war over it." He shook his head. "It just seems to me that he's got a lot less responsibility than you did two years his junior."

"The circumstances were different," I said stiffly.

"Granted you lost your mother, but you had a roof over your head and a father to depend upon. You've lost one now and you're probably on the way to losing the other."

"We haven't lost the homestead yet," I said steadily, the color draining from my face at his prediction.

"You'd be wise to sell," he suggested, finishing off the last drop of bourbon in his glass. "If your brother isn't interested, why would you want to stay on it?"

I searched his face suspiciously. That was the second time he had suggested we sell out. Had Mace put him up to this conversation?

"Leave go, Dad," Mace said, walking into the room. My muscles jerked to attention, my head spinning to face him.

"Why? Seems the only sensible thing the girl can do," Mister Donovan retorted. "Here. Pour me another one, Mace. My bones ache ungodly."

Mace obliged, handing the full glass back to his father. "Because . . . Kathryn Durham is not a sensible girl."

My mouth tightened but I forced myself not to say anything. Mister Donovan was looking between the two of us again.

"Then maybe you should talk some sense into her," he suggested, smiling slightly.

I did not like the way they spoke about me as though I was not even in the room, or lacked sense enough to understand English. I stood up, intending to leave.

"Sit down, Kat," Donovan drawled.

"Thank you, no," I said glaring at him.

"Testy little thing, isn't she?" he commented to his

father, who was smiling broadly. Then he looked back at me. "Sit down." It was a command this time. Who did he think he was?

"I am not going to sell our homestead, Donovan! Go ahead and try all your clever tactics with Jeremy, but it's going to change absolutely nothing. I am not selling!"

The smile dropped from Mister Donovan's face as he looked from me to his son's grim countenance.

"What's going on here?"

"I think what she's inferring is that I am deliberately showing Jermey that he has other choices in life besides the homestead." He looked at me steadily. "Don't you want him to know that, Kat?" He turned away before I could answer and poured himself a drink. "At least it's an improvement over accusing me of murder," he said dryly, turning back again and looking at me over the glass.

"Murder?" Mister Donovan repeated. "What are you talking about?" My face had reddened.

"The first time I laid eyes on Kathryn Durham, she was aiming a rifle at my heart and accusing me of murdering her father."

Brian Donovan's eyes swung to me. "You couldn't seriously have thought such a thing," he said, stunned.

Seeing a way out, I grabbed at it. "Under the circumstances, I can certainly understand that you would not want me in your house after . . ."

"You're going to stay, Kat," Donovan said firmly.

"It's your father's ranch, not yours!" I flared. "It's up to him and I'm asking him if I can please leave!"

"It's not my ranch," Mister Donovan said flatly. "I signed it lock, stock, and barrel over to Mace when I could no longer manage it."

"You're still his father!"

"You're wasting your breath, Kat." Mace set the glass down and crossed his arms. "Dad knows this is between you and me." He smiled slightly, taunting. "Just what are you afraid of? That you might change your mind about me?"

"There's no chance of that happening!"

Mace drew his breath in slowly. "Well, at least you don't believe I murdered Roger anymore. And a lot of other things are going to change while you're here as well."

There was a warning in his tone and I searched his expression for some indication of its meaning. His face was enigmatic.

I swallowed hard. Just what was he planning? To pull out a note with my father's signature on it saying that I owed him money and that I would have to forfeit the homestead? Perhaps some kind of personal revenge for all my hurled insults?

I did not realize how pale my face had become, nor how vulnerable my expression. Mace turned away from me, sensing his father's dismay at our scene.

Before Mace turned around again, I left the room. I fled up the stairs to Jeremy's room, where I found him washing his face. He dried off and grinned at me.

"Mace took me riding all over . . ."

"There isn't time to talk about that, Jeremy. We've got to leave here, and now."

"But why?"

"You know why. If we don't go back to the homestead and work it, we'll lose it! Oh, please, Jeremy, try to understand? The garden is the only thing we . . ."

The door opened behind me and I knew who it was without looking.

"Leave the boy alone, Kat," Donovan said quietly.

I did not look at him. "Jeremy," I said pleadingly, but my brother was looking at Mace for guidance now. There was respect and something more in his eyes.

"Jeremy!" I reached out and grabbed his thin shoulders, shaking him. I needed him now and he couldn't let me down, he just couldn't! His eyes widened at the shock of my unusually rough treatment. Mace gripped my shoulder and pulled me away, yanking me across the room and out the door.

"What have you done to him?" I demanded accusingly. Was my own brother's loyalty so easily swayed?

"Not a damn thing!" he said through his teeth, catching my wrists as I tried to flail at him. I yanked hard, trying to pull free, but instead found myself slammed against the wall. Mace's body swung against me as he clamped my wrists against the wood panelling. His face lowered to within an inch of mine, and the gold eyes were blazing.

"Katie . . ."

"It's all right, Jeremy. Go back in your room for a few minutes while I talk to your sister," Donovan instructed. The door closed.

"Let go . . ." My voice was high and I was out of breath.

"Not until I get a promise out of you," he growled. My breasts were crushed against his chest and I could feel the rapid, hard thud of his heart. He shifted slightly and thrust his hips against mine so that the entire length of him stretched against me. I felt the hard muscles of his thighs, the overpowering strength and maleness of him. It sent a shiver through me.

The look in Mace's eyes changed subtly. There was still anger, but his eyes were darkening, smouldering. I was sure he could feel my heart pounding against my ribs. I remembered what he had said to me in the Madrone park about how good it felt to feel me against him. I could hardly breathe with the emotions that were caused by nearness.

"Just a promise," he breathed, his voice husky. He lowered his head, pressing his mouth against the curve of my neck. My body jerked taut, warmth licking through my blood.

"Don't! What . . . what do you want me to promise?"
I got out quickly.

He laughed harshly. "Scared to death, aren't you?" he
raised his head to look into my pale, tense face.

"What do you want me to promise?" I stammered. He
sighed.

"That you won't leave Tasajara until your well is
completed," he said, moving away a fraction of an inch.
When I hesitated, he moved back again, his mouth hov-
ering dangerously near mine. I was more terrified of his
kiss than anything else and responded quickly.

"I promise." When he didn't move back, my eyes
widened in alarm. "I promise, Donovan!"

"In the nick of time," he drawled mockingly, kissing
my cheek briefly and releasing me. I let out my breath in
great relief. My knees felt shaky and I stood frozen
against the wall as he looked me over. "I mean to hold
you to that."

"I haven't any choice, have I?" I said bitterly.

"You had a choice," he said. "I almost wish you had
decided not to promise. It would have been very en-
joyable convincing you . . . what was the sensible thing
to do. And the outcome would be just the same, you'd
stay." He smiled derisively, his eyes moving down over
me and back up again.

I did not know why, but I hurt inside. What a hopeless situation I was in. How could I fight a man like this?
Even my own brother looked to Donovan for guidance
rather than to me, his own flesh and blood.

Closing my eyes, I leaned back wearily against the
wall. "Why don't you just take it all away from me now,
Donovan?" I said, unaware of how hopeless I sounded.

"When you leave here, I hope you will understand
that I don't want to take anything from you," he said,
his voice gentle.

"I suppose you want me to give it to you," I said,

trying to sound scathingly sarcastic, but unsuccessful.

His mouth curved up slightly. "Something like that."

"Did you loan my father the tax money last year?" I asked, needing to know. Mace's eyes widened and then narrowed.

"What makes you ask that?" His expression was unreadable.

"Hattie said she heard you and my father talking about it;" I admitted flatly. Donovan was silent.

"Hattie mishears a lot of things," he said, finally.

I took a shaky breath and let it out slowly. Looking up at him, I frowned with confusion. "You could have lied to me."

"Then why bother to voice such a question."

"I have to know."

"Why? If it were true, what could you do about it."

"I suppose I could wire our relations in Virginia and ask them for a loan," I said.

"And what if they asked you to come back to Virginia?" he asked, his expression cold and withdrawn.

"If we lost the homestead, where else could we go?" I shrugged. Mace looked suddenly depressed and frustrated.

"No, I don't suppose you'd go any place else."

"I won't lose the homestead," I said to myself, to rebuild my flagging confidence. So much was against me, I needed all the assurance I could get.

Mace looked at me expressionlessly. Turning slightly, he tapped on Jeremy's door. "Come on, Jeremy. Hattie is holding dinner for us."

My brother opened the bedroom door and looked at me and our host. His eyes came back to mine, where they remained. He looked worried and I gave him a smile. He smiled back, reaching out to take my hand.

On the way down the stairs, I held onto him as though my very life depended on it.

CHAPTER TWENTY-ONE

Jeremy was up and about all the next day. He looked healthy and happy for the first time in months. I resented the fact that it was Tasajara fare that was bringing the color back into his cheeks.

I did not see him all morning after breakfast. He went out with Mace to work. When he came in, he was covered with sweat and dust, but grinning from ear to ear. And all he could talk about was Mace Donovan!

It seemed futile to keep up a war against such a man, so I decided to curb my tongue and learn all I could about him. After all, I reasoned, how could I fight unless I knew the man's weaknesses—if he had any.

I spent the afternoon working with Hattie in the kitchen and then visiting with Mister Donovan in the library. From him I learned that Mace had studied back East and then traveled extensively in Europe before returning to California. My father had spoken of Donovan's travels numerous times. Brian Donovan said that Mace had always spoken very highly of my father's knowledge. He left any further comments about papa's homesteading abilities unsaid, for which I was grateful.

Later that day, Mister Donovan retired to his bedroom, in need of rest. He said he had had a couple of bad days with his arthritis and sometimes he just needed to sleep in order to fight the pain. He took a full bottle of bourbon with him.

I was alone in the parlor, having finished some chores Hattie gave me and having been shooed out of the kitchen. Mace came in after freshening up from a hard day's work. He looked at me in surprise and then walked to the decanter to pour himself some bourbon. Finding it empty, he opened another bottle without comment. He poured a second glass from another elegant decanter and carried it to me.

"Sherry," he answered my silent question. "Or perhaps you'd prefer bourbon as well."

"This is fine," I lied, wondering how I was going to force it down. It smelled sweet but very strong.

"Whatever you wish, Kat," he said. "Where's Dad?"

"He wasn't feeling well," I answered, sipping the sherry. It passed over my tongue and dropped like a hot rock into the pit of my stomach, where I was sure it was burning its way through to my skin. Donovan grinned broadly, seeing my expression.

"Do you like it?"

I forced myself to swallow another sip without showing my distaste. "It gets better," I answered, though it tasted not a whit better than the first time.

"Of course," he drawled, eyes laughing.

"Papa always liked his brandy," I said for conversation, and then felt driven to add, "good French brandy." I gazed out the window, remembering other things Papa had liked; sunflowers in June, mockingbirds, the church hymn my mother taught me, and especially fine, fat cattle. Many things made Papa happy, gave him pleasure. Even when things were at their worst, he had smiled for us.

"You and your father were very close," Mace said quietly, all the laughter gone from his eyes. I could feel all my defenses rising again, searching for some slight or mockery in his statement, when apparently he had meant none. I relaxed, breathing in slowly before answering.

"Yes. As close as you and your father are . . . perhaps more so."

"I can understand that. He protected you from the world, kept you neatly locked away at the homestead taking care of Jeremy."

"There was nothing wrong with that!" I flared. "It was necessary. And I went into Madrone on occasion. It wasn't as though he kept me at the homestead *all* the time."

"I think he kept you there a good deal of the time so that you'd be spared knowing what was going on in town," he told me quietly, sipping from his glass.

"Things might have been easier on him if he had chosen to confide in me."

"And a lot easier on you as well, I would think." He lounged back on the other end of the couch. "I'll probably be just the same way with any daughter I'm lucky enough to have."

Something in his tone caught at the muscles of my stomach and tightened them. "You're thinking of getting married and starting a family soon?" I don't know why I asked the question so derisively, but managed to keep my tone polite enough anyway. Donovan smiled at my efforts.

"I'm getting old enough, wouldn't you say?"

"I wish your wife well," I muttered, taking another sip of sherry.

Mace laughed. "She'll do very well. She'll have security, plenty of help in handling her household duties . . . and she'll have all the . . . attention from her husband that she could possibly want."

I could hardly misunderstand that and pain jabbed at my midsection. I wondered vaguely if the sherry was poisoning me, and then knew despondently that it wasn't.

"Charlene will make you a fine wife," I said carefully.

"Charlene?"

"Charlene Bellows," I said, sipping the loathsome sherry again and finding the taste less despicable.

"So you think Charlene will do well for me," he said, watching my face closely. "Do you like her?"

"I don't know her," I said blandly. "But she's . . . she's very pretty." The words almost choked me.

"A man couldn't ask for more than a pretty wife, I suppose. Now could he?" Mace smiled slightly. "Otherwise, what do you think of her?" he pressed. I glanced at him curiously. Why was he so interested in my opinion about a woman he wanted to marry? Surely he could make up his own mind about her?

"I said I didn't know her. She seems nice enough. Her father's very nice."

"And her mother?"

"I've only met her half a dozen times and briefly." Thank God!

"You really were kept on that mountain, weren't you?" he baited.

"There didn't seem much sense in going into town all the time to socialize," I answered shortly.

"Didn't you ever want to go to school, have friends your own age, be a part of what was going on in Madrone?"

I had, of course, but why wish for something that was not possible? It made no sense for me to ride sixteen miles round trip to school. And I had been needed at home from the day of Jeremy's birth. While other girls my age were playing with dolls, I had my brother to raise. My interests would not have been the same as theirs even if I had gone to school. And everything I needed to know or wanted to learn, I learned at the homestead. Thanks to Papa.

"No."

"Liar. The answer isn't that simple, and you know it."

I glared at him. "And just when I was changing my mind about you!"

His brows lifted, the gold eyes becoming intense. I didn't know why it was so important that he know that now.

"Indeed?" he drew out the word. "Would you mind elaborating a bit?"

I had to think about that for a moment. "If you had wanted my father dead so that you could take over the homestead, why would you care about us? We stand in your way now just the way Papa did then."

"Kat . . ."

"All right," I conceded, seeing that my choice of words had made him angry. "I don't believe you murdered my father. Let's leave it at that."

"Thanks." He looked away, sipping his bourbon, a muscle in his jaw tightening.

"You've been . . ." I had to say it, but it stuck in my throat. He glanced at me. "You've been a *concerned* neighbor."

He grinned. "Hmmmm. Go on, Kat. Anything else?"

I seethed. Then I reminded myself of my resolve. "If you hadn't come by the cabin when you did, Jeremy would be dead . . . and so would I."

"So you owe me your life, hmmmm?" The thought seemed to give him obvious pleasure. "How're you ever going to pay me back for all I've done for you?" he asked mockingly, baiting me.

"I can't possibly know. But I'll think of something," I said through my teeth.

"Anything else that's changed your low opinion of me?"

"Does there have to be a catalog of reasons?" I

snapped and then tried to force my temper down.

"I'd just like to understand this . . . rather sudden and inexplicable . . . change of feeling about me," he said dryly, finishing the last of his bourbon. He stood up and I watched him walk back to the decanters, all too aware of the casual smoothness of his movements and the breadth of his shoulders. There was a raw masculinity about Donovan that struck a chord deep inside me. He was dangerous in more ways than one.

"You've said often enough that there's nothing at the homestead you need or want," I hedged. He turned slightly and looked at me. Then he laughed low.

"Did I really say that?"

That question was highly unsettling. "There's the ridge, of course. It would give you such a clear view of your vast domain," I said, giving in to my urge to stab back at him. He smiled unpleasantly, turning all the way around.

"Do you think I'd sit up there dreaming over Tasajara the same way your father did?" he retaliated.

"My father worked damn hard!"

"Not all that hard, Kat, or you wouldn't be in such a mess now. What was that you just said about Roger enjoying *good* French brandy? How could he afford that, hmmm? By using the money that should have been spent on more needed things . . . a decent pair of shoes for you, for example. And how many hours a day did he spend up there on the ridge dreaming? Or in town at the hotel?"

"Don't you dare criticize my father!" I was on my feet, hands fisted angrily at my side.

Mace poured more bourbon into his glass and then slammed it down. "I'm trying to make you see a few facts! Your father was a good-hearted man . . . a loving father. But as a worker, he left a lot to be desired. He could have worked harder, made things a hell of a lot easier on you. He would have been better off in town with a steady job rather than settling out here. He bought a piece of land totally unsuited to running cattle or farming if that's what he had in mind. It's nothing but a hunk of rock with trees sticking out here and there and some pathetic meadows not big enough for anything, nor rich enough for good yield." He laughed insultingly. "Sure, it's got a magnificent view of the valley. But that's all its got! All that ridge did was to draw your father further into his dream world when he should have been working his cattle, saving to buy more and better land. Roger didn't really know what the hell he wanted except for life to be fun. I think you grew up a long time before he did . . . if he ever did!"

"Stop it!" I said desperately. "Just stop it!" I did not want to hear the truth from Donovan, especially since many of those doubts about my father had already begun to niggle at me before this.

Mace walked across the room. "When I've finished," he said coldly. "Let me tell you something else you should have known about your father. He dreamed big dreams, Kat. He used to talk a lot about you, weaving wonderful little fairy tales of his perfect little daughter, more woman than child. I used to see the way he looked down on Tasajara, and I was pretty damn certain just what he had in mind. I can tell you I wasn't all that eager to make your acquaintance, knowing that he was building hopes of you becoming mistress of *my* ranch! I wasn't going to get roped in and hog-tied that easily!"

I stared at him aghast.

"Horrifying, isn't it?" he sneered. "What man in his right mind would be interested in you? God, he'd be asking for a lifetime of constant battling and endless sexual frustration!"

I felt as though he had punched me in the stomach. He made it even worse.

"A man prefers someone soft and yielding, warm and gentle, someone who has a kind and loving heart . . . not some girl with a stubborn streak as wide as the Sacramento River and who is as prickly as a barrel cactus. Someone like Charlene Bellows, for example," he bit out. "Life would be damned easy with her!"

"If not dull. But then all you men really want is someone to drop you a baby, preferably a boy, once a year!" I threw his own words back in his face.

There was the harsh sound of air being sucked through gritted teeth. I backed up, afraid of what he might do. He breathed deeply for a few seconds.

"And what about you? Who'll want to marry you?"

"I don't plan to marry anyone."

"Sounds like an exciting life . . . single and stuck on that homestead playing nursemaid to your brother. Of course, you could always plead your case to Bigelow. But he'd still be a little cold about it, to my way of thinking."

I lifted my chin and deliberately cocking an eyebrow, gave him a faint smile. "Les never seemed the least bit cold to me. A little too warm, I'd say."

Something very unpleasant flickered briefly across Mace's face before his eyes became veiled and his face a mask of cold contempt.

"Let's say then, he's a little too practical. Did he also check your teeth?"

"And what about your requirements for a wife, Donovan?"

"There's nothing the least bit practical in my choice of a mate," he said. Then he hesitated. "Charlene and her parents are coming out here for a few days, by the way."

"Here?" I gasped.

"That's what I just said."

"After I've left . . ." I said hopefully, the news wiping out all my anger.

"No. You'll still be here."

"But what'll they think!"

"They'll probably not think a thing, except that you and your brother needed a charitable hand during a trying time," he mocked. Tears burned, but I blinked them back out of sheer willpower. This man was not going to make me cry!

"I would think you would be concerned about Charlene's feelings," I said levelly. Just the thought of being here when she was made my stomach churn. Having to watch the two of them would turn me inside out. It had been bad enough seeing him with her that one time in town.

"Charlene knows how I feel about her," he drawled, unconcerned. "And I know how she feels about me as well. She has no need of feeling jealous over you." He made it sound like I was the least attractive female in all of California. "If you're worried about it, I'll spell it out very clearly that you're only here out of charity."

I flinched, and felt my face turn white. But wasn't it the truth? How could I deny it? Charity!

"I'll repay you."

Mace muttered something under his breath in exasperation. "Why you? Why not Jeremy, too?" he demanded hoarsely. "Why do you take every damn thing onto yourself?"

"Jeremy's a child," I said, feeling emotionally drained from this argument and not even able to remember what had started it.

"Oh, Kat," he sighed, his anger gone. He rubbed the back of his neck. "You can make me so mad I can't think straight."

My throat ached and I averted my head, blinking rapidly as I stared unseeing out the front window. So much for my resolve to make peace, I thought ruefully.

"Can we try for two weeks to be civil to one another?" he asked quietly.

For a moment, I could not speak at all. He waited. Finally, I looked up at him.

"I'm tired of fighting you . . . and everything else."

"Then, we'll call a truce until you're rested again," he smiled.

If I had not still been thinking of Charlene Bellows, I might have even smiled back at him.

CHAPTER TWENTY-TWO

The sun was barely up when I heard someone tapping on my door. I moved stiffly beneath the covers, rolling over onto my back to force my eyes open. I had had a long night with very little sleep. What sleep I did have was intruded upon by Donovan. It bothered me a great deal that it wasn't his insufferable arrogance that had made me toss and turn most of the night, but rather his overpowering sensuality. This was not the first time I had suffered such shocking revelations in my dreams, but it bothered me more occurring in his own house.

I had to get out of here, somehow. It was frightening the way he could make me forget all my responsibilities with just a few words. In a few weeks, I would lose everything! It didn't matter at all to him. Why should it? Look at the massive empire he possessed! How could he possibly understand what my tiny plot of earth meant to me . . . and Jeremy?

Jeremy! What was I going to do about Jeremy and his dreams? I was beginning to realize that he would no longer be satisfied with the homestead, no matter how well things might turn out. If I wanted to be perfectly honest with myself, I had always known that. The thought was not comforting.

There was another tap at the door, more insistent this

time. "Just a minute, please," I called huskily, pushing the bedclothes aside and sliding my legs off the bed. I didn't have a chance to get further than that. The door opened and I stared wide-eyed and shocked as Donovan strode into the room.

"I just wanted to make sure you were awake before I barged in," he said, barging in. I dived back under the covers, feeling hot color surging under my skin.

Lord in Heaven! Why did he have to appear right now, just after I'd been dreaming about him in such appalling ways! I felt guilty and embarrassed at the same time and was sure that he could read my thoughts just by looking at my face.

"Donovan!" I protested loudly. He did not stop until he was beside the bed looking down at me with the covers up to my nose. He grinned broadly.

"Relax," he drawled easily, obviously enjoying my embarrassment immensely. "I never ravage a woman before I've had breakfast!"

"Get out of here!"

"I was curious how you look when you first awakened. Now I know. Flushed and bright-eyed."

I decided to try another tactic. "Please, Donovan, would you go away?"

"You're a lot more polite in the morning as well."

"Tell me what you want, and then get out of here!"

His grin grew lopsided and he considered me from my concealed form to my glittering eyes. "Now, what would I want from you this early in the morning?" he provoked.

"So much for our supposed truce," I said tightly, glaring up at him.

"Okay," he said, raising a conceding hand. "I'll go. But I want you up and downstairs in five minutes . . . ten, at the most."

"What for?" I asked warily.

"You and I are going riding together this morning," he announced.

"We are?" I challenged irrepressibly. "Why? Are you planning to show me more of your great empire, Donovan?"

He leaned down, putting his hands on either side of my head. "Truce, remember?"

I gulped. "Yes. All right, I'll be downstairs in five minutes," I stammered hurriedly. I would have agreed to almost anything to get him out of this room and away from me. Every muscle in my body was heating up with him this close. And there didn't seem to be enough oxygen in the room either.

"Good girl," he teased, patting my cheek like a big brother. He straightened. "Hattie put some riding clothes in the wardrobe for you," he said. Then he grinned wickedly. "I hope you like them."

With that cryptic remark, he strode from the room. As soon as the door closed, I jumped out of bed and ran over to lock it. Donovan could not have taken more than three steps when the lock clicked. He laughed.

"Five minutes!" he repeated.

After a hasty wash, I threw off the nightgown and put on my underclothes. I found a pair of boy's denim pants and a plaid shirt in the wardrobe. Holding them up, I glared at them. No self-respecting female would be caught dead in such a getup, I thought furiously. But after a moment's hesitation, I admitted grudgingly that these clothes made more sense than riding in my gingham dress. I pulled the pants on, surprised to find that they fit well, if a little snugly. The waist was a bit loose, but a leather belt at the bottom of the wardrobe would solve that problem. The shirt fit well and I tucked it into the pants, buckling the belt. Glancing at myself in the mirror, I shrugged.

"You'll get a good laugh out of this, Donovan," I

muttered to myself, leaving the room. Donovan gave me
a long look up and down when I met him in the foyer.
But thankfully, he made no comment.

Two horses were tied up out front. Donovan's sorrel
stallion was impatiently pawing the ground and snorting. The dark, glistening mare next to him looked aloof.
She lowered her head slightly and tossed her silky mane
while the shifting stallion rolled his eyes at her.

"What do you think of her?" Donovan asked, glancing at me as we stood at the top of the steps.

"I love her attitude," I said with a slight smile.

"You would," Donovan chuckled. "Come on, before
Diablo gets too frustrated." He took my arm as we
walked down the steps. His touch set my skin on fire and
bothered me more than a little. Did he think I was going
to fall headlong down the steps? I debated whether or
not to pull my arm away from his disturbing touch, but
knew just how much amusement he would get from that.
There certainly wasn't any need to let him know how
nervous I was.

When he came around the mare with me, I glanced
over my shoulder at him warily. "I can mount by myself,
thank you."

He was not deterred. Bending slightly, he cupped his
hands. "I just thought you might like the opportunity to
step on me," he said with a teasing smile. I couldn't help
but laugh.

"Hmmmm. Yes. Thank you." I put my foot in his
hands and let him bear my full weight before I mounted.

"Not as light as I thought," he needled.

"There's a pity," I grinned at him from my perch. I
picked up the reins, watching him swing into the saddle.
"Where are we going?"

"I lead, you follow," he said, baring his teeth at me.

"For the moment," I agreed.

It was a brisk morning, but the ride was warming me

up fast. We had passed between the two larger barns and were heading south onto the stretch of grazing land that lay cradled below the mountains to the east and the lower range of hills to the west. From here I could just see our stony ridge. Around us, oak, rather than pine, studded the land. Along the meandering stream there were alders with round, quaking leaves rustling faintly in the breeze.

There was plenty of thick, rich grass down here, I observed enviously. And plenty of cattle eating it as well. Fat, healthy cattle. I remembered our mangy herd and smiled ruefully. Les Bigelow had been more than generous with his price, I suddenly realized. But then he had had ulterior motives.

I found my eyes straying to Donovan again and again. My gaze travelled over him languorously, from the proud tilt of his dark head, to the breadth of rippling shoulders, lean hips, and long length of hard-muscled legs. My heart pounded slowly and hard, almost in cadence with the steady, leisurely walk of the horses.

He must have felt me watching him, for he glanced back over his shoulder. "Bored?" he asked.

With my entire system long ago awakened with desire, I was anything but bored, I thought frantically. "A little," I lied, yanking my eyes away with an effort and trying desperately to maintain a poker face. He laughed slightly. Drawing in his reins a little, he waited for me to come up beside him.

"Well, we can't have you bored," he said. He stretched out his arm, pointing southeast. "Race you to that outcrop of rocks," he challenged.

My heart quickened. "Hardly fair, considering your mount," I said, giving him a droll smile.

"You can have a head start."

I didn't wait! I snapped the reins over the mare's strong rump and took off. She was fast and I leaned

down, loosening the reins. I heard Donovan start a few
seconds later and snapped the reins again knowing that
if she didn't get more of a head start our meager lead
wasn't going to last. The mare stretched out and she
almost flew over the grassy earth. Her dark mane
whipped into my face. I laughed. This mare wanted to
beat the stallion as badly as I wanted to beat Donovan!

"Go, girl!" I urged her. I could hear the thunderous
hooves of the great stallion, and felt the answering,
straining muscles of the mare. My heart was racing wildly. Donovan drew up beside me suddenly, turned his
head and grinned. With a tensing of his leg muscles, he
moved the stallion over, almost brushing against me. It
was enough to ruin our stride and force me to shift. He
shot forward, arriving at the outcrop of boulders seconds before me.

I swung down, furious. Marching around the mare, I
put my hands on my hips and glared at him in frustration. He was standing with one booted foot raised triumphantly on a large rock below the mass of boulders.

"You cheated!" I railed.

"I won," he grinned, not the least bit ashamed.

"You cheated!!" I repeated a little louder.

"I don't remember setting any rules," he said in-
nocently. "You're just a very sore loser."

"Oh, hell's bells! What's the use?" I said, out of
breath from the ride. I flung myself down and sprawled
back against another boulder, drinking in the fresh air.
Donovan laughed.

"You're not half bad for a girl," he provoked me.

"Truce, remember?" I reminded him, flicking him a
brief glance. I noticed the stallion sidling up to the mare,
nosing her gently. Apparently, she was a sore loser, too.
She snapped at him and he snorted in surprise. I started
to laugh.

"A horse after your own heart," Donovan drawled,

walking over to stretch out beside me. I was still laugh-ing. "Would you like to bite me, Kat?"

All my hostility was momentarily forgotten. "Give me your arm, Donovan!"

"Only my arm?" he asked, pretending disappoint-ment. He leaned back, his arms behind his head, and stared up at the blue sky. He sighed deeply, a little too deeply. "I should have let you win," he said. "I can think of a few places I'd like to bite."

My smile froze and my mouth dropped open slightly. I turned my head slowly in his direction, staring at him. Heat surged up into my cheeks. His mouth twitched. He turned his head slightly and looked directly at me.

"You're a little red, Kat," he observed unkindly. "Are you feeling warmed up from our ride?"

"A little," I said, knowing the steaming heat in my body had very little to do with the ride, but hoping he would believe it did. He smiled, eyes laughing but in-tense.

"So am I."

I looked away, feeling very dry mouthed.

"There's a canteen on my saddle," Donovan said, grinning at me. I glanced at him in surprise and then stood up abruptly.

"Thank you," I said, walking away. I took the can-teen down, opened it, and drank thirstily. Before I put the cap back on, Donovan was beside me, reaching out for it. His fingers brushed mine as he took it and he watched me as he drank. I turned away, my heart ham-mering.

Slinging the canteen back on the saddle, Donovan leaned on his stallion. "Have you ever been up the ridge by way of the Tasajara trail?" he asked.

"No," I admitted, grateful for conversation. "But I . . . I'd like to . . ."

"Let's go."

Before I could protest, he lifted me easily into my saddle, his hands lingering for just a second before he turned away. I tried to pretend that the contact had not disturbed me, but it was several moments of riding before my heart stopped knocking against my ribs.

The trail was steep, winding up through the trees south of the ridge and then doubling back as it neared the top. It was precarious in places and I swallowed hard as I looked down.

When we reached the top, I dismounted before Donovan could touch me. He gave me a mocking glance and then tied up both horses. I walked toward the boulder where my father had sat. Standing there, beneath the huge pine, I stared out over Tasajara. It was beautiful, I admitted grudgingly.

Donovan came up behind me. Putting his left hand on my hip, he stretched his right arm over my shoulder, pointing outward. "See the range of hills over there?" he asked, his warm breath fanning my ear and cheek. I nodded, unable to speak. "Most of the Tasajara herd is over there." His fingers spread over my hip, turning me slightly as he moved his arm south. "Right along there . . ." His body was right behind me almost brushing against mine. I started to shake.

Why did he keep touching me? My breathing felt constricted. I moved determinedly away, pretending interest in what he had said.

"How . . . how many head did you say you ran?"

"Are you interested?" he asked. His fingers curved around my arm, drawing me back. "Watch out there. A few more steps and you'll go right down that cliff."

I drew my arm away and walked in the other direction. Donovan followed, watching me with a faint smile on his face. I was growing more nervous by the minute.

I stopped in the middle of a rocky ledge, a foot or so above the level of the boulder. I thought of my father and the pain squeezed my throat tightly.

"Donovan?"

"Hmmmm?" He came up to stand next to me. As I was starting outward, he was looking down at me.

"Who killed my father?" I asked in a choked voice.

"I don't know, Kat," he said quietly. "I don't know anyone who would have had any reason to kill Roger."

"Then who? And why?"

"I don't know," he repeated. "There are a lot of strange people in this world. Some are no better than animals. Maybe there was no reason. Maybe it was someone passing through. I couldn't tell you, Kat."

My mouth quivered and I closed my eyes, averting my face. Don't cry! I told myself fiercely. Don't cry in front of Donovan!

I walked back toward the mare. "Ready to go back already?" Donovan asked, walking more slowly behind me.

"I . . . I'm going to go down to the cabin," I told him, swinging up into the saddle after untying the reins.

"No."

I glanced at him sharply. "Why not?"

He let out a sharp breath. "Because you'll only get yourself upset."

"Upset? Why?"

He raked fingers back through his hair and a quick frown creased his face. "Because your garden is dead." My shoulders slumped.

"I'd still like to . . ."

Donovan swung up and reached across to draw the mare in the opposite direction. "We haven't had breakfast yet, remember?" he said. "And I'm starving even if you're not. Come on."

"We can go down that way, you know," I said indicating the trail by way of the cabin. It was the easier route, by far, even if it added a little distance.

"No." He was practically herding me back toward the Tasajara ridge trail and I had little choice but to follow. Why didn't he want me to go by the cabin?

"You're being a little high-handed, aren't you?" I demanded, angry at not having had anything to say about the decision.

"I can't think of any other way to handle you," he grinned. "The carrot and sugar method doesn't work."

CHAPTER TWENTY-THREE

I was greatly relieved to part company with Donovan when we returned to the ranchhouse. My emotions were in too much of a turmoil. The less involved with him I was, the safer I would be. I had had too much pain over the past few months to open myself up to the kind that I was sure he could inflict on me.

Jeremy was waiting on the veranda. When he saw us coming, he came down the steps waving and grinning broadly. I caught the speculative gleam in his eyes when he glanced between Donovan and me. After what Mace had told me about Papa's pipe dream concerning me and Tasajara, I was not going to have my brother humiliating me with any more ridiculous notions.

Sliding from the mare before Donovan could dismount and touch me again, I turned and handed the reins to Jeremy. I almost fled up the steps to get a few feet between me and the man looming close by with that all-too-knowing smirk on his face. Stopping midway up the steps where I felt safer, I glanced back.

"Thank you for the ride, Donovan," I called sweetly and gave him a mocking salute. Before he could put in his two-cents worth, I disappeared into the house.

I managed quite deftly to avoid Donovan for the rest of the morning by insisting that Hattie put me to work in the kitchen. When she flatly refused to have me underfoot any longer, I used my own resources to find things to do.

"What in Hades do you think you're doing?" Donovan demanded, having tracked me down like a bloodhound. Why wouldn't the cursed man just leave me alone?

Sitting back on my heels, I looked up at him standing there arms akimbo, legs spread. My gingham dress was as dusty as his denim pants and work shirt. And I was sure that there was as much perspiration on my face as on his. He looked angry and it gave me an odd sense of power. It was very hard to maintain a cool smile when looking up the solid male length of him and finally meeting those golden eyes narrowed by frowning brows. I think I succeeded admirably under the circumstances. I wished heartily that he had seen fit to button his shirt, however. It made things a little uncomfortable for me. Forcing my gaze away, I used my handkerchief to wipe the perspiration from my forehead and then fingered back the loose strands of hairs into the neat braid hanging down my back.

I dismissed the inclination to get up. Perhaps kneeling at his feet like this would make him feel enough the conqueror that he would not have to pursue the matter further.

Donovan never gave up easily.

"What do you think you're doing?" he repeated, exasperated.

"Now, any man with half a brain could figure out what I'm doing," I said teasingly. He was aggrieved enough at finding me weeding his vegetable garden, without my resorting to my usual tone. I was proud of my restraint.

"I didn't bring you over here to grovel around in the dirt," he said slowly. "Now, get up out of there!"

Imperious as ever! God, how he irritated the hell out
of me when he ordered me around! I stood up and
brushed myself off. "I'm well now, Donovan," I said
trying to remain calm and polite. "And I'm bored to
death. Please . . . please, can't I work a little out here? I
enjoy it!"

"I'm sure you do," he said, obviously not believing a
word I said. "Why don't you ride, or read, or sew—or
do whatever ladies usually do to entertain themselves,
instead of coming out here in that threadbare dress and
crawling around on your hands and knees like a field
hand."

I ground my teeth for a second or two before thrusting my chin out. "Just because some fine-feathered lady
friends of yours don't like getting their lily-white hands
dirty does not mean that I'm like that!" I said quietly
enough. "I like the feel and smell of productive soil!"

His eyebrows shot up and the gold eyes laughed. He
smiled, all irritation gone. "To what fine-feathered lady
friends with lily-white hands were you referring, Kat?"

He knew exactly to whom I was referring. But how
could I get myself out of this without sounding like I was
jealous? Jealous! That was ridiculous!

"No one in particular," I said with a faint lift of my
shoulders and then decided a quick change of subject
would be my best tactic. "Please, Donovan," I appealed,
deliberately batting my eyelashes. "Please. I'm going to
go mad here if I don't have something to do!"

He laughed. "All right," he conceded. "Follow me."
He seemed to delight in having me follow him around!
But I did what he asked.

"You want to work? Fine," he said, slowing and waiting for me. He put his hand at my elbow and pointed.
"You want to work the soil? Great! There's your domain."

I stared in open delight at the flower garden. "Really?

You mean it?" I breathed, looking up at him. "But what about Hattie?"

"Hattie will be delighted. She has more than enough to do in the house. She'd appreciate the help . . . *here*" he pointed again to make it emphatic. "But so-help-me-Hannah, if I catch you in the onions and rhubarb again, you're going to be in deep trouble," he warned.

I laughed. "Don't worry," I guaranteed.

"This is your domain . . . for the moment."

Ten days in a flower garden sounded marvelous to me. I glanced up at Donovan. He was obviously pleased about my agreement, but something else was pleasing him as well. Whenever Donovan had that self-satisfied look, I began to worry. Just what was he thinking?

"You can handle cutting and arranging all the flowers for the house," he said.

"Fine."

His smile broadened. "Just in case that won't keep you occupied, you can do my mending for me."

"Mending?" I smiled forceably. "Fences?" I asked hopefully. He laughed again.

"Shirts."

A thought struck me and I smiled back at him. "All right. If you wish, Donovan. You may be disappointed in my skills."

He eyed me warily. "You can manage to put a button on, can't you?"

"Oh, I think I can manage more than that," I said walking away from him, practically sashaying with amusement. I could hardly wait!

My opportunity came quickly enough. Following dinner, Donovan gleefully deposited a pile of work shirts in my lap. "So you won't get bored," he said. His father was chuckling. Jeremy was grinning. I smiled back sweetly and went right to work.

"She seems to be coming around nicely," Brian

Donovan observed, giving me a teasing wink.

Donovan didn't say anything and I glanced up to catch the worried frown on his face. Obviously, my zeal for this chore was worrying him. Poor lamb! I tried hard and succeeded in giving him a blandly innocent look before I threaded a needle and began sewing on a button. He watched, eyes narrowed.

I finished the work later in my room upstairs. My fingers were sore and stiff by the time I finished. But my spirits could not have been higher. The following morning, I turned the pile of shirts over to Hattie. They were then given to the maid, who had them washed, ironed, and folded away into Donovan's armoire. For the next two days, I was in high spirits. I even found it easy to be friendly with Donovan, though I maintained my distance.

On the third morning, I was rewarded for my efforts.

The sun was barely up when I heard a door upstairs slam with a violence that put a smile on my face, a *big* smile. I dressed hastily. Footsteps were coming down the hall.

"Kat!" Donovan pounded on the door.

"Just a minute, Donovan," I called out politely. I sat down on my bed and counted to five. Donovan pounded again and I covered my mouth to hold the laugh. Then I walked to the door and opened it.

"Is something wrong?" I asked, looking up at him. He shoved the door open. In his other hand he had a shirt which he thrust under my nose.

"You ungrateful little wretch!" he exploded.

"Is there a problem?" I widened my eyes. "I did sew your buttons on, didn't I?"

"You did," he drawled. "And you also sewed the sleeves shut!"

I started to giggle because I couldn't help it. I spread my hands in an apologetic gesture. "I'm really very

sorry, Dono . . ." Then I couldn't contain it any longer.
I burst out laughing. He stood in the doorway staring at
me and then after a second or two joined in.

"I ought to strangle you," he said after a minute.
"And just when I thought I had you eating out of the
palm of my hand."

"Carrots and sugar! Yes, I know." I pointed at the
shirt. "You deserved that!"

It was the first time we had laughed together. The expression in his eyes changed subtly, making my heart
thud. The laughter ebbed as we stood staring at each
other.

"It's good to see you laugh, Kat," he said quietly.

"I haven't for a long time," I admitted, reminded of
everything that had happened in the last few months. I
sighed, reached out and took the shirt from his hand.
"I'll fix them all."

He gave me a smile that turned my heart over. "Damn
right you will," he growled mockingly. Then he walked
out of the room.

Living here on Tasajara, seeing Donovan every day, I
was learning things about him I didn't want to know.
There were many sides to this man. Telling myself not to
feel anything for him was no longer possible, and the old
fears stirred inside me. I didn't need any more pain. And
Donovan would bring me nothing but heartache.

Don't be a fool and fall in love with him! I told myself
fiercely. Remember who he is and who you are! A man
with his power and wealth could never be seriously interested in you. I remembered the burning scorn in his
voice when he had told me of my father's dreams for me.
That was humiliating enough!

Les Bigelow might not have wanted anything more
than a healthy woman to bear him equally healthy sons.
But Donovan would be a lot more selective in his mate.
He would want a woman with a proper background,

proper manners, and all the refinement that a formal education cultivated. Someone like Charlene Bellows fresh from her eastern school.

And why was I even bothering to think about it? It did not concern me, I told myself again and again. I realized I was holding Donovan's shirt in a death grip and tossed it onto a chair. I shook my head and turned away from the open doorway. I wished for the thousandth time that I was far away from here and home again.

Jeremy was full of talk about Tasajara and Donovan when I saw him at lunchtime. We had so little time together lately and I missed him terribly. He was moving further away from me each day, becoming a little more distant and independent. I began to realize that it was not that he loved me any less, but that he desperately needed and longed for a man's company. Mace Donovan was filling that need, giving Jeremy the attention he craved, providing the affection he missed since my father's death. My love wasn't enough anymore.

The growing closeness between Donovan and my brother worried me almost as much as my own deep feelings for the man. In another week, we would be leaving Tasajara and returning to the homestead. Our lives would pick up exactly where they had left off. There would not be time for Jeremy to go gallivanting off to visit with Mace, nor for me to sit in a flower garden and spin idle dreams like my father had done on the ridge.

I was lying awake one night thinking about that, when Hattie tapped at my door. I knew something was wrong the minute I opened the door.

"It's Jeremy, Kathryn. He's asking for you," she told me.

"Asking for me?" I repeated dumbly while wrapping myself in the voluminous robe she thrust at me to cover my thin cotton gown.

"He's having trouble breathing."

I did not need to hear more. I rushed past her and ran for the stairs. When I got to his room at the end of the third-story hall, I found Donovan sitting on the edge of his bed talking in a low voice. I came across the room and around the bed to the other side. Leaning down, I brushed the hair back from Jeremy's forehead. He looked up at me, eyes wide and frightened.

"When did it start, Jeremy?" I asked in a quiet voice, trying hard not to show the old fear. No matter how many times I went through this agony with my brother it never became easier to bear. It frightened me half to death to see him struggling for every breath of air.

"About two hours ago," Donovan told me from the other side of the bed.

"Two hours?" I repeated. "Why didn't you send for me sooner?" I demanded, and then shook my head. "Never mind." Sitting down on the bed, I took Jeremy's hand and gave him a smile. "We've been through it before, Jeremy. It'll pass."

Donovan looked at me. "This has happened before?"

"Yes. Less frequently during the last couple of years. I thought he was outgrowing it."

Donovan frowned slightly, looking down at Jeremy thoughtfully. "Is he sensitive to anything in particular?"

I smiled slightly at my brother, who was staring at me. "Dogs and cats, unfortunately."

Jeremy's guilt-ridden eyes moved slowly to Donovan. Donovan smiled and shook his head.

"Why didn't you tell me that?" he asked my brother. Jeremy was having too much difficulty breathing to answer but his lower lip was quivering.

"Where is he, Jeremy?" Donovan asked gently.

"Where is who?" I asked. Donovan neither looked at me nor replied. He was waiting for my brother's answer. His face was gentle with understanding and Jeremy's eyes filled with tears. My brother slowly lifted his hand

and pointed across the room. I looked. There was a large box against the back wall in the shadow of the big wardrobe. I hadn't noticed it before.

Donovan got up and strode across the room. He bent down and reached into the box. When he straightened, he was holding a mongrel pup with shaggy hair and large, soulful brown eyes.

"Kat, I'd like to introduce you to Chaps."

Jeremy sniffed. I looked down at my brother's stricken face. "Oh, Jeremy, how could you be so foolish?" I asked. Looking more closely, I could see the pup's hair all over the bed. No wonder Jeremy was in trouble.

"Come on, you scamp," I said, throwing off the offending covers. "You can't stay in this bed or this room." I started to lift my wheezing brother when Donovan came over. Hattie had taken the animal out of the room.

"Here, I'll take him," Donovan said, nudging me aside. He lifted my brother easily. I followed him out of the room. When he carried him into his own bedroom I protested.

"Why don't you bring him downstairs?" I suggested.

"He can stay in here until this spell is over, and Hattie can make up the other guest room down the hall."

I was standing in the doorway feeling very uncomfortable. "I can take care of my brother, Donovan," I said, unable to keep the stiffness out of my voice.

"I'm well aware of that, Kat. Come on in," he said, hardly giving me a look. He lay Jeremy down in the center of the large bed. He squeezed my brother's shoulder comfortingly, and then sat down. "Relax, Jeremy. You're as tense as Chaps was after he squatted in the middle of Hattie's kitchen floor."

My brother tried to laugh but couldn't. Fear transformed his eyes into huge round saucers as he tried desperately to pull in air through his straining lungs.

"Easy, boy," Donovan whispered, kneading my brother's knotted muscles. He looked straight into Jeremy's eyes and smiled, giving him confidence. As Jeremy relaxed under Donovan's touch, his wheezing lessened slightly. The blue of his lips was fading too.

"Where's Katie?" Jeremy managed.

"I'm here, sweetheart," I said, sitting on the other side of the bed and taking his extended hand. Donovan eased away and I took over. He left the room, coming back later with a tray on which was set fresh coffee and a couple of sandwiches. I wasn't hungry, but I had several cups of the invigorating brew.

It was close to four in the morning and I was exhausted. Jeremy was sleeping restlessly. My hand was cramped from his tight grip, but he didn't want to let go. He never did when he was going through this. I looked down at him, absently stroking his hand and remembering things he had done as a baby. He had teethed on my favorite volume of French poetry.

"Why don't you lie down next to Jeremy, Kat, and rest for a while?" Donovan asked. He had been sitting in a chair by the window, getting up every so often to check on Jeremy.

"I'm all right," I said, my voice husky. I was very tired, but the thought of lying on Donovan's bed for any reason was unthinkable.

"I promise not to join you there," he drawled lightly.

"Not now, Donovan, please," I murmured quietly, unable to answer his needle, feeling perilously close to tears as I looked down at my brother.

"I'm sorry," he whispered. Standing up, he came across the room. When I felt him sit on the edge of the bed behind me, I tensed.

"He'll be all right, Kat."

I swallowed hard. "I know."

"I'm sorry I gave him the dog. I didn't know . . ."

"I know, Donovan. It wasn't your fault. I should have told you that that time we'd discussed it at the cabin." I said without facing him.

I felt his fingers in my hair, lightly stroking it away from my neck.

"Donovan . . ." I began to protest weakly.

"Shhhh . . . don't wake Jeremy," he whispered. His hands moved along the curve of my neck across my shoulders. The warmth of his body behind me was enticing, frightening. He began to knead my shoulders gently as he had my brother's, only without producing the same effect. Those warm, hard hands sensously increased my tension, building it to painful proportions. I started to shake.

"Hmmmm, you smell so good," he murmured against my hair. Then his hands dropped as though he suddenly realized what he was doing and saying. He got up and moved away from me to stand near the window. I glanced at him and then looked away, closing my eyes against the sting of tears. His gentleness was more devastating than anything else. I wanted him to hold me. I wanted to sob out all the pain of the last months, all the fears I had of tomorrow. And, at the same time, I wanted to get away from him.

When dawn came, Jeremy was sleeping soundly, his breathing eased, his color good. Hattie made up the other guest room upstairs and Donovan carried Jeremy in. Bending down, I brushed my lips against his pale forehead. Jeremy smiled, rolled over, and curled into his usual sleeping position.

When I straightened, I looked back toward Donovan, who was leaning against the doorway watching me. I motioned him into the hallway and quietly closed the door behind us. Then I looked up and smiled wearily at him, almost too tired to hold my eyes open.

"He'll be fine now. Thank you," I said, reaching out and lightly brushing his arm with my fingertips.

"Can you make it back to your room on your own legs or would you like to be carried?" he smiled.

"I can walk."

CHAPTER TWENTY-FOUR

The truce and friendly feelings growing between me and Donovan died a sudden death with the arrival of Charlene Bellows and her doting parents.

I was helping Hattie clean up the lunch dishes brought back from the cowhands' bunkhouse. The stack was diminishing slowly. Pot after pot of hot water was dumped into the sink for washing and rinsing. After rinsing, I set each plate in a rack for Hattie to dry and put away. We were working on the pots when I heard a commotion in front of the house.

"The Bellows must have arrived," Hattie said, hanging a pot up on a hook above the butcher's block in the middle of the kitchen. My heart plunged into my stomach.

"They were expected today," she added casually picking up another pan and watching my face as I scrubbed a skillet over the sinkful of hot sudsy water. My fingertips and hands looked like the skin on a prune. My hair was coming loose in places and hanging in damp curls around my temples. I brushed it back impatiently and continued to scrub.

"Mace brought your trunk over from the homestead this morning," she told me. I looked at her blankly.

"My trunk? I don't have a . . . oh! You mean he

brought my mother's trunk here?'' The thought of Mace
Donovan going to the homestead without my knowledge was annoying. He knew how much I wanted to
check things out, make sure everything was all right.
What right did he have to go into our cabin without me
and take anything out of it?

"Now don't go getting that headstrong look of yours,
Kathryn,'' Hattie said. "He thought you would want
some clothes. You won't be wanting to sit with Charlene
and her parents in that . . . gingham.''

"I don't plan to sit with Charlene and her parents.''

"Where do you plan to sit, if you don't mind my asking?''

"Here with you.''

"Oh, no,'' she shook her head.

"Hattie . . .''

"I think you'd better go on upstairs right now and get
fixed up. I'll send up water for a nice, scented bath,'' she
smiled.

The door swung open and Mace bound inside. He
looked me over and grinned in a way that could only be
described as malicious.

"Come on, Kat. I want you to meet Charlene.''

My eyes widened and I shook my head. "Oh, no. Not
like this, thank you.''

"Nonsense. What difference does it make? I can assure you it doesn't matter to me what you're wearing!''
He took my arm, giving me no choice, and my face
burned as he pulled me through the door and down the
hall.

Charlene Bellows was wearing a charming and expensive lavender ensemble that put me to shame. Her
clear blue eyes swung from Mace to me and she smiled.
There was no disdain, no condemnation, not even an
element of surprise at my untidy appearance. She was
young, exquisite, and very sweet. I loathed her on sight.

Her mother's expression, however, was one of distaste. Her gaze roved over me, taking in the grubby, worn gingham dress, my hands still wet and shriveled from washing dishes, my wild hair starting to come out of its coil, and my flushed cheeks. Jeremiah Bellows merely gave me his usual polite smile of greeting.

"Kathryn and Jeremy are staying here until a new well can be dug on their property," Donovan announced.

"What happened to their old one?" Harriet Bellows demanded, eyeing me suspiciously.

"It was fouled."

"How unfortunate for you," Charlene said quietly, looking at me blandly. Her smile seemed vacuous to me and I glanced up at Donovan, who was looking at his lavender lady.

"Yes, it was unfortunate," I agreed, smiling sweetly.

"She wasn't very enthusiastic about accepting my hospitality for so long, but she finally gave in gracefully," Donovan informed everyone.

"Really," Harriet said slowly. "Wouldn't it be more seemly for . . . Miss Durham and her young brother to stay somewhere in town?"

"Nonsense, Mother," Charlene put in. "She's close to her homestead here and she can ride over and check on things for herself any time she wants. I'm sure Kathryn wouldn't want to be ten miles away without a chance of seeing to everything herself."

Apparently, Mace was right about his sweet Charlene. She wasn't jealous of me. Her lack of concern over my presence in Donovan's house even disturbed me. Was I really so unattractive? John Saunders hadn't thought so. Nor had Les Bigelow.

Charlene smiled at me again and I made a valiant effort to smile back politely.

"Mace told me that your father died recently," she

said giving the appropriate frown of concern. "I'm very sorry. I hope everything will work out for you and your brother."

And what could I say to all that? "Thank you, Miss Bellows," I murmured tight-lipped.

"Oh, please. Call me Charlene. I'd like to call you Kathryn."

"Of course." I ground my teeth. How could I possibly loathe someone so *nice*? There wasn't anything in her eyes to indicate she was insincere.

"Jeremiah, I'm putting you and Harriet in the bedroom on the second floor. Charlene will be right next door." Donovan picked up the two cases and gestured with a movement of his head for the others to precede him. Then he took a step back to me, bending down to whisper.

"Why don't you go up and sit in a bath for a while, Kat?" he suggested with a devilish gleam in his eyes. "You might even brush your hair into a pretty chignon."

I wanted badly to slap him, but turned and stormed back to the kitchen instead.

Hattie was just hanging up the last pot. "What's the matter with you, Kathryn?"

I plunked myself down on a chair, fisting my hands in my lap.

"Damn his hide," I muttered.

"Mace, you mean. Of course, who else," she said, chuckling. She gave an exaggerated sigh. "So much for the lull before a storm. It didn't last long, did it?"

I glanced up at her curiously.

"Skeedaddle, Kathryn. Whether you like it or not, you're going to be sitting at the table with those people. And Mace won't hesitate to drag you in there in what you're wearing now. I'll have the water up for you in half an hour."

Pacing in my room upstairs, I wavered between tears
of mortification and the desire to scream in rage. Mace
Donovan was a heartless devil! He had almost convinced me he was human. I had begun to like him, to
trust him. And now this. He had deliberately set out to
make a fool of me in front of Charlene Bellows, dragging me in for inspection in my grubby little urchin
dress. I wanted to die.

Harriet Bellows had obviously heard all of Les
Bigelow's lies. I could tell from the ugly expression she
gave me, looking me over like some snail. And Jeremiah
Bellows? I could not begin to fatham his expression
when he paused on the stairs and looked back at me
standing by Donovan.

Sitting on the edge of the bed, I put my head in my
hands. I had never been embarrassed by my poor means
and appearance before. What could I do about it now?
There was no money for fine clothes or for pretty rib-
bons for my hair. And I didn't really need them! But
seeing Charlene in her dainty lavender frock sent a disturbing jab of envy through me. I felt pathetic in comparison and began to realize just how Donovan must see
me.

I hated him! I told myself over and over, his taunting
smile swimming before my tear-filled eyes. It was his
fault I was feeling this way. If only he had let me alone.
A sick feeling of frustration filled me, tightening my
chest painfully.

Hattie had the water sent up as promised and I tried
to still my turmoil of thoughts in the warm, scented water. It was useless. I kept seeing Mace Donovan marrying pretty Charlene with her vacuous, perfect smile.

A tap on the door announced Hattie's entrance. She
walked to the wardrobe and swung it open, revealing my
mother's dresses and evening gowns. Even her wedding
dress, which sent a sudden stab of pain through me.
Everything had been aired and pressed.

"I think this would be nice," Hattie suggested, taking out a green gown that was as beautiful as it was outdated. I could almost see Harriet Bellows's lip curl in contempt.

"I'm not feeling well, Hattie," I said and it was true.

"You're fine and you know it," she argued. "Mace hasn't asked anything of you, but he asks now that you join him and his guests. Jeremy has already gone down."

"You don't understand," I said tremulously.

"I think I understand a good deal more than you do," Hattie answered, taking the dress out and carrying it across the room. Undergarments had already been laid out by some unknown hand. "Now try this on. If it needs any alteration, we'll do it right now.

"I can't, Hattie. Please, don't make me," I pleaded. "Harriet Bellows has obviously heard the rumors that Les started and I'm not sure what Jeremiah Bellows thinks. Charlene . . . Charlene . . . Mace was just trying to make a fool of me. He's had his fun, so . . ."

"If you think that, then it's all the more reason for you to go down there and show them what you're made of," she said, thrusting the dress at me.

"Donovan would do well to marry Charlene," I said dismally, doing as she bid.

"Call him Mace."

I smiled brittlely. "I don't like to think of him in intimate terms."

"Because you're afraid to?" she sniffed, buttoning up the back of the dress expertly.

"I'm not afraid of him!"

"You're scared to death of him, and for all the wrong reasons."

"I don't know what you mean," I said stiffly, chin in the air.

"He's a man. More of a man than you've ever known. And I've seen the way he looks at you." She made an impatient gesture. "If you were a little more cordial to him, you wouldn't be going back to that hovel on the hill."

I swung around. "It's not a hovel! It's our home, a home my father built with his own hands."

"And never improved. Fifteen years . . . and still you're living in a sod house. If that don't beat all. And don't give me that crushed look."

"My father worked hard . . ."

Her look was bland. "And how do you think you're going to manage what a man couldn't? You, a mere slip of a girl. Give it up! It was a foolish dream from the start."

My mouth tightened mutinously. "So everyone here at Tasajara keeps saying. A lot of other people have the same dream and they're making it."

Hattie sighed in exasperation. "Let's forget the homestead for a while. You've got to go downstairs tonight."

"Why should I?"

"Because that little Bellows girl is pretty and charming enough, but she lacks spirit and real intelligence. Mace would be bored with her after one week."

I stared at her aghast as I realized what she was really saying. Then I felt a rise of hysterical laughter. "You want *me* to marry him!" I accused.

"Think of it as keeping your land, if you must," she shrugged, "and if you move again you're going to have this needle in you instead of in this dress!"

I felt as though I were going to faint. How could Hattie think such an abominable thing?

"I wouldn't marry Mace Donovan if he were the last man west of the Rockies!" I told her, just to be sure she understood my sentiments.

She sniffed. "He is as far as you're concerned."

My face suffused with color. "You're wrong, Hattie! If you knew how wrong you were. I don't even like him!"

Hattie stepped away, smiling. "There, finished! You're prettier than a picture. And you're going downstairs!" she added sternly. "Don't embarrass your little brother by sitting up here hiding or staying in the sulks."

She marched from the room before I could argue with her. I rubbed my temples, wondering what to do. She had said Jeremy was already down there with them. I couldn't sit up here indefinitely. Taking a deep breath, I walked to the door and opened it. As I came down the stairs, I could hear voices coming from the parlor. Jeremy was there.

Charlene was sitting on the couch with my brother, whose rapt face was clear indication that she had made yet another conquest. Donovan was talking to Jeremiah, and Harriet hovered nearby like a mother hen. She was the first to see me and her displeasure was immediate. However, she forced a smile and invited me to join her by the window.

I opened the conversation by saying how much I had appreciated her husband allowing me the extra time to repay my father's debt.

"Jeremiah can be overly charitable at times," Mrs. Bellows said, bringing a faint flush of color to my cheeks. But she did not stop there.

"Are you really planning to join us for dinner?" she asked, snidely.

"I . . ." I began to stammer self-consciously and then anger swelled up inside me. "Yes, I am. And so is my brother, Jeremy. Do you have any objections?"

"Several," she said in a low hiss. "You must realize what's been said about you in town."

"By Les Bigelow?"

Harriet Bellows colored. "I'm not one to repeat rumors, and I don't want Charlene touched in any way by them either."

"I can understand that. But if you did hear a rumor

started by Les Bigelow, I can assure you it is false. I am here solely on sufferance, if you must know the truth. Your daughter need not be hurt by any of this."

Harriet Bellows stiffened. "You take your reputation very lightly."

"What do you suggest I do, Mrs. Bellows? You apparently have already made up your mind to believe what you want, regardless of the truth."

"How dare you speak to me like that!" she snapped. There was suddenly a stillness in the room that could only mean that all conversation had stopped. I turned and met Mace's questioning glance. He looked at me and then at Harriet Bellows, whose face was now an angry, mottled red.

"How can you have this disrespectful girl in your house?" she asked Mace, who was looking at me grimly.

I was embarrassed enough by Harriet Bellows's comment without having him looking at me as though I had deliberately set out to ruin his fiancee's visit.

"What was she saying to you, Mrs. Bellows?" Mister Donovan asked, having entered the room unnoticed. That was a question she couldn't answer without accomplishing what she said she wanted to avoid. She stammered some inane comment about not feeling it was worth repeating.

Tilting my chin, I turned away, pretending an interest in the garden. Mister Donovan wheeled over to sit beside me. I felt him watching my tense expression and gave him a forced smile.

"You're feeling better?" I asked. He had been in his room for days.

"I'm feeling fine. You look a little pale, however."

"Nothing that couldn't be cured by a few solitary hours in my room," I said, looking at him hopefully.

"No, I don't think that would suffice. Now, what did that busybody say to you?"

"As she said . . . nothing worth repeating," I answered firmly. Mace strode over to pour more drinks and he turned his head to one side to look at me. I couldn't read his expression and gave him a hateful glance. His mouth tightened, and I noticed a muscle moving in his jaw.

How long did it take to dig a well? And why couldn't Jeremy and I just leave?

"Why don't you have her stay in town?" Harriet Bellows was suggesting again. "It would be much more proper for an unattached female like her than having her here with you, Mace."

Mister Donovan laughed heartily. "Now, Harriet, Mace is out working most of the day and too tired for shenanigans when he gets home. And as for me . . . you don't think I'm chasing the girl around in my wheelchair, now do you? Besides, Kathryn has her brother with her. What better chaperon than that?"

Charlene Bellows's laugh tinkled. "Oh, Mother, really, you're so dreadfully old-fashioned." She glanced up through her lashes at Mace, who was standing next to her, bending down to give her a crystal glass of fine sherry. "I'm sure Mace is exemplary. I trust him implicitly."

Mace lifted her free hand and kissed it gallantly. "Thank you, Charlene. I'm grateful for your glowing report."

I wanted to vomit! Mace Donovan exemplary! Charlene Bellows could have him, and luck to her!

Dinner was a feast obviously meant to impress. Prime ribs of beef, mounds of mashed potatoes and rich gravy, garden fresh peas, carrots, beans and squash, fresh butter and milk, sweet breads flavored with apricot preserves, and one of Hattie's superb chocolate cakes. I couldn't eat a thing.

Poking my food around and around on my plate, I had to listen to Charlene's endless, silly chatter about her friends back East and in town, the parties she had attended, and the harmless gossip she apparently reveled in. It might take Donovan a week to become bored with her, but it took me only an hour.

When Charlene's monologue began to wind down, her mother wound her up again with a few careful posed questions. There was little attempt made to draw anyone else into the conversation. Jeremy was so busy staring at Charlene's radiant face that he almost forgot to eat until prodded by my sharp elbow. Then he shoveled the food in, his eyes still focused on the lavender visage at the end of the table near Donovan.

Mace Donovan listened to the endless dialogue. He twirled his glass of wine and smiled, nodded when appropriate. Anything he did say was uttered in a warm, polite voice he had never used to me. Once he laughed at a story Charlene told, but I could see no humor in it. Did he really find her so amusing?

Following dinner, we all adjourned into the main living room. There was brandy for the men and sweet wine for the women.

There was a piano in the room and Harriet Bellows exclaimed over it passionately, encouraging Charlene to play for everyone's enjoyment.

"Only if Mace insists," she laughed softly, gazing up at him teasingly. And of course, he did. Charlene spread her skirts over the needlepointed bench and poised her graceful lily-white hands over the keys.

After a few moments, I realized with a wrench that she was playing a hymn that had been one of Papa's favorites. He told me he used to sing it while mama accompanied him on the piano or guitar. Papa had always talked about how she had had such a light touch on the piano keys and could play many of the masters by heart. After Mama died, he never sang again. But sometimes when I was alone, I would sing that hymn and think of my mother.

In the middle of Charlene's performance, which included singing in her dulcet voice, I left the room. I could stand the flood of memories no longer. There was a door which opened from the parlor out onto the veranda. It was the closest exit, and I took it. I knew it was rude, but perhaps they would all think that I was suddenly indisposed and badly needed a visit to the outhouse. I really didn't care. The last thing I wanted was for Mace or Harriet, or even Charlene, to see the tears burning in my eyes and the trembling of my lower lip.

"Kat?"

Without realizing it, I had put my hands to my face while leaning heavily against a pillar on the veranda. My palms were wet. I rubbed my eyes quickly and dropped my hands. My back straightened immediately.

"You've had your fun, now leave me alone, Donovan," I said coldly.

Amazingly, he did. I listened to his footsteps going back to the parlor, where Charlene was playing some polonaise by Beethoven. A few minutes later, Jeremy came outside. Without saying a word, he took my hand.

Perhaps he understood. I had taught him that hymn, telling him all about Mama.

Staring out into the darkness, I wondered if there would ever again be any happiness for either of us, any sense of security. My brother longed for an education that we could not afford even if we sold the homestead, and I clung to a piece of worthless, rocky land that would probably be the death of both of us.

And there was still Donovan. There would always be Donovan.

CHAPTER TWENTY-FIVE

I slept fitfully that night and arose very early the next morning. When I went downstairs the Bellows family was still sleeping. Hattie was up and making elaborate preparations for a breakfast fit for a queen. She willingly put me to work and I was grateful. I did not want to be sitting in the dining room when everyone came down, and I did not want to have to watch Donovan smiling at Charlene anymore. Last night had been sufficient.

I hadn't been helping Hattie for more than ten minutes when Donovan came into the kitchen.

"There you are," he said, looking squarely at me with something akin to exasperation. "Come into the library for a minute. I want to talk to you." He turned and strode out of the kitchen before I had a chance to say no. Hattie gestured with a flour-coated hand.

"Go on with you, Kathryn. For Heaven's sake, don't start battling at five-thirty in the morning."

I followed after Donovan. He wasn't looking toward me when I came in, but he gave me an order. "Close the door, Kat."

His tone made me bristle. "Just what is this all about, Donovan? And what did your 'there you are' just now mean?"

He turned slowly, eyes narrowed with irritation. "Close the door . . . softly," he said when he saw my rapidly rising temper. "And so help me, if you slam that door, you'll regret it."

I didn't doubt that for an instant judging from his expression. I closed the door with exaggerated deference and turned back to face him, hands on my hips.

"How was that?"

His smile was almost grim. "When you weren't in your room, I thought you had high-tailed it back to the homestead," he admitted coolly.

My eyebrows shot up tauntingly. "I wonder what the Bellows thought about you going to my room at five-thirty in the morning," I said stiffly. "Or perhaps they thought you'd never gone to your own."

"Kat," he said through his teeth.

"I'm sure you were very careful," I drawled. "We wouldn't want to upset the apple cart, now would we? And as for 'hightailing it' back to my home, the thought occurred to me. But I remember making you a promise. I'm not in the habit of breaking promises."

"And if you were, you'd have found yourself dragged back here by your hair!"

I thought it wise not to comment on that. This conversation was quickly degenerating into open combat. Donovan seemed to be of the same mind as I, for he sighed heavily.

"Just when things were going smoothly," he muttered to himself, not looking at me. I thought I heard him hiss an unmentionable word.

"Charlene is going to want to ride this morning, and I want you along with me," he told me.

"No, thank you."

"That wasn't an invitation, Kat."

"No, thank you," I repeated, emphatically. The last thing I wanted to do was to ride with Donovan and his precious little darling, Charlene. The thought was nauseating.

"You're going to go with me whether you like it or not," he challenged.

"Really?" I drew out between gritted teeth, my heart pounding. "I should think that this would be your grand opportunity to sweep your lady fair off her dainty feet, Donovan. A nice romantic ride over your vast domain," I waved my hand airily, "a stop by the river . . . far enough from the house to offer a little privacy . . . and a few lightly stolen kisses to convince her of your interest. The lady's more than willing, I'm sure. And I'm just as sure she wouldn't appreciate an audience!"

"It's just because of all that, that I want you along," he said flatly.

"If you think I'm going to go along as some sort of . . . of chaperon, you're badly mistaken!" I exclaimed, eyes burning. I drew a slow, shaky breath. "I'll work in your kitchen, your garden, your *stables* if you want. I'll do *anything*, Donovan . . . but I will not act as a chaperon for you and Charlene Bellows."

Donovan's foul temper had miraculously dissipated. He was watching my face closely and he smiled slightly, almost tenderly.

"Anything, you said," he murmured suggestively.

"*Almost* anything," I amended. "I won't ride with you and Charlene."

"But *anything* else? Hmmmm?"

"Donovan," I said warningly.

"You're in one very bad temper this morning, Kat. Any particular reason?" he drawled.

"There wasn't a thing wrong with my temper until you started ordering me around again!"

His smile became playful. "Come to think of it, you were in a foul temper yesterday . . . just after the Bellows arrived."

My mouth tightened. His implication was clear. "You think I'm *jealous*." I said sneeringly. I gave a short laugh, insulting in its brevity. "I'd have to feel something for you in that case, wouldn't I? And I don't feel a thing!" His eyes blazed golden fire, but I continued heedlessly. "Of course I was angry. What did you expect when you dragged me out of the kitchen to be inspected like a pinned moth by the Bellows? How did you suppose I would feel dressed like . . . like . . ."

"A turndown from a church rag bag?" he finished brutally. I didn't know anything Donovan could say could hurt quite so much. Was that really how he saw me? My fingers twisted painfully into the gingham of my worn dress. I had but two, and I alternated between them. It wasn't by choice that I had no wardrobe. It was a fact of life. At least I was always clean and neat!

"We can't all have satin and lace, Donovan," I said quietly. Turning away, I walked with as much dignity as I could toward the door. Donovan got there first, flattening his hand against the dark panels so that I couldn't open it.

"I'm sorry," he muttered half-angrily.

I gave a faint shrug, feigning the utmost indifference to anything he said or thought. "I'm not embarrassed about it. Anything I buy, I work hard for. And any money I make goes into a jar to save for mortgages and taxes." We all couldn't be like Charlene Bellows, who had everything handed to her on a silver platter.

"You looked very pretty in that dress you wore last night," he said quietly, not moving his hand.

"It was my mother's."

"Hattie could . . ."

I cut him off with a glance. "I'm not here to make your lady friend think she has any competition, Donovan."

"Can't you ever shut up!" he demanded harshly.

My eyes smarted and I averted my face from his angry one. He let out his breath impatiently, dropping his hand from the door. As I reached out to open it,

Donovan's fingers curled around my wrist, turning me to face him with a harsh twist. My pulse leaped and my entire body stiffened at his touch. The heat of his hard fingers swept up my arm and then spread through me until I felt like I was in a furnace.

"Please, Kat," he said huskily. "I haven't asked much of you while you've been here, have I? But this is vitally important to me."

I stared up at him. So having things absolutely perfect for Charlene was that important to him. My throat ached and I didn't want to figure out why.

"All right," I answered quietly, extracting my wrist and rubbing it unconsciously, concentrating more on dispelling the feelings coursing through me. He noticed my movements.

"Did I hurt you?"

I shook my head, just wanting to get out of the library and away from him. "I'd better change if we're going riding," I said, turning away. He didn't stop me from leaving.

Breakfast was filled with Charlene's exuberant conversation. After one glowering look from Harriet Bellows, I was flatly ignored. Not that I minded. I drank coffee and managed to make it appear that I ate some breakfast. Brian Donovan was listening to Charlene with a wry look on his face. Mace sat at the end of the table deep in thought.

When I came downstairs later in my denim pants and plaid shirt, Harriet Bellows stared at me aghast. Charlene giggled. She was wearing a perfectly tailored riding outfit that probably would have paid for a month's groceries for Jeremy and me.

"Dear me," she twittered, "I wish I had nerve enough to wear something like that."

Donovan didn't say anything, but there was a grim look about his mouth as he ushered Charlene out the door with me trailing behind. Harriet Bellows caught my arm just before I reached the front steps.

"Just where do you think you're going?" she demanded in a fierce whisper.

"Riding," I answered casually.

"I don't think they need or want your company," she hissed. "Why don't you go back into the kitchen where you belong?"

Donovan had stopped at the bottom of the steps and was looking back up at us.

"Coming, Kathryn?" he asked coldly.

"Excuse me," I said, snatching my arm away from Harriet Bellows's clawing hand. She almost sputtered with rage. Donovan's face was a hard, cold mask as I came down the stairs.

While Donovan was helping Charlene onto her sorrel mount, I swung myself up onto the dark mare. He gave me an irritated look as he mounted Diablo. I ignored him. Did he think I had said something to annoy Harriet Bellows?

I waited for them to lead off and then followed at a leisurely pace, pretending interest in the countryside around me. My eyes kept straying to Donovan's back, watching his broad shoulders, the play of strong muscles beneath the cotton shirt. My stomach muscles tightened and I looked away.

Charlene was laughing at some witty comment Donovan had made. She asked many questions and Donovan answered patiently, politely, warmly. When Charlene complained that she was getting a little tired, he was very solicitous.

"There's a nice stretch down by the river," he commented, pointing toward a cluster of white oaks near the bank.

As we approached them, I looked up toward the hills and noticed cattle there. Not far away, I recognized a

man astride a pinto. John Saunders! Surprised relief
spread through me as I saw a way out of my uncomfortable predicament and a chance to leave Donovan
alone with his lady love.

I waited until Mace was gently lifting Charlene from
her mount before I made my escape.

"Excuse me, but I see someone I know. I'll be back in
a while," I told them, and slapped the reins over the
mare's glistening rump to set her off at a canter toward
John.

I drew reins, turning to walk my horse beside his. "I
thought you said you were going home," I accused him
with a slight smile.

"I am . . . at the end of this month . . . after I get my
pay," he smiled back. "God, but you're a sight for sore
eyes!" he said, looking me over admiringly. "You look
damn good in men's clothes, Kathryn."

I laughed, reaching out to take his extended hand.
"Why didn't you come to see me if I'm such a sight for
your poor sore eyes?"

"Because Donovan sent me to the opposite end of his
ranch, that's why!" John told me. He glanced toward
the river. "Uh oh," he drawled. "Something tells me I
am about to be exiled again."

I turned and saw Donovan riding toward us. Where
was Charlene? I glanced back toward the river and saw
her standing there staring after Donovan, hands on her
hips. My heart began an uneasy staccato beat.

"I think you'd better get a move on, Kathryn," John
suggested. I didn't want to get John in trouble, so I lifted
the reins, turning the horse slightly. John caught them
for an instant. "Would you meet me tonight? I'll be back
at the bunkhouse."

"Meet you? Where?" I repeated hurriedly, all too
aware of the look on Donovan's face as he approached
us. He was furious!

"By the pepper tree out front. As soon as you can after dinner. We can walk by moonlight," he teased.

I laughed back at him. "All right," I nodded, flicking the reins over the restless mare. "As soon as I can manage," I agreed, gently heeling the horse forward to meet Donovan. I didn't want to cause more trouble for John. Once at the homestead had been enough. I remembered Donovan's blistering tones when he had spoken to John then.

Donovan swung his stallion around sharply beside me. The mare sidestepped nervously, but Diablo sidled closer.

"Goddamnit, Kat," Donovan snarled. "What in hell do you think you're doing?"

His vicious tone caught me unawares. "I thought you might like a few minutes alone with Charlene," I said simply, not adding that it had grown almost intolerable to watch them together. "And I was within sight, so you were still technically chaperoned. The Bellows won't be . . ."

"If I want to be alone with Charlene, I'll damn well let you know. Have you got that straight?" he cut me off.

I blinked, surveying his face carefully. "Are you afraid of her, Donovan?" I drawled, deciding that a lighter note was called for. "Surely not Charlene. She's too much of a lady to bite you, I'm sure."

My teasing was not improving his disposition, I noticed. Lord, but he was mad! And I could see no earthly reason for it. I would have thought he would have cheered at my timely departure. Charlene had certainly looked appreciative.

"Donovan, you have it made," I assured him. "You won't even have to dangle that carrot and lump of sugar to have Charlene eating out of the palm of your hand. With a word, she'd follow you to the ends of the earth now."

He glowered unappreciatively at my humor. "I suppose I ought to thank Saunders for putting you back into a better mood," he growled.

"Just so you don't fire him," I said sweetly.

Charlene seemed well rested when we reached her, for she said she was ready to return to the ranch house. Her questions were not as frequent on the return ride and it was left to Donovan to make conversation. I held back though he periodically looked around at me. Did he think I was going to sneak away with John and leave him and Charlene in some compromising situation that would raise the Bellows's disapproval?

As soon as we tied up at the hitching rail, I excused myself, not allowing Donovan a chance to argue. I went around the house and set to work in the gardens. What better way to make it very clear to the Bellows and Charlene that they had nothing to worry about as far as I was concerned? And Donovan could have all the time he needed with Charlene. My altruism was wearing very thin though. Seeing them walking around the house and toward the paddocks, I had to force my eyes away.

Lunch could best be described as a tense affair. Charlene was quiet—for a change. Perhaps she had talked herself out during her walk with Donovan. Her mother was casting worried glances at her fledgling and leaving conversation up to her less-than-loquacious husband. Jeremiah Bellows had one interest: business. After a short discussion on the topic, he lapsed into silence. Brian Donovan asked polite questions, made a few erudite observations and then returned his interest to his lunch. Jeremy spent the entire hour staring moon-eyed at Charlene, who had changed into a fashionable blue frock that matched her eyes.

As for Mace Donovan, he sat at the end of the table saying nothing. Every now and then, he would look at me with a cool, pained expression. Things were obvious-

ly not going the way he wanted them to go. I wondered
if he and Charlene had had some kind of misunderstand-
ing. It would certainly explain her unprecedented silence.

The thought of Donovan with Charlene weighed
heavily on my mind all through the meal. I tried to keep
my eyes away from the two of them, but it was useless.
I kept wondering how they were together and I didn't
want to think about it. My growing feelings for
Donovan were hard to ignore in the face of what was
going on. If I cared nothing for the cursed man, why did
it hurt so much to see him with her? I shouldn't care a
whit what he did. But I did. A lot.

I worked in the kitchen that afternoon, flatly refusing
to budge when Hattie broadly hinted that I was probably wanted elsewhere. I managed to help her a lot in
spite of herself. And if she had aimed a cannon at me, I
would not have left the safe refuge of the kitchen. Nothing was going to get me into the parlor with Mace
Donovan and his lady love. Not to mention Dragonlady
Bellows! If things went wrong for Donovan, he was not
going to be able to use me as an excuse. His concern that
everything go perfectly during the Bellows's stay on
Tasajara was clear indication to me just how deeply he
felt for Charlene. And that thought brought me im-
measurable pain, though I stubbornly refused to acknowledge the reason.

I did not know where Mace and Charlene spent the
afternoon, but I knew that Jeremy had wrangled an invitation to join them. Harriet Bellows had been voicing
her utter disgust about that when I put the fresh flowers
on the dining room table. She had been standing in the
corridor and must have known I was present, but she
made no effort whatsoever to lower her very audible
voice when speaking to her husband. I left the dining
room, seething.

"You've been hiding in here behind my skirts enough, Kathryn," Hattie told me sternly. "Now you get on out of here this minute and get cleaned up in time for tea."

"Tea?" I repeated, stunned. Since when did they have afternoon tea at Tasajara? But of course, how foolish of me! Since Charlene Bellows! I grinned at Hattie. "My, but Donovan is setting a fine trap."

"You've got thirty minutes," Hattie told me, shoving some delectable-looking pastry into the oven.

"Hattie, the last person on earth that the Bellows want in the parlor is me," I told her frankly. "Especially Charlene."

"That may be true, but this house belongs to the Donovans and not the Bellows."

"Hattie," I sighed.

"Don't you 'Hattie' me, young lady."

I approached her. "Listen. Donovan made it very clear to me this morning how much this visit means to him. He wants everything to go perfectly for his . . . Charlene. And my being in that parlor for tea will only ruffle Madame Bellows's fine feathers. Can't you understand that?" I had to swallow the lump in my throat. "I'm not going to be blamed for spoiling this for him. If he wants Charlene Bellows, you should be happy about that."

"It doesn't bother you at all to think of him marrying that girl?" Hattie asked, eagle-eyed. I stared back at her.

"Of course not. Why should it?"

"It doesn't bother you to think of them having babies together?" she went on relentlessly. I flinched but managed a disdainful smile.

"Hattie, you've known all along how things are between me and Donovan."

"I thought you were changing your mind the last couple of days before the Bellows descended on us like the hoof and mouth disease!"

I couldn't contain my laughter. "Hattie!"

"Well?"

"Donovan wouldn't appreciate your sentiments," I told her more seriously. "And what objections can you possibly have to Charlene? She's everything you should want for Donovan. She's pretty, she has all the social amenities, and she has a formal education . . . not so common out here, you know." I swallowed, turning away slightly before I finished. "And besides, Donovan is in love with her. That should be enough for you."

"You think so. I don't happen to share your opinion about Mace being in love with her."

I didn't want to talk about Mace Donovan any more, but I knew if I lingered in the kitchen, that was all Hattie was going to talk about. So I gave her an affectionate hug and a peck on her cheek.

"Did any one ever tell you that you're plain bull-headed, Hattie?" I teased, sauntering toward the door.

"Look who's calling the kettle black," she muttered, having the last word.

Brian Donovan was showing the Bellows the garden when I started out the back door. Seeing them, I turned back inside and headed down the corridor toward the parlor. Charlene was playing the piano again and she had my serious-minded young brother singing some ridiculous ditty from the East. I could imagine Donovan lounged on the sofa enjoying the pretty picture Charlene made. I headed for the stairs.

"Kat," Donovan's voice startled me. I looked back and saw him coming out of the library. What was he doing in the library?

"We're having tea in the parlor in twenty minutes," he told me.

"So Hattie said. I hope you enjoy it, Donovan. Be sure to keep the pinky out slightly," I told him instructively, giving a mock demonstration.

"I'll remember that," he grinned.

I started up the stairs. "Oh, Kat," he half whispered and I glanced back at his grinning face and glittering eyes. "If you aren't down here in precisely fifteen minutes, I'll come up and drag you down. Got that?"

"And what would Charlene think of that?" I hissed down at him.

"Don't challenge me, Kat. I'm not in the mood for your sparring!"

"I just went through all this with Hattie, Donovan. Things will go much more smoothly for you if I *don't* come to the parlor."

"What're you doing, Kat? Relegating yourself to the level of a servant . . . or do you want the Bellows to wonder just what exactly your position is in this house that you have to sneak around corners and hide in the kitchen all day." His implication was clear enough. I stared down at him, furious.

"Fifteen minutes, Kat," Donovan said with a taunting smile as he turned and walked into the parlor.

I cleaned up and put on my mother's dress. Brushing my hair furiously, I wound it into a neat coil and jabbed pins in. Shoving my feet into my houseshoes, I went out the door. Did the Bellows seriously think that Donovan would have a mistress in residence when entertaining them? Of all the idiotic notions! I fumed.

Entering the parlor, I found Donovan just where I expected him to be, lounging on the sofa, laughing at something Charlene had just said. Jeremy was in attendance on her as well.

"Oh, Miss Durham," Charlene said in exaggerated surprise. "There you are. We haven't seen you all afternoon, but I expect you've been very busy doing . . . whatever it is you do."

"I was helping Hattie McFadden in the kitchen," I answered frankly, walking the rest of the way into the room and then suddenly not sure where I should sit.

"Paying for my room and board, as you will," I added for good measure. Donovan's mouth tightened and he gave me a warning glance.

"Oh, I'm sure Mace doesn't expect you to repay him for all he's done for you. How could you?"

Before I could retort to that, the Bellows came in behind Brian Donovan. He wheeled over to the windows and swung the chair around. He looked tired and bored. Harriet Bellows spotted me immediately, and her displeasure was obvious.

"The garden is absolutely marvelous," she enthused to Mace. "Immaculate."

"Kathryn keeps it up for us," Mace told her flatly, bringing Harriet's thick dark brows down again in disapproval.

Hattie came bustling in with the tea things on a trolley. She pushed it across the room and placed everything on the long table in front of the sofa. Charlene knew her duty. She elegantly poured while everyone watched and smiled over her perfection. The teacups were handed around, Jeremy delivering mine.

Donovan sipped his tea with aplomb and when he saw that I noticed, he wagged his little finger at me, eyes laughing. I couldn't prevent a smile. Harriet Bellows noticed everything and she was obviously drawing her own conclusions. So much for alleviating her suspicions, I thought ruefully.

Dinner was less strained than lunch had been, but several times the conversation lagged. Donovan seemed relaxed and not the least bit worried that others were searching for something to say, especially Charlene. Silence seemed to unnerve her.

It was close to eight that evening when I finally managed an escape. John Saunders was leaning against the pepper tree, waiting for me. He straightened as I came down the stairs.

"I didn't think you were going to come," he said, tak-

ing my hand and leading me away from the house toward the paddocks.

"Why wouldn't I?"

"I thought maybe Donovan might have said something to you," he shrugged.

"Donovan is mooning over Charlene Bellows," I told
him. He glanced at me.

"You don't sound too pleased about it."

I laughed slightly. "It doesn't have anything to do
with me."

"You still hate him? He saved your life . . . and
Jeremy's."

"Did you ask me out here to talk about Donovan?" I
asked lightly, wanting desperately to change the subject.
My spirits had already plunged into my shoes from
watching Donovan with Charlene. On the way back into
the parlor following dinner, she had wrapped her arm
through his and he had smiled down at her.

"No, I didn't invite you out here to talk about him,"
John drawled, grinning at me. "It's a full moon tonight.
Have you noticed?"

"They say it brings out the beast in people," I teased
back. He gave me a low, mocking growl, and I made my
fingers into a gun.

"Bang!"

We laughed together like two children.

"So what do you think about Tasajara?" he asked as
we walked along the fence, gazing out into the green
field where animals were exercised. I lifted my shoulders.

"It's not my home," I said quietly, looking out across
the stretch of green pastureland to the homestead. Since
coming to Tasajara, everything had become complicated, not the least of which were my emotions where
Donovan was concerned. Charlene had asked me how I
could repay him, and I had wondered about that myself.

If it hadn't been for him, my brother and I would be dead. But everything was so tangled up inside me. I didn't want to owe Donovan anything, especially not my life!

"All this doesn't make you wish things were different?" John asked.

"Different? How do you mean?"

"What would you do if suddenly you had a chance to live somewhere like this forever? So that it belonged to you? And you could have anything you wanted? And Jeremy, how would he feel about it?"

"Lord, what a question, John!" I laughed. "It doesn't matter anyway. It'd never happen."

"I'm speaking hypothetically . . ."

"Well, it wouldn't matter to me really. All I'd like is the money to pay off the mortgage and taxes. But Jeremy . . . that's a little more complicated."

"How so?" John asked, genuinely interested.

"Well, Jeremy hankers after an education. A real one, not the kind I can give him with mail-order textbooks. The kind you get in a big city where there's a university . . . and high tuitions." I sighed heavily. "I'd like nothing better than to be able to get that for him, but I'm afraid it's impossible. He'll have to face that soon enough."

"Too bad. He's a smart kid."

We walked on and John reached for my hand. I didn't take it back, allowing him to lace his fingers with mine.

"You're quite a woman, Kathryn Durham. I'm very proud of you."

I glanced at him in surprise. "What brought that on?"

He smiled down at me ruefully and shook his head. "I just needed to say it, that's all. I'd better get you back to the house."

We walked back slowly, saying little. John seemed very pensive. He stopped at the base of the steps, turning me toward him. He slid his hand up my arm and I drew back slightly, nervous without knowing exactly why. He smiled slightly, leaning forward to lightly brush my cheek with his lips. Then he walked off into the night.

As I walked up the steps, I heard Charlene's voice. Glancing up, I saw her standing with Donovan at the edge of the veranda facing outward over the front of the ranch. They could easily have been watching me with John.

"Mace?" Charlene said. "Did you hear what I just said?" she asked quietly.

I averted my face and continued up the steps, opening the door and stepping into the house. Every step I took I could feel Donovan's eyes searing the flesh on my back.

CHAPTER TWENTY-SIX

The Bellows left the following morning, cutting their visit a day short. No explanations were given, but the atmosphere was definitely cool. Harriet Bellows was frowning heavily. Jeremiah looked uneasy, and Charlene wore a perfect if somewhat strained smile. She reached up to kiss Mace on the cheek before they left and then climbed into the carriage to wave back to him.

Mace rode out somewhere for the rest of the day, leaving Jeremy to get underfoot until he was relegated to the library with Brian Donovan. I worked with Hattie in the kitchen all morning. During the afternoon, I totally engrossed myself in the flower garden.

That evening, Mace was quiet and morose over dinner. Hardly anyone spoke. Brian Donovan kept glancing at his son, watching him curiously. I asked to be excused before dessert and coffee, complaining of a headache. It was the truth. Lying on the bed upstairs, I stared into the canopy, trying not to think about Donovan and Charlene Bellows.

Hours later, I was still awake so I arose and went downstairs. It was a warm night and with everyone in bed asleep, I saw no reason to put on the heavy robe Hattie had loaned me. I made it all the way downstairs and into the corridor when I heard the door of the li-

brary open. Startled, I jerked back and hid behind the
grandfather clock just outside the parlor. Whoever had
started to come out changed their mind. They walked
back into the room without closing the door. I could
hear the rumble of voices. There was no way to go back
up the stairs without taking the chance of being seen.
And I was not exactly dressed for conversation with
anyone!

"Are you going to marry that Bellows girl?" Brian
Donovan asked his son. Guiltily, I strained to listen,
moving as close as I dared.

"She's built for children, and pretty enough, wouldn't
you say?" Mace drawled.

The elder Donovan snorted derisively. "But give her
another ten years and she'll be just like that harridan
mother of hers."

"Not with the right man she won't."

"And you plan to be that man, hmmm?" came the
wry comment. "Somehow I can't quite see the match."

"She'd be a hell of a lot easier to live with than some
women I know."

Brian Donovan chuckled. "Women? Or woman?
Kathryn Durham, you mean." My stomach muscles
contracted and I felt hot and cold all at the same time.

Mace mumbled some growling comment. I couldn't
hear it but knew well enough what it must be. I didn't
want to hear any more, but couldn't see any way to escape without some risk. After what I'd just heard, being
caught here would be the height of humiliation. They
might think I'd been eavesdropping deliberately.

"Well, hell sakes, Mace!" Brian exclaimed. "You
know what you've been after since day one. She's not
going to be here at Tasajara much longer. I'm surprised
she hasn't made a run for it already. You'd better get on
with your plans or you'll lose your chance completely."

My ears sharpened. What were they talking about?
What plans?

"It's not quite that simple, Dad," Mace said dryly.

"It damn well should be," his father answered flatly. "Things were a lot different in my day. When we saw something we wanted, we took it. That's the way things are. The strong win. It doesn't matter how they do it . . . short of murder. It's a fact of life, Mace. You know what you want, so take it. It'll all work out, believe me. I know it. I feel it."

A glass clinked down on a wooden surface. "What kind of hell are you prescribing for me? Or haven't you really gotten to know Kat Durham at all?"

"What kind of hell are you already in? I've watched you. I know you. Take the land. Why leave little Kathryn any choice at all? Or do you think she'll listen to what you're offering?"

Mace laughed slightly. "She hasn't listened so far."

"Then lay your trump card out. What can she do then?"

"You're forgetting John Saunders?"

"What can he do?"

"I've got a pretty damn good hunch what he'd like to do," Mace drawled harshly. "I don't like the son-of-a-bitch sniffing around Kat."

"Afraid he'll ruin everything, hmmmm?" Brian commented and then laughed low. "You'd better do something fast then if you don't want him to take it all."

The voices dropped again and I leaned heavily against the wall, feeling sick. So Mace Donovan really did want the homestead after all.

Closing my eyes, I thought about how deeply betrayed I felt. Somehow, somewhere along the line, I had stopped believing Mace wanted to take anything from me. I had begun to trust him, to believe everything he repeatedly said.

The library door opened wider and I flattened myself back further against the wall alongside the clock. It suddenly struck two, almost making me faint in shock.

The sound of Mister Donovan's wheelchair came into the corridor.

"If you're smart, you'll take my advice," Brian Donovan said. And I had liked him!

"And if things don't go the way I want, my life won't be worth living," Mace said, apparently right behind his father, probably pushing the chair toward the back of the house to his father's large rooms off the garden.

"Things will work out. I know it. From where I sit, it looks so damn easy. If I were your age again," he sighed expressively and then laughed low. "You know what you want. Take it. Use every weapon you've got."

There was silence for a moment. The wheels of the chair squeaked down the hall.

"There's one thing I can think of that you haven't tried yet," Brian Donovan said.

Mace laughed low. "I've thought about it," he said dryly.

Brian Donovan laughed. "I'll just bet you've thought about it. So what's stopping you? If it helps any, you've got my blessing. Use any means you have to to get what you want. Any means."

"At what price later?"

"I think you might be surprised on that score."

"I'll tell Kat Durham that," Mace said without humor. "It'll make all the difference."

The wheelchair continued down the corridor. I didn't move for a long time. Mace finally came back and went up the stairs slowly.

I was shaking badly. I needed to sit down and collect my turbulent thoughts. I went around the clock and into the parlor, throwing myself onto the sofa. Moonlight filtered in through the windows, giving the room an eerie glow. I felt beaten and miserable, and angry. All this time wasted, sitting here on Tasajara, when I should have been working. Had Donovan ever intended to dig another well, or had he deliberately held off, knowing what it would mean to me when the garden died and I lost my last means of making money to pay the mortgage and taxes?

You fool! I told myself fiercely, tears burning, throat aching. You utter idiot!

So deep was I in thought, that I didn't even see Donovan until he was all the way into the parlor. He stopped by the table with the decanters, reaching for one. Then he saw me. He froze, staring at me, his eyes glittering in the semidarkness.

"What're you doing in here?" he demanded.

I didn't answer him. I sat in silence, feeling all the old animosity stirring up inside me, swirling higher and higher until it grew to greater proportions than it had reached the day I first laid eyes on Mace Donovan. He must have felt it crackling in the room.

"How long have you been down here?"

I drew in air slowly before I answered in a low, cold voice. "Long enough to know that every blessed word you've ever uttered to me about the homestead has been a goddamn bloody lie!"

"Eavesdropping, Kat?" he mocked unpleasantly, pouring himself a drink and downing it before he continued. "It's obvious you didn't hear the whole conversation. Why didn't you come into the library and get everything straight?"

"I wonder if everything was a coincidence after all," I said incitingly. He slammed the glass down.

"What're you talking about?" His voice was strained, angry.

"The broken fence, my stampeded garden, the burned barn, the fouled well . . ." I cataloged, baiting him further. I didn't believe he could have done anything to harm us physically, but he *was* perched in waiting to buy up the mortgage. That much was clear enough from the conversation I had overheard.

Donovan moved slowly forward. I felt a tremor of fright travel up my spine at the look in his gold eyes. I had seen him angry before, but never like this. I stood up shakily and stumbled back against the sofa. He came slowly toward me.

"You stay away from me, Donovan!" I told him, eyes widening.

"If you'd hit me with this tomorrow, after some sleep, I might have been able to answer you . . . reasonably," he sneered. "But you've pushed me too far this time . . . and at the wrong time." He came closer and I darted around the back of the sofa.

"It's time you learned a few elemental things about me," he growled.

"I think I know more than enough already," I flung at him and then ran for the door to the veranda. I heard him coming after me and for one terrifying moment I was afraid I wasn't going to get the door open fast enough. Gasping in fright, I nearly flung the door off its hinges and plunged into the night. I raced along the veranda and almost fell headlong down the front stairs. Ducking to the right beneath the pepper tree, I ran back around the side of the house.

My first thought, irrational though it later proved, spurred me toward the barns where Dionysus was stabled. If I could get to him, I could ride home, get away from Donovan. I ran across the yard, my loose hair flying back across my face, my gown whipping against me. The rocks cut into my feet and I tripped, barely catching myself as I scrambled up the path. The stables loomed ahead in the moonlit night, stark and silent against the background of the mountains.

Opening the door, I swung it back behind me and entered the darkness. Moving forward more slowly, I tried to adjust my eyes to the blackness, feeling my way along the stalls. I needed a lantern, but didn't know where to find one. I couldn't remember which stall housed my horse.

Moving further into the stable, I could hear the nervous shuffling of hooves and the soft whinny of a horse nearby. There was a sharp sound behind me and I turned in time to see the door swing shut. I heard a bar drop. I froze and then started to run toward the other end as I realized I was trapped. That door swung open, halting me in my tracks, and Donovan stood there.

A match struck and I saw Donovan's hard face as he held a lantern. He lit it casually, shaking out the match. Then he began to walk slowly toward me.

I stood frozen, staring at him, my breath coming in frightened gasps. He smiled slowly though his eyes were still cold and angry.

"I couldn't have picked a better place to mete out your punishment, Kat," he said advancing steadily toward me. "It's going to give me the greatest pleasure to give it to you."

I backed away, turning to look behind me for some means of escape. With the other door barred, there were only a few windows and they were latched. The fear aroused my ever incautious fury.

"And to think my father trusted you, called you a friend!" I railed at him. "The minute he's dead and buried, you're plotting to take our land away from us!"

"You never know when to shut up, do you?" he grated, still advancing. I looked around frantically again, and then spied a glint of steel in a vacant stall. Looking back at Donovan, I recognized the look in his eyes. It wasn't a beating that he intended to give me. There was a frighteningly sensual purpose in those glinting gold eyes and I remembered too late his warning in the upstairs bedroom the night I had almost fallen out the window.

"One of these days that wide-eyed, frightened virgin look isn't going to help you one damn bit!" The words came back in all their force. I started to tremble.

"I'll see you dead and in hell before you ever touch me, Donovan," I managed, my heart beating a hard staccato beat. I backed deliberately into the stall, my hand behind me.

Donovan laughed low. "That's not a good place to hide, Kat," he mocked. My hand jerked out and closed on the pitchfork. I swung it up and aimed the deadly points at his chest. He laughed again, hooking the lantern on the front frame of the stall.

"So now you're going to try to skewer me."

"If you come one step closer, I will," I threatened, my voice wobbling nervously.

"Come on, then, Kat," he drawled, stepping forward. "This is your last chance to even the score you think you have!" He spread his arms wide, stepping forward yet again to make an open target of himself. I stared at him, unable to move. He looked back at me for another second and then, with a suddenness that caught me unprepared, he moved. I tried to follow through with the fork, but he sidestepped it, gripping the handle and yanking it from my nerveless fingers.

I tried to twist past him and almost succeeded except that he managed to grab my hair, pulling me backwards. I flattened with a thud against the end of the stall, eyes wide, scalp stinging. Donovan flung the fork out into the walkway and closed the stall door, latching it securely.

Then he stood there, hands on hips. "Where's all that courage and defiance now, hmmmm?" he asked sardonically, moving forward slowly. I moved to the side, shaking visibly now and unable to stop it. "There's nothing but fluff and hiss to you," he taunted. "At the first hint of real danger, you panic . . . like you're panicking now." He followed my movement toward the side of the stall, sending me scurrying toward the opposite end.

"If you touch me, I'll kill you. I swear I will!" I said, the threat sounding meaningless and weak.

"Touch you?" He raised his brows slightly. "I warned you about pushing me, Kat. Do you remember? Well, you had your warning and you didn't listen. I'm going to do a lot more than just touch you this time. You've got this coming to you. And I'm going to give you everything you deserve."

He stripped off his shirt and tossed it onto the hay in an angry motion. His hands went to his belt buckle, and I watched, stunned, as he shed his clothes.

"No . . ." I whispered, my lip trembling.

"Did you think I'd take your insults and accusations indefinitely? Did you really think I'd never retaliate? I've put up with your verbal harangue since the first day I met you. You've torn at my guts with your vicious little claws, and by God, it's time you paid your due for the pain you've caused me every day you've been on this ranch and in my house!"

Anger rose, giving me some small defense to stand on. "Pain *I've* caused you, you miserable bastard! When you've been planning all along to take our home away from us!"

"That's the last time you'll ever say that to me!" He bolted forward. I ducked and darted to one side, but his fingers caught the back of my gown, ripping it. I turned and swung at him but he dodged me. His hand curved around my waist, hauling me backwards as he pried my fingers from the stall doorlatch.

"Let me go!" I gasped tearfully, kicking and scratching, striking blows anywhere I could. I could hear the horses in the side stalls pacing nervously at the commotion and hoped someone would come to in-

vestigate. And if they did, what could they do? This was
Mace Donovan! This was Tasajara!

I twisted my body sharply, swinging hard again, and
succeeded in striking him hard and full across the face.
Momentarily stunned, he released me. I stumbled back
without his support and fell against the back wall. Pulling myself up, I tried to hurl myself past him to reach the
door again.

The gold eyes were alive with fury. "Not this time!"
he said through his teeth, the mark of my hand clear on
his face. He caught my hair again and twisted it brutally
around his hand. I cried out, trying to claw my way free.
He entrapped my hands behind me, drawing me relentlessly against him. Then he forced me backward, his
body lowering over mine.

"I could wring your damn neck!" he breathed, all
control gone. He pinioned my body beneath his
crushing weight, shoving my hands under me with one
strong hand while the other forced my chin up. His
mouth came down on mine, hard and punishing. I tried
to pull away and the pressure increased. Tears streamed
down my face into my hair as I tried desperately to twist,
roll, buck free. There was no escape and finally I lay
still, exhausted and feeling faint from his brutal,
smothering kiss.

Mace raised his head then and glared down at me.
"You've had that coming. How far did you think you
could go with me?" he demanded harshly. My breath
came in rasping sobs of panic.

For a long moment, Mace remained above me, staring down into my terrified face.

"Oh, Kat," he sighed, lowering his head again, holding my face still when I would have turned away. His
mouth was gentle this time, his tongue lightly caressing
my bruised lips. The pressure increased slowly,
persuasively, and I knew then why I had never wanted

Mace Donovan to touch me like this. I moaned, trying desperately to struggle free and evade the insidious feelings tingling through me, but he stretched his length on top of me. Heat began to spread from a central point in my body through my limbs as I felt every hard angle of his body.

"God, you feel good," he murmured huskily. "But I told you that once before, didn't I?" he said, kissing me again. Mace used more than his mouth in his war on my senses. His body moved over mine, the pressure of his hips increasing against me while he held his weight away slightly from my breasts. He rubbed against me while nuzzling my neck, returning again and again to possess my mouth.

"Don't . . ." I groaned.

"Don't you like it?" he asked throatily, laughing slightly before kissing me into silence. Shifting his weight to one side, his hands began a slow, exquisitely sensual exploration through my thin nightgown, making my skin hot and trembling. My breasts swelled and my nipples hardened against his palm. When he kissed me again, my lips parted naturally and he hungrily devoured the soft moist interior of my mouth. He was no longer restraining me, and my arms entwined around his neck of their own accord, drawing him even closer as I arched my body against him. I could feel the growing tension in his body, the explosive pressure hardening him, and my own empty, naked longing.

Groaning, Mace dragged his mouth from mine and rolled away. His breathing was ragged. Uncaring of his nudity, he stood up, making no attempt to hide the fact that he was fully aroused. Shamefully, I couldn't look away. My eyes moved over his body, loving it, wanting it, craving it. He reached down, grabbing up his pants, his face rigid.

"Mace . . ." I whispered, confused and frightened,

aching inside. I didn't realize how eloquent my voice was in that instant. And I had never willingly called him Mace before. He stopped, but he did not look at me. I could see him trembling, his knuckles white.

"Mace . . . ?"

"Shut up!" he said savagely, casting a furious glance at me and then looking abruptly away again.

So this was what he had meant by giving me exactly what I deserved. Rejection. The most humiliating, degrading, aching rejection he could have planned. My eyes filled with tears and I put a hand to my mouth to stifle the sob.

His breathing hadn't eased and he knelt down, bending at the waist, holding his head in his hands. I heard a harsh sound from his chest and his eyes were tightly closed as though he were in some kind of agony.

My body shook with silent, painful sobs and I felt sick. After a moment, Mace opened his eyes slowly and turned his head to look at me. The front of my nightgown had been torn open and the hem had ridden up around my thighs. His eyes seemed to burn over me as they moved upward past my hips and breasts to stop on my agonized, tear-streaked face. Muscles tightened and then worked in his jaw.

"Don't, Kat," he groaned. "For God's sake, don't cry . . . not now."

I closed my eyes tightly, feeling I would suffocate with the pain in my chest. My body ached with longing and frustration. I wanted to die of humiliation.

I heard the rustle of hay as Mace moved back beside me, close enough to feel the warmth of his body but not so close as to touch.

"Kat . . ." he whispered, still not touching me. "You just don't understand . . ."

I opened my eyes and he reached out to push my hand away from my mouth. He kissed me tenderly, our lips the only parts of our bodies touching, and I moaned, rolling onto my side to arch against him. He shuddered and the gentle caress deepened. His fingers shook as they plowed into my hair, tilting my face up as he drew back to look at me again. His eyes were almost black.

"Kat . . ."

"Mace, please . . ."

He sucked in a breath of air through his teeth. "Damn you," he groaned, kissing me again and again, opening my mouth with his thrusting tongue to an intimacy and passion I had not dreamed possible. His mouth moved away finally to trail hotly across my cheek to my ear.

"It's gone too far . . . too far," he groaned and moved my body beneath his. He kissed me hungrily melting any resistance I might have had. There was none, instinct having long ago taken over. My hands roved down his back, kneading his hard, smooth flesh. I could feel the muscles tighten and there was a moment of pain, sharp and frightening as he entered me. He held my face, kissing me over and over, slowly, druggingly, until I was totally unaware of the pain and a whirlwind of uncontrollable sensations took over.

"No, Kat," he moaned against my hair. "Don't move yet." His fingers were rough as he held my face for his deep kiss. "Don't move. I won't be able to hold back . . ."

But I couldn't obey. My body moved against his instinctively, drawing the response from him against his will. When it was over for him, I was still aching inside. He didn't release me, nor move away. He kissed me again and again, his breathing growing more uneven.

"Again . . . now . . ." he told me, kissing my swollen, responsive mouth. He prolonged my pleasure, carrying me to a high peak and then restraining me before drawing me up yet again. My fingers tangled in his vibrant hair, pulling him closer.

What my body and mind had denied me the first time, was relinquished now and a flood of feeling drowned me. "Mace . . . oh . . . Mace . . ." I cried out.

For a long time afterward neither of us spoke. Mace didn't release me completely. His hand slowly moved over me, stroking, exploring, lightly tracing every hill and valley of my body. The heat of our bodies warded off the night coolness.

Mace sighed heavily. "I only meant to scare some sense into you. I didn't intend to carry it quite so far." There was faint mockery in his voice, still husky and warm from our lovemaking. His lips moved against my hair, moving down to lightly nip my earlobe. Even now, languid, his touch could arouse me.

"I've wanted you for a long, long time," he whispered, nuzzling my neck, running his tongue along a sensitive spot. "You taste good, too."

A picture arose in my head of the woman at the hotel in town and the way Donovan had kissed her. Then I thought of Charlene and how he had wanted everything to go so perfectly. I closed my burning eyes tightly.

"You got what you wanted, Donovan."

His hand stopped moving and he raised himself up on one elbow to look down at my stricken face. "And didn't you?" he demanded ruthlessly.

I pressed a shaking hand over my eyes to block out his face. How could I have let this happen? He grabbed my wrist and forced it back against the hay. "Well, didn't you?"

I stared up at him miserably. He frowned, eyes moving slowly over my face, trying to read it. "Kat, stop beating yourself. You're a woman. At least now you know it. I never made a move toward this before because I was afraid it was too soon. Hell! It would have saved a lot of time and frustration on my part at least if I hadn't held off."

What was he saying? Did he think he could add me to that woman he had in town and then marry his perfect Charlene as well? It hurt unbearably.

"Droit du seigneur?" I managed, referring to an ancient custom of the old world whereby a landowner had the legal right to take any virgin he wanted.

Mace froze. His eyes widened and then chilled. He stared at me and I felt driven once again to say more.

"Now that you've taken what you wanted, Donovan, I think it's fair to say that all my debts to you are paid in full," I said shaking.

He stood up in one lithe motion and then stopped to grab his pants. Then his belt. Every movement jerky with anger. He snatched up his shirt, not bothering to put it on. With a violent swipe of his hand, he unlatched the stall door and kicked it open.

Turning, he glared down at me. "We're not through yet, Kat."

"You probably will get the homestead just the way you said," I said, sitting up. "By buying it out from under Jeremy and me when taxes fall due. But you're never, ever, going to get me again, Donovan. Never."

He just stared down at me, a muscle jerking in his jaw. Then he walked out of the stables, swinging the door shut. It reverberated.

I lay in the stall crying for hours. Then I returned to the darkened ranch house, tiptoeing up the stairs to Jeremy's room. There was light beneath Mace's bedroom door and I was afraid if he heard me he would try to stop me. He didn't.

Jeremy and I were back at the homestead by dawn. We would have to search out John Saunders to cut Constance and Don Juan out of Donovan's herd, and to return my mother's trunk.

The new well had already been dug. Touching the brick and mortar, I realized it must have been completed some time before. There was even new grass on the mound of dirt from the digging. Looking toward the side of the house, I saw that someone had been tending the garden.

I had never been more confused in my life.

CHAPTER TWENTY-SEVEN

After returning to the homestead, I did not allow myself time to think about Mace Donovan or what had happened between us in the stables. Only at night when I fell into bed exhausted from the day's labors did thoughts of him betray my resolve. Sleep was a traitor, dredging up all those ecstatic moments in his arms, the times of warmth and closeness, the feel of his presence. But during the day, I paid dearly for what I had done. Paid in shame and guilt.

Mace's last words echoed in my mind. I was filled with a miserable confusion and dread that grew worse as the days passed. I almost wished he would come. "We're not through yet, Kat!" he had threatened. And I knew what he had meant. Soon there would be nothing left, not even this modest piece of land that was my home.

There would soon be produce to take to town, for someone had seen to watering the garden during Jeremy's and my absence. I was afraid of what I would learn in town, sure each time I went that someone would say that Mace Donovan's engagement to Charlene Bellows had been officially announced. I knew that he could never love me, that he must now hold me in the worst kind of contempt for what I had allowed to happened. But the mere thought of him with another wom-

317

an, doing the things he had done with me, gnawed constantly at my brain.

John Saunders returned Constance and a stronger Don Juan. Jeremy had ridden the mare and I Dionysus, back from Tasajara. Both were now in our small corral eating our own forage rather than Tasajara feed. The day after we left, another cowhand was sent over with my mother's trunk. Everything seemed back to normal, teetering on the same state of financial ruin that we had always known.

Knowing something of the rumors in Madrone started by Les Bigelow, and expounded even more so now by Harriet Bellows, I dreaded my days there. The snide comments and speculative glances wore at my already lowered self-esteem, adding to my nightmarish nights. Worse, my sales had gone down. Iverson agreed to buy the bulk of it each morning for his store after I almost begged him to do so, and I left town immediately afterward, seeing fewer people each time I went. Jeremy still rode to Tasajara to see Mace and Brian Donovan and I felt more and more isolated.

Charles Lambert stopped me early one morning and reminded me that another mortgage payment would be due at the end of the month. So would taxes. The sum was staggering and might as well have been a million dollars. We did not have it, and had no prospects of raising it. Lambert knew by the look on my face that things had gone from bad to worse.

After finishing my work at the end of the day, I took to wandering the hills and thinking of Papa when I was not thinking of Donovan. The good memories flooded me and made my longing for my father's company worse. Would I ever know who had murdered him and why? I knew if Sheriff Collins was not able to find Papa's killer, I would never be at peace. When my dreams were not filled with Mace Donovan, they were of Papa dying on the ridge or of people throwing stones at me in town.

During the daylight hours, I worked until my back ached and my eyes blurred with exhaustion. It seemed the only way to fight off the emotional agony that assailed me. Jeremy watched me silently, knowing something was very wrong but not knowing how to help. Each time he attempted to talk to me about it, I brushed away his questions with evasive answers and changed the subject. He took to riding to Tasajara every chance he had, staying there for hours. During the evenings, he buried himself in his books, never raising his head or speaking until it was time to go to bed.

And the loneliness closed in around me.

Finally, when the deadline drew within days, I used my last resort and wired our Virginia relatives. Explaining the situation as briefly as possible, I asked their immediate assistance.

John Saunders rode by on occasion and he was the only brightness in my life. He always brought some news of Mace. Charlene and her parents had been back out to Tasajara, this time for two days and nights. Donovan had been into Madrone half a dozen times and each time had been seen with Charlene Bellows. It was only a matter of time before they announced their betrothal.

I tried not to let it hurt. But it only seemed to emphasize how stupid I had been, how Donovan had used me to ease his own physical needs while meting out what punishment he thought I deserved.

No man would want me now, sullied as I was by another. But no other man would ever be able to match Mace Donovan either. I remembered what Hattie McFadden had said about Donovan being the only man west of the Rockies for me. And it was the depressing truth.

No answer came to my cable and the homestead was

posted for public auction. There was nothing I could do and I stayed away from town. I knew exactly what the outcome would be. All that morning, I stayed in the cabin laying out all our belongings and packing them in separate piles.

Early in the afternoon, I heard a rider approaching. I was still sorting through things, setting aside what could be sold. If we could sell enough, we might find lodgings in town until I could find work. Jeremy could go to public school. He would like that very much. At least, something good would come from all this misery and my ultimate failure in holding onto Papa's land.

Pushing my wayward hair back from my temples and wiping the nervous perspiration off my hands, I went to the door and opened it. Mace Donovan was dismounting and I felt a hard lump form quietly in my throat.

Jeremy had seen him and was running across the spread from the corral to meet him, a welcoming grin splitting his elfish face. He chattered excitedly, seemingly unaware of the fate that had just befallen us. Or perhaps he just didn't care what it meant to me.

Deep inside, I had always known Mace Donovan would win, but it still hurt intolerably. After the first hasty glance at me since getting off his restless stallion, he didn't look at me again. I was no better in his eyes now than his Marcela Juarez. Good for a roll in the hay, but nothing else. Perhaps worse, for I had been reared differently.

My fingers clutched convulsively at my skirt. I knew why he was here, of course. I had known all along that he would come.

Donovan seemed in no hurry to end his conversation with my brother and after a few seconds I turned away, feeling the warning sting of hot tears. I went back into the sod cabin, looking around bleakly at the now bare walls and feeling an ache inside that threatened to consume me. I mentally walled myself in, breathing slowly and deeply, dulling my thoughts to blankness. Then I set back to work sorting our possessions.

The door opened a few minutes later. I did not look up, but kept on with my work.

"You knew I'd buy the homestead, didn't you?" he said bluntly. It was not really a question, more an accusation voice half in anger. My shoulders stiffened instinctively as I heard his footsteps moving closer.

"What's all this?" He reached down to finger my mother's silk wedding gown. Something twisted sharply inside me as I saw that strong brown hand touching the delicate white silk.

"We're selling that," I said quietly without looking up. I laid aside an embroidered pillow case that matched some sheets. Mama had been an artist with the needle. She had carefully packed these away for me to use someday, and now the set would fetch us a good price. Perhaps Charlene would even buy it for her hope chest and use it at Tasajara.

"Sit down," Donovan said hoarsely. "We've some talking to do." His order was terse.

I put my hands flat on the pile of things we were to sell and shook my head. "You've bought our land. There's nothing more to be said. We'll be packed and off in a day, unless you want it sooner."

Fingers curled cruelly around my arm and jerked me around. Mace shoved me roughly toward the table and chairs.

"Sit down before I really lose my temper," he growled harshly. There were deep-etched lines about his eyes and mouth that I had never noticed before. But the glittering gold anger I was familiar with was there and my eyes fell away from his. I remembered the last time I had seen him and a stain of humiliation and shame filled my cheeks. I bent my head so he wouldn't see, but it was too late. Everything I felt had been in my wide, swimming eyes.

Once seated, Mace had difficulty saying what he wanted too. His hands clenched and unclenched at his side. I wondered what was bothering him. Didn't he have everything he wanted now?

"The last piece in the valley! Think of it, Mace. It's right in the palm of your hand. Take it." And he certainly had. After he had taken me as well. There was nothing left now. Nothing.

Except my brother—my love for him and my responsibility to him.

"It's been a month . . ." Donovan said and then stopped, muttering a sound of self-contempt. He sat down, putting his hands out flat on the table and looked at me. I gazed at those hands, remembering how they had caressed my body, made me ache and yield, and how I had then become demanding myself under their guidance. I shut my eyes, trying not to think of all that now.

"Kat, there's no need for you and Jeremy to leave," he said quietly. "I don't need or want this place. You can stay as long as you like."

I looked up at him, eyes wide and filled with pain, and then back down again quickly to avoid those all-too-piercing golden eyes.

"We don't need your charity. You've no need . . ."

He cut me off. "Work the land and pay me a percentage at the end of each year!"

I had to smile at that. "You know very well there's never been anything left at the end of the year, just more debts. You might as well pull down the fences and add the last piece to your Tasajara. It's all yours now, Donovan. The whole valley."

"This isn't the time to be stubborn or proud, Kat," he said holding his temper. "Where do you intend to go?"

A resurgence of pride brought my head up. "Why should you care or be interested? You took the land legally. You needn't feel any guilt or . . ."

"I don't feel guilty!" he snapped, straightening. He scraped the chair back and walked away, raking a hand through his hair. Then he swung back again. The lines seemed to have deepened about his mouth and eyes.

"It's been just over a month," he began again. Was he trying to make everything worse, reminding me once more of what had happened to us in the stables at Tasajara? He rubbed the back of his neck.

"You know what I'm trying to find out, damn it," he said in frustration. I looked up at him in bewilderment and he stared at my face searchingly, frowning.

"God, you look so pale," he muttered. "Are you feeling all right?" he asked in an oddly tense voice. "Jeremy said you've . . ." He shook his head.

"I'm fine," I said expressionlessly, looking away because it was too hurtful to look at him and to remember. Why should he be concerned about how I felt? How did he expect me to feel?

Mace sat down again watching me intently. "A month is enough time to know," he said in a low, intimate voice.

I stared at him blankly, uncomprehending. "Know what?"

"You can't be that naive! Didn't your father ever . . . oh, hell!" he growled. He took a deep breath. "Kat, are you pregnant?"

All the color drained from my face until I felt about to faint. I stared at him for a stunned second and then a sob died brutally in my chest. My limbs were fired with action before my brain could think. I was out the door and running before Mace had a chance to react. I did not even know where I was going until I found myself in the shaded redwood grove where my father and mother lay buried side by side. I turned away, hugging the hard bark of an ancient redwood, pressing my tear-stained face against it as though to find some comfort there.

Mace's voice came from behind me.

"Does that mean yes or no?" he demanded, relentless as ever.

I didn't know! But how could I tell him that? Why did he want to know anyway? Just for the sake of his damn male pride? Or was he afraid of what such an event might do to Charlene Bellows and her parents?

"This is of vital importance to me," he had told me that day in the library. There had been a plea in his eyes that day, a silent plea that I not spoil this for him.

My silence seemed to goad him into violence. Brutally, he pulled me around to face him, uncaring that the bark had scratched the tender skin of my inner arms. I cried out in pain and protest, and he shook me.

"Damn you, Kat! I want an answer!"

I knew why he was so worried, so distraught. It was for Charlene Bellows! If I were carrying his bastard, she would be hurt. She might possibly refuse to marry him. Charlene was a *nice* girl, while I had simply been convenient. All those vicious lies in town about me and Donovan would be proven true if I suddenly found myself with child. Mace Donovan didn't care about me, not in any way that counted.

"You needn't concern yourself, Donovan," I said with quiet, bitter hurt. My neck ached from the jolting he had given me and I tried to pry his fingers loose from my upper arms.

"If I gave you a baby that night in the stables, it damn well does concern me!" he declared through his teeth.

"There's no baby."

His eyes narrowed disbelievingly on my face. "When did you last bleed?" he asked frankly and my pale face turned bright red. How could he know such private things about a woman or speak of them aloud!?

"A . . . a week ago," I lied. He shook me again, violently.

"When? Or have you?" he repeated. "I'm not going to let go or leave until I'm sure you're not lying to me!"

I knew he meant it and was driven by the devil to answer. "I haven't been regular in my cycle since my father was murdered. Does that satisfy your disgusting curiosity? Maybe I can't conceive! That would be even better for you, wouldn't it? No embarrassments for you! No little Donovan bastards running around loose to be explained away." I tried to pull free again and failed as his fingers tightened painfully. Speaking slowly, I stared up at him. "Rest easy, Donovan. If I do find myself in a family way, I'll kill myself so you won't have to . . ."

I fell backwards, slamming against the tree. My hand pressed against my stinging cheek. His face was white and strained but his eyes were terrifying.

"I hate you," I said, my voice devoid of emotion. I felt dead inside. The only thing I did feel at all was my burning face where he had slapped me.

"It wasn't hatred that softened your voice and made you cry out for me that night in the stables! I remember trying to stop things before they got out of control. But you? God, you were asking me, begging me for it. And I gave it to you."

His words were worse than any physical abuse he could do me. "I hate you now, Donovan." My voice was barely above a whisper and I couldn't prevent the flooding tears burning my throat and eyes.

"No doubt you'll try to hate me. What other defense have you left?" he said hoarsely.

I felt my chin grasped and jerked upward. My eyes opened wide and frightened.

"But let's just prove something, shall we?" The gold eyes glittered with determination. I remembered that look and tried to break free.

"No!"

His mouth descended to take mine, forcing my lips apart ruthlessly to plunder the softness within. It was force of will alone that kept me from melting against his hard-muscled body. But when the kiss continued, more demanding still, sapping my resolve, my fingers clutched at the smooth, soft leather of his vest and finally slid around his waist, spreading over his back, pressing myself closer. He moved his legs apart, drawing me closer, crushing me against him.

I sensed the exact instant he lost control. His hands trembled as they cupped my breasts, moving downward to arch my hips against his.

"Oh, Kat," he breathed and there was an age-old question in it. He started to draw me down, his fingers loosening the buttons of my bodice. "Give in to me. Give in . . ."

"Katie!" Jeremy called from just beyond the grove, his voice worried. "Katie, where are you?"

Mace's body tensed and stilled. He dragged his mouth away and my head sagged against his chest, where I could feel the hard, rapid pounding of his heart. It gave me some small bit of satisfaction to know that I aroused him as much as he did me.

"Katie!"

Mace groaned, holding me tighter, and I could feel the hard frustration in him. "Not now, Jeremy . . ." he whispered against my hair. "Go somewhere else for a while . . ."

Just long enough for Donovan to relieve his need with me, I thought miserably. "Let me go . . ." I choked, fighting myself as much as him. His fingers tightened convulsively, trying to keep me against him and a shudder racked me.

"Let me go . . ." I whimpered. Mace looked down at

me wordlessly. I couldn't hold his gaze and turned away as soon as he released me. After a moment, he strode from the grove. I heard him talking to Jeremy.

Then Donovan rode away.

Trembling violently, I sank to my knees beside Mama's grave and cried. My hands spread over the cool earth, pressing my cheek against the mound.

"God, make him stay away. Please, make him just leave me in peace," I prayed fervently.

Then I went back to the cabin. It wouldn't matter if Donovan did come back. We would be gone by tomorrow morning.

CHAPTER TWENTY-EIGHT

The next morning, I packed all our things into the cart. The furniture would have to stay behind. There was no room for it and it would not be worth selling anyway. I awakened Jeremy at dawn and we started out for Madrone. He protested all the way, sitting glumly in the cart as I went from one place to another selling our most cherished and valuable belongings.

The Jacobsons agreed to purchase all the linen and figurines my mother had brought from Richmond. They even bought some of Papa's classics. The few pieces of jewelry which had also belonged to our mother I sold to the milliner, Mrs. Perkins. My father's prize rifle fetched the most money, from the gunsmith. He admired the glistening sheen of wood and perfection of balance. He complimented me on the care of the weapon and handed over a few dollars more than I had been asking.

All told, combined with what we already had, there was almost enough for the mortgage payment and taxes. But it was too late to think of that now. The homestead was gone and there would have been another mortgage payment in a few months anyway.

Money in hand, I went to the first local boarding house. After two houseladies told me they were full up,

I began to understand the closed expressions I had received all day. Les Bigelow might have been precipitate in his claims about my relationship with Mace Donovan, but I could hardly deny now that Mace had had his way with me and with my fullest cooperation. My reputation was ruined and no decent boardinghouse intended to take me in.

There was only one other place in town that had lodgings. The hotel at the edge of town. The hotel where Marcela Juarez worked along with four or five other women of varying ages. With no other prospects in town, there was no choice but to go there and ask if they had a room available for Jeremy and me. Residing in the same building as Marcela Juarez and her friends did not have to make me one of them.

My feet dragged as I walked down the street, staring at the garish edifice of the hotel. A big sign in front with block letters announced "Madrone Hotel and Saloon." A small sign in the window said "Entertainment Nightly."

The place was almost empty, it being morning. I went up the steps and into the dim interior, looking around with curiosity at the red-velvet wallpaper and gilt mirrors.

The clerk at the desk was working on some papers and did not look up until I was standing right in front of him. His eyes widened in surprise.

"Ma'am?" he stammered.

"I'd like to speak with the proprietor, please," I said. Looking around further, I cringed. But other than this place, I could only move my brother and myself under the bridge with Milan Davis, the vagabond.

The clerk seemed about to say something and then decided against it. He left his desk for a few minutes and then returned.

"Mr. MacMillan will see you, ma'am."

I followed him along the hall and entered an opulent office when he stepped aside. A man in his late forties was sitting behind a big desk. He had dark hair, gray at the temples, and dark eyes. His gaze was indolent and all-encompassing. I looked at him coldly.

"You're Roger Durham's daughter, aren't you?"

"Yes."

"What're you doing here? Your father must be turning in his grave." He pushed his dark coat aside, reaching in his inner pocket to take out a cheroot. Striking a match with his thumbnail, he set the flame to his smoke. He drew hard and as he exhaled, there was a wry twist to his full mouth. I did not trust or like Foster Mac-Millan.

As quickly as possible, I explained Jeremy's and my plight.

"So Mace Donovan took over your homestead," he said with a smile. "I didn't think he was the kind of gent to push off tenants."

"He isn't throwing us off. He said we could stay, but we don't want his charity. The sooner we leave and find lodgings, the sooner he can tear down the fences and run his cattle in."

"And you want to live here?" he said, his eyes flickering over me.

"Every other place in town is full."

MacMillan raised his dark brows a fraction. "You believe that?" I flushed.

"I haven't much choice but to believe it, have I?"

"Is it true what they say?" he asked bluntly. "About you and Mace Donovan?"

"No." Guilty color darkened my cheeks and Mac-Millan smiled slightly. Then he laughed low, standing up and coming around in front of his desk. He sat down, hitching one leg over the corner.

"So you played for high stakes and lost. Well, I'd better warn you. I'm not running a charitable institution here either, Miss Durham," he said and stated the price he wanted for a room. It was high.

"I have enough to pay for a month, plus meals," I decided, my voice flat. "By then I should have work."

"You're optimistic. The only jobs open now are for cowhands. And somehow," his eyes roved down over me again and back up slowly, "I don't think you're suited to that kind of work."

"You've nothing here?"

He laughed again. "There's always something, but I don't think you're right for that either . . . yet."

"I can cook and clean. And my father taught me to cipher."

MacMillan rubbed his chin. "Would you consider serving drinks in the bar?"

"Don't you have anything else?" I asked hopefully. The thought of working in a saloon was devastating.

"It's that or nothing," he said and there was a sparkle of malicious amusement in his eyes.

I had already asked all over town for work and found nothing. Madrone had had several bad years and I was not the only person in need. Worse, I had less experience and strength to offer than a man.

"Well?" MacMillan pressed.

I could work here long enough to save money for Jeremy and I to return to Virginia, providing our relatives took us in. We would be charity cases there, but at least it would be within the family. What did it matter if I worked in a saloon until that time? Where else could I work?

"I'll do it," I answered.

"I'm sure you'll find it not unpleasant, and all the pretty girls get tips. I bet you'll be making fifty dollars a month."

My eyes widened at the possibility and he laughed.

"Don't look so surprised. There's money in sin, little girl . . . and the worse you get . . . and the more you're willing to give, the more you'll make. Think about it! Someone with your looks wouldn't have to work long to put away enough . . ."

"I don't plan to do more than serve drinks, Mr. Mac-Millan," I said, hoping my position was clear.

He grinned. "We'll make sure they understand your duties are limited to just filling their glasses then . . . and not to filling their other needs. Hmmmm?"

The situation became more depressing by the minute. I felt as though I had just consigned myself to hell in a drawstring purse.

"Cheer up, Miss Durham," he said, smiling. "You might even find yourself a husband among my clientele. California's native son is born of a whore and gambler. So a . . . barmaid . . . has an even better than average chance, wouldn't you say?"

I gave him a cold stare and turned away. "Which room?"

"Ask Howard. He takes care of the register."

I closed the door behind me.

Jeremy was appalled at what I had done. He talked about Papa until I angrily told him that we had no choice unless he wanted to sleep under the bridge. I tried to console him with the promise that he could go to school now. But he remained adamant and grimly disapproving. When he threatened me with Donovan, I told him I would slap him if he ever so much as breathed the man's name to me again. Stunned, he dropped his arguments and lapsed into sulky silence.

Emptying the cart, we moved into the hotel. The room was better furnished than our sod cabin had been and it was large and clean. Jeremy sat silently on the bed, staring moodily out the window and ignoring me. I would start work that afternoon.

I wasn't in the hotel an hour when I met Marcela Juarez. I had just returned from downstairs with instructions for work when I met her in the upstairs hallway. We both froze and stared at one another. She was the first to speak.

"*Dios!* What are you doing here?" she gasped, her Spanish accent thick. She was dressed in a long robe that barely concealed her voluptuous figure and her long, dark hair tumbled down about her shoulders. The heavy makeup was gone though and lines of fatigue showed around her eyes and mouth. She could not have been more than twenty-five, but the deep-brown eyes were years older.

"Living here, same as you," I answered stiffly, moving again down the hall. She stepped casually into my path.

"Is that all you're doing?"

I paled at her insult and then answered angrily. "I'm not competing with you, if that's what you mean!"

"Don't go shoving your aristocratic little nose in the air with me, *chiquita*. I was a good friend to your father and I don't want to see his . . ."

"That's a damn lie!" I shouted in her face. Marcela Juarez's eyes opened wide and then narrowed coldly.

"Every Friday afternoon."

I stared at her, stunned and horrified. Then I bolted forward, grabbing for her hair. Marcela Juarez was no novice when it came to fighting and I quickly found myself flat on my back on the floor, my cheeks stinging. I sat up, crying silently.

Papa had always come to town on Fridays. He never came home until late. The sheriff had said men knew him at the hotel. MacMillan obviously knew him well. I stared at Marcela Juarez as the truth hit me and the blur of disillusioned tears blinded me. Something flickered in her eyes and she reached down, hauling me up with surprising strength. She opened a door and pushed me in, slamming it behind us.

"*Sientase*," she ordered. "You look as though you need a drink as badly as I do." She poured two and thrust one into my hand, almost forcing it down my throat. "What did you think your Papa was, *niña*? A priest?" She swore softly in Spanish.

"He loved my mother!"

"Your mother has been dead for years, *chiquita*. There's only cold comfort for a warm man sitting by a grave."

I put my hands over my ears. Marcela Juarez stood up and walked to the window. After a while, I dropped my hands to my lap. I couldn't shut out the truth.

"I don't suppose I should've told you that about him," Marcela said without turning around to look at me. "A girl likes to have her illusions about her father. And you've got problems enough. Les Bigelow's mouth is bigger than any other part of him. Looks like he succeeded in putting you right in the boat with the rest of us." She turned and lifted her glass in mocking salute. "*Salud y pesetas, senorita.*" She downed the entire glass of amber liquid.

I just stared at my hands, miserable.

"What does Mace think of your moving in here?" she asked, refilling her glass.

I stiffened at the mention of his name and remembered with a jolt this woman's relationship to him. My eyes flickered over her again. "It's none of his business where I live. He's got the homestead now. That's what he was after."

Marcela raised a brow. "And that's all he wanted?" she questioned dubiously. When I didn't answer, she lifted her shoulders. "He hasn't been coming to see me for the past few months. I thought maybe you were the reason." I looked at her in surprise.

"He hasn't? Me? No," I answered everything. "He's going to marry Charlene Bellows," I volunteered.

"Jeremiah Bellow's daughter? *Dios!* I wish him luck with her." She gave a faint laugh. "Maybe if he marries her, I will be seeing him again. No?"

"You know Jeremiah Bellows?"

She laughed mirthlessly, crossing the room to recline in a wing chair. She didn't bother to cover her long, slender brown legs. "You are going to learn a lot about life here, *chiquita*. There aren't very many men in this town that I don't know."

"Do . . . do you know Mace Donovan . . . very well?" I could not help asking. I knew the answer and didn't know why I had asked a question that could only hurt me more. Perhaps I hoped the answer, bluntly stated, would drive him out of my mind.

Marcela looked at me blandly. She sipped from her glass. "He never had a wife to rush home to, and he was the only man I've ever taken to my bed that I didn't have to pretend to enjoy. Mace knows all there is to know about what pleasures a woman. And he's considerate enough to use it . . . even with someone like me." She finished her drink. She watched my pale, distraught face.

"You should have gone to Mace," she told me. "He was a friend of Roger's. He would have helped you."

"I'd rather be dead than ask his help," I said gratingly.

"You know you ruined your chances of salvaging your reputation the minute you stepped into this place? It's only a matter of time before MacMillan has you taking in men like the rest of us."

"I'm not planning to be around that long."

"Oh?" Her expression was sarcastic. "What makes you any smarter or better than the rest of us?"

"As soon as I have enough money, I'm going to buy

train passage for my brother and me to Virginia. We have family there," I confided.

She laughed low. "And you think they'll take you in after you've been here?"

"They're family."

"Family!" she snorted derisively. "Don't count on their kindness."

"They don't have to know we were living in a saloon."

"A saloon? Saloon is a polite word," she said flatly. "But let me tell you, *niña* . . . someday some *hombre* will pass through your Virginia and tell your family all about how you lived in Madrone. And it won't matter how good you've been since, *chiquita*. They'll toss you right out on your backside."

I looked at her and then shook my head. "Virginia is a long way from California."

"My home was a long way from Mexico City, but someone told my husband a lot about where I grew up and how I survived. So here I am in Madrone." She waved her hand about the lavish room.

I searched her face, but it was unreadable. She leaned over to pour herself another drink.

"My man wasn't much," she told me with a shrug. "I forgot him quick enough. But the baby . . ." Something flashed across her face and then disappeared. She looked away and I saw the hard tension in her body.

"You had a child?"

"A little girl," she admitted quietly. "She would be five now. Jorge wouldn't let me take her. Said I wasn't fit to be a mother," she said, pretending it didn't matter. "I don't suppose I am . . . now."

I felt sudden compassion for this young woman who had lost all her chances and was now trapped in a life she had tried to escape. Marcela got up jerkily when she saw the look on my face.

"Marcela . . ."

"Don't feel sorry for me, *chiquita*," she told me with a lift of her chin. "I enjoy my work, and I can put men right where they belong . . . most of them anyway." She stepped behind a screen. She slipped out of her robe and tossed it over the top.

"You'd better get out of here. Our illustrious town mayor is coming in soon, and he doesn't like people knowing where he is on Tuesday afternoons." She gave me a cynical smile. "Gotta make a living."

CHAPTER TWENTY-NINE

The bartender pushed a tray of beer mugs across the bar to me, winking as he did so. I avoided his eyes and picked up the tray, trying to ignore my nervousness. It was my first hour on the job and I felt I was the cynosure of all eyes in the room. Leering men followed my every movement and several had already made whispered suggestions that brought flaming, shamed and angry color into my cheeks.

Standing by the door was Foster MacMillan and he was watching me right along with the rest of the congregation. I wondered what he was thinking behind that cynical smile. Marcela had glanced at me once when she entered the room and ignored me afterward. She was presently sitting on a man's lap in the corner and she made no attempt to remove the hand that had crept up to her ample breasts. In fact, she was laughing. I kept my eyes averted.

Most of the men in the room I did not know and did not care to. But there were a few familiar faces. Jeremiah Bellows sat in the corner, right across the room from Marcela. He was with the milliner's husband, Herbert Perkins. They talked in low voices, drinking beer.

I wondered what Jeremy was doing upstairs and decided he was probably still sulking. He had barely

338

spoken to me since we entered the hotel.

Two hours after I had begun work another familiar face entered the saloon. I tensed immediately.

Les Bigelow sat at a table near the bar and the look he gave me was decidedly unpleasant. He let his eyes sweep insolently over me, then raised his hand and snapped his fingers for service. I desperately looked across the room at MacMillan and he looked back at me, casting a second glance at Bigelow to indicate I was to do the man's bidding. When I did not move, he jerked his head in silent command. Gritting my teeth, I moved toward Lester Bigelow.

"So Donovan bought the place out from under you," Bigelow sneered. "I could have told you so. You were a fool, Kathryn."

"Since you have no order, excuse me. I've work to do," I said, turning away. He caught at my skirt, imprisoning me. I looked down contemptuously at his hand and then at his face. He flushed, but his fingers tightened.

"You'd better be a little more polite. I happen to be a damn good customer at this place. One word to Foster and you'll be out on your pretty little ass." He grinned maliciously and took a swipe at my backside. If my hands had been free I would have slapped his face. As it was, I jerked back and spilled beer all over the tray. I had already been warned that any accidents would come out of my salary. I could not afford four beers, but they had already splashed down my front. My hands gripped the tray more tightly.

"There was a time when I might have offered you everything. Now, I'll give you ten bucks for twenty minutes in your room," he said insultingly and loud enough for the men around to hear. Some chuckled in encouragement.

My lip curled. "You did offer me everything, Les.

Even your supposed famous prowess as a man. And I said no. So you came to town to start your lies about Donovan and me. If it weren't for you I wouldn't be in this place and my reputation wouldn't be ruined." I was aware how loud my own voice was and that I had attracted even more attention.

"You're nothing but a foul-mouthed pig, Bigelow. And a very poor example of a man."

He grasped my wrist so tightly I thought my bones would be crushed. The tray fell crashing to the floor, the beer running down my skirt to form a puddle at my feet.

"Let go of her, Bigelow!" Came a chilling voice from across the room. I swung my head around and saw Mace standing menacingly in the doorway. He strode into the room, his eyes more frightening than I had ever seen them.

"I said let her go!" he repeated more quietly, yet more threateningly. Bigelow's fingers tightened more painfully, and he twisted my arm until I gasped and fell down on my knees to ease the punishing hold.

"You had her already, Donovan. Now, she's up for any man to . . ."

Bigelow didn't finish his sentence. Mace grabbed him, dragging him up out of his chair and connecting a sickening blow to his mouth. Blood spurted from a split in Bigelow's lower lip. He flew backwards over the table, knocking over the one beyond it and sliding against yet another.

Men scattered and women screamed. MacMillan casually removed money from a poker table, gave a signal to the bartender and stood back out of the way. The bartender removed the gilt mirror and swung a wood slat over the liquor bottles. Nothing could have been more carefully organized! I looked around frantically, not knowing what to do.

Bigelow shook his head, clearing his senses. But before he could stand on his own, Mace had hauled him up. Les made a swing and then grunted as Mace hit him in the stomach and then again in the face, propelling the man backwards again. He slid against the wall, where several people scrambled out of Donovan's way as he advanced. He stood over Bigelow.

"Get up, you lousy son-of-a-bitch!" Donovan said in a low, fiercely impassioned voice. Bigelow looked up at him out of a rapidly swelling eye. He started to push himself up and saw the muscles tensing in the younger man. He sank back, putting up a hand to indicate he'd had quite enough.

Mace turned away in disgust, glancing around the room until his gold eyes fastened onto me with cold fury. Raising a shaking hand to my cheek, I looked around hastily for a quick means of escape. Before I could move, Mace had crossed the room and grabbed my arm. When I resisted he gave me a hard yank and half dragged me toward the doorway. Foster MacMillan moved to stand in the way.

"You'd better get out of my way, MacMillan," Mace warned grimly.

Foster raised a ringed hand. "Right away, Mace. Just wanted to tell you her brother's upstairs. Room seven."

Donovan pulled me behind him into the entrance hall and bellowed up the stairs for Jeremy. My brother's running footsteps could be heard in the hallway. He appeared at the landing within seconds.

"Pack and meet us at the homestead," Mace ordered.

"Yes, sir!" Jeremy grinned and disappeared again.

People were watching us from the barroom. No one had spoken yet. They all seemed to be in a state of shock. I turned and looked back, humiliated beyond words. Marcela was looking between me and Mace Donovan. She caught my perplexed look. Smiling, she gave me a wink before turning away.

Donovan propelled me before him out of the hotel. I
stumbled and his arm looped tightly around my waist. I
felt myself swung roughly up and deposited none too
gently on his stallion. He leaped up behind me, pulling
me back against him with a hard jerk at my waist. I
could feel the full length of his legs against the back of
mine. Grabbing the saddlehorn I tried to draw myself
away from the disturbing contact, but his hand
tightened ruthlessly. His legs tensed and the stallion
turned from the hitching post and began a canter out of
town. Just past the hotel, Diablo was sent into a hard
gallop.

Donovan did not slow the painfully punishing pace
until we were several miles from Madrone. When he
did, I finally managed to speak.

"You had no right to interfere!" I gasped brokenly.

"Shut up!"

Furious, I snatched at the reins, trying to tear them
from his hand and succeeded only in startling the high-
spirited stallion. He stumbled to a stop and reared back.
Donovan uttered a sharp sound deep in his throat, controlling his steed. The stallion came down, snorting and
shaking its great head.

"Goddamnit!" Donovan said, incensed. "That does
it!" He threw the reins over the horse's head and dismounted in one swift movement. Reaching up, he
hauled me down as well.

"What . . . what're you doing?" I cried, really frightened by his roughness and the burning look of purpose
in his eyes.

"You've had this coming for a long time!" he ground
out, propelling me toward the side of the road. "You
think you can push me to the ends of the earth and back,
and by God, it's high time you learned you can't!"

He sat on a boulder and dragged me face down over
his hard-muscled thighs. It dawned on me then what he
had in mind and I kicked and fought frantically, scream-

ing at him. I tried to roll off his lap but his hand was like a steel trap. He shoved my skirt and petticoat up and began the first stinging blow.

"Mace!" I kicked harder, but it was useless. He was not satisfied until my cries of pain had diminished to tearful whimpers of protest. Then he pushed me off his lap to fall on the ground and stood up. He moved away into the shadows of the madrones.

I hurt too much to move and the whimpering cries turned into silent racking sobs of hurt and degradation. There was silence for a long time. Even the insects had stopped their buzzing. It was near dusk and somewhere an owl hooted plaintively. I hid my face in my arms as I heard Donovan coming back. He hunkered down beside me.

"Kat . . ." I felt his hand gentle on my hair. "What are you trying to do to me?"

What was *I* trying to do to *him?* Oh, God . . . My shoulders shook with crying. Why wouldn't he just leave me alone? Didn't he have everything he ever wanted? Why did he have to keep tormenting me?

Mace turned me over and drew me into his arms. His hands caressed my wild hair back into place. Looking up at him, bewildered, I saw how drawn and pale his face was and frowned.

"I think if we keep on like this, I'll go insane," he said hoarsely. He forced my dusty, tear-stained face close to his. His mouth was gentle, as if he were afraid of what my reaction might be. I closed my eyes, relaxing against him and he kissed me again, his tongue probing, teasing. Drawing back a moment later, he searched my face, his hand trembling as he held my chin.

"You're going back to the homestead until I can make some plans," he told me.

Plans for what, I wanted to ask, but right then I didn't care.

"Don't ever leave again," he said harshly, his hand

forcing me to look at him when I started to look away. "Don't even think about it!"

He lifted me and carried me back to his horse. We rode the rest of the way to the homestead in silence. When he lifted me down from his horse in front of the sod cabin, I moved away from him and in through the unlocked door. The house looked barren, cold. All of the things that had made it a home were gone.

On the table was a large box filled with supplies. Some flowers, now wilted, lay scattered on the table as if they had been flung there.

"It was meant as a peace offering," he said dryly. He entered the room. "I'm coming back tomorrow morning. Be ready for me."

His expression was implacable and I felt my chin quivering again. If he wanted me for anything other than a convenient whore, he would have taken me back to Tasajara with him. How long would it be before he grew tired of me and then let me leave? A few months, a year!

"D . . . Donovan," I started to plead.

"I'm not going to stay tonight. You've got me too riled up as it is. And the next time we're together as man and woman . . . it's not going to start out in anger," he told me flatly. "Now, you go to bed and think about that tonight! And you just adjust yourself to the idea because I've damn well given up letting you have any choice in the matter. It's settled! And right now, I don't give a damn whether you like it or not!"

He turned and walked out of the cabin, slamming the door behind him.

Turning away, I stretched myself out on the bed, feeling desolate. I thought of Marcela being sent away from her baby and closed my eyes so tightly they hurt.

Would Mace someday do that to me? I doubted very much if I would escape conception with the way he felt . . . and the way I felt, for that matter. And there was still Charlene. She was the girl Mace Donovan wanted for his wife.

And what about Jeremy? What would all this do to him? If he had been contemptuous of me before when we moved into the hotel, how would he look upon me tomorrow, seeing Donovan arriving here, realizing his purpose.

When Jeremy came into the cabin, he looked across at me lying on the bed. He didn't say anything, but walked quietly across to Papa's room. He closed the curtain.

Putting my hand up over my face, I cried silently into the night.

CHAPTER THIRTY

"You can't go, Katie!" Jeremy wailed in protest. "You know what Mace'll do. And he'll be spitting mad!"

"Let him," I said bleakly, turning back to the wood-stove after having just delivered my decision to my brother. I was going into Madrone to collect the advance money I had given MacMillan for room and board at the hotel, and then I was going to wire our relatives in Virginia again. There was no choice. It was either that, or stay here accepting whatever Donovan decided to dole out. And I couldn't bear that. I wanted him desperately, but the price he was asking was too dear. And if we didn't leave Madrone soon . . .

Pushing eggs around in the cast-iron pan, I tried hard not to think of Mace. His efforts to keep us here were as bewildering as they were frustrating. He could have any woman he wanted. Why me? Or had I simply challenged his masculinity by fighting him from the beginning?

My mouth softened. Even these eggs had been brought to us by Donovan in his accursed charity basket which he had called a "peace offering". A whole dozen snowy white eggs not brown ones. Even the coffee that was filling the sod cabin with its rich aroma had come from him. Things only seemed worse when I thought of

346

the slip of paper I had found last night stuffed in the family Bible. A note written in a strong hand with my father's perfect italic signature at the bottom. Donovan had loaned my father five hundred dollars. Why hadn't he told me?

"But Katie, he said . . ."

"It doesn't matter what Donovan said, Jeremy," I cut him off impatiently. "He has no say in how we run our lives. And we've flat run out of choices. We can't stay here any longer!"

"Why not?" Jeremy persisted with the blindness of a child wanting his own way.

"Don't you understand anything, Jeremy? The homestead doesn't belong to us anymore. And I found out last night that Donovan loaned Papa the tax money, plus a sizable amount, two years in a row. He could have taken this place from the beginning."

"But he didn't," Jeremy said, his lower lip protruding stubbornly. "That says something, doesn't it? And I understand plenty! You don't want to stay here because you love him! That's why you're in a hurry to leave. You're scared he won't like you because you've been so terrible to him all along. A real bitch, in fact!"

My lips parted at my brother's tirade and I stared at him for a stunned moment. Then, I turned away, pulling the pan from the fire.

"Breakfast is ready," I said chokingly.

"It's true! You're just too stubborn to admit it!" Jeremy accused hotly. I divided the eggs onto two plates in silence, not looking at Jeremy's flushed, angry face. My eyes burned and my throat felt as though it were closing up.

"I won't leave!" Jeremy decided, sitting at the table and lifting his fork. I took a deep breath.

"We can't stay here," I said reasonably. "Try to understand and accept that, please." I sat down opposite

Jeremy and looked at him. His face whitened.

"I won't go, I tell you! I won't," he fumed. "I don't want to go to Virginia and live with people I don't know and who don't want us anyway. If they cared, we'd have gotten an answer from your first wire, now wouldn't we? Mace said we could stay here as long as we want and that's just what I'm going to do."

"Jeremy," I pleaded.

"No."

I was beginning to feel angry frustration. Did he know just how cruel he was being to go on like this? Couldn't he understand anything?

"Maybe they'd pay for your schooling. You might be able to go to . . ."

"No!" Jeremy almost yelled at me. "I'll work and get there on my own."

"Oh, Jeremy . . ."

"You don't think I can do it?"

"You won't agree to go to our own flesh and blood for help, but you'd be willing to stay here forever living off Mace Donovan's charity?" I asked.

"We'd . . . we'd work . . . just like always."

"How? Grow vegetables for Tasajara, raise a few steers to his thousands, and at the end of each year owe him more than we did the previous one?" I sighed heavily. "Jeremy, I love you so much. I'd do just about anything to make you happy. But there's so much more to this whole situation than you can understand."

"What's the difference whether we accept charity from Mace or from some relatives in Virginia we've never even met?" he asked bitterly. "I don't want to go to Virginia, Katie. It's so far from home." His voice wobbled, warning of impending tears. Then he drew himself up. "If we've got to take charity, it'll be from Mace. I . . . I like him."

My face felt drained of blood.

"You know we don't have to go," he whimpered, the bravado gone. He looked at me beseechingly.

"Jeremy," I said faintly. "Will you please stop this? It's not easy for me either."

"He . . . he likes you, you know."

My face crumpled and I looked away quickly. "He's going to marry Charlene Bellows, Jeremy."

"Maybe . . . maybe he won't marry her. He told you to stay. He came after you at the hotel. He said he was coming back today." I looked back at him, surprised. A rush of guilty color came into his face and he looked down.

"Did you hear him talking last night?"

My brother's face turned crimson. "I didn't mean to listen."

"Jeremy," I swallowed hard and forced myself to speak. "Mace Donovan was not talking about marriage. That never once entered into what he said he wanted."

"Maybe he'd change his mind if you'd be nice to him for a change."

Feeling sick, I got up from the table and walked away from him, shaking violently. "I wonder if you love me at all . . ." I said, wrapping my arms around myself and feeling cold inside.

"Katie, I do love you," he said and I could hear the tears in his voice. There was a long silence in the room as I fought to regain control. It would be so easy to give in to the torrent of emotions I was feeling, but there was no time and I could not afford the liberty. I stood near the back window, head against the frame, staring out at the mountains. The ridge was up there. I longed to go there just as Papa had done.

"We still don't know who killed Papa," Jeremy said. "What about that?"

"We'll just have to trust the sheriff to find out and bring him to justice," I said. I had never called a place home, except for here. I felt a wrench at leaving this place. My insides ached. It was better not to dwell on it. Turning away, I crossed the room and picked up my shawl.

"What do I tell him when he comes?" Jeremy asked and I knew he was still hoping for Mace's interference in my plans.

"Tell him the truth. Tell him that I've gone to get our money back from MacMillan and that I'm wiring our family in Virginia to ask if we can go to them."

"If they'll have us," Jeremy said grimly. "They didn't answer your first wire. Maybe they'll ignore this one too."

"I wouldn't hope for that, Jeremy," I warned. "Whatever happens, we will not stay here on this homestead or in Madrone."

He must have heard the pain in my voice for he relented. "Is there anything you want me to do around here while you're gone?" he asked gently.

"Do what you want. It doesn't matter anymore. Nothing does." I left the door open behind me.

On my ride to town, I tried not to think about our dismal future. It was a beautiful morning, the sun glittering through the dewed pines and madrones and streaming onto the road. As I realized how much I loved this place, the quiet of the morning became less soothing.

When I entered the dispatcher's office, Horace Elderman looked up over his wire-rimmed glasses. Then his head jerked up and he stood.

"Miss Durham!" he exclaimed, smiling broadly. "Perfect timing. I was about to send someone out to you. The answer to your wire came yesterday, late afternoon. By the time I got to the hotel, you were gone." He bent over his desk and sifted through his papers until he found the right one.

"Here it is," he produced it dramatically, waving it at me. My heart was pounding.

Tearing open the envelope, I unfolded the sheet of canary yellow paper and read hurriedly:

"River's Bend belongs to Jeremy. Michael Durham looking for you. Last contact Placerville. Condolences on Roger. Come home.
                              Melissa Durham"

Stunned, I reread the telegram. So few words, so much said.

Then suddenly, it all came to me. A chilling coldness brought dreadful prickles to my skin as I remembered Papa lying on the ledge.

The words of the telegram screamed out at me.

"Michael Durham . . . last contact Placerville." *MD Tasajara.* Papa had managed to say both just before he died. And words of my brother and his safety.

Michael Durham had found my father. He was not in Placerville. He was at Tasajara. Suddenly I understood everything and was filled with an urgency to get back to the homestead. Jeremy was alone!

I thrust the paper back at Elderman. "Get this to the sheriff right away!" I said in a rush, turning for the door.

"The sheriff, ma'am?" he asked blankly, pushing his spectacles up onto his nose in surprise.

"Tell him '*MD* Tasajara,' " I said, not stopping. "He'll understand!"

Swinging up onto the mare, needless of the whirl of skirts that exposed my calves, I rode out of town, raising a cloud of dust behind me. People stared, shaking their heads.

Using my heels and the reins, I set the mare into a hard gallop. My body jolted painfully with the hard riding after a few miles, but I couldn't slow down. The horrible premonition was still there. Jeremy was in danger and he would be dead if I didn't get to the homestead in time. I thought of Mace and for the first time prayed to God for his presence. Let him come, oh, please, God! Get him to Jeremy before Michael Durham got there.

Just before I reached the homestead gate, I heard the shot. I didn't stop to unlatch the fence, but whipped the mare into a jump. She took the fence, stumbling once on the other side before catching herself. I thundered through the garden, trampling our precious vegetables in my wake and skidded to a stop before the sod cabin.

Jeremy was gone.

There was another shot. *The ridge!*

Never had I wished so much for Papa's rifle. I started running just as another shot cracked.

"Jeremy . . ." I screamed, terrified. The scene of several months before filled my mind as I raced up the hill trail. Papa shot, shoved off the ridge to fall to the narrow, precariously unsturdy ledge below. And left to die there . . . *by his own brother.*

Was it happening again? This time to Jeremy?

Dear God in Heaven, please, let him be alive! I ran harder.

My lungs were burning and the pain in my side grew until I could barely breathe. Reaching the top line of trees I saw a man standing on the boulder where Papa used to sit to look out over the valley below. The man was searching below, gun cocked and ready to fire again.

"Michael Durham!" I shouted, racing out of the trees without thinking of my own danger.

John Saunders swung around and stared at me, stunned. His face was white and drawn in concentration. His eyes flickered and then cleared.

"Kathryn!" he said harshly. "What're you doing up here?"

It had been there all the time, plain to see and yet I had been so blind to it. I looked at John Saunders now, closely. The color of his eyes, the bone structure of his face and that barely concealed Southern drawl all combined to present a younger vision of my father. Why had I never seen these things before? Had I been drawn to this man because he looked like Papa?

"Where's Jeremy?" I demanded, moving a step closer, still breathless from my run. My heart was pounding with exertion and the beginning of comprehension as to my own dangerous position.

Amazingly, Michael Durham holstered his gun and jumped down from the boulder. He walked slowly toward me, eyes cold.

"Jeremy!" I cried loudly. I heard his voice from below, frightened and full of warning, and I felt a flood of relief. At least he was alive!

"Get away, Katie!"

Too late.

There was a grim smile on Michael Durham's face. "Now I've got to kill you both."

I heard Jeremy again and shouted. "Don't move! Stay where you are!"

The man I had known as John Saunders continued toward me steadily. "If only you'd stayed away a little longer. It'd all be over and you wouldn't have to die too."

"Why do you have to kill either of us?" I asked, stalling for time.

"Since you know who I am, you must know why I'm here," he laughed bitterly. "I was sent to find Roger and bring him back to River's Bend." His mouth twisted. "Roger, at River's Bend. After he had deserted her. After I'd worked my whole life on the place, fought to keep it going after the war, poured my guts into it. Roger would get my land handed to *him* on a silver platter."

I stepped back. "But there were four brothers."

"Tad was killed at Gettysburg. Then Charles was

next. He had consumption, and Melissa never had a son. Then came Roger, my big brother, who left home before I ever knew him. I was last. Melissa sent me out here to find the lost lamb, the prodigal, and bring him home."

"And you killed him."

"I couldn't let him have River's Bend!" he exclaimed defensively. "He never cared anything about it. He always hankered after some big dream, like coming West. Working with the rest of us wasn't good enough. And, God, just look at this place, this miserable little piece of land. Everything Roger touched failed. I wasn't going to let him destroy River's Bend."

Michael had stopped, his face intent with his memories and determination.

"But you can't murder Jeremy! He's your nephew. He's just a boy."

"He stands in the way of my getting River's Bend. If it weren't for the damn senselessness of the Durham family custom and father's will, I could let him live. Tad had no children. Charles has a daughter, Marie, but a girl can't inherit. But Roger had Jeremy and no damned ignorant, arrogant little ten-year-old boy is going to take everything away from me!" His eyes were glazed and fierce.

"You poisoned the well?"

The question momentarily distracted him. I need not have asked, however. The answer was in his face.

"While you were out back washing." He laughed slightly. "I knew you'd think it was Donovan. You've always believed it was him. That just made everything easier. But nothing seemed to go according to plan. I tried to kill Jeremy when he was rounding up the cattle, but he got off with a broken leg. It had to look like an accident . . ."

"If you shoot us, it won't look like any accident," I reasoned.

"I haven't any more time to worry about details like that. I've been away too long already. I've got to get back and see to things. I left the place in the hands of an able overseer, but I want to make sure everything is going all right." His smile was wry. "You see how much we have in common, Kathryn."

"Everyone will know it was you," I told him.

He gave me a derisive look. "How?"

"I wired Virginia. They said you were looking for us. I sent the wire on to the sheriff's office. He's probably on his way out here now."

"Everyone knows me as John Saunders . . . drifter," he said, devilishly sure of himself. He moved forward again, and I stepped back.

"What if Jeremy were to sign a paper saying he forfeited his rights to River's Bend?" I tried. Michael smiled mockingly.

"And give up that grand education he wants? I'm not that big a fool! And you'd still know I was the one that killed Roger. You wouldn't rest until you saw me hanging from the nearest gallows. I've seen the way you can hate, Kathryn. No . . . I'm going to kill you both . . . now, before the sheriff gets here."

His hand moved toward his gun and I knew I had no more time to think or argue. I threw myself at him, fingers curled in readiness to drag my nails across his face. He fell backward with a cry, with me on top of him. I punched, kicked, tore at him, knowing that at any moment his superior strength would be unleashed against me. He grunted with pain, trying to catch my hands. I used my legs to hold myself on top of him. Michael rolled, trying to shove me away. Still I held fast, like the moss on a tree trunk. Grabbing my hair, he yanked my head back and slugged me hard in the face. My grip loosened and he thrust me away with a sickening thud of his boots to my stomach.

"Damn you," he hissed, rising and touching the painful, bloody scratches on his face.

Scrambling up, I lunged at him again, making a successful grab for his gun while he was trying to clear the blood from his vision. He felt the gun slide free of the holster and swung, catching me across the side of the head with a blow that sent me tumbling to the ground. I retained my hold on the revolver and tried to aim it up at him. He dived for it grasping my wrist and twisting it behind my back. His weight drove the wind from my lungs. I tried to scratch him with my other hand, but he caught it too.

There was an explosion next to my head as my fingers tightened on the gun now behind my back. If I used up his bullets, he at least couldn't kill Jeremy though he would probably bludgeon me to death. How many shots had he fired? I tried to pull on the trigger again, but he twisted hard until I cried out in agony, my fingers loosening.

Suddenly, Michael's weight was off me. I saw Mace Donovan behind him, hands dragging him back. Michael's face was like some savage beast as he turned to meet his attacker, catching Donovan in the stomach with a foot and sending him sprawling backward to the boulder. Not allowing Mace time to catch his breath, Durham came at him like a battering ram, kicking dust before him and blinding Mace.

"Mace!" I screamed, seeing Durham charging again I rose from the dirt and attacked him from behind. Jumping on his back, I grabbed his hair, entwining my legs around his waist. But Michael Durham's fury was uncontrollable now. He twisted sharply, breaking my hold and reeling me backward with a blow to the jaw. I sprawled out on the rocky ground, dazed. But my action had at least allowed Donovan to clear the grit from his eyes. I doubted he would be caught by that trick again.

My uncle clearly had no honor. He was fighting to

survive now, with a desperation that was deadly. The two men were about the same size and there seemed to be no advantage in either direction. They swung and connected blows back and forth, clutching at each other and rolling in the dirt, perilously close the edge of the cliff.

Pulling myself into a crouching position near the rock where I had landed I searched the ground frantically for the gun. The sounds of blows and grunts of pain rang in the air. Spying the revolver across the clearing, I scrambled for it and tried to aim it at Michael Durham. But the two men were moving so fast and furiously that I was afraid if I fired, I would hit Mace.

Michael succeeded in bringing up his knee into Mace's groin, buckling him to the ground near the ledge. He kicked him backward again and almost had him over but Mace rolled a few inches away from the edge. Durham lunged at him, stunning him with a blow to his jaw as he tried to get up. Then he grabbed for a rock, raising it high in the air and intending to bring it down on Mace's skull. I fired once, then again.

Jerking upright, Michael Durham stared in my direction. The rock fell from his hands, landing a few inches from Mace's head. When he turned to look at me, he threw himself off balance. He started to fall backwards over the ledge. Making a desperate attempt to save himself, he grabbed onto Mace's shirt. With a scream of terror Michael Durham fell backwards over the cliff, dragging Mace with him.

I screamed, standing up and running forward.

"Mace!" Falling to my knees I looked over the edge. Michael Durham's body was still falling, stopped only momentarily by protruding boulders and leaving an ugly red trail down the cliff. His screaming had stopped and finally the body slid to a stop at the base of the cliff against a scraggly pine.

"Mace!" I screamed again, tears streaming down my

face. He was lying on the ledge where my father had
fallen months before. There was blood on his face, but
his eyes were partly open. Rocks were breaking loose
beneath him and cascading down the cliff. The narrow
ledge was crumbling!

I looked frantically for some way to reach him before
he fell down the ridge as Michael Durham just had.

Movement caught my eyes. The sorrel stallion paced
restlessly among the trees to the south of the ridge. I
darted toward him. He backed, spooked by the hysterical picture I made, but I made a grab for the dangling
reins. He whinnied warningly and reared back.

"Easy!" I commanded, bouncing off the ground as he
reared again. I dodged the snapping teeth. His second
attempt set them deep into my shoulder, wrenching a cry
of pain from me.

"Damn, you devil horse!" I cried, hitting him hard
across the nose several times and pulling his ear down.
That startled him and I dragged heavily on the reins.
The stallion moved forward nervously, eyes rolling at
me. I unlashed the rope on the saddle, tying one end to
the saddle horn and running forward to the ledge, dropping the other end down to Mace Donovan.

"Grab the rope, Mace!"

When he moved, the ledge began to give. He turned
over from his back, clutching at the rocky protrusions,
his booted feet scraping below to push himself up precious inches.

"Grab the rope!"

Amazingly, he laughed. "You aren't strong enough to
pull me up. Or did you plan to let the other end go?"

"Damn it, Mace," I said in frustration and fright.
"It's tied to Diablo."

"He stood still for you?"

"Will you stop yapping and get the damn rope! You
can't hold . . . Mace!!!" I screamed as his fingers slipped

momentarily, but then he caught himself again.

"You actually sound concerned, Kat," he grunted, pulling himself up another inch. I cursed him as I had never cursed anyone or anything before in my life and he laughed.

"Lord, but I didn't know you had all those words in your vocabulary."

Pulling at the rope, I urged Diablo forward. The rope dangled nearer to Mace.

Hoisting himself up the rocky edge, Mace grasped it. He pulled hand over hand, feet against the ridge. When he reached the top, I grabbed at his shirt, pulling him up until he rolled away from the edge.

Without the weight on the end of the rope, the stallion backed with a jolt. He whinnied, blew out, and then dropped his nose to a clump of grass.

Donovan sat up, putting his head on his knees. He was breathing heavily. The skin near his temple was raw and bleeding and there were bruises already showing on his chin. I tried to assess the rest of the damage but he didn't raise his head sufficiently for me to get a good enough look at him.

Exhausted and not without a certain amount of pain myself, I crawled forward until I could touch him. "Mace, are you all right? Mace?" My voice broke and he turned his head to look at me. The cat-gold eyes were alive and sparkling in a way I had never seen before.

"I will be in a minute," he drawled. I felt myself grabbed and propelled forward across him until I was flat on my back, with him above me. He grinned then, before obliterating the sunlight with his body. His kiss was hard and demanding deepening intimately until my body was on fire. Then it softened to tenderness, not ending until I could hardly breath. He leaned back studying my flushed face leisurely.

I suddenly remembered other very important things.

"Jeremy!" I gasped.

There was a slight cough from above us on the boulder. We turned our heads, startled, and looked. Jeremy was sitting cross-legged on the top, arms folded. His face was a little too red, but he was grinning.

CHAPTER THIRTY-ONE

Mace brought Jeremy and me back to Tasajara. I was beginning to hurt all over and the swelling around my eyes was very tender. What other bruises and abrasions I had suffered were secondary to the pain I felt looking at Donovan's back as he strode away from me, after depositing us in Hattie McFadden's care. I tried not to admit my disappointment and discouragement. Perhaps that devastating kiss on the ridge had meant nothing to him after all.

Hattie ordered hot water for a scented bath. Allowing me the privacy of undressing behind a screen, she dumped my clothes unceremoniously in the hall.

"They're rags. Not worth keeping," she decided.

"But . . ."

"There's somthing nicer in here," she said, walking to the wardrobe. It was almost full and she extracted a silk robe that tied around the front.

"Put this on when you've finished your bath," she told me, laying the gorgeous thing over the coverlet. I stared at it, feeling sick. These things were intended for Charlene Bellows. They had the same rich, pampered aura about them that had surrounded her when she had been here.

I stayed in the bath for a long time, letting the gradually cooling water soothe my tense, aching muscles. My mind whirled, returning always to the thought of being hurt all over again.

Having dried myself, I touched the silken robe. I loathed it passionately, but had no choice but to wear it. The feel of the silk was luxurious against my skin but torture to my mind. Charlene would wear this for Mace. He would untie the sash and remove it . . . I thrust the thought away.

"You're going to have a very black eye, Kathryn," Hattie said, reentering the room. "Who in Heaven's name were you brawling with . . . and couldn't you have kept it a little less physical?"

I smiled wanly. Hattie knew nothing of what had happened and I did not feel up to explaining anything at the moment.

Setting the laden tray on a small table by the window, Hattie beckoned. She poured out rich coffee as I approached.

"We'll have Doc come out and take a good look at you," she said.

"I'm fine."

Hattie gave a tight-lipped look. "Sit down and eat something."

Donovan! I kept thinking about him. He had walked away from me without a backward glance. And all those expensive clothes in the closet . . . for Charlene Bellows. The kiss had meant nothing to him but it had torn me inside out with longing and hope. I wanted Mace Donovan! I loved him! Damn him! I loved him! Tears burned at the back of my throat, but I kept my face controlled.

"Just relax. I'll send someone up for the tray later."

I was not listening. I thought of killing my own uncle and was surprised that I felt no remorse. I pressed my fingertips to my throbbing temples and tried not to think of the body at the bottom of the cliff that might have just as easily been Mace's. Had I always loved him like this? With the pain swelling my heart so badly I thought I would die of it?

When he had walked away from me, I knew it was useless. I couldn't stay here or anywhere near Madrone feeling about him the way I did. Jeremy and I would make plans to go back to Virginia. Jeremy would adjust in time, and he would have the money to obtain the education he had always wanted. As for me . . . I hoped I would adjust in time, too.

Hattie was keeping up an endless flow of chatter meant to soothe me. She uncovered the plates. One displayed a rare steak with a mound of potatoes; another a bowl of steaming peas. There were rolls, butter as well. I felt ill.

"I don't think I can eat anything, Hattie."

"Eat what you can," she said gently. "At least try, you might find you're more hungry than you realize."

The door opened behind us and we both turned to see who it was. Mace stood negligently against the doorjamb looking squarely at me. He smiled slowly, making my heart constrict.

"You have a beauty of a black eye, Kat."

"Mace Donovan! You get yourself right out of here this minute! And what's the big idea of walking in here without so much as a knock. Kathryn might have been in her bath!"

"Too bad she wasn't," Mace laughed and walked forward, undaunted by his housekeeper's shocked and indignant countenance.

"I brought us some wine," Mace said, holding up a bottle in one hand and two crystal glasses in the other.

"You've no business being in here!" Hattie insisted, standing between us. "Your father . . ."

"Hush up, Hattie!" Donovan cut her off with a sternly impatient glance. "This has been a hard enough day all around without your needless expostulations or well-intentioned meddling. If you want to do something constructive, bring up another tray. I'm starved. And then, for God's sake, leave us alone!"

Seeing that there was no arguing with him, Hattie sniffed and marched out of the room. She stopped at the door. "I'm coming right back up here!" she warned.

Once alone, there seemed nothing at all for either of us to say. My back was stiffly erect and I looked at him warily. Mace opened the wine. He poured out the clear, red liquid and offered a glass to me. I accepted it, glancing up and barely meeting the penetrating look in his golden eyes. He sat in the chair opposite me, twirling the wine in his glass before sipping it. He wasn't trying to hide his triumph.

The silence rang in my ears and became unbearable. Why wouldn't he say why he had come?

One short tap announced Hattie's return. She had not been gone more than five minutes. She looked between the two of us and set the second tray on the table with a thud. She seemed in no great hurry to leave. Mace looked at her with a wry smile.

"That's all, Hattie. Thank you very much," he said softly.

"Oh, no, you don't, Mace Donovan. You might have a thought for the girl's reputation," she said disapprovingly, making a sharp clatter with the dishes as she uncovered them.

Mace smiled slightly, rubbing his knuckles along his jawline. "Well, I guess I'll just have to marry the girl then, won't I, Hattie?"

That brought two pairs of eyes to his, but his expression was filled with amusement. At my expense, I thought with sudden anger. Hattie's mouth was open. Mine slammed shut.

"You had better," she managed when her vocal chords worked again. "So you finally see some sense!" she said as a parting comment. She closed the door behind her.

"Was that necessary!" I flared.

"It got her out of here, didn't it?" he shrugged, unrepentant.

I slammed my glass down and stood up, unable to bear being this close to him. "I think Hattie had the right idea. You'd better get out of here. My reputation is bad enough as it is without you making matters worse." I moved to the opposite side of the room, away from him. It wasn't far enough for the way I was feeling.

"I've no intention of leaving this room. Not for a good, long time," he drawled casually, making his position perfectly clear. I heard him stand up and walk across the room to stand behind me. My skin prickled with awareness.

"We've still got some things to talk about, Kat," he said softly.

I shook my head, feeling dreadfully emotional and wishing desperately that he would leave before I made a complete fool of myself.

"What was Saunders doing?"

I explained as succinctly as possible what had happened and who John Saunders really was. Mace whistled between his teeth. Then he didn't say anything for a moment.

"So, what now?" he asked finally, in an odd voice. "Do you want to go back to Virginia and get everything sorted out? Or are you going to stay here?"

I didn't look up at him. "It's all up to Jeremy."

"Jeremy's a boy," he said harshly. "He's not capable of making that kind of decision. And this affects your life too, you know." I glanced up at him and he raked fingers back through his hair, turning away.

"With what he's had up to now, living on that home-stead in that sod cabin, I suppose a grand plantation would appeal to him," he went on, sounding bitter.

"Jeremy's not like that. But, then, I think we'll go," I said, pressing a hand against my stomach and trying to make the fluttering sensation stop. Mace turned and stared at me.

"What about you? What do you want, Kat?" he demanded in a hard voice, eyes narrowed.

I want you to love me. I want to stay here with you. But not if it means having to watch you marry someone else, giving them your babies, while I wait for whatever attention you decide to dole out to me. I answered silently. Outwardly, I showed nothing. I gave him a wry look and shrugged.

"How's Jeremy?" I asked, to change the subject.

Mace's mouth tightened ominously. He breathed in deeply before answering.

"Sleeping. He was worn out. He saw . . . Durham . . . coming and went down the face of the cliff. There's a ledge just below the one I fell to, and some deep cuts into the granite. He pressed himself into one of them. It saved his life. Thank God, he's as surefooted as a mountain goat!"

I shivered, remembering how Michael Durham had fired repeatedly down at my brother.

"You're cold," Mace said softly, solicitously. His fingers curved over my shoulder to trail along my collarbone. I shivered more, but from another emotion just as primitive as fear. "Your hair is still wet."

"I'm all right."

Other thoughts crashed in on me. The body at the bottom of the ridge loomed in my mind in all its gruesome detail. I had killed my own uncle. The reason why didn't matter. I had killed a man. Then an image of my father's body superseded my grisly memory of

Michael Durham. I stared blankly, starting to shake and unable to stop myself. And Mace, oh, God, Mace had almost been killed.

Donovan turned me comfortingly into his arms. There was nothing of the lover now in his embrace, and that somehow seemed to make everything worse. He could stand here holding me without feeling anything while my body vibrated with awareness of him. I put the flat of my hands against his chest and pushed away.

"I said, I'm all right."

"Sure you are!" he said sarcastically. "Nothing ever penetrates that cold little mind of yours." He turned away and I hid the trembling of my mouth and quick, hurt tears. When he came back, I was in control again. He held out the wine glass.

"Drink it!" he ordered imperiously. I glared up at him.

"Don't you order me around!" I took thankful refuge in anger.

Mace stared at my white face. His fingers tightened uncontrollably and the glass shattered in his hand, spilling wine on the floor. I gasped, reaching out without thinking and prying his fingers open. Blood oozed from a cut on the fleshy part of his thumb and seeing it seemed to sap me of strength and control.

"You've cut yourself," I whimpered.

"You're not leaving, Kat," he said, paying no attention to me.

"Why did you do that? Look at your hand! You're bleeding to death!"

"I'll take care of everything for Jeremy. I know a few people in the East that can take care of everything from that end. There's no need to go anywhere. We'll work things out right here. But you'll leave Tasajara this time over my dead body," he growled, still oblivious of his wound.

I looked around the room for something to stop the bleeding. There was a towel by the wash tub and I started for it only to be brought up short by his free hand. Mace's eyes glittered.

"Did you hear what I said?"

"Your hand . . ."

"You killed a man today."

"He would have killed you!"

"I thought that was just what you wanted all along," he snorted.

"Will you stop?! Your hand . . ."

"You could have let him bash in my brains and *then* shot him," he told me. "You always made it so damnably clear how much you hated me. Why the sudden switch?" His face was pale and tautly controlled.

"You know why I hated you at first. I thought you'd killed my father."

"And later? What about later? And now? How do you feel now?" he asked, his fingers touching my hair, traveling downward to lie at the pulsing vein in my neck. "Hmmm? Tell me, Kat."

"I . . . I'm sorry for all the vile things I said to you," I managed.

The gold eyes glittered. "That's all?"

"What more did you expect?" I countered. His hand dropped away as his eyes flared. I turned away, grabbing the towel and wrapping it tightly around his hand to staunch the flow of blood. Mace was watching me closely and when I looked up slowly there was a smile on his face that was in his eyes as well.

"It's not funny!" I snapped, not sure what he was laughing about anyway.

"No, it's not," he agreed. "I was so sure of everything at the ridge. So damn sure."

"What are you talking about?"

"I was sure you were in love with me." The smile was

teasing and my heart contracted.

"Don't be absurd!" I avoided his eyes. "You're going to marry Charlene Bellows!" As if that made all the difference . . .

There was a pregnant pause.

"And what makes you so sure about that?"

"Everyone knows. She's been here with her parents several times . . . They said . . . you were . . . she . . ." I shrugged, unable to say anything coherently.

"Charlene is very pretty, wouldn't you say? Charming too. Don't you think? And she's been real nice to me, never speaks back, minds her manners like a lady should . . ."

I bit down hard on my lower lip and the pain in my chest was excruciating. I shrugged my shoulders slightly and turned away.

"Do you think she's right for me?" he asked dreamily. I wanted to hate him all over again.

"Why ask me? Can't you make up your own mind?"

"Oh, I've made up my mind all right. I just thought you might be interested."

I gave a hoarse laugh. "Why should I be? It's your life. Hattie says you'll be bored with her in a month though," I blurted out. Mace laughed slightly, the sound cutting into me.

"Hattie is absolutely, one-hundred-percent right."

I looked around at him, round-eyed. "Then why marry her?"

"I won't."

"I don't believe you."

"So what's new, Kat? You never believe anything I tell you. Never have."

"You invited her out here with her parents!" I accused. "Not once, but a couple of times. Not to mention all the times you've been with her in town. Were you just dallying?"

"So now you're more concerned with Charlene
Bellows's feelings than you are with mine," he mocked.
"Just to set the record straight, I didn't invite them out
here willingly. They practically invited themselves, with
their eyes on the remote chance that I might take more
than a lukewarm interest in Charlene. So I used them.
Why the hell shouldn't I? I already had someone else in
mind."

"Marcela Juarez," I said automatically.

"Marcela . . ." He tipped my chin. "I haven't been
with Marcela in that way since the day you saw us at the
hotel."

"No?"

"No."

"Well, I'm sure she'd love to see you again. Any-
time." I turned away.

"We're getting nowhere fast, aren't we?" he drawled
wryly. "We're going to have one hell of a life com-
municating the way we do."

I turned back to him, eyes widening again. "You talk
as though . . ." I stopped, narrowing my eyes, suspiciously and scrutinizing his face. "You needn't worry
about my reputation, Donovan. I'm not going to hold
you to anything you said in jest to Hattie." Who did he
think he was, amusing himself at my expense? I was
hardly a suitable match for a man who owned thousands
of acres of land, not to mention cattle.

Marching across the room, I snatched up another
towel, intending to wipe up the wine still puddled on the
floor. Mace unwrapped the towel from around his hand
and cast it there instead.

"What're you doing?" I exclaimed. "Your hand . . ."

"Has nothing more serious than a minor scratch," he
finished. "Were you really worried that I would bleed to
death?" He was laughing openly at me now.

I rubbed at the stain on the floor. "When are you

going to admit you love me, Kat?" He looked overly patient, all the laughter gone.

I froze. "What do you want? Revenge for every rotten thing I ever accused you of . . . everything I ever said to you?" I managed, wanting to sound cruel but only sounding very vulnerable and close to tears.

"Maybe. You do owe me something . . ."

"All right," I conceded, putting my head down. "I love you. Is that what you wanted to hear? Laugh. Go ahead."

But he didn't. He didn't move either, but continued to look at me with a strangely smouldering expression in his eyes. "That's revenge enough for the moment," he said finally. "We'll get down to the rest of what this is about later. Right now, I think we should have something to eat before everything gets cold."

My stomach twisted into a tight, hard lump. "I'm not hungry."

"Aren't you?" he asked, raising one brow and then shrugging. "Well, I am." He walked to the table and sat down. I watched in amazement as he dug into his steak with gusto.

How could he possibly eat now? And what exactly had he meant about discussing the rest later?

Mace looked up at me, sensing my gaze, seeing my confusion. "Why don't you sit down and at least try something? It's good and Hattie did make an effort for you. Jeremy told me you hadn't eaten breakfast."

I sat down. After the first forced bite, I realized I was famished. We ate dinner in silence and Mace kept replenishing my wine glass until my head was spinning. It was better than feeling the miserable longing and bewilderment that constricted my heart.

Finishing half of the enormous steak, I pushed the rest aside. Looking up, I met Mace's eyes. He smiled slowly, a warm smile that lit his face with a tingling

speculation. My heart started to pound heavily and I
looked away from that compelling gaze.

"I wanted to buy the homestead for all the reasons I
gave you," he started. "When I bought it at the auction
I wanted the land for only one reason . . . as a means of
getting you." I frowned.

"You could have taken it from us in the beginning. It
was your money that paid our taxes last year."

That surprised him. "How'd you learn about that?"

"Hattie told me first, but you denied it. Then, last
night, I found the note when I was reading my father's
Bible."

"You had enough hanging over your head without
knowing anything about that," he dismissed it. "I didn't
insist on writing that note, your father did. And it was
his debt, not yours."

"I inherited my father's debts."

"Well, we'll just have to think of a way for you to
repay them, won't we?" he needled.

"I got the money back from MacMillan this morning.
I've got it in . . ."

Mace was shaking his head. "That won't do."

"What do you mean, it won't do? Do you want me to
go back to work at the hotel? MacMillan says that I
could probably make up to fifty dollars a month . . ."

"Do you want another tanned hide?" he said through
his teeth. "You almost drove me out of my mind when
I found out you were there. Every time I make an attempt to reach out to you, you slap me away like an
angry cat." He was angry again and I paled. "Can't you
trust me?"

"I . . . I . . ."

He looked grim. "What?"

"I probably would have trusted you from the first if
Papa hadn't written those initials in the dust and mentioned Tasajara. And then everything would have been

fine until you came around . . . and when you did, things seemed to happen . . . terrible things.''

His eyes were penetrating, trying to see into my mind. I reached out for the first time and touched him reassuringly. I drew my hand back almost immediately.

"I'm sorry . . . Mace, I'm really sorry. I was terrible to you.''

He smiled at that. "You were. A regular harpy from hell. I can't tell you how many sleepless night's I've had because of you.''

I forced a smile. "Well, that's all over now. I promise to treat you civilly from now on. And you needn't worry over Jeremy and me. We'll work things out for ourselves.'' He had had his pound of flesh. I wasn't going to hack myself to pieces for him.

He ignored all that. "You made up for a lot of my agony that night in the stable,'' he grinned. I flushed a humiliating, painful red and glared at him resentfully.

"Why don't you just forget about that, Donovan?''

"And then you saved my life,'' he went on heedlessly. "Twice, on the ridge. You even killed a man to save me.'' His smile was gone as he considered me with grim concentration. I stood up and walked away, unable to bear it.

"And,'' he continued softly, rising as well. "You just admitted, not thirty minutes ago, that you're in love with me.''

I pressed cold hands to my face.

"Kat,'' Mace said from right behind me, his warm breath on my hair, his hands caressing my arms. "I'll admit that I wasn't too eager to meet you, ever. Not with your father telling me all his nice, enchanting little dreams about this perfect angel of a daughter he had who was just right for me. Dangling bait in front of my nose like I was some stupid hungry fish. God, I've had plenty of Charlenes in my life, greedy-eyed at the thought of being mistress of Tasajara. And I learned young to steer wide of them whenever possible. I liked Roger a lot and I didn't want to hurt his feelings."

His hands moved slowly, arousingly from my shoulders upward, caressing the sensitive cords of my neck. "Then he was murdered. The sheriff rode over and told me about it. Your father was my friend and I knew what the situation was and that you and Jeremy would need help. So I rode over." His lips moved against the curve of my neck. "The minute I laid eyes on you, I knew what would happen. And you fought me every damn inch of the way!"

I was shaking, heart pounding. "Papa always talked about you with such awe. I resented you long before I met you. And then, when you came to the cabin that first time, you scared me to death. I thought you'd murdered Papa . . . and I knew just how much power you wielded around Madrone."

Mace laughed. "Awesome! Me? You should have seen yourself that day in front of the sod cabin with that gun pointed at my chest. Speak of awesome! Your father had me convinced you were soft, gentle, loving . . . all the things a woman should be."

"And you found out differently."

"I found a lot more than I'd ever bargained for in a woman, that's for sure," he admitted with a laugh. He turned me slowly, lowering his head to kiss me. "But I saw all those other qualities as well. The way you were with Jeremy . . . and Hattie . . . and my father. It was only with me that you turned into a vicious little witch!" When I started to speak, he kissed me again, lingeringly. "You know, you're beautiful even when you look like a fighter who's lost," he smiled.

The heaviness inside me lifted more every minute. "You don't look particularly flawless yourself, Mace Donovan," I smiled up at him. I touched the cut at the corner of his mouth gently and trailed my fingertips along his bruised jawline. He sighed with profound relief.

"Finally I can say it. I love you, Kat. Why, I'll never know. You're absolutely impossible."

I leaned against him, cheek turned and pressed against his chest. I could hear the sudden quick rush of his heart and smiled.

"Will you marry me, please? You've had me in agony for months. I've even got your mother's wedding dress in a package downstairs. We can have the preacher out here tomorrow morning."

"Anything you want, Donovan."

He laughed, a low, husky sound that rippled through my body. "Don't go completely docile on me, Kat. I wouldn't know you," he teased. He drew me toward the bed.

"And now, for that tax bill you owe me," he grinned wickedly.

"But your father . . ."

"He told me a long time ago to use *any* weapon I had. We've got his blessings."

"So that's what he meant," I breathed.

He laughed slightly. Sitting down, Mace drew me in front of him between his legs. He pushed aside the front of my dressing gown, exposing my breasts. He was no novice when it came to a woman's body and for a moment I remembered Marcela Juarez and the smile she had given me when Donovan had dragged me from the hotel. She had known what Donovan wanted all along.

His mouth moved over the curved flesh. "This bed is going to be a lot more comfortable than hay . . . hmmmm?"

My fingers curled tightly in his hair, my breath quickening. "I can't think when you do that . . ." He chuckled, not stopping. His hands gently pushed the gown back off my shoulders. Then I heard him stop and draw in his breath.

"My God!"

I looked down curiously at his distraught face. "How did that happen?" He touched the ugly, painful bruise on my shoulder.

"Your charming horse did that to me," I told him, laughing slightly, my fingers stroking through his hair.

"That damn beast! I'll shoot him tomorrow!"

"You'll do no such thing! He's magnificent and you know it! And besides, he and I have an understanding now. I slapped him rather hard across the nose a couple of times and he seemed to mind me fairly well after that. So much for your carrot and sugar technique."

Mace pulled me over so that we were both stretched out on the large bed. I could hear the rumble of laughter deep in his chest before it burst out. I laughed with him, all the tensions, fears and uncertainty of the past months falling away.

Propping himself up on one elbow, Mace grinned down at me.

"Is that the treatment I've to look forward to over the next fifty or sixty years?"

"Only if I find you need it."

The gown was open completely now and Mace's mouth moved slowly down to linger over my taut abdomen. "Are you sure there's no little Donovan in residence?"

"I'm fairly sure." I had his shirt unbuttoned and was working on his belt buckle.

"Well, let's see if I can't prove my own staying power tonight," he teased hoarsely, assisting me.

I sighed. Flesh against flesh had to be the most wonderful feeling in the world. Who cared anything about silk?

"Mace?" I breathed dreamily.

"Hmmmm?" He was too busy to raise his head.

"Are you only going to make love to me when you want me to have a baby?" I kept my serious expression with difficulty as he raised himself up to glower down at me.

"What the hell do you think?"

I laughed and drew him down again.

DOUBLE CAMEOS

A Double Cameo novel means you get two thrilling novels of romantic suspense for the price of one. You'll get twice as much enjoyment, with your favorite authors —Sheila Bishop, Janice N. Bennett, Eva Zumwalt, Diane LaPoint, Naomi Smith, and many others.

☐ **BURIED REMEMBRANCE/DARK SUN AT MIDNIGHT**
Smith & Wagner   08397 $2.25

☐ **FEAR AMONG THE SHADOWS/DARKNESS AT BROMLEY HALL**
Hoffman & Morgan   22870 $2.25

☐ **THE HOUSE WITH TWO FACES/THE CASTLE ON THE RIVER**
Bishop & Bennett   34456 $2.25

☐ **MASQUERADE OF EVIL/FLAMES OVER CASTLE**
Zumwalt & LaPoint   52091 $2.25

☐ **DEATHBED OF ROSES/RIEVAULX ABBEY**
Scott & Davis   14183 $2.25

ACE BOOKS   R-07
P.O. Box 400, Kirkwood, N.Y. 13795

Please send me the titles checked above. I enclose _____.
Include 75¢ for postage and handling if one book is ordered; 50¢ per book for two to five. If six or more are ordered, postage is free. California, Illinois, New York and Tennessee residents please add sales tax.

NAME_____

ADDRESS_____

CITY_____STATE_____ZIP_____

Interlude Romances